CONTEMPT OF CONSCIENCE

Aidan de Vries

CONTEMPT OF CONSCIENCE

Erser & Pond

Cover design by Benjamin Beaumont

Printed in the United States by Erser & Pond Publishers, Ltd. 1096 Queen St., Suite 225, Halifax, N.S., Canada B3H 2R9

Library and Archives Canada Cataloguing in Publication

De Vries, Aidan
    Contempt of Conscience / Aidan de Vries.

ISBN 978-0-9781761-7-4

    I. Title.

PS8607.E975C65 2008   C813'.6   C2008-900254-7

10 9 8 7 6 5 4 3 2 1

First Edition

This book is dedicated to my wife,
my children, and my grandchildren.
May you share the sentiments that Wolsey
expressed in these Shakespearean verses:

I feel within me a peace
above all earthly dignities –
a still and quiet conscience.

Henry VIII, Act III, scene ii

Conscience is the voice of the soul, the passions are the
voice of the body. Is it astonishing that often these two
languages contradict each other, and then to which must
we listen? Too often reason deceives us; we have only too
much acquired the right of refusing to listen to it. But
conscience never deceives us; it is the true guide of man.

Jean-Jacques Rousseau

CHAPTER ONE

Mike Slayton was suddenly interrupted by a phone call. He had just been on the verge of convincing Margo Watson, an aspiring young journalist, that their business relationship would be noticeably enhanced if she allowed him to cement their personal bond on a deeper level. He had been about to congratulate himself for making yet another conquest on the office couch when the phone just had to ring at that particular moment.

Margo, for her part, was glad for the interruption, as she was not interested in Slayton in a physical way. She had known, though, that it would eventually come to this some day. It always did, so she had already made up her mind to have sex with him in order to further her career. It wouldn't be the first time that she would use her body to advance her job prospects.

She straightened her clothes and sat on the edge of the couch, staring at Slayton's thick neck and sloping shoulders. There was something off-putting about the obsequious way he was responding to the caller.

"Yes, sir. Right away, sir. I'll take care of it at once," she heard him say.

At that point Slayton knew he was not going to be able to pick up with Margo where he had left off. He also knew he would have to fire her as soon as he could find cause. He wasn't too sorry about losing her, however. The world was too full of willing young journalism students for him to be concerned about seeing the last of this one.

But Margo had other plans. Observing that even Slayton himself had to curry favor with the people above him, she made up her mind to find out who they were and what they were like. If she had to play around to advance her career, then she might as well start at the top.

Mike Slayton was actually a figure of some importance in the media world. It was true he was only the front man who put a face on news management at the network, but as far as visibility was concerned, he was undeniably the head honcho of Washington TV news. He was the one who decided what stories to put on the air. He was also the one who assigned reporters to cover specific news stories. He usually made the decisions about the spin that was put on the items, but he sometimes received orders from his employer about what the editorial policy was to be. Even so, Slayton still wrote the pieces that he felt needed delicate handling. People usually respected him because he'd been around the newsroom for a long time, even before TV news casting had become show business.

Mike didn't like it that the newspaper business was in the toilet. He hated the internet bloggers who pretended to have inside information that ordinary investigative reporters had been unable to dig up. He despised having to hire pretty faces to read the news. He got cranky when he was forced to stretch programming time with filler stories of no real value, or to repeat the same items over and over again. The news had become mostly junk, and Mike Slayton wondered what an experienced editorial news hand like him was doing in show business.

At fifty-seven Mike was too young to retire, but too old to be fooled about when news was news, and when it was merely opinion. He had a reputation for grouchy toughness that went back to his days as a newspaper reporter and city desk editor. His unseen boss was capitalizing on Slayton's talent for putting across ideas that didn't always correspond to the actual events. Slayton was too old to quit, and with three kids in college he couldn't afford to be without a job. Finding a comparable new job wouldn't be easy at his age, and besides, he didn't want a new job anyway.

He would have liked to get more respect from the owner of the company, however, who had succeeded in acquiring him along with his previous company. He had stayed on after the merger because he had been given a good raise. He convinced himself that no matter where he worked, there would always be a certain amount of news slanting that had to be done to satisfy the editorial will of any publisher.

Phone calls like the one that had suspended his plans for seducing Margo Watson were his main complaint about his job. He would have liked to have more self-respect, and he could tell that Margo had been turned off by seeing him taking orders from the higher-ups. It turned him off, too. He was an employee, after all, just like her. She shouldn't have been surprised to find that out.

"Don't go," he said to Margo. "We were just getting to know each other better."

He had been concocting a scenario whereby he would allow Margo to share with him in the common employee's complaint of having to take orders from above. His idea was that they would commiserate with each other for having to obey the dictates of a self-important superior. They'd get even with him by having a little extra recreational activity on the boss's time that afternoon, and Slayton would emerge the winner.

Margo read him perfectly. She was young, but she had been in similar situations before.

"This wasn't such a good idea," she said, slipping on her jacket. "Let's just keep things on a professional level."

She left Slayton's office knowing that she had gone too far when she had allowed him to get his hopes up. Now that she had rejected her boss she expected that her career would be in trouble, and her suspicions were correct.

Mike's wife had left him years ago. She had refused to put up with his drinking and philandering. Slayton was still bitter about her hard-line, nit-picking attitude toward what to him had been convenient little rolls in the hay. It was all part of the reporter's life-style, after all, and he was news hound through and through. Developing sources and cultivating contacts were two of his strong suits. He could write rapidly and meet deadlines. His writing style – terse, fact-filled, and bluntly descriptive – was ideally suited to news reporting. Give him a political scandal to write about, and he was hard to beat. If you needed to put an American spin on an international story, Slayton was your man.

Mike had been given his job, however, not because of his strengths but because of his weaknesses. When his new boss was in merger and acquisition negotiations to buy the company, he had studied the situation and had decided that he could capitalize on Mike's standing in the news business, and at the same time use his character flaws to keep him under his thumb. From his boss's point of view, the deal had worked out perfectly.

Ivan Welland had been Secretary of Defense for three years. He had achieved considerable recognition for having helped the President implement his world peace program. Even though it had been Ivan's idea to silence the guns of anger in the world by halting the production of ammunition, he hadn't minded that the President had been given most of the credit. Welland was not concerned about credit. He was interested in results. In this case the first step towards world peace was to stop the killing.

Except for a few small-scale incidents, the guns had at last gone still. Most of the world's leaders had welcomed his announcement that the U.S. would purchase, for the period of one year, all the chemical explosives they manufactured while their factories found other uses for their facilities. It hadn't worked perfectly, of course, for several nations had to be convinced that beating their weapons into ploughshares was a requirement, not a recommendation. But after the second year of Ivan's tenure in the job and several pinpoint missile attacks by the U.S. Air Force on the ammunition dumps of non-compliant nations, the ammunition demolition derby had finally ended.

Efforts at diplomatic solutions had taken a serious turn for the better. The intensity of work at the State Department had escalated, while the energy at the Defense Department had shifted from large-scale military operations to mopping-up missions. These changes in direction suited Ivan and the President, but there were others in the U.S. and overseas that were not satisfied to give peace a chance, so Ivan had called a meeting of his special investigations team. This group of four had been with him since the beginning of his meteoric rise in government circles. They had helped him plan and execute missions in Saudi Arabia, on the high seas, and throughout the world as well as at home. Now he had called them together to consider a new conundrum.

Ivan Welland, PhD, was a Harvard-educated Russian scholar from Texas. He had fallen into government work as a result of an episode in Chechnya, during which time he had killed an imam in self defense. The experience of taking a life had had a profound effect on him. As a result he had undergone an epiphany, and had chosen to follow a different, more results-oriented career rather than the placid, scholarly one he had previously envisioned. His involvement in the dangerous world of international intrigue in Grozny had given him an indication of what his contribution to his country could be if he accepted the job that the Secretary of State had offered him at the time. From that moment on he had never looked back, nor regretted his abandonment of an academic career. Nevertheless, he was still a professorial type of man in his love of education and in his intelligence, personality, and demeanor.

Ivan's staff meetings were like no others in government. They were far more like university seminars than top-down conferences. The four members of his team – Brooklyn, David, Damian and Abdul – had grown to love their boss, and their loyalty to him was absolute. On that particular day in Washington they were just winding up their portion of the

President's peace plan and they were anxious to hear what their next assignment would be. They were certain that the meeting that was about to begin would reveal Ivan's plan for the immediate future in which they would all become heavily invested. They were also pretty sure that Wacky Welland, the Weird Wizard of Oz (a synonym for Washington, D.C.) would present them with a unique challenge.

"What if we're living in a world of make believe," Ivan said to his little team, "and everything that we've been told *is* happening, or *has* happened, is actually just a figment of someone else's imagination?"

"Here we go again!" exclaimed Brooklyn, his assistant, sensing that her boss was off once again on one of his flights of imagination.

"No, seriously, what would you say if I told you that most of what we read in the newspapers is made up, or at least totally modified to suit the purposes of the media?"

"Isn't that the way it was, is, and always will be?" David Feingold asked.

"Perhaps, but the people who read the newspapers and watch the news programs are receiving this information as though it were gospel truth," Damian Rutledge observed.

"Exactly my point," said Ivan. "The media can tell us anything they want, and we'll most likely believe it. What's worse, we may even act on the information."

"But doesn't competition from other sources even out the picture?" Abdul asked. "I mean, what about the time when suicide bombers attacked the consulate in Jerusalem? Al Arabiya reported it as a great victory for Islam over Israel and its American lackeys, and a giant step on the way to recapturing Jerusalem for the Palestinians. The American media described it as a cowardly sneak attack on innocent people with diplomatic immunity. So which is it?"

"Being a Jew and an American, I have to take the same position as the American press," Brooklyn said forcefully.

"That's just the point," Ivan said. "The same action is interpreted in diametrically opposed ways, and who's to say what's true? We're back to the same old question Pontius Pilate asked: *What is truth?* Suppose the attack in Jerusalem had never happened at all? This isn't a very good example, though, because in this case, unfortunately, we have the dead bodies and the destroyed building as hard evidence. But suppose we didn't have any evidence, just the news report? This happens in lots of news stories. So what do we do?"

"Is this going to be one of those *Dr. Welland and Mr. Hide the Purpose of the Meeting* meetings?" Damian asked.

"Probably," Ivan smiled. "But I'm a bit puzzled, and I'd like your help. So let me give you a couple of examples of media coverage control. Three years ago I was shot at six AM on the street in front of the White House. My assailant didn't get the desired result, as you can see, because here I am. My security agents shot the assailant, and we disposed of the evidence before the newshounds got wind of the affair. In line with my preference for cohabiting with the media as little as possible, the story never got out.

"Anyhow, the assailant's boss, whoever he was, wasn't happy with the result, so my house was bombed. That was too big an event to keep out of the papers, so it got a lot of ink. Now suppose for a moment that a headline-hunting media baron ordered the hit on me because I'm known to be anti-press? He gets a double header, a big splashy story, and the departure from the scene of a government guy who isn't living his life to be in front of the cameras."

"Are you suggesting," Brooklyn asked, "that someone in the Press Corps at the White House arranged to have you shot, and when that attempt failed he bombed your house?"

"Whoever it was, he was smart enough to get away with it, and he hasn't been caught yet," Damian said.

"I don't think it was someone in the Press Corps," Ivan said. "Someone higher up, perhaps. Someone who decides what makes news, not just a reporter."

"How are we ever going to find out who that is?" David wanted to know. "If he's clever enough to make the news, or if he can decide what the news actually is, and if he can get huge numbers of people to believe what he publishes, then won't he also be astute enough to cover his tracks?"

"That's exactly it," Ivan agreed. "That's why we've formed this little group of stinkers – oops, I meant thinkers. Anyway, the media use their freedom of speech rights under the First Amendment and then they pretend their job is to clean up politics and government by shining their righteous investigative light into the dark corners of polity. But what if the free press is not what it seems? What if its subliminal purposes are something totally self-interested?"

Ivan reached into his pocket and withdrew a newspaper clipping. "Take this article, for instance. It appeared in the *Times* yesterday. It's too long to read aloud, so I've made copies for each of you."

He passed the copies around, and gave his team a few minutes to read the article.

"As you see," he continued, "it's a seemingly routine report of the latest conference of environmental experts that was held here in Washington. I'm not familiar with the author's byline, though. Her name is Margo Watson. Does anyone recognize that name?"

They all shook their heads.

"Well," Ivan went on, "for the moment she's probably not all that important. But the article she wrote is interesting for several reasons. For one thing, she sows the seeds of dissonance among the various groups. The ones who have deepest feelings about the environment are portrayed as being lopsided in their views. She assumes that the animal rights people, the global warming guys, and the air polluters all have their own axes to grind, so she says they'll never be able to get together to raise a unified voice for the good of the environment. She even castigates Dr. Laura Murphy, the well-known, highly-qualified professor who favors a sane policy that puts the environment first on our list of priorities.

"And in a raw example of yellow journalism, the article insinuates that she's engaged in a sell-out to the petroleum producers. So how does the author come up with this idea?

Her conclusion is based on the fact that Dr. Murphy is married to a former officer of a large oil company, who was also an erstwhile representative of the Petroleum Producers Association. So with that item of supposedly scandalous material, she tries to make us believe that Murphy is selling out the entire environmental lobby.

"But she never mentions that Dr. Murphy is the wife of Ambassador Bradley Burke, the diplomat we all know and respect as the man who did the most to bring the world to its present relatively peaceful state by influencing most of the world's governments to adopt the President's program for the reduction of ammunition. This little omission detracts from Dr. Murphy's personal credibility. It makes no note of the fact that she has traveled the world with her husband while working in her own area of specialty, which is to end pollution in the world's environment."

"This certainly is a nasty piece of tripe journalism," Brooklyn said indignantly, "but what has it got to do with you being shot, or your suspicion that there's a media maven out there who controls what the public is handed out as *All the News That's Fit to Print?*"

"Actually, I don't know that it has anything to do with those two things," Ivan replied. "I'm just putting it forward as an example of what the press can do. In this one article they've sabotaged the chances for a unified front among the organizations that are interested in moving the environment higher up on the list of government policy issues. They've possibly damaged the moral reputation of Dr. Murphy by insinuating that she's involved with a man who's supposed to be opposed to her opinions on environmental issues. The article doesn't do anything to raise the moral status of the environmental movement, and it misrepresents both sides of the issue. All this is closer to slander than to investigative reporting."

"Slanderous yellow journalism is nothing new," Damian said. "So what do you propose we do with this article?"

"What I'm proposing is that we take this article, which is relatively innocuous except to the people involved, and trace it all the way back to its source, and even beyond, if possible. I'd like us to use this as a test case. My hypothesis is that the news is being controlled, even generated, by a clever egomaniac of a media executive, or possibly a coterie of such people. But my idea needs to be tested against the facts. That's what I'd like us to do."

"Okay boss, dole out the assignments," Brooklyn said.

"Right. I'll start with you then, Brooklyn. See if you can find out who this Margo Watson is, and who she works for, and anything else you can dig up. Abdul, read the Arab press and tell me if what I suspect is happening here, is also happening there. Is there a media caliph skulking around somewhere? Damian, try to find me some connections from corporation to corporation, from continent to continent, and from individuals to individuals. David, as usual, you do the math. See if you can create an algorithm that will facilitate the analysis of masses of data about papers, TV stations, journalists, media barons – the works."

"Our problem," David said, "is going to be with our own U.S. media entities. I don't think we'll find any linkages until we get all the way to the top. I also have the feeling that we're not going to like what we find here."

"Well, do what you have to do. Check in with me from time to time, all of you," said Ivan. "Keep me posted about your findings, but don't give up on your other projects. I'm still interested in completing the war on ammunition. David, we've still got to prepare to meet the computer honchos who are going to work with us to build the virtual world court. Abdul, we've got to prepare the rules of engagement for the religious elders meeting that will take place after we've got all the ammo corralled. Okay, back to work now. Remember, *Blessed are the peacemakers, for they will be called children of God.*"

CHAPTER TWO

Robert Thomaston was the scion of the publishing empire founded by his grandfather, who had come over from England as an immigrant and had quickly found employment in the pressroom at the New York Times. He had attended New York University on a part-time basis, finally completing a journalism degree. His reputation as a dependable worker and his tenacity in earning a degree the hard way had opened the door to the club room.

He gradually became a staff reporter of some note, but when he'd had the chance to purchase a small newspaper in upstate New York, he couldn't pass up the opportunity of becoming self-employed. He'd learned the newspaper business from the bottom up, and he soon parlayed his first paper into several others. By the time he died, he owned over a hundred small-town newspapers. The torch passed on to George Thomaston, Robert's father, who continued to build the business, through hard work and parsimony, into one of the largest newspaper holdings in America.

Robert was sent off to Yale to be educated. He was pledged to the Skull and Bones, and soon became an active participant in all its arcane rituals and secret connections. After graduating from Yale, he went directly into the family newspaper business, where he showed considerable acumen. His greatest coup was to widen the base of the newspaper and magazine business by acquiring radio and TV stations. He rolled the business into one of the largest privately-held media conglomerates in the world. His wealth was legend, and his influence was felt all over the world.

During the course of his successful business career, his path crossed with those of two men whose backgrounds were not unlike his own. They were Baron Friedrich von Aragon, who lived in Germany when he was not on board his yacht, and Geoffrey Lord Pressman, who resided in London and also owned media empires. The three moguls competed for years to make their companies prevail.

Baron Fritz, as he was familiarly called, had a brilliant idea one day as he was sunning himself on the foredeck of his enormous yacht. Why not invite his two competitors to join him for a cruise? It would be interesting to converse with his fellow moguls, who were probably the only other two in the world with experiences similar to his own.

Fritz ambled over to his yacht's communications center which was, short of that of an aircraft carrier, the largest telecommunications center afloat. He fired off an invitation to Thomaston and Lord Pressman to join him for a week of cruising in the Balearic Islands, off the coast of Spain. The Englishman and the American were surprised to receive such an invitation from someone that they had both regarded as a competitor. Each was afraid to turn down the offer, thinking that perhaps the Baron was planning to sell off some of his properties, and neither man wanted to be absent should this be the reason for the invitation. In any case, the three men couldn't help being a little curious about one another, so the first of what became an annual event took place on board the titanic motor yacht, *Sternlicht*.

Robert Thomaston arranged to pick up Geoffrey Lord Pressman and his wife in London with his private plane, as it was en route to Palma de Majorca anyway. From there Baron Fritz would send his helicopter to fly them to the yacht.

After the businessmen had landed on the helipad of the yacht, they were led into the magnificent saloon to meet their host. The guests and the host were seated informally, and drinks were served.

It immediately became obvious that these three men had a lot in common. The commonalities went well beyond being in the same business, and in a short time genuine friendships began to take root. Lord Pressman and Thomaston felt both disappointed and relieved that von Aragon had no business to transact with them. He genuinely wanted to meet them and thought it would be an interesting time for all of them. He was right.

Wealth, and the power that derives from it, was laid to rest, as those present were comfortable with their money and status. They were surprised to discover that they bore no hostility toward one another, despite the competitive nature of the media business. They soon realized, to their surprise and tentative delight, that they actually enjoyed each other's company, maybe even more than their long-term friendships. On the third evening Baron Fritz suggested that they have an honest, freewheeling discussion of the state of the world. His two guests thought that was a wonderful idea.

The Baron led off. "Since none of us needs any more money, why are we still so actively involved in business?"

"Umm, to catch up with Bill Gates and Warren Buffet?" Robert Thomaston asked, with feigned ingenuousness.

"Perhaps so we can leave some kind of mark to indicate we've been here," said a more serious Lord Pressman.

"I don't think it's that, Geoffrey," said Baron Fritz, "as we've all gone to a good deal of trouble to keep out of the public eye. We put the spotlight on those we choose, but we control the focus of the camera lens very carefully."

"So why do *you* think we work so hard in the business, then?" Robert asked, looking at the Baron's tanned face.

"I think the unpleasant truth is that we thirst for power in a most Machiavellian way. We want to wield power, but we need to have political fall guys in case things don't work out the way we'd like them to. We operate behind the scenes, but with full awareness of the outcomes we're trying to achieve. We wish to manipulate our people, the nations, and the world at large. We use ideas as our weapons, and we paint them in exciting, provoking words to cover the fact that we're spreading propaganda. I've noticed that the three of us have parallel ideas in almost every situation. That's really what prompted me to call this meeting of the minds."

"So you're suggesting that some sort of alliance be made between us, right?" said Lord Pressman.

"That's correct, Geoffrey. We already have an unspoken alliance of mutual interests. I'm merely suggesting that we acknowledge it, and strengthen it by giving voice to it."

"I think the Baron is right, Geoffrey," said Robert. "We all operate the same way. We have unanimity in most things. We all support democracy as the best method of governance. We approve of market economy, competition, and free trade. Freedom for the peaceful practice of religion is central to all three of us. I don't think the Baron is advocating that we change the rules of free enterprise, or that we show each other's corporations monopolistic favors. I think he means that on matters of philosophy, peace, and morality we can agree on some firm general principles that will be helpful in the world of tomorrow. That's it, isn't it Baron?"

"Precisely. I couldn't have said it better."

"All right then, let's have an open discussion and see what we can agree upon or disagree upon," Geoffrey said, composing his bespectacled, heavily-bearded face into an expression of solemn expectation.

The three arbiters of pubic opinion eagerly engaged in a discussion of the world's problems and how they might be resolved. They began with the situation in the Middle East, easily concurring that Israel must survive and not undergo the second holocaust that some Islamic countries seemed to want to inflict on the Jewish state. They discussed the ways they could coordinate their efforts to refute the absolute lies that were coming out of the Arab media companies. They talked about the methods that they could use to persuade the governments of America, Germany, and England to come to a common agreement in opposing the imposition of Sharia law around the world. By the end of the day, the three men had come to an understanding that would have far-reaching effects on the knowledge of good and evil for all the world's peoples.

News editor Mike Slayton had delegated Margo Watson to cover the conference on the environment. He had done it more as a punishment than anything else. He didn't regard the conference as being of much importance, and he didn't think she did either. He felt she was sexually unenthusiastic about him and needed to be taught that if she took care of her boss, he would return the favor by giving her some more challenging assignments.

Sometimes fate has a way of making a totally ordinary situation into something special, and this was one of those times. Margo was sitting in the section of the auditorium that was reserved for the members of the press. On her right a well-dressed, middle-aged man was glancing at her nametag. Robert Thomaston didn't know her name, but her affiliation was familiar to him, as he was the owner of the company. After his surprisingly agreeable discussions on board the *Sternlicht*, he had returned to Washington D.C. for meetings with his editorial staff. He had decided to stop in at the Conference Center to see what the vocal left wing was up to, but he hadn't expected to find anything of interest to him there. The conference had turned out to be more enjoyable than he had anticipated, however. It had provided him with the opportunity to listen to what was being said about some important issues of the day, and the speeches had given him an idea that he felt he could use. Best of all, it had given him an opportunity to meet an attractive young woman.

Thomaston decided to get acquainted with his employee without telling her who he was. They bantered back and forth a little bit during the session, and Margo began to warm to him. She assumed he was a reporter, since he was seated in the press section, so she asked him where he worked. Thomaston decided to play it cool.

"I'm with the CBC, Canadian Broadcasting Company."

He felt she wouldn't catch that lie so easily, as it was less likely that she'd know any Canadian media people.

"That's strange," she said, looking puzzled. "I thought you were from somewhere else, judging from your accent."

"British Columbia," he replied. "We're wannabe Brits out there, and our accent is intentionally not American. We do have a beautiful environment, though, no matter how you pronounce it."

When the conference broke for lunch, Thomaston asked Margo to join him. He struck her as a reasonable guy, and she could use a free lunch, so she accepted his invitation.

He guided her into an elevator and took her to the Roof Garden restaurant. He had no idea where ordinary reporters ate, so he invited her to the only place he knew. Thomaston stayed in this hotel whenever he was in Washington, and the senior staff of the establishment knew him well. Margo was impressed that the maitre d' had recognized her escort and had quickly seated them at a table by the window.

"How is it that Canadian reporters are treated so well here? I never get treated this well in any restaurant."

"You'll never be treated badly when you're with me," Thomaston assured her. "I'll see to that. Shall we have some wine with lunch, or would you prefer a cocktail?"

"I'd like a scotch and soda please, Robert." She felt the occasion warranted the use of first names.

"We'll have two scotch and sodas," he told the waiter. The waiter had already been informed that Thomaston was a VIP, and should be served nothing but the best of everything.

Robert Thomaston was enjoying this rare moment of anonymity. Usually he was fawned over to an embarrassing degree everywhere he went. He relished the fact that Margo worked for him, but didn't know it. His usual dates were fabulously beautiful, and incredibly spoiled. Margo was not an ugly duckling by any means, but although she wouldn't have stood out compared with most of his women, there was something down-to-earth about her utilitarian appearance that appealed to Robert. He asked her how she liked her job.

"I like journalism, but I'm not keen on my boss."

"Why? What's he like?"

"He's always trying to feel me up. You probably know the type. He promises me he'll help me in my career if I sleep with him. Mike's one of those old-line newsmen – lots of booze, broads, and cynicism. I hope I don't have to leave this job because I won't sleep with him. Do you think I'll be fired because I turned him down?"

"I'm sure not."

"I hope you're right."

"I'd bet on it," Thomaston said, patting her hand to reassure her. "Mike Slayton won't fire you."

"How did you know his name was Slayton? I only said Mike. There must be a lot of Mikes in the news business."

"I just guessed. It sounded like the kind of thing Mike Slayton would do."

"So you know Mike Slayton?"

"Yes, I'm acquainted with him."

"You won't tell him what I said about him, will you?"

"No, certainly not," Thomaston assured her.

They had a leisurely lunch. It was the best meal Margo had ever had, but she didn't want to praise the food too much for fear of seeming provincial.

After lunch they returned to the conference to hear the afternoon speakers. Margo took prodigious quantities of notes, using her laptop computer. Thomaston was impressed by her zeal for the job. As the afternoon wore on, he asked her if she'd like to attend a small cocktail party after the conference broke up for the day.

"I'll need some time to file my story," she said, "but after that I'm free."

"Good. I'll meet you in the lobby at 5:30. Can you be ready by then?"

"That shouldn't be a problem," Margo smiled. "Unless, of course, I can't find you in that huge lobby with all those people milling around."

"I'll wait for you under the blue clock to the left of the registration desk."

Margo was impressed that he had even noticed the clock, let alone its color and whereabouts.

"I'll be there," she said.

"See you then." He waved at her as he walked away.

"What's your name, by the way?" she called after him.

He stopped and turned around. "Robert," he said, then he disappeared into the crowd.

CHAPTER THREE

Thomaston had several gripes with Ivan Welland, but the most serious and obvious one was Ivan's penchant for secrecy in dealing with the media. Security and defense matters were big news to TV watchers, but ever since Ivan had assumed the reins of U.S. security policy and later the Department of Defense, the flow of information had slowed down to a trickle. His reporters and his producers hadn't uncovered any newsworthy items, except to say that Ivan's department was working feverishly on something, but no one ever seemed to know just what that was.

The iron-fisted clamp on information that Welland had imposed had plugged up all the usual leaks. Thomaston and his media-savvy executives were at the end of their rope. They were working behind the scenes, trying to bring the pressure of the Fourth Estate to bear on the government by stressing the First Amendment rights of the citizenry to know what its government was up to. They had loosed the ACLU, with all its abusive invective and legal posturing, on the Washington bureaucrats, hoping to suck a little information out of the beleaguered civil servants. They had allowed their creative juices to flow in fabricating rumors and anonymous reports by "trusted sources." They had also floated lots of informational trial balloons in order to get some advance notice about the business going on in the White House and the Pentagon, but mostly to no avail.

Welland's disdain for the press and his lack of interest in sharing information with the media were not the only causes of irritation for Robert Thomaston. What really bothered him was that Ivan Welland seemed to be sniffing around in the sacrosanct private realm that dealt with the motivations, agendas, and aspirations of the media moguls. In what he thought was an inspired moment, Thomaston had made up his mind to get Welland out of the picture once and for all. He had chosen a Colombian gang leader known as *The Viper* to do the job.

The first telephone conversation between the Viper and Thomaston had been unusual from the Viper's point of view. The pompous client, who seemed egotistic and supercilious, had carried on as though he were entitled to a free trial hit. Thomaston's self-importance came through in every word he spoke. The Viper had been made to feel as though he were the applicant for some low-level job.

When the contract negotiations had reached the breaking point, Thomaston had counter-offered some free publicity as part of the payment for killing Ivan Welland. The Viper thought it over carefully, but he finally decided that publicity was not something a hit man needed. If a little bad publicity could be dished out to his competitors, however, then there might be some wiggle room on the price of the Welland hit.

"I'll have to think about it," the Viper said.

"Well, don't take too long about it," Thomaston warned him. "I could change my mind, you know."

"I'll let you know when I've made up my mind."

Thomaston had hung up without saying goodbye, angry that there was nothing he could do to shame this little snake into acquiescing. Time, he decided, would no doubt present him with exactly the right opportunity.

The Viper recorded their phone call, as he always did. Transcribing his conversations was a precautionary routine he had instituted for self-protection in case a client was later tempted to testify against him. It could also form the basis of a future blackmail scheme in which he might use the tape-recorded and possibly photographed contract hit arrangement to threaten the client. What the Viper didn't know, however, was that this time he had bitten an animal so large he could choke on it.

Three years previously, Welland had been shot three times in the chest during the first attempt on his life. But Ivan happened to be wearing a bulletproof vest. Thomaston could understand how an assassin would be unlikely to have guessed that his intended victim would be so well prepared for the unexpected. The shooter had himself been shot to death, so although Thomaston was disappointed with the results of this arrangement, he was able to sympathize to a certain extent. Unforeseen things happen in every business, so he had allowed the Viper's hired killers to try again.

In the second attempt CNN reported the death of some Secret Service Agents in a bombing in Georgetown. Robert Thomaston was fit to be tied when he found out that Welland was not among the dead. This time Thomaston was furious not only because he still had to deal with the problem of Welland's continued ability to stay alive and well, but his own news channel had been scooped on the story.

He decided at that point to try to get rid of the pesky Welland some other way. He reamed the Viper out over the phone, assuring him there was no way in hell that he'd ever even *consider* giving him a third chance. Rafael Alvarez had never in his life had to deal with the flood of verbal invective that Thomaston heaped upon him. He was ordered to cancel the contract they had made, as two strikes were all a hitter in Thomaston's league was entitled to.

Thomaston thought he could get away with breaking his contract with the Viper by refusing to pay him for a service not rendered. He would pretend to take it for granted that the little snake would be too ashamed of his two failures to insist on being given the payments that had been stipulated in the contract. Thomaston decided that his best tactic would be to get him to think that although he was hugely disappointed, they were square.

But failure to perform in Robert Thomaston's ballpark carried a penalty. Thomaston needed time to think about what that penalty would be, but in this case it must be severe. Not getting paid was a type of fine, but it was insufficient. The Viper must be suspended, or do jail time. Thomaston, acting as both judge and jury, decided upon the latter as his penalty. He reasoned that the slickest way to get even with the Viper was to take the ironical path of arranging to have his intended victim collar the anonymous villain and put him in prison. For the time being he abandoned his plan to have Welland killed. Instead, he would leak some information to the government that would enable them to arrest the Viper. Thomaston would deal with Ivan later.

Thomaston sat at his desk doodling. In a flash he had an idea and began making notes about it. He wrote an outline for an investigative reporting series that would reveal the workings of a drug-dealing, gun-running, murder-for-money organization that was terrorizing everyone from its base in Cali, Colombia. He would leak information garnered from unnamed sources. He'd claim to have interviewed credible witnesses who were in hiding, too frightened to come out into the open until the venomous leader of the Latino Mafia was either dead or imprisoned for life.

Thomaston's story would be true, of course, but the picture he'd paint in his Sunday Supplement feature section called *True Modern Crime Investigations* would make it seem even more glaringly violent. In the end he would leak a piece of contact information from an anonymous source that the police could use to track the Viper to his jungle headquarters. The articles would hint that the DEA and the U.S. Secret Police were pressuring the Colombian authorities to arrest the Viper.

The publicity generated by the articles would obviate any efforts from the corrupt, colluding, cowardly police to allow the Viper to continue his illegal activities. He would be caught and brought to justice, and he would never know it was Thomaston who had betrayed him.

The power of the press to galvanize the public and the police into action was immense, and Robert Thomaston was a master of its use. He could make up any story he wished to publish, and by overt or covert means, he could make it fully believable. Truth or fiction, both worked to create whatever Thomaston wanted the public to know.

Behind his back his editors called him the master baiter, because he knew how to lure the lurid and entrap the sordid segments of the population into revealing the details of their webs of wickedness. His newspapers were purveyors of yellow journalism, but by using subtlety and creative flair they posed as investigative journals, but often their research was only a figment of Robert Thomaston's imagination. He had learned that the public wanted entertainment *more* than they wanted truth. True or false, the Thomaston School of Reporting made little distinction between the two, as long as the stories weren't libelous to the point of judicial penalty, and as long as they sold newspapers and advertising time on TV. Robert Thomaston sat atop this pile of accumulated, organized, and processed baloney as he selected, packaged, and published lip-smacking news for the world's readers and listeners. And when there wasn't any hot real news, he just made up whatever came into his head.

In the case of the Viper, Robert Thomaston didn't have to strain his imagination, for the truth was that the Cali cartel was involved in every possible criminal activity, and few in the Colombian justice system hadn't been corrupted by huge bribes from the cartel to allow things to continue as usual. Thomaston let his Latin American editors know that he was appalled at the amount of drugs moving into the U.S. from Colombia. He made the suggestion, which was as good as an order, that they should feature some articles that portrayed drugs in the worst possible light. Articles about addicted babies, deserted children, and stories that touched the hearts of the sympathetic public and turned them against the drug lords should be placed in prominent places in the media they controlled. The Baron of Bullshit, as one of his competitors called Thomaston, wanted to make things hot for La Víbora, as he was called in Colombia. Like the cold-blooded snake he was, the Count of Cocaine would be made into the most despised person in the western hemisphere. Pressure would be brought to bear on him, and the police would be forced by public opinion to find him and bring him to trial.

When he had put all these plans into action, Robert began to think about some dirty tricks to play on his Arabic competitors. When they crossed the line from broadcasting in Arabic to offering English language programming, they crossed Robert Thomaston's boundary line. He was not a man to be crossed, as he would soon make them realize.

The journalism giants had always dictated the subtle emphases that were being used to move public opinion closer to their own point of view. The power the media wield in picking the stories to headline, the characters to feature, and the items to intentionally ignore is so subtle as to be hardly noticeable. But in reality this power is much stronger than the heady wine of fame enjoyed by democratically-elected politicians, who must periodically solicit votes from their supporters. The unelected media barons, on the other hand, could make or break celebrities or high-profile entertainers by manipulating the facts while they amused their audiences. Meanwhile they secretly pursued their perfidious ends, using the news items to push their hidden agendas.

Each of the members of the trio of press barons worked in exactly the same way. They were interested in controlling fashions, popularizing idiotic brain candy, and standardizing standards, all of which suited their ever-increasing need to grow their businesses and extend their power bases. Their goal was to make every idea that was favorable to their own interests appear to be someone else's agenda. In supporting the politicians, parties, and policies of their choice, they used their governments to do their bidding without ever having to worry about being elected by a fickle electorate. This way they always managed to avoid being blamed for any failures that occurred.

Being in a position of power for the better part of a lifetime had made the press barons increasingly bold. When the news of the world didn't move smoothly or quickly enough to suit them, Thomaston, Pressman, and von Aragon tweaked things by producing a little news of their own making. The steady accrual of power had made these three men into megalomaniacs who were script-writing the events of the world to suit themselves, as if they were the directors of a giant play and the people of the world were their actors.

Having a difficult performer replaced on the stage was well within the director's purview, so Thomaston's desire to remove Ivan Welland from his role was foreseeable. It was amazing to Thomaston that politicians failed to realize that they were mortal. As their legends grew and they achieved star status, famous people always seemed to end up believing their own publicity. The famous no longer remembered who made them famous. They become lost in their own egos.

Thomaston's problem with Welland was that he was that rare individual who didn't seek personal aggrandizement, and he was therefore unpredictable and uncontrollable. Put a man like Ivan Welland in charge, and you can never predict what he will do. When a politically incorruptible man is given great power, the results can be very damaging to the puppeteers who pull the strings from behind the scenes. Famous men such as Jesus, Gandhi, Martin Luther King, or Abraham Lincoln had created revolutions of great moment, much to the consternation of those who thought it was they who held the power. All those heroes of the people had eventually been snuffed out, but the legacy of their work had lived on. Thomaston feared that Welland might be like them, and he wanted him silenced before it was too late.

This time Lord Pressman had already arrived on Baron von Aragon's luxurious yacht, and he and his host were waiting for Robert Thomaston. They were about to start their second meeting in Majorca – the one that would determine what actions they could sponsor to foster their businesses. One of the hot concerns of the trio of media giants had been the impressive growth of the Arab networks, Al Jazeera and Al Arabiya. It was to be expected that these purveyors of news would be well received and appreciated in the Arab world. But what really bothered the trio was that their broadcasts in other languages, including English, French, Spanish, and German, were reaching an increasing audience around the world. Some of their editorials were even finding surprising acceptance with naïve people in traditional Western media markets. The billionaires meeting on the yacht were planning to address the growing problem of this new competition.

The helicopter bearing Robert Thomaston was noisily landing on the deck of the yacht, and the other two men were eagerly awaiting him so they could begin their discussions. The isolation they enjoyed aboard the yacht at sea had made it the venue of choice for their meetings.

They met the American media giant on the pad as soon as he landed, and they immediately whisked him off to the conference room to begin their deliberations. The three men were angry with the Arab governments who had put up the money to create and support their own media groups. The Emir of Qatar had put up $150 million in 1996 to get Al Jazeera started in its headquarters in Doha. Al Arabiya was financed in 2003, by $300 million of Saudi money after the royal family witnessed the success of the Emir's investment. It operates out of Dubai. Money was no problem, due to the oil revenues that supported their investors.

These two media enterprises were now operating news bureaus in Washington, London, and many other unlikely locations. As Thomaston, Lord Pressman, and von Aragon saw it, these companies were nothing more than government-supported propaganda machines. They complained in all their newspapers, magazines and TV news broadcasts that these Arab news disseminators were government subsidized and not independent, and that they were merely propaganda machines for Islam. The existing big three media empires openly contended that since Al Jazeera and Al Arabiya weren't even attempting to present the truth, they shouldn't be allowed to operate in competition with the publications and broadcasts of the world's free press. The recognition of sins in others is greater when they are the same sins as one's own. The world was evidently not listening to their protests, so something had to be done. Thomaston was furious.

"The incredible gall of these Islamist jihadist journalists sitting in the newsroom of the White House, in Whitehall, and the Bundesrat, is enough to make a sane person favor bombing them back into the Stone Age," he thundered.

"Look at how cleverly they have publicized the golf tournaments in Dubai and Qatar in order to buy good will," Pressman observed. "It's amazing what can be done with unlimited supplies of money. Just building a golf course in an unlikely place like a desert is a monumental achievement, but putting up huge prize money to attract the best golfers in the world to play there is a veritable masterstroke. The appeal of golf as a genteel occupation is intended to lull the world into thinking that the desert marauders of the past have suddenly become benign sportsmen. The concept of having the world's best golfers shill for them is brilliant. It is almost worthy of *us*," Pressman concluded.

"Yes, they must be laughing themselves silly," Von Aragon agreed. "We host them, and they want to kill us. They tell their audiences that we're infidel dogs, and they point out how stupid we are to let them sit in our capitals and churn out hate messages. They're making us eat our free speech words."

"Yes, and they're right," said Lord Pressman. "We're stupid to allow it. This whole business of a free press is a farce. It's never been free. The Israelis don't allow them in the Knesset, so why the hell should we open all our doors to them? I believe we allow this in order to maintain some sort of principled democratic free press. What is the principle of a free press worth if it paradoxically exists only long enough to permit them to use it to incite their jihadist terrorists to kill us?"

"Now that maniac Iranian is making alliances with any idiot leftist that hates the U.S.," Thomaston remarked. "Do those poor peasants in Latin America really think Iran cares about them? Not until they all, every single one of them, are shouting Allah Akbar in the plazas and squares, and their Socialist asses are pointing heavenward as they face Mecca."

"You're right, Thomaston," Von Aragon agreed. Only then will the Islamic government in Tehran be satisfied. If these peasant leftists think they have the sophistication to deal with this *new* Persian Empire, they have a big surprise coming. If they think it's horrible to be a lackey for the Americans, just wait till they become the dhimmis of the ayatollahs."

"Well, we all certainly agree on this issue. The point is, what are we going to *do* about it?" Lord Pressman asked.

The three men knew that fuming and fulminating wasn't going to help. They had to get down to business and think of some ways to fight back.

"We've been trying to cast the Arab media in a bad light for a long time, but it doesn't seem to have helped. The problem is that we're the problem," von Aragon said.

"What do you mean?" Lord Pressman asked.

"Well, aside from giving them seats and time to speak in the question periods," Von Aragon said, "we also supply the telecommunications systems with which they blast out their crazy false messages. Our companies sell them the electronic weapons with which they shoot us. We allow them to build their mosques all over our countries, while they prohibit us from putting churches and synagogues on their soil. Their sheikhs are growing fat on Western foods, and their harems are full of Western women, while they extort the money to pay for these things from us. It's extortion to organize a monopoly and manipulate the price of a commodity like oil. Why do we allow it, Robert?"

"The problem is we've castrated ourselves," said Robert. "We've got all the resources we need to correct the mess, but our governments are composed of incompetent men and women. Our President evidently thinks Islam is going to love us for removing their ammunition, but he's just a foolish optimist. With them it's still going to be, *convert to Islam or else*. We have to manufacture some news that'll promote our interests. If the Arab press can utilize the 'Big Lie,' then so can we."

"Exactly," said Von Aragon, with growing excitement. "Let's have our respective newsrooms crank out anti-Arab propaganda by the ton. Let's saturate the airwaves and the print media with every known disparaging thing we can find to say about them. Let's blame them for everything bad that happens in the world, it's mostly true anyway. Let's get everyone in the West so riled up that every Arab will be cringing in his hovel for fear we'll nuke him. Then maybe they'll back off. The Israelis got it right. If the Arabs mess with the Jews, they get it right back in spades. It's the only thing they understand."

"That's true, Friedrich, I totally concur," said Geoffrey. "We should also ask our leaders, who've promised to get us off the oil tit, to actually *do* it. A good program of promoting the environment always goes down well with the public."

"It's time to play the hydrogen card," Thomaston said. "Let's send a few fat checks to the extreme ecologists and environmentalists, encouraging them to push the President and our Prime Ministers to get on the hydrogen bandwagon. Hydrogen is clean. Hydrogen doesn't belong to the Arabs. If we get cracking we'll have the technology first, and then we can sell it to China and India, who are about to encase themselves in smog so thick they'll need chainsaws to cut through it, while they make the Arabs even richer. Let's get the lazy buggers at 10 Downing Street and the White House off their duffs. We need another Manhattan Project type of effort. Let's send Mecca a message. What do you say?"

"I say yes," said Von Aragon.

"And I say yes!" said Pressman.

"Then it's settled," said Thomaston. "As soon as we get back home we'll each get together with our staffs and put on one hellish big push to get our message out. We'll bury those bushy-beard Islamist bastards in media snow so deep they'll never be able to dig their way out, and at the same time we'll pull the oriental oil rug out from under them and replace it with a flying carpet of hydrogen."

The three men clinked glasses and laughed gleefully at the thought of their future successes.

CHAPTER FOUR

Margo Watson was relieved to have posted her story, and glad to have some place to go to relax. A butler admitted her to the suite where Robert Thomaston had said the cocktail party would be held. The elegant room was beautiful, with its panoramic view of Washington along one whole side. Margo wondered whose suite it was. She had no idea that her host was the reporter that she had sat next to, and with whom she had lunched.

She didn't recognize any of the guests. Most of them were well-dressed older men interspersed with a number of elegant younger women wearing cocktail dresses. Next to them Margo felt self-conscious and underdressed. She also was sure she outweighed every other woman in the suite.

Perhaps there was a fashion show going on somewhere in the hotel, she thought, otherwise where would all these thin, fashionable women have come from? As she stood at the bar to ask for a drink, a couple of the female guests stopped talking and stared at Margo as though they were looking at an alien being. Judging from their haughty expressions, Margo had no doubt that she had been found dismally wanting. They obviously felt she was not worth talking to, and they openly snubbed her by turning away to continue their conversation.

Robert Thomaston had been talking with a distinguished gentleman, but when he saw Margo at the bar he broke away and went over to her.

"How are you, my dear? I'm glad you could come. Did you finish your story?"

"I did," she answered. "Who are all these people?" She spoke to him like a confidant, as though she knew that they had both crashed this party.

"Just some friends and acquaintances," he said. "Would you like me to introduce you?"

"I'd like to go to the ladies room first. Do you know where it is? I'd like to park my laptop, too."

"The washroom is in there," he gestured with his head. "You can leave your computer on the bed."

When she turned to leave, Thomaston gave her derriere an appraising look as she walked away.

Margo wondered how Robert knew precisely where the bathroom and the bed were located. On a whim, she took her laptop into the bathroom with her. While she sat in the stall she flashed up Google, and searched Robert Thomaston. What came up on her screen nearly bowled her over. It turned out that Thomaston was the preeminent publisher of news and current events in the United States. He owned hundreds of newspapers, radio, and TV stations, including her paper, and was rated as one of the most powerful and influential men in the country.

"Good Lord," she thought, "what a piece of good luck to have been sitting right next to him at the conference!"

She left the room, walking on air to have had lunch with such an important man. She had thought him so unassuming in his demeanor that she believed him to be just another reporter like herself. He had listened so patiently to her story about her boss. She never would have expected such an important person to behave that way.

When she arrived back in the main room, she had made up her mind to continue to act as though she didn't know his true identity. Thomaston waved her over and introduced her to the gentleman he had been talking to, whose name she immediately forgot. Then he did something that amazed her.

"Your attention please," he called out loudly, so that everyone would hear. When all the voices in the room fell silent, he cleared his throat and continued.

"I'd like to introduce you all to Margo Watson. To those of you who don't know her already, she is one of America's most promising young investigative reporters."

Margo, although she was nearly floored, noticed that the superior expressions on the faces of the women who had snubbed her had not become friendlier, they just turned to envious hate. The men, however, were anxious to meet her. Although she was cordial to them all, she tried her best to stay within arm's length of Thomaston.

"Will you join me for a light supper after the party?" he asked her, when they found themselves alone for a moment.

She had smiled shyly at him and nodded her assent.

When Thomaston had seen his last guest out the door, he sidled up to Margo and put his hand on her shoulder.

"Miss Watson, would you like to have dinner now?"

"Yes, indeed I would. I purposely didn't eat too many hors d'oeuvres in order to leave room for dinner."

"Good for you. We can't have you bursting out of your clothes now, can we?" he said, giving her shoulder a little squeeze. He told himself that Margo would not burst out of her clothes, but she would be out of them by night's end.

It was the first time he had touched her, and she wasn't absolutely sure if he was being inappropriate or just being avuncular. She guessed it was the former. She would have to wait to see what he did next, but she wanted to figure out what her response was going to be in advance, so that if she turned him down, she could do it right away before things got awkward. This man could be the key to her career development, she thought. She acknowledged that she had been willing to sleep with Mike Slayton to get ahead, so why wouldn't she do it with someone really important?

She was glad now that she hadn't gone all the way with her boss. You never knew what these guys might talk about in private, and she wouldn't have wanted Robert Thomaston to know that she would have done it with Slayton if he hadn't been interrupted by a phone call from his superior. On the other hand, if Slayton knew that she had slept with his boss, he would still hate her, but he might be a whole lot nicer to her, and that couldn't hurt.

Actually Margo had always used sex to get what she wanted, but it was only lately that it had become routine. As a teenager she had noticed how much control she could have over boys by just allowing, or disallowing them certain liberties. Later she had learned how to please a boy, while at the same time conforming the relationship to anything she wanted it to be. It was a lesson well learned, and one she had used to her advantage in other situations.

The garnering of this sexual knowledge of men had had its detrimental side for Margo, however. She didn't trust love, particularly platonic love. Love for her had always been too mixed up with sex. She knew men couldn't tell the difference anyway, so she became unsure if she could either.

"Let's have room service send up some food. That way we can kick off our shoes and not have to go out. How does that sound to you?" Thomaston asked.

"You aren't going to try to seduce me if we stay in, are you Mr. Thomaston?"

"We'll have to see how that goes, Miss Watson. You are over the legal age of consent, are you not?" It did not escape his notice that Margo had made the effort to find out his name.

"Yes, of course."

"Good, then you may do anything you wish. I certainly will not force you into bed with me. Now I'm going to order the food," he said, lifting the phone with authority.

The waiter came with a trolley and an ice bucket with a chilled bottle of Mumm's. The table he rolled into the suite was covered with an immaculate white damask cloth.

"Shall I pour the champagne, Mr. Thomaston?"

"No, thank you, I'll do it myself."

The waiter removed the cloth from the table with a flourish, and retraced his steps to the door.

"Have a pleasant evening, sir," he said, as he quietly pulled the door closed behind him.

There was a quiet moment while Thomaston deftly removed the cork. Then came the traditional popping sound, and the effervescing of the wine as he poured two glasses and handed one to Margo.

"I feel a toast is in order." He raised his glass. "To a budding young star in the journalism firmament."

"Why thank you," she said, and kissed him on the cheek. They took seats opposite each other and sipped the wine.

"What did you think of the conference, Margo?"

"I thought they each had a separate axe to grind. Their sponsoring organizations all stand to gain if a concerted effort is mounted to curb air pollution, but I didn't think they'd ever pull together. Dr. Murphy was the only one who made any real sense. She provided some interesting facts, and her analysis of the data led me to believe that there was a case for immediate large-scale action to control automobile and industrial pollution."

"So you got the feeling from Dr. Murphy's comments that the situation was urgent, but that nothing was going to get done until after the crisis came. Is that right?"

"Exactly."

He poured them each another glass of champagne.

"Do you think the news media can do anything to help?"

"You bet I do. They could put on a real blitz, and get John Q. Public all riled up. Then maybe our do-nothing congress would actually do something for a change."

"So then, Margo, you visualize the media as being able to do things besides just report the news?"

"I certainly do."

"Well, that's a refreshing point of view. Usually people think journalists just stand around waffling and blathering on about nothing."

"That's not a very true picture, as far as I'm concerned."

Margo was impressed that a real force in the media business was asking her, a cub reporter, to comment on these issues. That seemed a pretty humble thing for him to be doing. He had done nothing to capitalize on how important he was. He seemed to be natural, normal, and not the kind of egomaniac that she imagined someone of his high status to be. She decided that she would not in any way indicate that she knew of his stature in the media world. If he thought she liked him for himself, and not for his money, fame, or position, things would go better for her.

She was right, of course.

"I don't know about you, but I have definitely exceeded my allotted calorie intake for the day," Thomaston said.

"Me too," Margo replied. "Everything was delicious, but we don't have to eat it all, you know. Let me put temptation out of reach."

She got up from her chair, pushed the wheeled table to the door and slid it out into the hall.

"Are you putting *all* temptation out of reach?" he asked, as he intently watched her hips.

"Not all."

Margo returned, took his hand, and led him to the couch. She went to the TV to find the remote.

"What kind of television programs do you like best?"

"I watch news all the time, sports sometimes, and the occasional movie. How about you?"

"Pretty much the same, only more movies than sports."

She handed him the remote, and sat down next to him.

"It's your room. We'll watch whatever you like."

Thomaston took the remote, but didn't turn the TV on. He gazed at her until she turned her face toward him. They looked into each other's eyes. He was studying her to see if he could assess her qualities from what he could see in her eyes. She didn't blink. She looked him foursquare in the eyes, trying to discern what this man had that made him so successful. She wasn't able to read him at all. She thought he might be looking at her as a way of getting permission to make love to her. She took his hand and placed it on her thigh. Permission granted.

It became quickly apparent to Margo that he had a good knowledge of a woman's anatomy. He lifted her from the couch, displaying unsuspected strength, and carried her to the bedroom. She could tell he was very experienced with women, and she was finding his matter-of-fact, authoritative attitude to be an enjoyable relief from the usual boisterous behavior of her younger lovers. How convenient that Robert happened to be rich and control a huge media empire.

As a cynical man of the world, Thomaston was surprised that his young bed partner had been so genuinely responsive. And she really didn't seem to know who he was, he silently mused. He was used to thinner women who were interested in him because of his position. Their true love, however, like that of Narcissus, could only be seen in their own reflections.

But Margo was different. She was totally natural about sex, seemed to honestly enjoy it, and was the equal of any woman, even those who made it a profession. He liked her strong, womanly body, too. It made a lovely change from the bulimic models and the egocentric actresses who sought his favors. She treated him as just a man, not the fountain of wealth that most women believed him to be.

He originally thought that he would lord it over Mike Slayton because he had bedded her and Mike hadn't. But now he decided that Margo was a keeper, at least for a while. Slayton would now have to learn of it accidentally. It wasn't exactly clear to him at the moment how he would handle Mike, but master him he would.

While they were dressing the next morning, Robert asked Margo if she would like to accompany him to Europe later that day. He told her he had been invited to cruise on a friend's yacht in the Mediterranean for a few days, and he would like it if she'd accompany him as his date.

"Robert, that sounds wonderful, and I'd give anything to go with you, but I can't afford to lose my job. As things are, I think Mike Slayton is going to fire me because I said no to him. All he needs is a reason, and I'm out of work."

Neither she, nor Robert, realized that it was Robert's own phone call that had kept her from making a big mistake with Mike. Had she known, she would have counted it as divine intervention. Going to bed with Robert was proving to be infinitely more satisfying. He had so much more to offer, and he was her best lover ever. The situation was almost romantic, and would have been, except for the fact that she knew all about him and was pretending not to. Robert, on the other hand, had the emotional characteristics of a pit bull. He could cuddle, or kill.

"Margo, trust me, Slayton is not going to fire you," Robert said, feeling the same pride as he would have if he had cuckolded Mike.

"How can you be so sure?"

"Let's just say that he owes me a favor."

"I've got to go back to my apartment and pack, then."

"I'll have my driver take you home and bring you back. Pack a bathing suit. I'm looking forward to seeing you in something skimpy."

"You can see me in less than that."

She kissed him and headed for the door.

Thomaston watched her go. He observed her black ponytail swinging rhythmically in time to the movement of her derriere beneath her skirt as she walked across the suite towards the door. She hadn't had time to rearrange her hair properly after the tousling it had suffered during lovemaking, so she had tied it up quickly. She looked girlish with it done that way, but as Robert appraised her legs from behind, he knew she was a female animal at the exact peak of her physical maturity. He congratulated himself for having the evening turn out exactly as he had planned it from the minute he had sat next to Margo at the conference. In fact, he noted with satisfaction, she had exceeded his expectations.

CHAPTER FIVE

Brooklyn entered Ivan's office with a sheaf of papers in her hand.

"I have the information about Margo Watson that you wanted," she said.

"Okay, what do we know?"

"She's young, no more than twenty-five. This is her first real job as a journalist. She works at the Post under Mike Slayton. You may know of him. He's been around forever. I can't say her manager is very impressed by her skills, but he told me she's pretty. I could almost hear him licking his lips as he described her. When I asked if she was in at that moment, he told me she was in Europe on an assignment, but that she'd be back in a few days."

"Thanks, Brooklyn. Anything else?"

"I followed up with some of her profs at the journalism school. They all remembered her, mostly because of her appearance. She must be a real looker. Her grades ranked her in the middle of her class. One of her teachers told me that even though she wasn't the smartest one in the bunch, she was very ballsy. In fact, she was the most assertive one when it came to getting in to see people who are difficult to interview, and things of that sort. A photographer who was detailed to the environment conference told me that she was sitting next to Robert Thomaston, and they seemed quite chummy. But he hasn't seen her since."

"Thomaston, the same guy who owns the conglomerate that operates a ton of tabloids, newspapers, magazines, and broadcasting companies?"

"That's the one," Brooklyn answered.

"Call his office, will you? Find out where he is right now, but don't speak to him or connect me."

"I've already done that, boss. He flew to Barcelona in his private jet. The manifest listed Thomaston, one female passenger, and three crew members. The passengers are listed as American citizens. After landing in Barcelona they'll be transferred to a helicopter. The chopper pilot has logged a trip for two out to a large motor yacht named *Sternlicht*. The M.V. *Sternlicht* is registered in Germany to a man named Baron Friedrich Von Aragon. In case you didn't know, he's the German media mogul who controls most of the papers and networks in Europe. The yacht is a super posh plaything of the rich and famous, and it's currently bound for Palma de Majorca."

"Anything else? Please don't hold anything back," Ivan joshed. "What color underwear is the Baron wearing?"

"I doubt very much that he's wearing any underwear, but that's only my opinion. Thomaston's plane is standing by for their trip home in a couple of days. Oh, and the chopper pilot took an English couple out to the same yacht on the day before he was scheduled to ferry Thomaston out to it. In my opinion it's a slam-dunk that little Miss Watson is amusing herself and Mr. Thomaston as we speak, in ways we can only imagine."

"Excellent work, Brooklyn. Your mother must be very proud of you. Don't spend too much time imagining what they're doing. We've got work to do."

Margo Watson was silently incredulous. Here she was, seated in Robert Thomaston's Lear jet on Florentine beige leather seats, having a drink and looking out at the east coast speedily retreating to the west. They were alone except for the crew, which included the pilot and co-pilot in the cockpit and a beautiful blond flight attendant. It crossed Margo's mind that perhaps Robert had had sex with this tall, shapely,

Scandinavian woman. Margo wouldn't have blamed him. She was certain that most men would consider her far more beautiful than Margo felt herself to be. She tried to detect from the woman's attitude toward her whether there was any envy or jealousy present, but strangely enough she couldn't discern any at all.

The flight to Barcelona was to take five hours or so. Robert was busy making phone calls, but because of the distance between them and the noise of the jet engines, she couldn't make out a word he was saying. She was riding with her back to the cockpit door, while Robert was facing forward. There was a table between them, and they each had a window seat. Once in a while their eyes would meet, but other than that they had been incommunicado since the plane left the tarmac at Dulles. Margo thumbed through several magazines. She had resolved not to speak to Robert while he was busy. The last thing she wanted was to annoy him like some dumb bimbo who needed constant attention.

While she had been packing in her apartment she had wondered what the plane ride would be like. She thought perhaps Robert would want to have sex. She felt silly about it, but she wanted to join the mile high club. She would never have admitted it to anyone, though. Especially not Robert.

She imagined the interior of a multi-millionaire's plane would look like an airborne bedroom. She had intentionally neglected to wear panties, partly as a surprise for him, and partly to make things easier in case the plane didn't have a bed on board. Margo was a little disappointed that he was either too busy or too disinterested to pay attention to her.

Whether it was Robert's vague apathy or memories of the night before, she found herself wanting him. The feeling was something new for her. She had always needed a fair amount of arousing before she felt the way she did at that moment, and normally she didn't get it. What was it that attracted her to him? He was middle-aged, a bit pudgy, could have used more hair, and all in all, no big bargain to look at. She had been with younger and handsomer men, but he had made her feel like she had never felt before, the way good sex was described in the women's magazines. She wanted to feel that incredible rush again and again, but she didn't want to be obvious about it. She got up and made her way to the W.C.

When she went back to her seat, Robert was working away at his laptop. She wondered if he had even noticed that she'd been away. He certainly had the ability to concentrate. After about an hour he finally looked up and glanced in her direction. She found it seductive that she had no idea what he was really thinking. There was an element of mystery about him, and of course he had the tremendous power of his riches and his station in the world.

She remembered how tender and polite he had been to her in bed, but she had a suspicion that he knew perfectly well from the beginning that she would sleep with him that night, even though they had only just met. He had seemed so relaxed, unhurried, and undemanding, but there was also something about the confident way he had touched her. It was as though he understood her body perfectly. What would the nature of their relationship be after this first night together? Obviously it was not going to be a one-night stand. He must have liked her, or why would he have invited her to come to Europe with him? The casual way he handled great power was not as she would have imagined.

She recalled the night in his suite, the things he said, and the way he said them. He gave pleasant little orders, and she was glad to obey. She would have done anything he asked of her. Why? What was it that made her so compliant? She liked the way he had handled her question about missing work, and how he had informed Mike Slayton that he wanted her not to lose her job. Everything was so easy for him to arrange, and well within his control to do so. It was the sheer application of great power without any fuss or bother that did it, she decided. Imagine jetting the world in his private plane, and spending time on a yacht in the Mediterranean!

She had always been attracted to alpha males, but this time she was in the stratosphere in more ways than one.

After three hours of concentrated work, Thomaston closed his laptop and looked over at Margo.

"Excuse me for being so preoccupied, my dear. I just felt I should get my work done so I could concentrate on you for the rest of the day."

"That's all right, Robert. I understand. But I'm glad to hear that you'll be able to spend some time with me now. If your ability to concentrate on your work is any indication of how you'll concentrate on me, I'll be a lucky woman."

"I'm glad you feel that way. Now let me see the article you submitted yesterday."

Margo dug around and passed him her copy. She worried that he wouldn't find it good enough. Thomaston took it, read it, and looked up at her standing in front of him waiting for his verdict.

"Good work, Ms. Watson. I told everyone that you were going to be a sensational investigative reporter, and I was right. You should be able to work that liaison into a veritable flurry of scandalous plots and pay-off possibilities. Why don't you write a longer piece about this strange liaison? We'll put it in the Sunday Supplement."

The plane descended and made a smooth landing at the Barcelona airport. Robert's aircrew transferred their baggage to a helicopter that was awaiting their arrival. In a few minutes Margo was having her first chopper ride. They flew south over the sparkling waters of the Mediterranean Sea until a large white ship came into view. The chopper circled the ship and landed on the stern deck helipad. The two new arrivals descended the kick stairs of the helicopter. It was Robert's third visit and he was familiar with the layout of the super yacht from previous tours. He led the way to the entrance of the saloon, and Margo took his arm.

Once inside, an effusive Baron Friedrich Von Aragon greeted them. He hugged Robert and shook Margo's hand warmly as Robert introduced her.

"Everyone calls me Fritz, and you must too," the Baron said to Margo.

Margo doubted that *everyone* called him Fritz, but she smiled and said that she would be honored to call him by his first name.

Baron Fritz led her off to the bar, and smiled at Karl the bartender.

"You must order something special," he said to Margo. "Try to make it a drink that Karl has never heard of. He says he knows the recipe for every drink there ever was, so we have a little contest going to prove that even the great Karl doesn't know everything. So far we have only managed to prove that he is right. He *does* know everything."

Margo ordered a dirty Martini, which was no challenge at all for the bartender who knew everything. Robert asked for a scotch and soda. Drinks in hand, the Baron led the couple over to the other guests. He presented Geoffrey Lord Pressman to Margo. Robert and the Englishman exchanged familiarities, while Baron Von Aragon led Margo over to two women who stood nearby.

"Margo, I'd like you to meet Susan Summercroft, Lord Pressman's companion. And this beautiful woman here is my special friend, Hilde."

After making the introductions he bowed slightly and left the women to talk with one another while he rejoined the men. Fritz was glad he'd asked his business guests to bring their girlfriends along this time. Hilde didn't like being left out, and when Hilde didn't like something she made things difficult for Fritz. The additional female company was pleasant, but most importantly it pacified Hilde.

Margo Watson suspected that she would be spending a lot of her time with these two women while the men talked business. She knew how dedicated Robert was to his work, so she decided she'd better get to know these women, if only to keep herself busy and not interrupt him or rely on him for her entertainment. Margo assessed them as they exchanged pleasantries, not because she felt competitive but to find out if they had anything in common.

Her immediate impression of Susan was that she was trying to play the role of Lady Pressman. She was elegantly dressed in an aqua silk printed dress that moved about her when she walked, as though it had a life of its own. She was wearing a straw sun hat with a wide brim that shaded her pale skin from the sun. Her shoes were made of expensive Italian leather with narrow little straps running in creative directions over her well-manicured toes and feet. She was the very picture of an upper-class English woman, and Margo could imagine her at Ascot as Lady Pressman.

Hilde, on the other hand, didn't strike Margo as being the quintessential mistress of an important man. She was a towering woman, with an undeniably Germanic heritage. She had authority and discipline written all over her. If Margo had been a casting director, she would have chosen her to play the colonel in charge of the women prisoners in a WWII German camp. Every part of her body not covered by her elegant clothing was tanned and muscled. Neck, arms, and legs spoke of the long hours she must have spent in the gym. She came just short of a professional bodybuilder's fitness level. Had she wanted to, Margo felt that Hilde could have been Germany's answer to Austria's Schwarzenegger.

Apparently the two women had been on board the yacht for quite some time, as they knew their way around. They decided, as a way to occupy their time, to show Margo the yacht and point out a few of its remarkable amenities. Margo was already impressed to the hilt before she even left the afterdeck. As the informal tour proceeded she realized she was on board one of the premier mega-yachts in the world. Her entire interior was built of cherry wood and teak. The deeply varnished red wood cabinetry added an undeniable nautical elegance to every stateroom. The yacht's lovely classic woodwork didn't prevent its German owner from installing every modern device designed by man. It had flat-screened TVs that rolled out of almost every surface at the touch of a button. The cabinetry contained a library of DVDs that ran from raw porn to Disney cartoons. The bathrooms had huge, deep tubs, obviously made for two simultaneous bathers. Margo was told that she didn't have to skimp on water because the yacht made its own supply of desalinated water from the sea. When they finished the tour, Margo thanked them and they went to their cabins to rest for a while before bathing and changing for dinner.

Margo was looking at the assortment of clothing she had brought with her, and realized that she was going to look like a scullery maid compared to the other women on board.

Later that afternoon Robert came to their stateroom to change for dinner. He gave Margo a quick kiss on the cheek, and stood back to admire her.

"Did you have a good time with the other women?"

"Yes, it was great. This is truly a magnificent yacht. So tell me, how did your meeting go?"

"It went well, thanks. We'll need several more days to finish our business, but we'll have all our evenings together. You look very nice, by the way," he added, hoping to change the subject.

He would never have been willing to talk to her about the subjects that he had discussed with the other two men during their collegial meetings. He didn't believe in giving information away gratis. In the media business, information is worth money.

CHAPTER SIX

Baron Fritz's ocean motor yacht was proceeding south toward Palma de Majorca while the three bigwigs of the media business were in conference. The Baron had arranged for the women to disembark for a little change of scenery. He had orchestrated a tour of one of the lesser islands, and organized a swim for them at a local private beach. The three men would stay on board and continue their discussions.

These men had participated in the great metamorphosis that had taken place in the news business. What had started as an agglomeration of thousands of independent newspapers serving their local communities eventually became, through acquisitions, mergers and takeovers, a nearly homogeneous world media machine. The news was now being gathered by news bureaus and distributed to the rapidly consolidating newspapers in the hinterlands. Ownership was centralizing and being controlled by fewer and fewer people. Editorial policy was likewise becoming so limited and constricted that the views of the few were the only ones ever seen in print. Consolidation was argued to be the only hope for salvaging the smaller papers, and it continued apace until the arrival of the new wave of electronic news dissemination.

First radio and then television news programming came along to usurp many of the functions that newspapers had once performed. Local papers in the smaller markets were finally reduced to weeklies and served mostly as vehicles for local merchants and classified advertisements. Any national or international news items that appeared in the papers were supplied like pulp fiction from headquarters. In most cases the public didn't know that the editorials, news and features weren't local at all, or that the opinions expressed came from news corporations far away from their home towns in both distance and philosophy.

The print media barons were at risk from competition coming from the airwaves, so they simply broadened their targets. Then, after receiving F.C.C. approval, they began acquiring stations and networks. Soon the corporations that had consolidated the newspapers into very few hands now proceeded to do the same thing to satellite and cable news communications.

Now these three kings of media realms were planning the next steps in their march to control public opinion. While armies of media lawyers and telecommunications lobbyists overwhelmed government regulators who were trying to get a handle on the distribution of frequency, cable, broad-band, and satellite rights to the various petitioners, the big players had already moved on to greener pastures. Being in control of the media gave the broadcasters the editorial clout to influence politicians to their way of thinking. Controlling huge budgets that could fund political campaigns, or not fund them as the case might be, also brought pressures to bear on those seeking public office. Influence peddling was becoming the national pastime, but influencing was not a sufficient guarantee of control to satisfy the dictatorial lust for power of the media corporations.

In the very first meeting with Lord Pressman and Von Aragon, Thomaston had noticed how they proudly carried their titles. Coming from America, as he did, Robert knew there was never going to be a title in the works for him. He decided to ignore the fact that no monarch had ever knighted him – he simply created a title for himself without the help or approval of anyone else. He liked the alliteration of the title he had chosen: *Prince of the Press*. He also liked the fact that *Prince* outranked the lowly *Lord* and *Baron* titles of his friends. The title of Prince, although unofficial, also recognized his father and grandfather, who had founded the journalism empire over which he now reigned.

Once he had decided on a title, Thomaston saw to it that it was used as often as possible when referenced by any of his publications. In time Robert Thomaston, Prince of the Press, became a household name. His haughty manner with his employees led many to refer to him as Prince Robert. As far as Thomaston himself was concerned, a usurped title in America was just as valid as the ones that had been doled out by monarchies that no longer existed.

It was obvious that no politician seeking election could win without the support of the media operating behind the scenes. The royal trio of Thomaston, Pressman, and Von Aragon had not failed to notice the popularity of the movie personalities in Hollywood and their increasing visibility during political campaigns. Gradually they became involved with the film producers in their own geographic jurisdictions. Thus Thomaston became a source of investment financing for films being produced in Hollywood, Pressman financed films in Britain, and Baron Fritz was equally active on the continent.

In time they bought into the studios. The need to fill airtime on TV and radio soon led them to produce their own programming. Behind the scenes the media barons were consolidating their hold on the entertainment industry. The footage shot as news in the trouble spots of the world was also usable in the movies. The clear benefits of cost sharing between the news and the entertainment divisions of their corporations led to a blurring of the lines between the two.

The meetings on Baron Fritz's yacht were being held to review the history of their businesses, to clearly understand their present objectives, and to plan for the future. They had no trouble cooperating with one another, since none of the men's enterprises overlapped geographically, but all were linked philosophically. There was much mutual sympathy because of shared problems with government regulators and with new competition entering the marketplace, so the trio agreed to cooperate to achieve mutual goals. There would always be competition, but as long as they stuck together they could combine their efforts and maintain control of the industry among themselves. Besides, there was a genuine bond of friendship forming between them.

As the three friends sipped their drinks in the spacious saloon on board the Baron's yacht, Robert Thomaston was outlining his vision of the future.

"As I see it," he was saying, "news and entertainment are blending into one entity. I think we should go with the flow and merge these two aspects of our businesses, both of which we control. We're forced by our callow and fickle audience to make the news entertaining, and we're creating entertainment on newsworthy topics of interest to the same public. So why not combine the two?"

"Can you elaborate on how you visualize this merging of fact and fiction?" Lord Pressman asked.

"Well, you just put your finger on it right there," Robert pointed out. "No one knows anymore what's fact and what's fiction. Everyone depends on us to tell them the difference. I'm merely suggesting that we tell them what we want them to hear."

"Robert, do you mean that we should make up the news without regard to the facts?" Baron Fritz inquired.

"Yes, and why not? We're running all over the world shooting footage of news events that are repetitive, boring, expensive and prosaic. We could easily film this sort of stuff on our soundstages, or even better, we could pull existing film footage from our libraries and reuse it. We already run the same footage over and over again, so what difference does it make? When we shoot footage of the damage done by a hurricane, for instance, who cares if it was Katrina or Wilma? A bunch of demolished shacks or mobile homes look pretty much the same whether they're in North Carolina or Louisiana, right?"

"Maybe to you, but not to the people whose shacks they once were," said Geoffrey.

"But the owners of those shacks already know that they have been destroyed, so they're not the ones watching it on TV," Robert said. "We can save big bucks by not actually going to the disaster sites to report on them. But these are just details. What I'm really talking about is constructing the news to suit our purposes. Suppose we three decide we want to stamp out terrorism in the Middle East. We can just film a series of terrible defeats for the jihadists in our studios, and keep airing them till the support of the traditional Muslims for the jihadists just dries up. Unsupported, unpaid, and unappreciated, the terrorists would soon lose their appetite for violence. Wouldn't that be a better outcome for the world?"

"So you're saying perception is reality," said the Baron.

"Well, isn't it?" Robert asked. "We're sitting in this yacht right now, and it's a beautiful and stable vessel, but the money that paid for it came from people's desire to learn or be entertained by your presentation of the news, and not from reality. If you write about someone being shot, and that person is unknown, who's going to know the difference? But if the person who gets shot happens to be Yitzhak Rabin, for instance, then he'd better be dead if you say he is. In our business we deal in stories, fiction or non-fiction, it doesn't matter. People like to believe what we print when it's a lie, especially if it's an entertaining lie, but often they won't believe it when it's just the plain old truth."

"Truth is duller than fiction, in other words," said Von Aragon.

"Look," Robert continued, "somewhere to the east of us right now a Mullah is haranguing his followers to blow up our newspaper office because he says we're printing insults to Muhammad. It's a lie, but will the bomb be less deadly? All I'm saying is that we're the ones who make the news. The news doesn't make itself. If a large bomb goes off in a forest, does it make a noise if we don't report it? It's our perceptions that are the reality for our audiences of millions. If we don't report it, then it didn't happen. Between the three of us we can admit it without shame, but thank God no one else knows it. Our job is to make the things that happen be the things we want to happen, up to and including actually making the news we broadcast."

"We're in a very privileged position, and we've always slanted the news events to suit our own political purposes, but we've never just made the news up as though it were a work of fiction," said Lord Pressman.

"Well it's about time we started," Robert said. "Do you think those Arabs at Al Arabiya are having this discussion?"

"No. They're propagandists, pure and simple. But do we want to be like them?" Lord Pressman asked.

"No, but I'd like to survive them. How about you?"

"*Wunderbar!*" exclaimed Baron Fritz. "Who would have thought that competitors could have such a frank discussion? I side with Robert in this matter because the politicians can't get elected without our help. Once elected, however, they become either lazy and do nothing, or they get cocky and do things we don't want them to. I believe we have the right to get what we paid for from our politicians. If they fail to perform to our standards, I think they should be dealt with in any way we see fit."

"Well, out of respect for you gentlemen, I'm willing to discuss this further," said Geoffrey.

"Good," said Robert. "I'll prepare a test case for us to talk about tomorrow."

"Let's adjourn for the rest of the day, then, and go see what the ladies are up to," said Baron Fritz, with a naughty glint in his eye.

Rafael Alvarez had been a contented Viper, fully aware of his good fortune and the irony it involved, when suddenly he had received a direct personal call from Robert Thomaston, the famous media mogul. He could hardly believe his ears. Thomaston wanted him to off Ivan Welland, the very same man that Saudi Prince Umar had contracted him to kill just the day before. What were the odds that two such apparently unconnected men would come to him to hire the services of his killers to do away with the same target at the same time? Alvarez rubbed his palms in glee. He was going to get two fat fees for the same hit. Of course he would bill each of the contractors for the job as though it were theirs exclusively. Every time he thought about it he had to laugh.

Business had gone along swimmingly until the Viper's men had failed on two separate occasions to complete the contracts with Prince Umar and Robert Thomaston. At this point Thomaston, in his anger at the hit men's outrageous incompetence, had turned his journalists loose on the Viper's drug cartel. They had spotlighted the Cali organization and demanded that the local authorities close down the criminal activities that had spiraled from drugs into gunrunning, and now had created a Latino Murder Incorporated.

Thomaston had been right – the power of the press was strong enough to send the Viper straight to jail. A surprise military-style police action in the jungle had caught him in an unguarded moment. He was captured and taken to prison to await trial in Bogotá. His captors were amazed at the docile and upbeat behavior of their prisoner. He treated his jailers with camaraderie rather than reacting to them with the usual fear and suspicion exhibited by other inmates. What the guards didn't understand, however, was that Alvarez had good reason to be content, for everything was going exactly according to plan.

Thomaston believed that he had chastised his inefficient contractor, and that the Viper would be given a life sentence in prison, but Thomaston hadn't figured on the tapes that Alvarez had made of their telephone negotiations, nor had he reckoned with the mettle of the man who was the Viper.

Prince Umar had also been furious at the Viper's failure to finish off Ivan Welland, and he withdrew his hit order. He demanded a refund and proclaimed proudly to Alvarez that he would have his al Qaeda friends do the job instead.

The Viper's scheme to receive a double payment for a single whack job had been foiled. Marine guards at the scene of the crime had killed one of his men, so Alvarez felt there was no need for him to suffer further penalty. The vengeful Viper had already dealt with the second would-be assassin on his payroll, leaving his corpse in Chicago. The police could not identify the body nor explain the motivation for the gangland-style killing. To the constabulary in the Windy City it was just another unsolved drug-related murder that would end up in the cold case files.

The Saudi Prince of Oil and the Prince of the Press both thought themselves far too important to receive short shrift, so they informed Rafael Alvarez that their business with him was concluded. The Viper, however, was not through with the two upstart princes. He had been the king of his jungle, and he had earned his throne in the life-and-death world of the serpents, where turning on the king was likely to be fatal. Pride of self and pride of place are not exclusive to the world of the rich and famous. It flourishes in the underworld too, as the princes would soon find out.

Neither of his two customers had anticipated that the Viper was looking for a way to shed his snake skin and move on. Thomaston's bad press and the Viper's subsequent imprisonment had given him the best possible alibi. Neither his underlings nor his dangerous, ambitious competitors ever suspected that it was *his* failure that had called attention to their operations in Colombia, because he was the first cartel member to be exposed and put in prison. All of this was fine with the Viper, for his scheme was to slip silently away into anonymity anyway. Over the years he had managed to stash away many millions of dollars in laundered cash, and he was looking forward to retiring to a secret destination with his new skin intact, just as he had planned all along.

Revenge was deliciously sweet for the calculating Viper. He had already succeeded in killing off both Prince Umar and his repulsive consort, DeeDee Dunbar. Now the revenge he would exact from the other self-appointed prince, Robert

Thomaston, would be the icing on the cake. That egotistic big shot used the law whenever it suited his purposes, but he broke it whenever he wished, and always considered himself to be above it. Well, he would be writhing from his sting soon enough. The Viper's tape recordings and his supporting affidavit would be like the biting fangs of a venomous snake. Worse than its bite, the lengthy throes caused by the Viper's lethal poison would expose him to a slow and painful death. Alvarez believed that once Thomaston was incarcerated with hardened men who had murdered professionally, the law of the survival of the fittest would take over and Thomaston would succumb to vicious, primitive forces. The King snake would outrank the Press Prince in this jungle.

In an atmosphere that was the polar opposite to that of the Cali prison, Robert Thomaston's ego was buoyed when that night, after the men's meeting, Baron Fritz and his guests had played cards and Margo had emerged as the big winner. It was not just the winning that had pleased Thomaston so much. It was the way Margo had suckered them all in and then bluffed her way to the largest pot of the night. He was proud of her. The woman had something special. He vowed silently that he would reward her later with an unforgettable night of lovemaking.

The prospect of his anticipated pleasure was abruptly dissolved, however, when he received a text message from his Washington office informing him that the head of the Secret Service wanted to see him as soon as possible.

Usually when a high-ranking official of an investigative arm of the bureaucracy wanted to see him, it had to do with a request for information. It was amazing to him how often the information in his files outstripped theirs in detail and accuracy. He shook his head and smiled. Their business was investigating criminals and law-breakers, after all. They had subpoena power. They had the weight of the entire federal government on their side. They even carried weapons to quietly threaten their sources, but they still came to him for information. Thomaston's ego was completely wrapped up in newsgathering, and he was pleased when his informants passed information to his reporters before the police got it.

The Prince of the Press leaned back in his chair and smiled as he put away his cell phone. He easily convinced himself that the head T man just wanted to find out about something that his agents hadn't been able to dig up.

He had decided to return to the United States the next day anyway, as his meetings with Baron Fritz and Geoffrey Lord Pressman had been concluded after a strategy had been worked out among them to cope with the unfair competition coming from the Arab media. The main problems that the cruising trio had with Al Arabiya and Al Jazeera were two-fold. Their first complaint was that they were both financed and supported by Arab governments, which precluded their being representatives of a free press. Their second objection was that journalism coming from these Arabic sources was complete fiction and pure Islamist propaganda.

In spite of this the Arab networks had been granted accreditation and sat side-by-side with the other legitimate members of the world press. The worst of it was that they were establishing themselves as the voice of the Middle East by employing the same techniques that had been used for years by the three media barons. Once the Arab reporters took the giant step from reporting the news to interpreting it with editorial license, the next step came immediately to mind. Why not fabricate the news from start to finish?

The Russians, jealous that the American moon landing overshadowed their triumph with Sputnik, had subsequently had Pravda put out a story that described how the Americans had never really gone to the moon, but had simply made up the story in complicity with special effects provided by Hollywood. That was bad enough, but when the Arab press suggested that it was really the Israelis who had blown up the World Trade Center buildings and were trying to blame it on the Arabs in order to get world opinion on their side, that was too much for the Western media to take. If truth was not a consideration in reporting the news, why bother trying? Why not just create any situation that suits the purposes of the news media, and print or broadcast it? Thomaston's media empire had been using staged events and special effects for years in the making of documentaries. And when his interest in filmmaking took him to Hollywood, he had learned how easily the eye of the beholder could be tricked so that nobody could tell the difference between perception and reality on the screen. It was at this point that Robert Thomaston's megalomania took over.

In his studios he began to make TV serials and feature-length films that were based on actual real-life events. His staff of producers, directors, and actors became so good at portraying fictionalized reality that the media no longer needed *actual* reality. Whatever came across the TV screens of the world looked real enough to convince the audience that they were watching real events. The viewing audiences began to see events such as copycat killings of killings that had never occurred in the first place. Arrests, trials, fights, conventions, battles, or any event of interest to an audience could easily be staged and performed. The participants in these pseudo events didn't even have to get out of their beds in the morning to create the illusions.

If one had sufficient funds one could order a custom-made film depicting a particular conflict and have it resolved in any way the purchaser wished. The footage was kept in Thomaston's film library, and clips from his movies could be borrowed, interchanged, and reused at a tremendous cost reduction. Film editing, directing, and script writing had become some of the fastest growing occupations in America. Biographies in film were being made in profusion, regardless of truth. Documentary films had outstripped fiction in the number of productions underway. In the book world, non-fiction titles exploded and fictional works decreased year by year. There was less need for fiction, since everything was becoming fiction anyway. With enough money you could buy history. You could buy Jewish chronicles, for example, with the holocaust in or out, depending on your audience.

Certain limitations existed, of course, but Thomaston made those up as well. The tag lines *based on real events*, or *based on a true story* became ever more prevalent. Very few people knew which events actually happened and which ones were manufactured on film. Robert Thomaston was the king of the mountain of manufactured reality, and he sat on the throne like King Solomon making judgments for his people. But Thomaston had not been appointed by God, nor elected by citizens, to make their choices for them. Still, he never hesitated to grab all the power he could get his hands on, like a huge magnet drawing iron filings to itself.

Geoffrey Lord Pressman and Baron Von Aragon both feared and admired his many accomplishments. Their meetings usually evolved into sessions in which Thomaston would encourage them to follow his usually diabolical lead. His interests were unfailingly self-serving, so he was totally comfortable with his motivations in currying their friendship. He knew that the more closely his two European colleagues followed his lead, the easier it would be to merge them into his growing empire when he acquired their companies at a time of his own choosing.

After an amorous night with the triumphant Margo the Card Shark Watson, whom he now saw as a potential female counterpart worthy of greater respect, Thomaston fell asleep dreaming of future glory. The next morning they packed, showered, and had breakfast sent to their stateroom, after which Robert ordered the helicopter to come out to the yacht to pick them up. When they had thanked their host and said goodbye to the other guests, they made their noisy departure in the mechanical locust that whisked them off to the airport.

As Margo looked out her window in the departing jet, she thought how easy it would be to become addicted to the life-style of the rich and famous.

CHAPTER SEVEN

The private jet landed at Dulles International Airport in Washington, D.C. As it was five hours later in Europe, Robert Thomaston and Margo Watson had a head start on a case of jet lag. When they cleared through customs, Thomaston's limo was waiting to take them to the penthouse suite in the hotel where they had first met. Robert called the Secret Service and made an appointment to meet the Director the next day. He handled several other matters via phone and e-mail, and then they had room service send them a light supper. Now that they were back in the U.S., things seemed a bit dreary to them. After their royal cruise, nearly everything else would be a let-down.

Margo knew she had to go back to work unless Robert arranged for her to be with him on a more permanent basis. She wasn't looking forward to being under Mike Slayton's thumb again. She began reading the Washington papers to see what she might have missed while she was in Spain. In the little section devoted to upcoming events she noticed that the President was going to have a press conference for the international media. She decided to ask Robert if she could be assigned to that conference as a reporter for one of his newspapers. Even if he said no, it would be a reminder to him that she needed some sort of assignment in order to keep busy and earn her salary.

Because of the time difference, Robert and Margo woke up early. International travel, though exciting, takes its toll on people no matter what their station in life. They were a bit fuzzy-headed, but they ordered their breakfast, showered and dressed. Now that Margo was back in the U.S., she noticed that even getting up in the morning had a quicker pace to it than in Europe.

The breakfast arrived, accompanied with a thick pile of newspapers. Robert dove into the stack and began to read avidly. It was said of Thomaston that he could tell the profit margin of a newspaper to the dollar just by hefting a copy. Margo couldn't keep up with him. He would scan each paper for a couple of minutes then throw it aside. As soon as he was finished with the pile of papers he switched on the TV and moved the channels frequently between CNN, ABC, CBS, NBC, PBS, and Fox. In the course of half an hour he had managed to satisfy himself that they had not missed very much while they were away.

"How do you absorb all that news in such a short period of time?" Margo asked.

"It's not so difficult really," Robert answered. "Nearly all of it is rehash, so there's no reason to burden your brain with repetitive information. You can count the reporters who actually dig up worthwhile news on the fingers of one hand. The spin that's usually put on stories is coming from editors whose positions on important issues are well known to me."

"So all this dull, repetitive stuff must be bad for sales."

"People don't seem to care. They don't have time to go into the details any more."

"But aren't newspapers in trouble? I thought sales were going down."

"They are. They're in a free-fall decline that's been brought on by the advent of the internet service providers who digest everything and spit it out onto the screens of the world's computers. Most people are satisfied with the news at this shallow level."

"So what's happening to the newspapers, then?"

"The flagship newspapers like the New York Times, the Washington Post, and the Wall Street Journal are struggling to stay alive, that's what. They're mostly being used for archival purposes by researchers, professors, and the like.

I've been switching my investments into media companies based on telecommunications."

"Is this a nice way of telling me to find another job?"

"Not exactly, although as readership declines there'll be fewer jobs for reporters on newspapers and magazines."

"So what do you think I should do for a career?"

"Well, you're very attractive, so you could go into TV reporting. You could be an editor or a producer, or you could get a specialty and be an expert commentator like Sanjay Gupta or what's her name, the religion editor. Unfortunately those jobs tend to have a short shelf life, unless you can find the secret of eternal youth. Then, of course, there's the good old path of least resistance..."

"Which is?"

"You stay with me. The devil you know, so to speak."

"Robert, is that an indecent proposal?"

"Yup."

"Then I accept, but with one condition."

"What's that?"

"Occasionally I get to write a story of my choice."

"Why do I think you already know what that story is?"

"I can't imagine, Robert, but I wouldn't mind covering the President's speech. He's going to make another special announcement to the international press."

"I'll arrange it for you then, but I expect some special treatment tonight. Why do I feel so manipulated, I wonder?"

"I have no idea," Margo said, batting her eyelashes.

Robert bent down and gave her a quick kiss.

"I have to go and find out what that damn Secret Service guy wants from me now. I'll call Slayton and tell him I'm assigning you to the press conference. See you tonight, my little manipulator."

"Spoken like a good little capitulator."

Robert Thomaston was not used to being kept waiting in an outer office, and he was impatiently cooling his heels, trying to imagine what on earth the head of the Secret Service could possibly want with him.

"Mr. Thomaston?" A middle-aged woman had poked her head through the doorway and was looking at him with a friendly, speculative expression.

"Yes, that would be me," he said, rising to his feet.

"This way please, sir."

She led him to the inner sanctum of the man charged with the duty of protecting the President's person, among other things. So many times when dealing with government employees, it seemed to Thomaston, the man who held the office took on the importance of the office, as if he and it were one and the same. He could tell immediately that this was going to be another one of those cases. The U.S. Secret Service had approximately seven thousand employees, less than 10% of the number who worked in Thomaston's own companies, but because the government had the force of the law on its side, the bureaucrat in charge considered himself to be much more important than Robert Thomaston.

The Secret Serviceman told him to take a seat in a tone of voice that immediately alerted Thomaston's radar. This was evidently not going to be a mere request for information, as he had expected. He sat across from the federal officer and waited to hear what he had to say.

"Mr. Thomaston, I'd like you to hear a tape-recorded message that has come into our possession," he said, aiming a finger over the play button on the machine that stood on his desk.

"Very well, let's hear it," Thomaston replied, as though *he* were ordering it to be played.

In a minute Thomaston realized that he was hearing his own voice in conversation with Rafael Alvarez. That slimy Viper had recorded their conversations and sent them to the Secret Service. Now he was trying to use them to bring him down, as Thomaston had brought the Viper down with his exposés in the Latin American press. He listened to the tape carefully to make sure they hadn't used names or specified any illegal activities during the course of their telephone conversation. He heard a reference to failing to take out the garbage and a few other veiled statements, but they were out of context and could in no way be considered evidence. Thomaston sat with a totally deadpan expression on his face and waited to see what the Secret Serviceman had to say.

"Mr. Thomaston, we have an affidavit from a prisoner being held in Colombia stating that he had this conversation with you. He stipulates that the garbage in question was Dr. Ivan Welland, the Secretary of Defense. He claims that he had a contract with you to have his men kill Dr. Welland. There was indeed an attack, in fact two attacks on Welland's life, but luckily they were unsuccessful. It is the duty of this agency to protect the lives of the President, Vice President, those in line to become president, and also those delegated by the President to receive the protection of the Secret Service. Dr. Welland is one of those people. Therefore, I am duty bound to ask you, is this your voice on the tape?"

"It seems to be," Robert answered.

"Did you in fact put out a contract on Dr. Welland?"

"I certainly did not. I don't know this Welland fellow. I never met him. Why would I wish him dead?"

"Well, how do you explain the tape?"

"I don't. It's not my job to explain a perfectly ridiculous tape. Perhaps it was put together from sound-bytes. I have no idea. In any case it's a long jump from what I heard on that tape, to an order for a murder to be committed."

"Why would a high profile prisoner go through all the trouble and effort to involve you in a conspiracy?"

"I have no idea who this prisoner is, or why he would do such a thing. Perhaps he felt pilloried by my newspapers and is seeking some sort of revenge," Robert suggested.

"Why would a man in his position, facing a long prison sentence, bother to involve you, of all the people, in this situation? He has nothing to gain from ratting you out. His sentence in Colombia, if he's convicted, will not be any shorter for his having made this accusation."

"I told you, I don't know. Who is this man, anyway?"

"His name is Rafael Alvarez. He's known as *La Víbora* in Spanish, or the Viper in English. He's been indicted, and he'll be tried in Colombia for many serious crimes. We believe he's the head of a huge crime syndicate that was born of money made originally in the drug trade."

"Well, I don't know him. Get him extradited so I can face him. I have a right to face my accuser, don't I?"

"He refuses voluntary extradition, and the Colombian authorities won't let him out of their control."

"So you've hauled me in here without any real proof."

"You were not *hauled* in sir, you came of your own volition. I merely wanted to ask you some questions."

"Well I'm leaving now of my own volition, and I'm telling you I don't appreciate the treatment I've been given. A person is innocent until proven guilty in this country, or at least that's the way it was before you raised your own suspicions and self-importance above the law," Robert said loftily as he moved towards the door.

Nobody could play lofty and self-righteous better than Robert Thomaston.

The Director of the Secret Service was explaining to the Secretary of Defense what Thomaston had said to him during their interview.

"We received some unsolicited tapes from a drug dealer in Colombia," he said to Ivan. "He's in jail awaiting trial, and he sent us the tapes along with an affidavit claiming that he was paid to perform a hit on you. He accuses Robert Thomaston, the media mogul, of paying to have you killed. We brought Thomaston in for questioning, but he's smooth as silk and denies the charge. The accuser is known as the Viper in Colombia, and he has avoided being caught for years by paying off the police. He refuses to testify in person, and we can't extradite him because the Colombians are holding him in prison, and they won't release him to us unless their court exonerates him. What, if anything, sir, do you know of him or Thomaston?"

"I haven't met either of these men, although I know of them by their unsavory reputations. The Viper came to our attention as being a dealer in illegal weapons. Thomaston's media empire has been the inspiration of some research my department is doing into the area of manufactured news. I don't know how either of these men would have gotten to the point where they would want *me* killed. I shouldn't have thought I was important or notorious enough for that."

"It could be that the fellow in Colombia knew nothing about you, and was just filling a hit order. How likely is it that either he or Thomaston got wind of your investigations, and decided to get you off the case? Is it possible that you have a mole in your department?"

"I've treated these matters as top secret. Only a handful of my most trusted people are aware of these investigations. I think the business practices used by these two gentlemen would make looking over their shoulders routine for them. They're very wary of anyone found snooping into, or acting suspicious of their activities. You must be cautious lest you provoke their anger before we have a solid case against them. We've already lost two agents too many. Meanwhile, I thank you for the information. I'll take extra precautions to protect my safety and the security of our work. I've got a beautiful young daughter, and I'd like to be around to see her grow up. Please keep me posted, and I'll do the same."

David Feingold had requested an appointment with his boss to discuss some interesting facts that he had turned up in his investigation of the media, and he wanted to talk to Ivan about his findings during the few minutes before he went to the Press Room.

"Boss, you're suspicions about the media are proving to be clairvoyant. In delving into the ten top stories in terms of media air time and print columns that appeared in the last few weeks, we came across some amazing coincidences."

"Such as?" Ivan asked intently.

"Well, the company owned by this guy Thomaston is so frequently the first to break news that he's either uncannily prescient or he's making it up, and the other media services just follow along so as not to be left out."

"Can we prove that?"

"Not really, but I understand statistics and I know you'll find it more than coincidental that in about 90% of the cases, Thomaston's media empire scooped all his competitors. I think it's also pretty coincidental that he owns a large TV production company and the largest library of news film footage in the world. He employs a staff of special effects guys, and more computer-enhanced filmmaking technicians than anyone else in the country."

"That's very interesting, David. So you think he has the capacity to make a movie depicting anything he likes, and he's putting his own slant on it. Is that what you're saying?"

"That's it in a nutshell. But you've got to hand it to the guy. He's created a sort of *perception-is-reality* business like no other on earth. Maybe that's why so many bigwigs in Hollywood are speaking out on political issues lately."

"Are you telling me that Thomaston makes a movie and passes it off as *real life* in the form of news reporting?"

"Yes. I think that's exactly what he's doing. He's very efficient at it, too. Some guys in Iraq have been killed fifty or sixty times each. Bomb explosions, wreckage, and funeral procession footage appear over and over again, interspersed with phony updates made to look like current events. His company may not be the only one doing this, either. Movie makers always claim that their slanted political work is art, but Thomaston is passing his artwork off as news."

"Isn't there a law against this?" Ivan asked.

"No. We have a free press here in the U.S., and we're proud of it. The Fourth Estate, short of slander, pretty much does whatever it likes. The media have browbeaten the government into submission with legal suits based on First Amendment rights."

"I just want to make sure I heard you correctly," Ivan said, incredulously. "You're saying that the media not only slant the news, but they make it all up from *scratch*?"

"I really think that's exactly what they're doing," David assured him. "Under the best of circumstances the viewing public believes they're receiving accurate reports of actual events, but these reports are always edited, abridged, and slanted. They're getting somebody's idea of *All the News That's Fit to Print*, and nothing that resembles *the truth, the whole truth, and nothing but the truth*. The media have forgotten that freedom carries with it the responsibility of truth and accuracy in their journalistic work."

"In the end it always comes down to the big questions, doesn't it?" said Ivan soberly. Questions like *What is truth?* The media don't even promise that they're going to give us the truth, or any part of it. They just spoon out what they call the news, and the people of the world are stuck with their versions of it. It's no wonder we're all suspicious of one another."

"Well," David said, "I think we all have built-in BS detectors, and they're working overtime these days. If the events portrayed on TV are false and the news is full of lies, we lose faith in the media. We no longer believe what we see and hear."

"Exactly," Ivan agreed. "We live in a Kafkaesque world that's served to us on a silver platter by the likes of Robert Thomaston. By the way, David, the Secret Service believes that it was Thomaston who was behind the attempts on my life."

"Really? Well, I can't say I'm totally surprised. When I do the math I have to believe that he, or his hirelings, are on the scene before the news is even made. In other words, in many cases, as we were saying, they're shaping the events that will *become* the news. You, and the work of our team, are probably the biggest obstacle to Thomaston's hegemony over the world of public knowledge."

"The only thing I can think of to do about this old world of ours is to silence the weapons. Conflict is news. Our *War on Weapons* program suppresses conflict, which of course silences much of the news, so it's no wonder that Thomaston wants to get rid of me. In the defense and security business it's best to be cynical first so we don't have to be sorry later. In the news business it works the other way round. Anyway, thanks for your good work, David. Keep it up. Just make sure you focus your cynicism on those who deserve it."

CHAPTER EIGHT

Margo Watson took her seat in the press gallery. She and the other reporters were waiting impatiently for the President to arrive. He had promised that a major announcement would be forthcoming. The Press Corps was reminded of the time three years before when the President had announced his intention to put a worldwide halt to the manufacture of explosives. He had begun at home, and his example in the U.S. had inspired the people of the world to influence their governments to give his plan a try.

Amazingly enough it had worked – not perfectly, but surprisingly well nevertheless. It had been necessary to destroy two armories in non-compliant countries and levy fines against some smaller operations run by entrepreneurs who thought being small would hide them, but other than that the vast majority of nations had complied with the terms of the President's initiative, and the world had enjoyed nearly three years of comparatively blissful peace.

At first the cynical press had had little confidence that the President's plan would work. But in time the surprising results of his policy to *speak softly, but carry a big stick* had amazed even the most dubious journalist.

Now, as the President mounted the podium, there was a sense of respect and deference apparent among the reporters attending the conference. Those who had expected the plan to fail were now expressing a tentative hope that a politician or an elected official might actually be able to change the world. There was an almost tangible sense of expectation in

the conference hall that day as the smiling Chief Executive
began to speak.

"Ladies, Gentlemen, and citizens of the world, I am
extremely honored to stand before you today to announce a
new initiative. Before I do that, however, I'd like to extend
my compliments to all of you for your work of the last three
years. Although incredible obstacles of hatred and suspicion
had to be overcome, our beleaguered world has finally seen a
tremendous improvement in international comity. Recently
peace has prevailed to a very large extent in the mostly sad
history of our species.

"But before I pass on to new matters, I should like to
admonish you not to rest on your laurels. The garden of
peace needs constant attention, and the weeds of war are ever
encroaching. I beg all of you who want our little dot in the
universe to be God's garden to stay alert, be brave, and pray
for wisdom. If we continue the efforts we have now begun
we shall succeed in the noblest cause of all – the gift of
peace to all people."

The President smiled benignly at the audience and into
the cameras of the world, and continued his presentation.

"Now I'd like to have you join me in another new vision
for the peaceful world that we are building together. Just as
it has been impossible for us to have peace between armed
men, it will be impossible for man to be at peace with his
environment until we have an end to pollution.

"Nature has done a magnificent job of staying ahead of
mankind's nasty habits, but I fear we are gaining on her. We
dare not get ahead of her or the human race will be the loser.
I am proposing, therefore, that we make an all-out effort, on
an international scale, to clean up the shameful mess we've
made, while at the same time we devise a common strategy
that will prevent us from ever mucking things up again.

"My assistants are right now passing out a written plan
that explains what must be done to beat back the harm we've
already caused, and how to prevent polluting activities in the
future. Copies of this plan are being submitted to the leaders

of every nation on earth. For several years now Dr. Laura Burke, née Murphy, has been traveling the globe observing environmental problems, speaking to leaders in the field, and formulating the plan you now have in front of you. Dr. Burke is a highly-respected environmental scientist and a passionate exponent of a well world. I've asked her to head up this effort for me, and for all of you. I'm asking you to cooperate with her as she labors to provide clean air for all to breathe, pure water to all who need it, and fertile soil in which to plant healthy food.

"When you have time to examine the handouts in detail you will find the results of Dr. Burke's research, and the statistics-based measurements upon which her calculations were based. Included are standards that need to be met by all nations if we are to begin making significant progress. I'm appointing Dr. Burke as my representative in all matters concerning the environment.

"I'm hereby asking for the full cooperation of all nations in this matter, because we live on one planet and the actions of one effect us all. Dr. Burke will now be the second Ambassador Plenipotentiary in her family, but the objectives of her strategy will be second to none in importance.

"For those nations who will complain that they can't afford to clean up their environments, we will offer help when it is necessary. Presidents are pragmatists, after all. We are elected to achieve positive results, and we must not fail to do so. Problems of greenhouse gas emissions, global warming, lack of potable water, and unproductive soil must be solved quickly. We no longer have the luxury of looking the other way. We need to face up to our environmental problems and begin to solve them now, not later.

"On the last page of the handout you'll find a list of the incentives the United States will offer for the successful attainment of the national goals we have prescribed for each country. You'll see that America's future policy with regard to foreign aid disbursements will be keyed into the results. Achieve half the prescribed results, and the nations receiving financial aid or trade incentives will have their funds cut in half. But reach the standards as outlined by Dr. Burke's program, and monetary incentives will be available in full.

"In order to successfully address the problems of the environment, we will require large changes in the way things are presently being done. There is absolutely no doubt about the correlation of air pollution with the use of fossil fuels. Solutions must be found for that urgent problem, so I'm asking you to pay particular attention to the section dealing with coal and petroleum products. We simply must get over our dependence on these fuels, but obviously we must have something to put in their place.

"The United States will therefore contract with the nations of the world to produce a clean fuel to substitute for the polluting fossil fuels of today. Research is underway on the development of hydrogen-fueled vehicles and stationary plants. We will be asking other nations to share with us in this research, but we must set a realistic goal ensuring that we will end our fossil fuel dependency as soon as possible. We will simultaneously focus on other non-polluting energy sources such as wind, solar, tidal, nuclear, and hydro.

"Now, ladies and gentlemen, I must stop talking about curing pollution and start doing all I can to see that it gets done. The problems are huge I admit, but I can tell you without hesitation that they can be successfully addressed if we use the available technologies, work together, and have a cohesive plan. The plan is now in your hands, and I strongly exhort each and every one of you to search your conscience and enter the next world challenge with the United States as your partner."

Having concluded his remarks, the President waved a copy of Laura's plan high above his head. He indicated with an upward gesture that each attendee also rise and wave their copies, and with his other raised arm he gave the V for victory sign. In seconds the audience was cheering and waving back to symbolize its agreement.

As they had three years before, those present at the announcement speech were left gasping at the immensity of the task the President had set before them, but they also felt inspired to follow the man that had since become known as the Peacemaker.

The Viper assumed that Thomaston had bought his way out of his involvement in the conspiracy to kill Dr. Welland. He believed, based on the many times he had successfully used that tactic himself, that bribery was universally the way to solve problems with law enforcement officials. Since he hadn't heard or read anything about Thomaston's being arrested or tried for his crime, he assumed that the matter was closed. He knew that Ivan Welland had been appointed Secretary of Defense, so he concluded that Thomaston must have abandoned his murderous plans, because as a Cabinet member Welland was now too well protected.

The matter may have been closed as far as the law and Thomaston were concerned, but the Viper could not ignore his need for revenge. In time, he might have forgotten about Thomaston's pressure tactics on the Colombian police that had resulted in his arrest and his premature flight from the country, but he had learned quite by accident that Robert Thomaston had a large house in Costa Rica.

The little Central American nation had throughout its history stayed close to the American way of life. It had enjoyed a brief flirtation with the left, but had eventually chosen dependence on the U.S. economy over communism, poverty, and dictatorship. It had become a democracy with a sensible constitution, peaceful people, and no income taxes, mostly made possible because it decided to have no army. With no military expenses, the tiny nation was able to spend its money on social programs that benefited all its citizens. It had quickly become a star performer in the Caribbean region, a destination for immigrants from the less successful neighboring nations, and a home to expatriates from colder climes seeking the comforts of warm weather.

One of the biggest problems for Costa Rica is illegal immigration. It is amazing how quickly ordinary people will desert economically and politically disadvantaged homelands to seek more promising opportunities over the border in a prosperous, free country. Like other democratic nations that had generously welcomed immigrants to their shores, Costa Rica had no procedures to ascertain whether the incoming people were intending to assimilate with the citizens of their adoptive nation. Of course, the arrival of crowds of poor immigrant people as well as opportunists like the Viper and Robert Thomaston led inevitably to a noticeable decay in the quality of government. The broad-scale opportunities that were offered to new immigrants who had no connection to the existing moral, cultural, and patriotic feelings in the new land, resulted in the formation of ghettos of disconnected ethnic minorities who were impatient to receive benefits equal to those of their hosts, but who were also unaware of, or unwilling to assume the responsibilities of citizenship.

The Viper had fallen in love with Costa Rica many years before when he had had occasion to go there to meet one of his drug dealers. He was not interested in the citizens of his host country except as possible candidates for exploitation. He was concerned with two things and two things only: his own welfare, and his macho self-respect. Thomaston was therefore on his black list, for he had spoken disrespectfully to him, and then had put the spotlight on his illegal business operations. Both of those errors were capital crimes in the eyes of the Viper, and for him there was no forgiving and no forgetting. His time in prison was only serving to keep his hatred simmering on the back burner, but it also gave him time to carefully plan his revenge.

Brooklyn was busy helping David, Damian and Abdul to formulate their report on the media's effectiveness in presenting the truth to its audiences. The upshot of the information they had gathered was that the tacit journalistic search for the truth either never existed, or it had come to an end. The money worms had eaten all the way through the framework of the free press in the United States.

Cynical electronic media had sprung up, and they bore little or no resemblance to the idealistic pamphleteers of revolutionary days. It was no longer the same press that the founding fathers had visualized when they wrote the Bill of Rights. Freedom of the press had become a license to print or say anything one wished. It didn't matter if the material were true or false, as long as it was interesting, which usually meant naughty, and/or entertaining, a prerequisite for every news item in post modern times.

It was a depressing task for the foursome, as each of them had uncovered termites that had penetrated deeply into the strong oak of the American free press. They found that it was the same all over the world, but in most places, like Europe and the Middle East, the cynicism was not a new development. The search for truth had long ago been thrown overboard like dead slaves from a slave ship, and no one had thought to blame the deaths on the ship's owners.

Corporate ownership of the news media had watered down and spread responsibility for journalistic truth so thinly that editors no longer needed to pay no attention to the truth at all. The only things they had to be concerned about were the editorial slant their corporate masters wanted to be put on stories of consequence, and the sales of print space and air time.

The end of unbiased journalism had arrived, drowning out the neutral, factual reporters of the past. Journalists of the left worked for left wing media companies, and reporters leaning personally to the right worked for conservative media corporations. They either shared the editorial slant of their publications or they hid their personal opinions, or else they didn't work at all.

The battle for the minds of the public had begun, and partisanship would emerge victorious. The viewers out in TV land had to choose their journalistic poison. Every news story was tainted with opinions that were cleverly presented to appear as absolute truths. While the evenly matched Democrats and Republicans were squabbling over the few remaining uncommitted independent voters, the extremely well financed and totally unified Arab media were having a field day.

The American public was trying to figure out where the truth actually lay between liberal and conservative opinions, but the Arab press knew where it stood, and it was united against American policies from the right, left, and center. The concrete certainty of the Arab press that it was right in everything it said was a perfect antidote for dissension, and in a war there is no victory possible for the confused.

Ivan Welland and his stalwarts were convinced of this scenario when they started their investigation, but once they got into it they found that the situation was worse than they had anticipated. The free economy had enabled a gradual agglomeration of media entities, which in time became concentrated in the hands of a few major organizations.

As Ivan's team probed the interests that controlled the American media, they were soon able to draw a picture of a segment of the economy that was dangerously undermining the nation from within. It had the potential to destroy American democracy more than any enemy from without. Capitalism and the free enterprise system had rolled back the attacks of socialism, communism, and fascism, but to prevail over Islamist extremism, the forces of America's competitive democracy were going to have to be united. But competition doesn't unite – it divides.

Ivan was worried when he looked over the draft of the report his staff had prepared. Lincoln's biblical admonition that *a house divided against itself cannot stand* kept running through his mind. He felt America was frittering away its chance to defeat the insurgency by engaging in petty political squabbles.

Representatives of the American people were more concerned about party loyalties and with being reelected than they were about the issues themselves. For intellectuals, patriotism had become a symbol of a closed mind, but they were dependent on the truthfulness of the information that they were being given. It was therefore not an issue of who was smart, but rather one of what was true.

Ivan took a dim view of the media, whose tactics had morally deteriorated over the years. Much of what he read in print and saw on TV would have been declared treasonous during WWII. What had changed? It seemed to him that the Fourth Estate had inflated its importance to the point where it could publish or broadcast anything it wished.

Slander and libel laws seemed no longer able to contain the bitter vituperation of the media against those of whom they disapproved. Patriotism and the national interests were becoming subservient to the economic interests of the media. Cynical, self-serving journalists, politicians, and religious spokesmen in general were leading American society around by the nose, and the Congress fiddled while the nation's citizens were burned.

Emperors, kings, queens, tyrants and dictators had had unlimited power at different times in history, but never had the rhetoric of a few private, anonymous citizens so clearly influenced the minds of ordinary men and women. If these media barons had been paragons of virtue, or the wisest of the wise, it would have been different, but they were just greedy, self-aggrandizing, morally deficient businessmen. They used their media power to further enrich themselves while at the same time they deprived common men access to the truthful information they needed for proper political decision-making. It got worse as Ivan read further.

These media barons had invaded Hollywood, and as though fiction could be made into reality at the wave of a hand, truth and fiction were wed. Pouring money into the outstretched hands of the movie producers, the media corporations gradually acquired the controlling interest in many studios, and folded them into their empires. It was not long before Warner Bros. became Time Warner, and News Corporation controlled Twentieth Century Fox.

Through stock purchases on the New York Stock Exchange, ownership of these companies became truly international. In time oil rich Arab Sheikhs, representing companies like the Kingdom Corporation from Saudi Arabia, bought into these media companies. They learned the media business this way and transferred the knowledge to the Arab media companies they formed, like Al Arabiya, Al Jazeera, and others.

These Arab companies were not regulated by the FCC, and having no rules but the ones they make themselves, they served as the propaganda wings of the Arab nations. While posing as independent media entities, they disseminate the messages of Al Qaeda, Hezbollah, and Hamas. Needless to say, they were not concerned about any inconvenient truths or conflicting opinions. Opinions that did not match their own were immediately censored.

Welland was impressed with the work of his little group. They had linked all the various subsidiaries, divisions, and associated media companies that operated in the United States. They had found the stockholder lists of the companies and cross referenced the major investors, discovering many conflict of interest crossovers.

The team had also discovered the FCC regulation that demanded that the owner of any TV station be an American citizen. It was disturbing to see how many media moguls had acquired U.S. citizenship in order to comply with this requirement. But just how loyal were these newly-minted citizens of convenience?

David Feingold, the gifted mastermind of the computer algorithm, had come up with a formula for comparing the interrelationships of individuals in the media businesses. When he ran his program, both he and Ivan, who was also a journeyman mathematician well versed in computer analysis and software development, immediately noticed one name that stuck out even further than those of the Thompsons and the Murdochs. It was Robert Thomaston.

Thomaston, whose name was similar to that of another one of the great media barons, had traded on the resemblance of their names many times, and to his great advantage. Now he owned more newspapers and Radio/TV stations than all the other barons put together.

The linkages between the producers of news and the producers of films were closer in his company than in any of the competing companies. Since it was Thomaston who was suspected of arranging for Ivan's assassination, Ivan's team felt that it was only reasonable for them to focus their work on Thomaston's companies first.

Ivan asked David to hack into Thomaston's computer systems. He hoped to get evidence that would enable him to get the FCC to pull his licenses. Even if they couldn't prove that Thomaston was not complying with the regulations, they might gain enough information about his operations to shine the light of public disclosure on his companies.

If it became common knowledge that Thomaston was creating news events in his studio and passing them over to his news outlets as breaking news, that might be enough to turn off his customers, ruin his reputation, and force him into bankruptcy.

Ivan wondered whether Thomaston's competitors would bond together like a pack of wolves, or if they would ignore his sins because they shone light on their own iniquities.

"Brooklyn, would you please get me the attendance list from the President's press conference?" he asked her.

"Sure, boss. I have it right here."

Ivan took it eagerly from her hands. He wanted to see specifically which reporter from Thomaston's affiliated companies had been present. He wanted to read his account and compare it to the accounts that had been reported by the other big five media corporations.

Within a few minutes Ivan had discovered that a woman named Margo Watson had attended the press conference as the representative of Thomaston's media empire.

CHAPTER NINE

The Viper was delighted when he found out where Thomaston lived in Costa Rica. He decided to have a look at the property, even though it was a three-hour drive from his hideaway. He jumped into the Range Rover four-wheel drive vehicle that he, like so many expatriates, had purchased expressly for driving on the rough back roads of the beautiful Costa Rican countryside.

When the Range Rover finally approached the gate of Thomaston's picturesque estate by the sea, it was clear to Alvarez that the media mogul was not there. He could tell because the gatekeeper was lounging around the entrance flirting with one of the local girls, and he never would have been carrying on like that if the boss had been around.

The beautiful vegetation was slightly overgrown and in need of a trimming, which would be provided at the last minute by the gardeners. They had learned long ago to wait until they got word of the imminent arrival of their *patrón* before knocking themselves out preparing the grounds for his visit. The Viper needed only to see the landscapers at work to know that Thomaston would be arriving soon.

When he made inquiries, Alvarez found that Thomaston seldom stayed in his villa. When he did come he generally had a woman with him. They would usually fly in, and a chauffeur would meet the plane and drive them to his house. He would stay a few days and be gone, not to return again for months.

Usually he would have a different woman with him every time. In fact, he learned, Thomaston hadn't been seen in Costa Rica for many months. He must be due for a visit, thought Alvarez. Like a true snake, he decided to wait for his prey to come to him. But like a criminal mastermind, he laid his plans with great care.

Robert Thomaston was pacing back and forth, fuming and grinding his teeth. He was in the vilest of moods. He was angry at having been interrogated by the Secret Service. He was furious with the Viper who had turned on him and betrayed him. He was deeply suspicious to have learned from his chief I.T. employee that someone was trying to break through the firewall of his computer system. He had seen the President's speech on TV, and the unflattering, critical comments he had made about the media lay like an invisible pall over the rest of the dismal events of the day.

Margo had e-mailed her account of the press conference to Mike Slayton, who was still her editor as far as she and he knew. Slayton had rewritten it and faxed the original, along with the edited copy, over to Thomaston for his approval. The approach Margo had taken was wrong, and Slayton had had to red line edit a lot of her ideas in order to make it fit Thomaston's editorial policies. After Thomaston added one or two of his own ideas, he had laid the copies down on his desk and continued to pace back and forth.

Some time later Margo knocked on the door of the suite. Thomaston had never given her a key. She guessed it was because he wanted to exercise control over her comings and goings, and she was correct, but it was also that he didn't want her snooping around in his absence.

She was cheerful, happy to have filed her story, and looking forward to discussing the President's environmental program with him. It was not difficult to see that he was in a foul mood. Margo thought perhaps she could get him to forget about whatever was bothering him by conversing with him about the press conference and the President's ideas.

"Did you listen to the President's speech?" she asked.

He nodded and grunted something unintelligible.

"Is it that you don't believe in peace, or are you just in a bad mood?"

"It's both."

"You don't believe peace is possible?"

"No. Ever since Cain killed Abel we haven't had one minute's peace. What makes this idiot think he can change that? Why not let the fools of this world just kill each other? I can't even abide looking at jerks like him. On the other hand, I don't mind looking at one that serves my purposes, so why don't you go into the bedroom and get undressed, and I'll be with you in a minute," Robert said, anticipating the sport to come.

"Okay, but first tell me what it is that's bothering you."

"Today was one of the worst days of my life. I think I'd like to get away from it all for a few days. I keep a place in Costa Rica that I'm quite fond of, and if you do what I ask of you, I'll take you along."

"That sounds lovely. I like coming along with you," Margo said suggestively, but actually she was not referring to the treatment that he had in mind right then. She had always wanted to see Costa Rica, however, and she was living like a millionaire even though she was dirt poor, so she supposed she had to pay for it one way or another. She winked at him and headed for the bedroom.

Rafael Alvarez answered his cell phone. It was Robert Thomaston's pilot. The Viper had bribed the man to call him when he knew he'd be flying Thomaston to San José.

"I'll be down there with Thomaston and his girl friend tomorrow."

"What time do you expect to get here?"

"In the late afternoon. Some time before dinner."

"Thanks for the call."

"No problem, you paid for it."

The Viper had thought long and hard about the various courses of action open to him, and had decided on one. Most people would have tried to make a murder look like an accident, but when a viper strikes out at someone, it's no accident. He wanted Thomaston to know that he was the one responsible for his death. Anonymous revenge is no revenge at all, or so he felt. The girlfriend would just be collateral damage. That would have to be her penalty for taking up with that *maricón,* Thomaston.

Rafael Alvarez was not a man to be taken lightly, and many an enemy, debtor, and traitor had found that out the hard way. In his newly-assumed role as a rich foreign gentleman, Alvarez had tried to leave the Viper behind, but beneath the soft exterior that he projected lay the hard-hearted, clever killer that was coiled inside him just the same as he had always been.

Successful criminals are generally more observant than the average person. They have to be, as it's their business to take advantage of opportunities. Small-time thieves and burglars in Costa Rica were gentlemen compared to the drug smugglers of Colombia. Except for the few paved main roads in the Central American countries, the vast majority of roads were dusty dirt trails that took a heavy toll on automobile suspensions even at slow speeds. In the rainy season many were simply impassable. A casual observer during the dry season might wonder why the roads were ditched so deeply, but anyone who had seen the torrential daily rains during the wet season would know the answer.

A policeman or a wise serpent would stay in his burrow during the warm tropical rains. A desperate man, or a man on the run, would have to have another way to travel. Most of the Costa Rican small-time criminals committed their crimes on foot. Cars owned by local people are as readily identifiable as the faces of their owners. As a result, burglars wishing to remain anonymous had to restrict their booty to what they could comfortably carry.

Local people in Costa Rica traveled from place to place on buses, ordinary tourists used taxis, and rich expatriates drove expensive four-wheel drive SUVs. Together with commercial vehicles they comprised 90% of the traffic. Crater-like potholes and serpentine mountain paths forced drivers to proceed with such caution that criminal escapes generally had to take place in slow motion.

The particular problems that thieves have to face in this part of the world have helped the police tremendously, as they needn't usually look too far to find their quarry. They could follow the tire tracks, or visit the hospital to search for snake-bitten miscreants who had attempted to escape on foot through the heavily snake-infested jungle. Most criminals were quickly apprehended – not by Sherlock Holmes detective work, but by local knowledge of the land and the people that lived on it.

The Viper could tell all this at a glance. It wasn't that different in Colombia, except that the cities were larger and the criminals more heavily armed with the latest weapons, so violent crimes were common there. A drug kingpin from Colombia who hadn't lost his touch could become Public Enemy Number One in Costa Rica in five minutes, without even trying.

It was not a difficult challenge for the Viper, therefore, to break into Robert Thomaston's vacation house and then make a clean getaway. It might have presented insoluble problems to a local thief, but it was a piece of cake to a rich, big-time criminal with a fast boat, especially since he was not motivated by robbery but possessed senior credentials in breaking and entering. Now that Alvarez knew Thomaston's ETA he would simply take a leisurely run down the coast in his cigarette boat, tie up at the dock, break into the house, and be there waiting when the cab from the airport dropped the couple off. He didn't need help to do this little job, and like a good mission commander, he knew that the fewer people involved, the less the chance of detection.

On the morning that Thomaston's flight was to arrive, Rafael Alvarez opened the doors of his boathouse and got aboard the boat. He turned the key in the ignition, then let the engines idle in neutral for a minute or two while he checked the fuel gauge and listened to the deep, throaty noise of the engines. Satisfied that he had sufficient fuel for the trip, and with the engines purring like a couple of contented lions, he loosed the lines and shifted into forward gear.

The long, low profile of the speedboat nosed out into the ocean and turned to the north. Alvarez would run along offshore, with the coast just in view, necessitating no real navigational skills. He had his charts spread out and he followed his progress from sea buoy to sea buoy until he was abreast of the narrow entrance to the cove that led up to the back of the house where Thomaston's sixty foot cruiser, *Breaking News*, was tied to the dock.

The wind was coming off the land and the clean, sweet odor of the tropical vegetation subdued any trace of engine exhaust fumes. The sea was cooperating nicely by being relatively flat, which kept the boat from pounding its hull noisily against the water. Were it not for the intended violence of the purpose of the voyage, it would have been just a scenic passage in a tranquil paradise for the Viper.

He slowed to enter the private cove, and pulled in abeam of Thomaston's yacht. When his boat was tied up he went aboard Thomaston's vessel, entered the bridge, found the key in the ignition, removed it, and put it in his pocket. Now it would not be possible for a pursuer to use Thomaston's boat to follow his boat without locating a duplicate key, which would take time.

The cruiser could never catch up with the faster cigarette boat, but it would be a lot more comfortable at its top speed than the Viper's boat, which was built for speed, not comfort. *Breaking News,* however, could possibly stay close enough to track the cigarette boat on its radar, and the Viper was unwilling to take that chance. It would be obvious to anyone that the criminal who had broken into the Thomaston house had come by boat.

You could never tell exactly what would happen in a caper like this one. Stealing the key of the *Breaking News* was a symbol of the thoroughness of the Viper's getaway plan, but even that master criminal was unable to foresee the part that Thomaston's yacht would play in his future.

As Alvarez walked up to the house he turned to check his escape route, and was satisfied to see the cigarette boat at the dock with its bow pointed in the direction of the open sea. He could make his escape in seconds, and there was no boat up and down the coast as fast as his. Smuggling drugs and guns had always called for boats that could outrun the coastal patrols, and that was good preparation for his present mission. Thomaston would be in the "Breaking News" this time, though he himself would never know it.

Rafael Alvarez had no idea that Thomaston had been making the news for a long time. This time his death would *be* the news, but the reporting would have to be done by someone else.

When he reached the house, the Viper found all the doors and windows locked, just as he had expected. He was preparing to pick the lock on the back door when he heard an old rattletrap of a vehicle pull up around the front of the house. A couple of Ticos, the local diminutive for Costa Rican people, got out and opened the front door with a key. They were the housekeeper and the gardener who were going to put the finishing touches on the house and grounds for the visit of the *patrón*. As usual during the times that Señor Thomaston was staying in the house with a woman, the housekeeper's services were not required. This time the boss had told her he planned to stay for five days, after which she could return to clean up and do the routine maintenance, as had become her custom.

The Viper was forced to retreat to the dock where he hid behind the *Breaking News* while the couple worked. He waited and watched. He could clearly hear them speaking to each other in Spanish. Eventually the housekeeper asked the gardener if he was nearly done with his jobs. When he replied in the affirmative, the woman asked him to cut her some fresh flowers to put in the vase in the front hall. The man did as he was told and took the flowers in to her. He left the back door ajar for a few minutes. The Viper took this opportunity to slip through the door and into a nearby closet. He listened to the man trying to cajole the woman into going upstairs to the bedroom with him.

Alvarez had the idea that the housekeeper had accepted this offer on previous occasions, but she told him she wasn't going to take a chance on the day the owner was coming. When she had the flowers arranged to her satisfaction, she went around checking to make sure the doors were locked. She discovered the back door was open so she upbraided him by telling him he should keep his mind on his business and not think so much about the bedroom. They filed out the front door, she in front, and he behind her grabbing at her behind while she swatted at his hands.

When the Viper heard the door close, he came out of the closet just in time to see the old pick-up truck taking off down the road. It had been easier to walk in than to break in. They hadn't even noticed the strange boat tied to the dock behind Thomaston's yacht. The Viper had prepared a good story for them in the event that he was discovered and they showed some interest in the cigarette boat. He was going to tell them that Thomaston had called to express some interest in buying the boat, and he was the salesman waiting there to take him out for a trial run.

It was a good story, but it was wasted now. The Viper took his time and looked into every drawer, closet, nook, and cranny of the house, as though he were the owner expecting guests. He didn't take anything, as he didn't want to be in possession of any goods that could link him to Thomaston. He sat in a comfortable chair, put his 9-millimeter pistol with its silencer on its barrel in his lap, and waited until he heard the cab pull up in front of the house.

The cab driver lifted the suitcases out of the trunk and put them on the stairs leading to the front door. Thomaston paid the driver in *colones* because he knew the driver wanted American money. As a matter of principle Thomaston never gave anyone what was wanted from him. The man drove off in a snit, with a handful of local currency.

The Viper stood behind the door on the inside while Thomaston fiddled with the keys. Finally he found the right key, turned the lock, and pushed the door open far enough to slide the suitcases into the entrance hall. With his back to the open door he took Margo by the hand and led her into the house. Thomaston reached behind him and pulled the door shut.

The Viper had been standing behind the door and now, as Thomaston turned, a hushed pistol shot sounded. Alvarez had shot him in the foot. He screamed and bent down to grab his foot to see what had happened to it. When he did that the Viper cracked him on the head with the butt of the Berretta, and he fell forward unconscious on the marble floor of the entranceway hall.

Alvarez wheeled around and pointed the gun at Margo. She raised her hands above her head, lifting her considerable décolleté and pulling her skimpy top up so that her bare, flat stomach was exposed.

"Sit there on the bench," he ordered, "and don't move."

The Viper went quickly over to the telephone. He pinched the plastic connection of the cord off the instrument, followed the cord to the wall, and pinched the other end of the wire free of the wall. He used it to tie Thomaston's hands in front of him, then led the cord to his ankles and tied them together.

He took note of the wound in the man's foot, which was bleeding profusely. He took hold of Thomaston by the shirt collar and dragged him along the smooth marble floor, bouncing him down two steps into the sunken living room, where he propped him up against the wall. The wounded man moaned, and seemed to be returning to consciousness. The Viper ordered Margo to move to the living room couch, facing Thomaston.

"Can I wash the blood off his face?" Margo asked.

"No, I'll take care of it," the Viper said, as he walked over to the vase of flowers on the hall table. He picked it up and dumped it over Thomaston's head.

"These flowers are for your funeral, Thomaston," he declared.

"What do you want from us?" Margo demanded, as a soaked, pitiful-looking Thomaston strewn with flowers was coming around.

"I want revenge. This traitorous excuse for a man informed on me, and tried to have me put away for life. He ruined my business, and some of my friends are dead or in prison because of him. He going to die for his betrayal, but I'm not in a hurry. In fact, I prefer not to hurry at all."

"Who the hell are you?" Thomaston slurred the words, as the pain in his head and his foot competed for his anguish.

"You see," the Viper said to Margo. "He doesn't know or care for anyone but himself. He can ruin my life and then ask who I am."

Alvarez stood over Thomaston and urinated on him.

"It is I, *La Víbora*, and I piss on you, Robert Thomaston. Did you really think you could get away with what you did to me?"

"What are you talking about? I didn't do anything to you. I didn't pay you, but you didn't deliver the goods. I never saw you before in my life."

"Yes, and I never saw your ugly gringo face either, before I pissed on it. You wanted me to kill Dr. Ivan Welland for you and he got away. Now the circle closes. I will kill you instead."

"Please don't kill anyone," Margo begged. "If it's money you want, we can get it for you, can't we Robert?"

"You understand nothing, *Puta*. This is about honor, not money."

For the first time Alvarez stopped and looked carefully at Margo. He had known instantly that she was attractive, but on closer inspection he realized that she was beautiful, and not whorish, as he had expected. His instincts told him that she was not a prostitute, but an impressionable young woman who had fallen under the spell of a powerful, wealthy man. It was then that the Viper devised one last way to take Thomaston off his high horse.

"There is nothing honorable about killing a wounded man who is tied up and can't fight back," Margo was saying, looking squarely into the dark eyes that were at that moment glancing at her appraisingly.

"Ah, perhaps not, but this is not a fighting man," the Viper replied. "This man slanders, libels, flatters, and betrays with words, not weapons. He must be put out of his misery like a horse with an injured leg, but first he must be taught the humility that fear inspires. This man has gone through life disrespecting others, and I bet he has disrespected you more than once. Hasn't he?"

Margo didn't reply to that question, but stared mutely at the gun pointing at her.

"Are you going to murder me too?"

"That depends on you."

"What do you mean?"

"If you don't give me any trouble, I will let you live. If not, I will kill you too," he said, gesturing with the gun.

"What do you want me to do?"

"Just come with me," said the Viper, jabbing her ribs with his pistol. "We are leaving now."

"*We* are leaving?"

"Yes, you are coming with me."

"Where to?" Margo asked him, looking apprehensive.

"Does that matter to you? Anyone remaining here will be dead very soon."

Alvarez went up to Thomaston and kicked him in the groin.

"Thank you, Roberto, for giving me this beautiful gringa *puta* as a parting gift."

He placed the pistol between Thomaston's eyes and pulled the trigger.

Margo gasped.   Robert Thomaston lay on the floor,
dead.   Poor Robert, and poor her.   Robert had been her
ticket to a big job in journalism, and a life among the rich
and famous.   What would she do now?   For the moment she
had no choice.   She had to obey this killer, or she might very
well be his next victim.

CHAPTER TEN

Margo Watson was looking up at the stars as the Viper's cigarette boat streaked through the water, creating a bright phosphorescent chartreuse trail. Her mind was racing. She didn't know where she was, except that it was off the coast of Costa Rica. She was the hostage of a killer. Where was this man taking her, and what did he have in mind to do with her?

She felt sorry for Robert Thomaston. She had been abducted by the man she had seen kill Robert, and who now had it in his power to kill her. She was involved in events that would make her a star journalist if she ever got a chance to write the story. The one thing she couldn't understand was why, under these dire circumstances, she didn't feel afraid. What she did feel was a strange kinship with the heroine of a bodice-ripping erotic novel who finds herself at the mercy of a masterful, mysterious sheikh who arrives on a white stallion, enters her tent, and takes her passionately.

The bow of the boat pounded into the swell of the sea as the silent Alvarez drove at nearly top speed. The wind was blowing Margo's dark hair straight back and out behind her. Her light summer clothing adhered to her body as the wind pasted them against her, a sight that the Viper didn't miss noticing as his ever alert eyes moved from the horizon, to the wake, to the gauges on the dashboard.

Margo was cool in spite of the warm tropical night air. Her mind was beset with bewildered thoughts. On the one hand she wanted to escape, but on the other hand a failed attempt might get her killed. They were traveling too fast for her to jump overboard, and they were too far off shore for her to swim to land.   Instinctively she knew that it was her sexuality that had kept her alive back at Thomaston's house. Had she been a woman of Robert's age, a wife perhaps, she would likely be dead now, and she didn't want to die. The only insurance she had was to do what he asked of her until such time as she could safely make her escape. In reality, she thought, what difference did it make? She suspected that she had already done with Robert whatever her captor could think of, and if it would keep her alive she would willingly do those things again.

She hated herself for thinking that her abductor was, in age and physique, a better match for her sexually than Robert had been. Why was she having all these sexual thoughts when she should be primarily concerned about staying alive? Margo felt ashamed of herself. Shouldn't these feelings be reserved for someone she truly loved, and not just given away to any man that fate threw in her path? Something must be wrong with her. She resolved to see a shrink or a minister about it, if she ever had the chance.

From puberty on she had always known that she had something, whether it was a certain ripeness, as one of her lovers had described it, or just her fit womanly figure, but males came to her like bees seeking nectar from a flower. Early on Margo had learned to trade on this attraction. Once she began to enjoy sex, the game became addictive. She was where she was now because of it. She wondered what this silent man was thinking about as he steered his speed boat through the waves.

It was just as well that she didn't know, because he was engrossed in developing an alternative plot to pin Robert Thomaston's murder on her in the event that he became a suspect in the crime.

Margo looked at her watch when she heard the motors rev down. The nose of the cigarette boat got lower as the speed decreased. It had been over two hours since they had left Thomaston's house. Her kidnapper deftly maneuvered the craft, backing it into a boathouse and tying it up. He gestured for Margo to get out of the boat. She lifted her small suitcase over the side and stepped onto the dock. He removed the keys from the ignition and followed behind her, flipping the electric door switch as he passed. He lifted the bottom of her suitcase to help her, and eyed her hips as she climbed the stairs that led to the house.

The Viper turned the lights on as they went through the front door. Margo was surprised at the spacious, tastefully decorated interior. The exterior of the house hadn't been visible to her because of the darkness. It was not as large as Thomaston's house, which was in the mansion category, but this house was no shack, either.

"Are you hungry?" the Viper asked her.

"Very," Margo answered.

"Can you cook?"

"A little."

"We'll see tomorrow. Tonight I will do it. Sit down," he said, pointing to the table and chairs in the corner of the kitchen.

Margo watched him move easily around in the kitchen. The appliances were of the highest quality stainless steel.

"Do you have a housekeeper?" she asked. "Everything is so clean."

"Don't ask questions," he said sharply. "I will tell you anything you need to know."

"Okay. It's just so pristine in the kitchen I assumed you had help, that's all."

"You assumed? What do you know about me to base your assumptions on?"

"You're right. I know nothing about you. It was just that you're a man. I know that much," she added, with the hint of a smile.

"You think because I'm a man I can't clean or cook?"

"Well, in my experience it's unusual that a man can do these things well."

"Do you have a lot of experience of men from which to draw your opinions?"

"I have some experience, but I guess I'm not much of an expert, since I've obviously misjudged you."

"I'm glad to see that you have some humility. Your friend Thomaston could have used some of that."

"You're right. He was proud and arrogant, but was it necessary to kill him?"

"It was. If you were me you would know that I had to do it," he said, turning some eggs in a pan on the stove.

He was making *huevos rancheros*, and the smell of onions and peppers frying in olive oil was making Margo salivate. He put two plates down on the table, along with some silverware and napkins. In a flash he was dishing the eggs out of the pan and onto the plates. He produced a loaf of magnificent crusty bread, from which he cut two large hunks and served them with the meal.

"This is delicious," Margo said, with her mouth full.

"It is a peasant's meal, but good. I don't expect you ate simple food like this with Thomaston."

"That's true. Usually we ate restaurant food. He never cooked for me, either."

She laughed at the thought of it as she said it.

"What is your name?"

"Margo Watson. What's yours?"

"I told you to ask no questions. However this one, and only this one I will answer. You may call me Rafael."

They finished eating and Rafael quickly put things in the dishwasher and tidied up.

"We'll go upstairs now," he said, grabbing the suitcase that he had left in the hall.

Several large bedrooms branched off the upstairs hall. Rafael stopped in front of the largest one.

"This is my room. You have two choices. Either you can sleep in my bed, or I will have to tie you up and lock you in one of these other rooms. Your choice."

"I don't want to be tied up."

"Very well," Rafael said, wheeling Margo's suitcase into the large room. "You may put your things in this dresser, and use this closet," he pointed to the left side of the room. "I sleep in the nude, and I will expect the same of you. The bathroom is there."

He watched her unpack her things while he sat on the side of the huge bed.

"I'd like to take a shower now," she said. "Is that okay with you?"

"Be my guest."

Margo went into the bathroom, undressed and stepped into the spacious shower stall. She turned on the water and began to soap herself up. A moment later Rafael jerked open the shower door and joined her inside.

The Chief of the White House Secret Service detachment came to Ivan's office to deliver some advisory information that he thought Ivan should have. The man explained that Robert Thomaston had been found murdered in his house in Costa Rica. Apparently a housekeeper had found him tied up, bloodied, shot in the foot, and fatally shot between the eyes. Evidently he had been dead for several days before his body was discovered.

"That's all the information we have at the moment," the man told him. "The Costa Rican police contacted the FBI because Thomaston was an American citizen. Thomaston had just arrived at the house, according to the police. They had flight information from the airport that confirmed that his private jet had arrived only a couple of hours before the estimated time of death."

"Did you question the pilot?" Ivan asked him.

"Of course. But he wasn't able, or willing, to add much to the information we already had. He just said that he had taken Thomaston and other young ladies to Costa Rica on previous occasions, and his instructions were to wait until he was called to make the return flight."

"Did he fly down there with a woman this time, too?"

"Yes he did, sir. Customs agents reported that a young American woman named Margo Watson had accompanied him on the flight. She is presently missing, and possibly kidnapped. The woman was likely Thomaston's mistress. Costa Rican law enforcement officers have asked the Bureau for forensic assistance in tracking down the murderer and locating Ms. Watson. An FBI crime scene investigative team has been dispatched. I knew you would want to be kept informed."

"Thank you, Chief. Please continue to keep me posted on future developments. This is a matter of top priority national importance."

"I'll keep you informed, sir."

After the Chief had left, Ivan began to hatch a plan. His research team had pointed to Thomaston's companies as being the worst offenders when it came to creating news that was subsequently reported as facts. The team had noted that the Hollywood subsidiary of his media empire was in the vanguard of new graphic computer applications. They were experts in special effects, had the largest computer database of films categorized by subject matter, and of course they had access to actors and directors.

David Feingold had indicated to Ivan that Thomaston could make a cow jumping over the moon look believably newsworthy if he wished. David had made up a list of the top news stories produced by Thomaston's media companies over the last three years. He had divided the stories into categories and compared those stories to events known by the U.S. Government to have occurred. He discovered that about 30% of the stories were either pure fabrications, or could not be substantiated by other news sources. In some cases government agencies had accepted the renditions of the news as fact.

The idea that was percolating in Ivan's brain called for more research to be done by his team. He gathered them together and assigned them their tasks.

"Damian, please find out how Thomaston's last will and testament disperses his assets, and who is to be his executor. David, determine how Thomaston handled the issuance of editorial orders dealing with what news items to publish or produce. Abdul, please check your Middle Eastern sources to see if Thomaston's companies were associated with any Arab media companies, and find out if they were using work put out by Thomaston's studios. Brooklyn, do the same for Israeli news sources, and as usual coordinate and assist the boys by facilitating things for them."

Ivan Welland was cracking the whip and simultaneously designing the plan he would use to unblock the political log jam that was building against the President's plan to wet down the world's supply of gunpowder.

After putting his team to work, he finally had some time to think. When the Chief of the Secret Service mentioned the name of Margo Watson, Ivan's photographic memory clicked in, and he recalled that this was the byline on the slanderous article written in Thomaston's tabloid about Dr. Laura Murphy. He had no doubt in his mind that this was the same person who had gone to Costa Rica with Robert Thomaston.

So where was she now? Was she on the lam? Had she been part of a conspiracy against her boss? Was she a hostage, taken against her will? Perhaps she was dead too, but her body hadn't yet been found. Then he remembered a report he had read some days before that said that the Colombian drug cartel boss, known as the Viper, had escaped from custody in Colombia. Was there a connection between the Viper of drugs and the other snake, Thomaston? Ivan called Brooklyn and put her to work to see if she could establish a connection between the two men.

The traditional way that items made it into print or onto the TV news broadcasts went like this: the reporter interprets the event and its sources and files his story. His editor decides, based on its importance, if it is big news or not. She assigns the page number or time slot to it. A desk editor, or a TV story producer/technician decides which parts of the film or story will be edited to fill the space. By the time a reader, viewer, or listener gets the news, it has undergone a number of biased interpretations. The audience then must make its own assessment of the importance of the item. With no information that hasn't been slanted, edited, tampered with, or lied about, the receiver of the story is not in a very good position to extract the truth from the dozen or so opinions, criticisms, comments, and editorial changes that may have already shaped the item.

Ivan spoke from the head and the heart several days later when he addressed the President and his advisors.

"My recommendations for the solution of the snag we are encountering in Congress and in the world at large are based on the concept that perceptions are people's reality. My department has been investigating the media for some time now, and we have come to some surprising conclusions. It has always been the policy of the news media to present the views of its owners on any given news event.

"Over time, slanted stories take their toll on viewers, and they become brainwashed into believing they are receiving truth in reporting, when in fact they are actually absorbing the news as digested, filtered, and regurgitated by media moguls pushing their opinionated ideas out as fact. The media has become emboldened after getting away with spreading more propaganda than truth, and they have lately gone off the deep end. In some cases they are just simply making the news up in their studios, with no regard for the facts. The mergers and amalgamations among the companies functioning as the *media* have resulted in the existence of fewer independent companies, and the consolidation of power into fewer hands. These remaining hands are by no means lily-white.

"Recent investigations by my departmental people have turned up information that, in and of itself, is shocking, but just at this juncture it can be of enormous help to us. If you take a look at the handouts I'm circulating, I think you'll see that the vertical integration of media companies is now complete. Controlling interest in a media conglomerate these days covers every aspect of news, from reporting and photographing to printing and distributing, or in the case of TV, from live reporting and taping to producing and editing. The companies owned by Robert Thomaston have been involved in using artistic license to create believable ersatz news in their studios, then passing it off as truth to one of its related corporate newscasters. Thomaston's companies seem to specialize in these activities, but they are by no means the only ones, of course.

"Nevertheless, this individual's control over the nation's sources of news information has been growing incrementally for years. He's reached the stage where he could give Josef Goebbels a run for his money when it comes to pumping out pure propaganda. It's possible that his influence on public opinion today might be even more dangerous than was Hitler's Minister of Information in the Third Reich.

"I say this because of the anonymity factor, and the technologies that are now available. At least we knew who was responsible for the lies in Germany, but the source of today's lies is much more obscure because layers upon layers of corporate entities are intertwined in such a way as to make anonymous the individuals responsible. My departmental investigative team is now involved in unraveling this mess.

"Unfortunately for Mr. Thomaston, he was murdered a day ago in Costa Rica, so he won't have a chance to clear his name by standing trial before a jury of his peers. He will, however, receive justice from the highest judge of all. Although few evidently will mourn his passing, I find myself celebrating not his death, but the opportunity it presents. In the vacuum that exists now as a result of his demise, we can, in the confusion of the moment, plant some news of our own creation."

"And what would that be?" asked the President.

"I'm glad you asked, sir."

Ivan passed him a small file folder.

"Inside you will find details of a comprehensive media campaign that will convince the naysayer at home, as well as those abroad. The media corporations now own many of the Hollywood film production companies. For many years they've been making fictional stories that have influenced the world's opinions of our country, and very much to our own detriment. It's about time the media did something to help the nation that gave them the freedom to get rich while they disparaged our citizens and exaggerated our faults.

"They've gotten away with this because the most liberal legal interpretation of the freedom of speech laws permits them to do it. This behavior has had appalling effects in our own country. Our citizens no longer have confidence in our government. In addition, this nation's morals have been shockingly corrupted in the eyes of the world. Our open mindedness and our desire to keep the government out of the private lives of its citizens have left the field open for blanket exploitation.

"The titillation and dumbing down of our citizens has become the focus of the media. Why would the press do that, you may ask? I believe it's because it benefits certain segments of the economy to keep the populace in a state of porn and drug-induced ignorance."

"Which segments, and how are they benefiting?" the Attorney General asked.

"Your segment for one," Ivan said. "Nothing produces budgetary generosity for your department like a good legal battle over the personal rights of our citizens."

Turning to face the Secretaries of Energy, Commerce, and the Treasury, Ivan continued his presentation.

"In the same way, nothing is as financially beneficial to energy stocks, the economy, and the tax base as a healthy boost in the price of oil."

"You might add the Department of Defense to that list," said the Secretary of Energy. "You have the largest budget of all, and your generals are always crying for money to buy bigger and better weapons. Stop me if I'm wrong."

"On behalf of all who have preceded me in this job," said the Secretary of Defense, "I admit that what you just said is true. But now, as you know, I have the responsibility of implementing the wishes of the President by changing the status quo and leading the world to disarmament."

"Now boys, we're not going start a petty internal war," the President interjected. "We're trying to do something good for the world for a change. I believe it will also be for our own good. Let's just hear Dr. Welland out, and then with your input I'll decide what to do. You were saying, Dr. Welland, that propagandists have been creating conditions that suited their purposes without regard to the truth?"

"Exactly so, Mr. President. And if persons in high positions aren't conscious of it, how can an ordinary voter know what to do? At last we have a President who is willing to buck the policy influencers and give peace a chance. Let's take this opportunity to do something glorious that benefits mankind. We may never get another chance, or another leader who will tackle the issues of peace and pollution head on."

"Thank you Ivan," said the President.

"As far as I'm concerned," said the Attorney General, "Welland's plan should be designated as the nation's number one Baloney Battle. It will go down in history as the first time anyone has tried to load America's guns with bullshit."

In the end he was outvoted. Finally Ivan was able, after much debate, to persuade the President's august group of advisors to reluctantly give peaceful means a try. What Ivan wanted approval for was a war of fonts and pixels. If objectives could be reached with no loss of lives and military expenses that drained the national treasury, it would be foolish not to make the attempt.

Ivan finished up his presentation by pointing out that in large measure the people who were making movies were also the people making the news. It was his job to convert them from pandering to an audience they regarded as stupid and vulgar, to becoming an industry that respected its clientele as well as itself. Perhaps only then could they put out films that were intelligent, morally upright, and patriotic. If Islam's opinion of democracy was to improve, then it was essential to clean up the nation's media portrayal of democracy as freedom to do anything that came into your head. It was high time that the confusion between freedom and license be clarified for the benefit of all. Having the freedom to point out the flaws in democratic systems didn't make them any less flawed, unless something was done about them.

CHAPTER ELEVEN

A report from the FBI crime scene investigators in Costa Rica was brought to Ivan's attention. They had pieced together a probable scenario of the events that occurred on the night Robert Thomaston was murdered. Judging from the blood trail leading from the front entrance to the location on the living room floor where Thomaston's body was discovered, he had probably been shot in the foot first, and then dragged down the steps into the sunken living room.

The body was also found to be covered with urine. The report concluded that the killer must have urinated on his victim in an attempt to humiliate him while he was still alive. The investigators collected hairs and other material from the crime scene and sent the samples over to their lab for DNA testing. The results indicated the presence of a sum total of eighteen different individuals, a relatively small number for a DNA sweep in an average residence. The DNA sequences were now on file, ready to be compared with those of future suspects.

The FBI team had not found any suspicious evidence of tire tracks or footprints, and that led to the conclusion that the killer or killers had come by boat, and left the scene the same way they had come. Arrival records showed that Thomaston had entered the country with a woman by the name of Margo Watson. Since they hadn't discovered a female body on the scene, they had to assume she was still alive until such time as they found her either dead or alive.

Working in concert with local law enforcement, the FBI checked the records of boats registered with the Costa Rican

Coast Guard and owned by or rented to foreigners. They discovered several vessels fitting that description, and they ran the names against their database of wanted criminals, as well as those of Interpol. This turned up a number of people of interest to both the Americans and other international policing agencies. Apparently opportunistic criminals from many countries had infested Costa Rica, the benign bastion of democracy in Central America. The unsuspecting Ticos had not realized that so many of the rich inhabitants of the walled, dog-defended palazzos were wanted by the police in other countries. Regardless of the Thomaston murder, the local law enforcement personnel were going to be kept very busy extraditing riff raff wanted elsewhere.

Among the many names discovered to be on the most wanted persons lists from other countries was the name of Rafael Alvarez. He was wanted in Colombia for many drug-related crimes, but he had always escaped from custody before being brought to trial. The Colombian authorities, according to their incarceration laws, had taken compulsory DNA samples of Señor Alvarez. When his DNA sample was compared to the eighteen samples found in the Thomaston residence, the FBI found a perfect match that put Alvarez on the scene which, if nothing else, was circumstantial evidence of his having had the opportunity to commit the murder.

The fact that his name was also on the Coast Guard's list of foreign boat owners raised him to the top of the list of the Thomaston murder suspects. An interagency note on the Alvarez file requested immediate notification of the Secret Service in the event of his apprehension.

When the Director of the FBI called the Chief of the Secret Service to find out why the President's bodyguards wanted Alvarez, he was told that he was implicated in an attempt on the life of Ivan Welland, the President's erstwhile Security Advisor and the present Secretary of Defense. The Chief was willing to hold off on the charge of complicity to murder in favor of the first-degree murder charge that the Bureau Director was trying to hang on Alvarez. The Chief called Ivan with the news, and that was how Ivan became aware of the events that had taken place in Costa Rica.

Now the FBI, in concert with the Costa Rican police force, was conducting a stakeout around the Viper's villa. They wanted to be sure that he was there, that he was the Rafael Alvarez they were looking for, and that he was alone. By the end of the day they had discovered that he was alone except for a woman companion. They needed to know if the woman was the missing woman that Thomaston had brought with him from the States. If she was the same woman, was she an accomplice in the murder, or was she just an innocent bystander being held hostage?

Special Agents of the Bureau were not allowed to carry or discharge weapons in a foreign jurisdiction. They had no idea what the Spanish-speaking Costa Rican officers' level of competency might be. They didn't know if they could shoot straight, or even if they would shoot at a man wanted by the authorities of another nation. It might have been different if the Viper had been wanted for a crime in Costa Rica, but he was only a suspect in the shooting of a Yankee tycoon. From the point of view of the Costa Ricans, there was some doubt over the issue of whether it was worth getting shot to make an arrest for the U.S. authorities.

FBI agents were not the best at conducting surveillances in the dense jungles. The Costa Rican police officers laughed at the Americans who were tripping over vines and roots, jumping at the sight of insects the size of mice, and dreading being bitten by venomous snakes, or being shot by a two-legged, erect viper. State-of-the-art scientific crime fighting was more in the FBI repertoire than was traipsing around in the bowels of a Central American jungle.

A Costa Rican Coast Guard patrol boat passed by just a little too frequently for it to be coincidental, and had the Viper not been otherwise occupied enjoying the considerable charms of his prisoner, he might have been alerted. As it was, the activity that the stakeout team was observing took place in either the bedroom or the kitchen of the large house.

It was not clear whether the woman was a hostage or a paramour, but either way the residents of the house were spending most of their time in these two rooms. The kitchen was in the back of the house, and the bedroom upstairs.

If the police had been in possession of a key it might have been possible for them to enter the house through the front door after the bedroom lights went dark, and by quietly climbing the stairs, catch the Viper in his nest. The Bureau solved the question of the key when it obtained a passkey from the American lock manufacturer.

In considering the next step, the question of how to interrogate the couple arose. It seemed extreme to go into full assault mode when they were not certain that the resident of the house was the Viper. They might learn something by just knocking on the door under some pretense or other, in order to observe the reactions of the suspects. If the American woman was a hostage she would behave one way, and if she was a lover or an accomplice, another. It would not do to have an innocent kidnap victim injured or killed. Politically the Tico police position was to be as invisible as possible when it came to foreigners. The greatest portion of the Costa Rican economy was composed of tourist-related activities, and the most damaging thing to tourism was violent crime in any form. No visitor wants to vacation in a country where they'll be robbed, attacked, or possibly killed.

In Costa Rica avoiding mistakes was as much a motive for good police planning as making a difficult arrest. The latter activity would get no mention in the press, while the former would be spread all over the news. Either way, getting involved in a shoot-out with foreigners was of little benefit to the police. As a result of this attitude there was more unreported criminal activity in the country than there should have been, and fewer arrests as well. Gradually the Tico police learned that a great many of the people they were hosting in their country were not the cream of the crop in their own countries. This, too, contributed to the lethargic response of the police in matters concerning foreigners, an attitude that the Tico criminal element had not failed to note, resulting in a large proportion of the crimes in Costa Rica being committed against visitors.

While the police and the FBI were consulting about the plan for the arrest, the Viper and his captive were creating another page for the Stockholm syndrome report. Margo was experiencing some emotional and sexual attachment for the outlaw who was holding her captive. Rafael, for his part, was knowingly using those feelings for his own convenience and pleasure.

Margo, had she known his true motives, would have behaved differently. She had occasionally consorted with the opposite sex in a manner contrary to her true feelings, but those times had not involved life and death consequences. The heightened emotions of the present circumstances were a sort of catnip to the kitty in Margo. Perhaps she should have been concentrating her thoughts on finding a way to escape the clutches of the Viper, but for the moment she was content to be entangled in his coils. Neither Margo nor Rafael were aware of the cadre of law enforcement officers that were assembling nearby.

An armed, out-of-uniform young female police officer was selected to carry out the first part of the plan to take the Viper into custody. She was to pretend she was a census taker, knock on the door of the Viper's house, and then take stock of the situation while asking questions for the census. This particular officer was selected because aside from being female and therefore less threatening, she had a friendly, outgoing personality that most people related to in a warm way. She had been provided with official blank census forms mounted on a clipboard. By law each person in the country had to fill out a census questionnaire. This procedure was widely known to residents of Costa Rica, and the police hoped the Viper would also know it. It was hoped that this ploy would allay any suspicions that the Viper might have about a stranger approaching his house. If possible the officer was to get the woman out of the house so that she would not be injured if a shootout occurred when the police arrested the Viper. People completing the census form were required to sign on the bottom line. On the last page in the sheaf of papers on the clipboard, just above the signature line, the FBI agents had written in English, *If you wish to escape from this house, step behind the census taker. She is a police officer and you will be safe.*

The police assumed that because he spoke Spanish, the Viper would be the one to come to the door when the officer knocked. They guessed correctly about that, but they could not have imagined that he would come to the door armed and furious that he had been interrupted during his lovemaking. He flung the door open, but before the policewoman could get an intelligible word out, the Viper grabbed her and flung her into the house and slammed the door behind them.

He pushed her face against the wall. The clipboard and pen had flown out of her hands, and the papers had come loose from the clipboard and fallen on the entranceway floor. Alvarez held his gun against the woman's neck and tore the shoulder bag off her shoulder and quickly looked inside. It held a small pistol, her badge, and police ID card bearing her name, María Escondido.

The Viper patted her down roughly while pushing his pistol hard into her neck behind the ear. He was searching to see if she had concealed another gun on her person. His hand passed over her body, seeking the feel of hard steel, but nevertheless taking tactile inventory of her womanly curves. Pressing her hard against the wall from behind, his hand slid across her chest from armpit to armpit, stopping momentarily to evaluate her breasts. With every movement she made to protest he pushed the pistol harder into her neck. Satisfied that she had no concealed weapon on her person he shouted, "Margo, come down here."

Meanwhile the police outside were conferring about what to do. The point was made that whatever the status of the American woman, whether accomplice or captive, the Viper now had a police hostage. The police reasoned that by now the criminal knew that María was a cop, so there was no reason to remain in the mode of silent surveillance. Perhaps if the Viper knew he was surrounded and could not escape, he would surrender. They were sure now, in the face of his hostile act against one of their officers, that this was indeed the man they were looking for. They decided to cordon off the house and advise the fugitive by loudspeaker that he was trapped. The desire to come to the aid of a fellow police officer was strong in Costa Rica, as it is everywhere else, and the fact that the officer was a woman only heightened the desire of her fellow officers to rescue her.

When Margo heard Alvarez call, she came to the head of the stairs to see what he wanted. She had heard the knocking on the door, of course, and she wondered who was there. Whoever it was, he or she was the first person to come to the door since the Viper had kidnapped her. She was surprised to see Alvarez holding a gun to a woman's head while he was obviously enjoying searching her with his free hand. When he completed his pat down he pushed the cop back against the wall. Papers were strewn all over the floor.

"Come down here," he yelled up at Margo.

Margo quickly did as she was told. Rafael pushed past her, grabbed Maria's coarse black hair, and still holding the gun between her neck and her ear, he pulled her into the living room and threw her down on the couch.

Margo bent over and gathered up the papers from the floor. She saw the handwritten note from the FBI, and put it in the middle of the blank census sheets. Then she clipped them to the clipboard and placed them on the hall table.

Wary that the policewoman had been trained in martial arts and might try to escape, Rafael kept the gun at her neck, and sent Margo to get a spool of rope that he kept in a closet.

As she performed this errand, Margo considered her options. It was obvious that there were other police outside the house and she didn't want to be caught in a crossfire should they forcefully enter and start a gunfight. She didn't exactly know what Rafael Alvarez had in store for her. She had tried to please him and she thought she had succeeded, but how much could you trust a murderer called the Viper? She wanted to be rescued, but more than that she wanted to stay alive. It was possible that the police would think she was Rafael's accomplice and shoot her. She would just have to decide when and how to get safely out of this desperate criminal's control.

When she arrived back in the living room with the rope, Alvarez told her to tie the woman to the couch. When the job was done to his satisfaction, he looked at his watch, took Margo by the arm, and led her to the front door.

"Will I ever see you again?" she asked him.

Margo didn't know why she had said that. She should have been very relieved to be set free, but she was obviously having mixed emotions about the prospect.

Rafael had been vaguely conscious of the hold he was gaining over his hostage. The present situation didn't lend itself to the continuance of the Svengali relationship, but her question betrayed her desire to continue the liaison. He had had no time to think about this possibility, and the Viper did nothing without forethought.

"No questions, remember. I will find you."

He opened the door and pushed her out into the sunlight. He was counting on the few minutes of confusion that would arise due to her sudden appearance outside. It would occupy the police and keep them from attacking the house while they questioned Margo about the officer being held inside. The FBI diagnosed the release of the American hostage as a sign that the Viper wanted to make a deal in preference to having a shootout against overwhelming odds. They started planning their negotiating strategy, carefully considering the points they would make to persuade the Viper to surrender peacefully. They were sure that time was on their side.

But Rafael Alvarez had other plans. While the cops were busy talking to Margo out front, he escaped through the back door and ran to his garage. He opened a trap door in the floor in front of a parked SUV and went down a short flight of stairs, pulling the hinged door down behind him. He followed a winding tunnel that led underneath the dense jungle above, emerging beyond the police cordon a few minutes later. He ran quickly through the thick brush until he came to a small clearing. He removed a camouflaged tarpaulin from a small helicopter, fired up the engine, and flew away to the north.

Although the police heard the noise of the copter engine, it was far away and didn't seem related to the Viper, who was known to be inside his house, or so they thought. Rafael flew directly to Robert Thomaston's house that now sat idle pending disposition of the dead man's estate. He landed on the back lawn and walked directly to the dock. He pulled the stolen key to Thomaston's yacht from his pocket, went aboard, started the engines, backed away from the dock, and headed north by sea.

It was several days before the police and the FBI pieced together the method of his escape. By then he had motored to Nicaragua, caught a plane, and went to Thailand, where he had previously acquired a property using a pseudonym as he had in Costa Rica. His revenge on Robert Thomaston had cost him millions, but it had been worth it to the man who had the foresight to stash away what was believed to be at least 300 million dollars in untraceable cash in various safe spots around the globe. Using Thomaston's boat, *Breaking News*, to make his own escape was the final insult to the dead media tycoon, who had overestimated his power and had suffered the fatal, venomous bite of the Viper.

When questioned by the FBI and the Costa Rican Public Forces, which is the name for the combined security force and police department in the only country without a formal military, Margo Watson made the following statement:

"I was with Robert Thomaston when we arrived at his house to find a man with a gun inside the door. He shot Mr. Thomaston in the foot, dragged him inside, tied him up with a phone cord, and took me hostage. From that moment on I was held prisoner, forced to do unmentionable things for several days, and held at gunpoint until my captor shoved me out the front door as a distraction to the police outside so he could make his escape."

María Escondido, the policewoman, confirmed Margo's story, which also gelled with the forensic evidence at the crime scene. In due time Margo was allowed to find her way back to the U.S., while María was given a commendation for having bravely entered the house alone where she had faced a dangerous and violent criminal who, but for a strict time factor and his need to beat a hasty retreat, might have caused her to share the same ultimate fate that he had dished out to Robert Thomaston.

CHAPTER TWELVE

When Margo Watson got back to Washington DC after her exciting and terrifying trip to Costa Rica, she found her little apartment dismal, cold, and unappealing. She also felt lonely and at loose ends. She had no job, and she wasn't sure what to do or where to turn. Robert Thomaston was dead, and Mike Slayton was not about to forgive her for ditching her job with him to join forces with the far more prestigious Thomaston. Margo was puzzling over what her next career step should be when the phone rang.

"Ms. Margo Watson?"

"Yes."

"My name is Brocklin. I'm the Executive Assistant to United States Secretary of Defense Dr. Ivan Welland. I'm calling on his behalf to make an appointment for him to meet with you."

"The Secretary of Defense wants to meet with *me?* Are you sure you've got the right Margo Watson?"

"I'm sure."

"What can he possibly want to meet me for?"

"I'm not at liberty to say, but I can assure you it's a matter of national importance. When is the soonest that you can spend an hour with him?"

"I'm not employed at the moment so if it's urgent I can come at any time that's convenient for the Secretary. How can I be sure this call is for real?"

Brooklyn had been through this exercise before, as most people receiving a call from her for an appointment with the Secretary of Defense assumed that such an inviatation was a practical joke.

"Just call the Pentagon and ask to speak to the Secretary of Defense, and you'll be put through to me. In order to save you time and inconvenience I'll send the Secretary's car to pick you up. Can you be ready in an hour?"

"Sure, I guess so," Margo replied.

"Good. I'll tell the Secretary to expect you."

Margo took her phone book, looked up the Pentagon's number, and called it. She had had too many peculiar experiences of late, and she was taking no chances.

"Defense Department."

"May I speak to Secretary Welland please?"

The next voice she heard was familiar to her.

"Secretary Welland's assistant."

"It's just me making sure this is on the level."

"That's okay. Now you know, Ms. Watson."

"I'll be ready when the car comes," she said and hung up. Instantly Margo remembered that she hadn't given her address. She thought about calling back, but decided that if the Secretary of Defense wanted to see her badly enough he could probably find out where she was.

Gambling was not normally something that Rafael Alvarez was interested in doing. He didn't want luck to be the most important factor in determining the direction of his life. Many times he had heard his associates refer to Lady Luck, and he had hated the entire concept of his success being attributed to an anonymous female fortune regulator. Any plans that he had ever made included a hedge against the unexpected. Planning for accidents, miscalculations, and coincidences were activities found on the negative side of the ledger. Accidents didn't just happen. Mistakes in calculating could be fixed by recalculating and testing assumptions. Coincidences could be statistically examined to assess the odds of such occurrences, and in none of his operations had he ever consulted any lucky ladies.

Divine interventions were anathema to the man they called the Viper. Hope did not spring eternal in the cold-blooded heart of this serpent. Alvarez didn't ask death where its sting was. He believed it rested with him. He was a conscienceless partner of the Grim Reaper. Expediency dominated most of his motives. In the big picture battle of good and evil he would certainly have been allied with the latter side. His superior knowledge of the foibles of people enabled him to disarm them. He used his good looks and considerable charm to prepare them for the dénouement, and then with well-oiled efficiency he disposed of any who stood in his way. He seldom had second thoughts once he had made up his mind about dispatching a victim.

That was what made his handling of Margo Watson so unusual. He had been resolved to kill her when he was finished with her, but he hadn't followed through. Why? Rafael examined his motives and decided that he had used her to buy time for his escape. Inwardly he knew he could have just disappeared, but unfortunately for his own high opinion of himself, he knew it was not true. It had been weakness that made him release her. Alvarez frowned. He had no patience for the weak, and less for his own frailties. Suspicion had always trumped fidelity in his experience, so it was difficult for him to face up to the simple fact that he liked Margo.

What was so wrong with liking a woman? She was beautiful, intelligent, pragmatic, and she had pleased him. He sensed clearly that she was coming to love him. He had no right to expect that she would. Nor did he care, except that it improved her ability to satisfy his needs. But now that she was gone, he was having withdrawal symptoms. All this was a strange kind of introspection for a lifelong misogynist loner. He toyed with the idea of getting her back one way or another. Finally he grew tired of mooning about Margo. He went out to one of the upscale bars in his neighborhood to find a woman who would, he hoped, put Margo out of his mind.

* * * *

Ivan sat at his desk in his office half a world away. He was visualizing his meeting with Margo Watson and thinking of the questions he would ask her.

Five minutes later Brooklyn buzzed him.

"Margo Watson is here. Shall I send her in?"

"Yes, please do," Ivan said.

"Ms. Watson," Brooklyn said by way of an introduction as Margo entered the Ivan's spacious office.

He rose to his full height behind his desk.

"I'm glad to meet you, Ms. Watson. Welcome to the den of iniquity that I call my office, which belongs as much to you as a taxpayer, as it does to this temporary occupant."

"I'm pleased to meet you too," Margo said, shaking his hand. "But I can't help wondering why I'm here."

Margo was surprised at his imposing size. She had seen him on TV before, but in person he was even taller than she had expected him to be.

Ivan offered her a cup of coffee, or a drink of her choice. He wanted to help her to relax before he proceeded with the interview. He was familiar with the awed effect his office and his position had on nearly all the first time visitors.

"Thank you, Mr. Secretary. I'd love to have a cup of black coffee."

Ivan poured some coffee into one of the blue and gold fine china cups, and presented it to his visitor. He helped himself to a cup, too. He directed Margo to an expensive leather couch, which looked suitably shiny, black, and austere. He took a seat in the oversized matching chair across from her.

"Ms. Watson, the discussion we're about to have is of great national importance. I shall have to ask you some personal questions that may be somewhat embarrassing. I'm sorry for any discomfort or chagrin that my inquiries may incur, but as I say, you may be able to help your country in a time of considerable difficulty. You can be sure we'll use all the discretion we can possibly muster to keep you safe and anonymous."

"I'll try to answer your questions with the honesty your position requires, but I must say, I haven't the faintest idea why you would think that I have any information to give that has national significance."

Margo also wondered why she didn't feel the sexual overtones that were usually present and almost palpable in these leather-appointed male bastions of power. Considering the seniority of his position in the government, the huge man across from her looked surprisingly youthful. Under normal circumstances she might have found his appearance a little disconcerting, but perhaps because he focused his eyes on hers, and didn't seem to notice or care about her body, she was able to relax to a certain degree.

It was important to Ivan to do his best to avoid gender issues when he was in one-on-one business conversations with women. But no matter how important the subject or the number of times he tried to keep gender out of the equation, he felt he never completely succeeded in this. Often the fault was not his, however. Women had a way of appraising men in the same way men did, although it was less obvious than the way men tend to look at women. But the speculative glances nevertheless had their roots in attraction, be it physical, emotional, or spiritual, and consequently it was always difficult to concentrate properly on the subject under discussion.

Women of mating age, like Margo Watson, possibly had some subtle motivations that answered to the requirements of nature. But Ivan still had the feeling that even women of grandmotherly age, often those in powerful positions, were not unconscious of unspoken gender dynamics when meeting with men face to face. In any case, Ivan was hoping to reach a mutual understanding sufficient to put matters of national security in the foreground, and all personal and gender issues as far out of the picture as possible.

"Ms. Watson, my questions for you aren't meant to be in any way personally or morally critical, nor do I ask them for prurient reasons, but they do concern two men, one of them now dead, with whom you had recent connections."

Margo blinked and swallowed.

"For the moment," she said, "I'll assume you have both the tact and the decency to keep this conversation on a purely professional level. I'm also assuming that this talk is off the record, and that I'm not legally required to testify in any court about my association with these men, whose names, I notice, you still haven't mentioned."

"That's understood," Ivan assured her. "The name of the first man was Robert Thomaston, now deceased. Would you tell me, please, how you came to know him?"

"I met Robert at a conference on the subject of the environment that was being held here in Washington. I was covering it for the newspaper I was working for at the time. He sat next to me at that conference and we got to know each other. I had no idea that he was such an important man in the media business."

"He never mentioned who he was when he introduced himself to you?"

"No, he just told me his first name, that's all. Anyway, we had lunch together, and later he invited me to a cocktail party after the conference had ended for the day. One thing led to another. Eventually I found out who he was, because he owned the paper I was working for as a junior reporter."

"Did your relationship with him continue?"

"Yes. He became my mentor and my patron, and I, in turn, became his mistress. That's the whole story."

"My sources tell me that you went with Thomaston to Palma de Majorca to spend some time on a yacht belonging to Baron von Aragon."

"We did. Is there something wrong with that?"

"No, not on the face of it. But surely the purpose of this yachting trip was not just pleasure. Who else were guests on board the yacht?"

"Aside from von Aragon, the yacht's owner, and his lady friend Hilde, there was Geoffrey Lord Pressman and his companion, Susan Summercroft. The men were locked up most days in a continuing meeting."

"What was the subject of those meetings?"

"I don't really know. I spent most of my time with the other two women while the men went into a separate room to confer with one another."

"Didn't Mr. Thomaston tell you what those meetings were about?"

"No. He was a man who kept such things to himself. He never said anything at all to me about the subject of the meetings."

"You have no idea what they were discussing?"

"Not really. As I said, the women were not invited. All three of the men were giants in the publishing and media businesses, so I presume they were talking business. We women didn't know anything about the topic, so that's probably why the men didn't invite us to join them."

Margo didn't know what Welland was really driving at. Whatever it was, she wasn't sure she wanted to part with any information, as she thought it might have more value as background for the articles she was planning to write.

Ivan was conscious of the wariness in Margo's attitude, but he couldn't tell what was behind her reticence. It was possible that she had been a co-conspirator with Thomaston in something illegal and she feared prosecution. It could also be that she had enjoyed access to his bed, but not his head, and consequently didn't know what the media mogul had been doing. Based on the fact that Watson and Thomaston had only known each other for a relatively short time, he decided to give her the benefit of the doubt. He decided to change tactics and aim his questions to her from another angle, intending to return to the question of Thomaston's business plans later.

"Ms. Watson, I understand you were present when Mr. Thomaston died. Is that correct?"

"Yes, I gave all the details of that horrible experience to the FBI. Must I go through all that again?"

"No, I read the FBI report, but there are a few blank spaces. For instance, Thomaston's killer must have known him. This was not a robbery, was it?"

"No, I don't think so. When we went into the house there was no mess or any other indication that a robber had been turning the place upside down."

"Where was the killer when you entered the house?"

"He was waiting right behind the front door."

"So do you think he was there for the sole purpose of killing Mr. Thomaston?"

"That would be my guess," Margo replied. "I can't imagine why else he'd be hiding behind the door."

"It also seems to me that this man wanted not only to kill Thomaston, but also to demean him. Does it seem that way to you, too?"

"It certainly was that way. He urinated on Robert. So I'd definitely say he wanted to humiliate him as well as me.

"How did he humiliate you?"

"He called me a *gringa puta*. I don't think I have to translate that, do I? The whole experience was terrible. Then he shot Robert in cold blood and forced me at gunpoint to go with him."

"I'm very sorry that you had to through that. According to the account that I read, you were taken from the scene of the crime by boat to another house in Costa Rica. Is that correct?"

"Yes. Rafael had a very fast boat tied up to the dock behind Thomaston's house, and we sped away in that. It was a very long, powerful motorboat."

"Rafael?"

"Yes, he had me call him Rafael. That's the only name he gave me. Does that have some significance?"

"Perhaps."

"Before he shot Robert he referred to himself as *La Víbora.* Do you know what that is?"

"It means *the Viper*. So you were alone with this Rafael the Viper for several days. What can you tell me about him?"

"What exactly do you mean?"

Margo didn't honestly know whose side she was on. Rafael was a murderer, but for all she knew he may have had cause. Robert was an impossible man and he very well could have done something to infuriate Rafael. All she knew was that the Viper had been mostly kind to her. He had his demands, but he was not brutal to her. In the end she felt they had developed a mutual understanding. She never expected to see Rafael again, but she wouldn't have minded seeing him again, and she didn't want to be instrumental in his capture.

"I mean, what was he like?" Ivan persisted. "What did he look like? Did he have any identifying marks? Did he speak English?"

"He had a dark complexion, black hair, and dark, piercing eyes. He was about six feet tall, nicely built, no tattoos or any other identifying marks, and he spoke perfect English."

Ivan noticed that she was answering his questions as briefly as possible, and never volunteering any additional information. He suspected, from her descriptors, *nicely built,* and *piercing eyes*, that Margo might have picked up a case of incipient Stockholm syndrome. Falling in love with their captor is a fairly common thing among female victims of kidnappers and other criminals, but it is very rare that they will ever bring themselves to admit it. Ivan decided to move the subject away from Rafael Alvarez and back to Robert Thomaston. Perhaps Margo would be less guarded about her relationship with a man who was dead.

"Let's go back to Thomaston again. You said he was your mentor?"

"Yes."

"What would you say was his journalistic philosophy?"

"I'd say he was a businessman first, and a journalist second. I found that working with him was nothing at all like taking journalism classes in school. Issues of morality, the public's right to know, and freedom of the press never came up. He was trying to toughen me up, and get the stars out of my eyes, and bring me down to earth. At least that's what he said."

"What do you think he meant by that, exactly? Could you give me a specific example?"

"He was always interested in making the news exciting. His idea of a really good news article was one that promised imminent death and destruction. If the item was less than earthshaking, he wanted to see lots of intrigue, corruption, suspicion, scandal, and innuendo in the copy. He was less interested in the truth of the reporting than in whether it would sell newspapers."

"Did he ever suggest that you lie or fabricate the details of a story?"

"I think it would be fair to say that his most frequent advice about my writing concerned punching up the copy. He was the world's greatest advocate of hyperbole. If the reporting in the articles was such that the story was actually not true, that was okay with him as long as it wasn't boring. To be boring was the greatest sin, according to him. He was also very careful about matters of legal liability."

"How did you feel about that approach?" Ivan asked her. "Ethically, I mean."

"I might have been more concerned about that when I was fresh out of journalism school, but my first reaction was that good journalists deserve to take artistic license the same way novelists do, otherwise nobody will find the writing either interesting or inspiring, and probably not even all that instructive, either. But eventually I came to realize that the so-called artistic license wasn't being used for creative purposes, but to sell newspapers. So at this point I'd have to say that my experiences in the real world of journalism have made me somewhat cynical."

"I'm sorry to hear that, Miss Watson. I know cynicism is rampant in our day and age, but I don't think one should have to separate personal ethics from one's work."

Margo wasn't sure she was hearing correctly. In her experience of the world a man in a high position such as Dr. Welland's would have let go of morality long ago. She had met several men whom the world would regard as important, but to her they seemed dishonest, devious, and generally unscrupulous. So she was completely unprepared to meet a powerful figure whose character was unsullied or at least apparently unchanged by his success.

Her first consideration was to regard Ivan as a possible master of deceit who was using idealism as a cover for his true purposes, but she still had no idea what they were. Until she knew better she was prepared to wait for the veil to drop, revealing the real Secretary of Defense. She would not have been the least bit surprised to find that he fit the same mold as those important men that she had encountered before.

"Journalists count themselves among the sophisticates of the world," Margo said at last, "and the nature of their work dictates that they must be suspicious and cynical. Tragedy, bloodshed, intrigue, sex, and scandal are the basic plot tools of the reporter's trade. Flamboyant prose accompanied by grisly photos, are the characteristics of the types of news items that sell advertising space, and TV and radio broadcast time. You can't blame the media for giving the public what it wants, can you?"

"Well, actually I do," Ivan said.

Margo was incredulous. Would a man who had risen to the high position of Secretary of Defense be so naïve as to think that it was the media's business to self regulate the moral content of its outpourings to its insatiable audience?

"Mr. Secretary, what makes you think that the media could afford to disappoint its customers and still remain in business, and what about the First Amendment right of free speech? Who is to decide what is, or isn't suitable news for presentation to the public?"

"I think the common good is the place to start, followed by strict adherence to the truth."

"And I think the regulators should stay out of it. It's just a case of supply and demand, like drugs. If nobody wanted drugs, there wouldn't be any. If people want to read the Bible instead of the newspapers, they should be perfectly free to make that choice."

"Yes, and in no time at all we would have the modern version of Sodom and Gomorra taking place in the United States, which is what the fundamentalists of all religions are warning us about."

Ivan was not interested in continuing the discussion of the oft argued issue of the place of a free press in an immoral world. He could already understand her point of view and he was merely attempting to discern if Margo was a wanton exponent of loose living, or merely the victim of it. He decided that their conversation, which had served to relax them and draw them closer to a mutual understanding, now needed a change of subject. Ivan thought that perhaps in time Margo would switch sides in the argument, but for his purposes now he would have to make do with things as they were.

Margo might have been a helpful and willing witness of Robert Thomaston's unprincipled media philosophy, but she was not a principal in its manufacture and distribution. She could, however, be instrumental in the capture of the Viper, but Ivan couldn't help feeling that she wouldn't be a willing participant in this enterprise. It was with no small amount of guilt that Ivan decided to use Margo, but not sexually, as so many had done before.

"Miss Watson, let's return to the matter of the Viper. Have you any idea where he went after he disappeared from the house in Costa Rica?"

"None."

"He never said or did anything to indicate where he was headed?"

"No."

"According to the police, he had a secret tunnel under the jungle which led to a helicopter which he used to escape. During your time with him, did you see the tunnel or the helicopter?"

"No."

"Did you see him talk with anyone else?"

"No, no one."

"So you would suspect that he flew the chopper himself when he escaped?"

"Yes, I guess so."

"Miss Watson, the ability to fly a helicopter is not nearly as common as the ability to fly a fixed-wing aircraft. Aren't you surprised that he knew how to operate a helicopter?"

"Not really. I didn't know it was harder to fly a chopper than an airplane. Anyhow, he seemed to be a very self-reliant and competent individual. He certainly was able to handle a speedboat, so although I don't know about his other abilities I wouldn't be surprised to hear that he could fly a chopper."

"Did our friend say that he would be in contact with you again?"

"Certainly not!"

Ivan's initial impression that Margo might be harboring feelings of attraction for her captor were aroused once again by the exaggerated vehemence of her response. Perhaps the lady protested too much? She seemed to have a high opinion of the Viper's abilities. Ivan couldn't shake the feeling that she might have agreed to meet Alvarez again at some time in the future, or at least that he would be in contact with her once more. Since Ivan felt that he had developed some sort of rapport with Margo during their talk, he decided to take a chance and turn the questioning to more personal matters. He hoped that he could draw some emotional responses from her that would confirm his suspected diagnosis that she had contracted an emotional connection to the Viper during her captivity.

"What did you do during your time as a hostage?"

"What do you mean?"

"You were with this man for several days, weren't you? Were you tied up? What did you eat? Did you read, or watch TV, or what?"

"I wasn't bound, but he had a gun with him at all times. I didn't know where I was. All I knew was that it was a lonely spot bordered by the sea on one side and the jungle all around. He wanted me to cook, but since I'm not very good in the kitchen, he prepared the food. We didn't watch TV. He had a lot of books, but most were in Spanish."

Ivan noticed that she had not really answered his question. He suspected that he knew how they had occupied their time together, but her disinclination to discuss and condemn the man indicated that her imprisonment was more like a honeymoon than she would like to admit. He didn't question her further on the matter, not wishing to alert her that he was on to her. He was quite certain that she would eventually lead him to the Viper.

CHAPTER THIRTEEN

David Feingold and the rest of Ivan's team of investigators were going through a difficult period. Discovering that the published news was often a total prevarication was one thing, but proving it was another. The biggest question of all was simply to find out if there were federal laws on the books to prevent the media from simply manufacturing the news as if it were fiction, and if so, did they have sufficient evidence to bring and win a legal case against the big three media conglomerates?

The team had scheduled a meeting with the Chief White House Counsel to discuss the matter. Damian and Brooklyn had been selected by the team to act as point men on the legal issues because they had the most knowledge of the workings of government, and the most government contacts with those who labored in its halls.

The Counsel was a gaunt, gruff lawyer in mid career. His general demeanor was intentionally intimidating and was intended to curb any languor or verbosity on the part of those who sought his advice. His tall thin frame was topped by a thinning patch of fluffy grey hair that had its own ideas about the proper coiffure that the President's lawyer should have. Garrison Palmer was his name, and his reputation as a legal expert was based on his several appearances before the Supreme Court on behalf of clients seeking clarification of various complex constitutional questions.

Evidently he had found standing before the austere bar of the nine most prestigious judges in the country to be exhilarating, for he had tailored his office in the White House and his judiciary demeanor to match those of his admired role models. It was apparent to Damian and Brooklyn that the man they were seeking counsel from aspired to a more lofty position, and that his present job was only a step on the road to greater things.

Ivan wanted to be on sound legal ground as he led the Executive Branch into the inevitable constitutional battle that would proceed from any presidential actions that the Fourth Estate deemed to be an infringement of its First Amendment rights. Welland's position was that freedom of speech didn't trump all the other rights. He needed to know how far the President could go to prevent sedition. He wanted to have an expert opinion on the legality of actions he might take to halt the purveyors of false information from poisoning the well of peace. He delegated his trusted assistants to ascertain what, if any, penalties there were for a free press that eschewed its responsibility to present the truth to the citizens who had been kind enough to grant them the freedom to say anything they chose.

It was Ivan's position that inherent in the freedom granted to the press was the tacit understanding that the free press would make every effort to ensure the truth of what they published. Individuals had some protection under the law against being slandered and libeled, but the government, not being an individual, apparently had no recourse. The President's program to blanket the arsenals of the nations had released the worst spewing of political invective that had ever been trained on an American president. The reaction from the international media was intended to be as deadly as any assassin's bullet. The organizations responsible for truthfully informing the public rose up as one and delivered a tidal wave of distorted, false, and calculatedly misinformed information.

Angry reactions were voiced by those segments of the economy that stood to lose out if the world no longer needed weapons. The President and his policies were excoriated. Condemnatory editorials were published in most of the major newspapers, and TV commentators and satirists were fully devoted to undermining his program.

Yet in spite of the efforts of the special interests in opposition, the world had become noticeably safer. Ordinary citizens everywhere were cognizant of this fact, so the dissenters had turned to subterfuge as the way to bad mouth the progress that had been made. Some subtle, and some not so subtle media attacks had been formulated to disparage the peace process and those who supported it.

So when Damian and Brooklyn took their seats in front of Garrison Palmer's huge desk they felt small, which was the aspiring justice's plan. They were, however, representing the views of their boss and of his boss, the President of the United States. The matter was of monumental importance now because after more than two centuries the playing field had changed greatly, mostly because of technology. The executives charged with directing the government's actions could no longer function efficiently without clarifications to the First Amendment. Brooklyn led off the discussion.

"Mr. Palmer, the Secretary would like to know whether there are any laws on the books to prevent the media from fabricating news reportage."

"Would you like to expand a bit on that subject?" the lawyer asked.

"Our department has put together enough information to prove that the largest media conglomerates in the country have acted in concert to create news that suits their purposes instead of simply reporting on events that happen. Over the years, through strategies involving mergers and acquisitions, three men have managed to consolidate a majority of the world's press into monopolies controlled by them. Their enterprises include the capacity to create fictional events that are seemingly so real and so broadly proclaimed that their renditions are perceived as true and actual by the general public, and by many governments as well. Technologists have harnessed the speed of light and communications are now done in real time.

"The authors of the Bill of Rights couldn't have foreseen that a believable lie could be spread all over the world in a matter of seconds, or that a missile could deliver destruction from another continent in a matter of minutes. We have to know if the use of free speech under the First Amendment is trumped by a tacit assumption that the matter spoken of is true. Otherwise we can visualize a scenario in which the missiles are crossing the sky because of an untrue report that one side or another released. We need to have grounds to stop this type of potentially subversive activity at once. Do we have any legal methods by which to do it?"

The attorney, trying not to look nonplussed by the information he'd just received, adopted what he thought was his most intelligent expression.

"I'll have to know more," he stated, "before I can render an opinion on such a large matter. You say you have proof that they have done this?"

"Yes, we have," Damian answered.

"You realize, of course, that proof of such an accusation would have to include proof of intent. I'm sure you know that either we'd have to prove that they knowingly intended to use their influence to gain unfair commercial advantages for themselves, and/or that their actions were seditious and clearly aimed at subverting the legally-elected government's policies. Show me what you've got on these people."

Brooklyn produced several files that summarized the team's recent findings and passed them across to Palmer. For the next hour Damian and Brooklyn responded to the Counsel's questions, and discussed hypothetical situations.

"All right," said Palmer finally. "I think I've got a grasp on things. I'll need a week to work on this, to do some research, and to consult with colleagues and legal experts."

Ivan's people were a bit disappointed that they couldn't get Palmer to give them an immediate yea or nay, but when they remembered that it had taken the four of them months to gather their information, it did seem inconsiderate not to give the lawyer a week to study it, so they agreed to wait and left his office to go back to their own less plush offices.

Ivan was not particularly disturbed to hear from Brooklyn that the President's Chief Counsel wanted to think carefully about the recommendations he was expected to make. Ivan needed the time anyway for other matters that were bubbling around in his head.

For one thing he wanted time to pursue his theory that Margo Watson and her hostage-taker were not through with each other. His sixth sense had been activated during their interview when she had not said even one derogatory thing about her kidnapper. Ivan couldn't believe that a woman could have nothing bad to say about the man who had killed her lover in cold blood right in front of her eyes. It wasn't a normal reaction in his book.

He believed it was a case of the Stockholm syndrome, where the victim falls in love with her captor, but with one variation: Margo was intelligent and beautiful, and not any kind of a shrinking violet. Usually the syndrome applies to lonely, introverted women with low self-esteem – the type of woman who has suffered from lifelong marginalization and then suddenly discovers that she is the center of someone's attention. In cases like this it is not surprising that she doesn't want to give up that new and heady feeling of self-worth. Even if Margo, however, didn't exactly fit the description, Ivan still believed that she would contact the Viper, or else he would get in touch with her. He decided to start making plans to have her watched.

Ivan realized that he would need the cooperation of other investigative governmental departments, as bringing Rafael Alvarez to justice was not specifically a Defense Department jurisdictional matter. He decided to pay a visit to his counterpart, the Secretary of Homeland Security. In a half hour of intense discussions he was able to arrange for the cooperation of the FBI, Secret Service, and the CIA. An inter-agency plan for Margo Watson's surveillance was also drawn up and activated. It was agreed that the two cabinet level officials would act in tandem and be part of every detail of the manhunt for Rafael Alvarez. The killings in Chicago, New York, Costa Rica, and the attempt on Ivan's life in Washington were all attributed to the man known as the Viper. These unsavory activities had moved him to *Most Wanted* status.

Rafael Alvarez, meanwhile, was beginning to feel that he had made a mistake by choosing Thailand as his second choice of a retirement location. It had never really occurred to him that he would have to use it as anything more than a temporary hideaway. Costa Rica had been his first choice, but he had squandered all the advantages of that country by opportunistically deciding to settle his account with Robert Thomaston there. So he had ended up in Thailand, without even knowing the local language and culture.

His primary motivation for settling in Thailand had been for reasons of safety and anonymity, rather than comfort and convenience. His secondary reason had to do with the many connections he had in Southeast Asian drug circles, and the excellent money laundering opportunities that they provided. Bangkok is the point through which the rest of the world enters Asia, and as a result it is the international business hub in its area. The Thai currency was relatively stable. The land and the climate were beautiful, and offered international tourists an attractive destination. One more foreigner was not likely to be noticed in the wild, commercial bazaar of the Thai economy. In these ways the Viper's choice had been sound, and gave him no regrets.

His complaints about his decision to escape to Asia weren't as practical as they were emotional. Although his personality was that of a natural loner, the permanence of always being immediately recognized as a racial outsider was wearing thin on him. He felt he needed to live with at least one person with whom he could communicate on a deeper level. It should be a woman – one who shared at least some common cultural experiences, and could provide him with companionship, sex, and intellectual stimulation. His ventures into the nightlife of Bangkok had produced either gold-digging Thai girls or Caucasian tourists looking for a merely temporary adventure. These women had provided only weak distractions for Rafael, and he soon found himself thinking frequently about Margo Watson.

As far as he was concerned, part of Margo's charm came from the fact that they had met each other unexpectedly. She was Thomaston's mistress, and she became his against her own will. Rafael felt that her connection to him, therefore, had been honest and heartfelt. In the beginning she had been in fear for her life, but as things progressed she had lost her initial apprehensions and moved in the direction of a mutual understanding. Although he could never completely trust anyone, woman or man, Alvarez felt closer to Margo than to any other person he could think of at the time. He decided he would send for her, but he had to carefully work out the details so that she couldn't betray him either knowingly, or by allowing herself to be followed. He decided to contact her by e-mail in order to test the waters.

He stopped in at the Cook's Travel Agency in Bangkok and bought a one-way, first-class ticket from Washington's Dulles International Airport to Bangkok, via London and Delhi. Next he walked up the street to an internet café and rented a terminal from which he sent this message. *First Class ticket to Bangkok in your name at Cook's. Use it if you wish to write sequel to Costa Rica story. No reply necessary. R.*

Ivan Welland had convinced the Secretary of Homeland Security and the Secret Service Chief to begin the Priority One surveillance of Margo Watson as a way to locate Rafael Alvarez. Ivan's hunches had panned out before, and the enforcement agencies had no other better leads as to the whereabouts of the Viper, so their resources were brought to bear on observing Margo's comings and goings. Every trick of the trade was employed to monitor her every move. The art of electronic spying had evolved to a degree that would surprise the average person. Margo would have been astonished to know the extent to which her movements were being watched, but since she had never been a subject of importance to government agents, she left her apartment at the usual time and went blithely and undeterred about her business.

When she checked her e-mail at work that morning, she discovered the message from R. She had no doubt as to R's identity. She looked forward to the opportunity of renewing her relationship with Rafael. She told herself that she really wanted to get an exclusive story about one of the world's most wanted men, which would also be a follow-up to her kidnap article. Of course she had another personal reason for seeing him again, but she was intentionally minimizing that.

It had also occurred to her that she might be able to combine her trip to Bangkok with a stopover in London to see Geoffrey Pressman. She contacted the English media magnate's office by e-mail and requested an appointment to see him briefly while she was in London between flights. The rapid affirmative response she received confirmed her intuition that Lord Pressman had at least some interest in her.

Margo Watson's plans were beginning to take shape. Rafael's plane ticket was a godsend, because now she could speak with Geoffrey without feeling obligated. Selling him her exclusive story about her captivity would be her cover negotiation. Finding out if he was interested in hiring her would be a second reason to see him. The third, and perhaps the most important one, was to determine if he was interested in her on a personal level.

She had felt the old, familiar vibrations emanating from him when they had met aboard the yacht, but since she was with Robert then, those feelings could not be explored. This more subtle level of negotiation would require time and delicate handling, and it would be the most costly to him. No longer would she give her youthful companionship away. At a minimum she would require a salaried job as a writer before entering into any personal relationship with him. Her dalliance with Robert had left her flat broke when he was killed. She should have had some sort of understanding with him that provided for her future, but she couldn't have known he would die prematurely, and consequently she was out in the cold after warming his bed for him. She resolved never to make the same mistake again.

Things would have to be different with Geoffrey Lord Pressman. He would have heard about Thomaston's death, and he was bound to be interested in an exclusive story of his rival's last hours. Margo had noticed the Englishman appreciatively looking her over on several occasions during their time on Baron Fritz's yacht, and now that she was free, perhaps he might be interested in a liaison.

The FBI agents assigned to shadow Margo had learned about her upcoming trip to London by tapping her phone, bugging her apartment, and monitoring her e-mail account. They found out the time and flight number, and saw that her final destination was Bangkok. The Homeland Security agents were excited by the news that the Viper's trail was hot and led straight to Thailand. Arrangements were made for two FBI special agents to be on the same plane as Margo. Interpol agents and the police in Thailand were asked to be on standby in support of the arrest that Ivan and his associates felt sure would be coming soon.

Jim Blake was comfortably ensconced in the first class section of the British Airways flight that had just lifted off the Dulles tarmac, headed for Heathrow Airport in Britain. Margo Watson was seated next to him, by the window. She decided to review her article during the flight, so she reached into her black leather briefcase and withdrew the folder. She was just about to begin reading it when the flight attendant came along with a glass of champagne. Her attention was diverted from her papers while she took the flute from the server. As she accepted the wine and settled back in her seat, she noticed that the attention of the man in the seat next to hers was firmly fixed on her legs. He accepted his glass of champagne and looked right at her with a pleased look in his eyes. Margo knew that the usual flirty conversation was about to begin.

"We might as well chat," he said genially, "because you're not going to be able to read without interruption until the dessert, coffee and cordials have been served."

Since he had spoken to her directly, Margo couldn't ignore the man without offending him.

"I guess you're right," she answered.

"Let me introduce myself. My name is Jim Blake, and I'm VP of Sales for United Fast Food Restaurants. I'm on my way to India to see if we can corral a few franchisees to open up Western-style restaurants as a change from the usual curry castles they have over there in India. I figure with all the folks in India we ought to be able to develop a nice piece of business with our cowboy ambience. So tell me then, what's your name, if you don't mind me asking?"

"Margo Watson. I'm a freelance writer and journalist."

Facing the inevitable, and remembering fondly her last trip across the pond in Robert's private jet, Margo reconciled herself to listening to her neighbor's palaver. It was an overnight dinner flight, and her only hope of escape was to go to sleep right after eating.

"Pleased to meet you, Ms. Watson. Anyhow, so like I said, the majority of Indians are Hindus and they don't eat beef."

"Mmm hmm. So how do you plan to get around that?"

"Oh, we've given that a lot of thought. We've got a whole line of non-beef hamburgers ready to roll out. We've got burgers made of ground turkey, chicken, lamb, pork, fish and vegetarian ingredients. Everything will be cooked on our patented open-fire cookhouse grills and slathered with our cowboy barbecue sauce that comes in all degrees of heat, like Texas chili comes at home."

"I see."

"Yeah, we've thought of everything. There are so many people in these countries over here. The market is huge, and we're going to carve out a piece for ourselves."

Blake looked confidently and approvingly at Margo as he waited for her reply, but she said nothing.

"It's great, isn't it?" he contined, unperturbed. "When we get through with the Indians, Pakistanis and Bangladeshis we can start with the Chinese. Boy, what markets! It's a salesman's dream."

Blake went on and on in his enthusiastic American way. If it were up to him, the various cuisines in the world would eventually give up and grant the hamburger its proper place at the top of the food chains. He likened it to Western movies, sports, and sex, and was absolutely positive that the world would convert to the American way of doing things. Margo wondered vaguely what this guy meant by American sex, but she wasn't about to ask.

Jim Blake was in his mid to late forties. He was surely making more money than his intellectual abilities justified. Margo noticed he hadn't surreptitiously removed his wedding ring when he saw her sitting next to him. At least he was honest enough not to try to get away with it. She thought he was the type who, when he had advanced up the corporate ladder sufficiently, believed he was entitled to have a young mistress. He would probably find one too, but after Robert Thomaston, this guy was small potatoes as far as she was concerned. She was fishing in deeper waters now. After the meal she excused herself, flattened her seat, and went to sleep.

In the early morning the lights in the cabin came on. Margo was first into the forward lavatory. She had to look her best when she met Lord Pressman, so she took extra care with her make-up and hair. She figured she had three, maybe four hours in which to make an impression on the master of the British media world, and then she had to be back in time to catch the plane to New Delhi. When she got back to her seat Jim Blake was looking rumpled, paunchy, and in need of a shave. He was squirming around in his seat, waiting for the red "occupied" sign above the door to the lavatory to turn green. As soon as it did, he fairly ran for the door. Margo was glad she was a woman and didn't need to scrape her face with a razor in order to look human.

Looking a bit better, Jim Blake picked up where he had left off the night before. He had never asked her even once what she had written or where she worked. He seemed to just assume that she knew no one in London, and that he was going to take care of her between flights. When Margo told him she had an appointment with Geoffrey Lord Pressman of Fleet Street, Jim Blake had acted deflated. His imagination seemed to have gone far down the road with his beautiful companion, and he feigned taking a hard ego blow when he found he couldn't follow.

When they disembarked, Margo hurried toward the exit to catch a cab. She glanced back and watched him looking forlornly at her while he stayed behind to wait for the next leg of the journey. He realized that she was more than she appeared to be, but she had suspected from the first that he was less than he pretended to be. Both were wrong.

CHAPTER FOURTEEN

Geoffrey Lord Pressman was the scion of a rich Jewish family that had escaped from Hitler's Germany before the advent of World War II. He had been sent to the very best English schools where he had been tortured by masters and fellow students, as were all the students who didn't come from the British upper classes. Having to survive in public schools by using his own intelligence instead of his father's influence, he ended up receiving an education in practical democracy from those who least deserved to live under it.

For years he had existed among people who doled out talk of justice and freedom from behind the protected walls of elitism. His family was not about to succumb to politics based on vague, arcane principles of royal dispensation, any more than they had submitted to the National Socialism of the Third Reich or capitulated to the heady strains of Stalin's proletarian communism. His people had come through the eons of persecution and slavery described in the Pentateuch, followed by the victimization of all the nations that led to the holocaust. They feared nothing from America's version of monetary democracy. In fact, they had learned to use it for their own purposes.

Geoffrey had distilled his personal political philosophy from history. He had arrived at a point where he felt he knew all the arguments, pro and con, and had rejected all of them except those in which he attained suzerainty. His expanding media empire was a tribute to his ability to construct an environment in which he reigned supreme. In this way he was no different from Robert Thomaston, except that he was even cleverer. As E.B. White once said, "It is easier for a man to be loyal to his club than to his planet; the bylaws are shorter, and he is personally acquainted with the other members." Pressman's club was his family, but his dynasty was running out because he had no children. He likened his situation to the Patriarch Abraham, whose wife Sarah had been barren for most of his life. He had become impatient, as had his wife, and he had begun searching for his Hagar to bear him a son and heir.

Susan Summercroft was supposed to have been the stand-in mother of his child, but when she caught on to his plan she refused to conceive unless he married her. Tucked away in his past was the wife chosen by his parents, but no longer suitable for a secular man in his position. Geoffrey's plan didn't include marriage to a gentile, so they had reached a state of limbo in which he had used Susan as a temporary showpiece, while his wife's value to him was as his protector from the double jeopardy of a second marriage – but neither woman solved the problem of his having no heir.

He was at the end of his patience with Susan, and had secretly begun to look for her replacement. He wanted to explore the possibilities with Margo now that Thomaston was gone and she was available. Unlike most men, Geoffrey was not put off by Margo's affair with another man. In fact, quite the opposite was true. He regarded her relationship with Robert as a very favorable reference.

During her time on the yacht, Margo had observed that most of the heat had gone out of Geoffrey's relationship with Susan. She had consigned that information to her memory in the event it might become useful in the future. She wanted to use her conclusion in the subtlest way possible to convey her availability without the slightest indication of lewdness. She had already rehearsed the scene of their reunion in her mind several times, so she was ready when Lord Pressman's secretary told her that he was ready to see her in his office.

"Margo, how very nice of you to stop in to see me."

Margo approached him in ladylike fashion and hugged him as she would a friend, but with just a hint of openness that would leave him wondering. He accepted her hug by momentarily placing his hands lightly on her waist just long enough to discern if she had any extra flesh that people call love handles. He detested the expression almost as much as the flab itself.

"It was generous of you to spare me some of your very valuable time," Margo said.

"Not at all, my dear. Please have a seat. You must tell me everything you've been doing since Robert's demise."

"I think I tell it best in the story I've written. I'm trying to market it. Unfortunately, with Robert gone, I've had to get back to work to earn a living. I was wondering if you'd be interested in reading it."

"Why, of course. I'll be happy to read it. I'm flattered that you brought it to me. Am I the first one to see it?"

"Yes. It would be an exclusive if you were to buy it. I thought either you or Baron Fritz might have a particular interest because of your personal relationships with Robert."

Margo hoped she hadn't been too businesslike in dealing with the article by referring to his European competitor Baron Fritz, and making it seem as though she would shop the story around if she didn't get a prompt offer from him. It was part of her ploy to make Geoffrey conscious of her need to support herself. She also hoped he would see it as a sign that she was not just a piece of arm candy, but a strong, talented woman in her own right.

"I'd be happy to read anything you write," he said, hoping to encourage her and to keep her closely in touch with him. "But I'll need some time to make up my mind about whether your story fits our present needs. I'm in negotiations right now to acquire Robert's interests, and I'd like to consult my legal team to consider the ramifications of publishing anything at this time that might affect the terms of the agreement."

Geoffrey, of course, was more interested in keeping her on the hook while he examined her candidacy to be Susan's replacement than he was in getting a second opinion on her article.

"You must be excited about the prospect of acquiring those rights. Such an acquisition, if you're successful, will make your companies preeminent in the media world. I'd be delighted if my story could be a part of the project."

Margo passed him the folder containing a copy of the account of Thomaston's last hours. Geoffrey accepted the manuscript with a gracious smile, and placed it on his desk.

"Good. Now that we've taken care of business we can relax. Would you care to join me for lunch?"

"Yes, thank you. I'd enjoy that."

"I generally eat here rather than at my club or in public."

Geoffrey was showing Margo through to his private dining room that doubled as a conference room when he wasn't having a meal. As she walked ahead of him she could almost feel his eyes examining her body while his chatter continued apace.

"We have a fixed menu here, I'm afraid, so you'll have to take what you get. The Chef and I work out the menus in advance, week by week, but seeing you again has disturbed my concentration and I can't remember what he's serving today. It will be something I like, to be sure, and I hope you will like it, too."

Margo, after her short time living the high life, had no doubt that his choices would be exquisite.

"Whatever it is, I won't have time to fully appreciate it," she said as she placed her napkin on her lap.

"Oh?"

"I'm afraid I'm just between flights today. I'll have to hightail it back to the airport right after lunch. I'm just passing through, but I wanted to stop in to say hello and show you my article," she explained, hoping he wouldn't ask about her destination and her plans for the future.

"Too bad. I thought perhaps you'd like to stay for a few days to give me time to see what we could do with your article, and so that we could expand our acquaintance. I would have liked to give you an insider's tour of London."

Margo heard his words and interpreted their meaning to be that he would have liked to squire her around on a sort of test basis to see how she handled his upper crust friends, and perhaps try her out in bed as well. It might have been fun for her, but she already had what she wanted – his attention. It was never wise to make oneself too available.

"I'd like that very much Geoffrey, but may I have a rain check? It's work that calls me away. But I could stop by on my way back home, if you wish." As an afterthought and to check the status of his present relationship she added, "It would be nice to see Susan again, too."

Geoffrey had been around the block a few times and realized what she was doing. He didn't mind playing the mating game. He knew that overcoming obstacles in the early stages served to enhance the pleasure of the end game. Her offer to visit again later proved her interest in him, and that was enough for the present. He didn't mind using Susan as an obstacle. It would add a little insecurity to Margo's position, and force her to be diligent in her pursuit of him.

"Susan will be happy to see you again, I'm sure."

Just then a waiter arrived and served them two small bowls of chilled gazpacho.

"I really fancy this kind of soup," Margo said, taking a spoonful. "It's refreshing, mildly spicy, and an excellent way to eat healthy, boring vegetables."

"I agree entirely. There's nothing worse than having to chew interminably on a serving of raw vegetables. But if one is to believe the nutritionists, raw veggies seem to be essential to good health. What do you think, Margo?"

"You're right. Vegetables might be boring, but they're definitely a necessary part of maintaining one's figure," she said, hoping to call attention to her best feature and keep the prize of the game in his sights.

It did, and Geoffrey offered the compliment that she sought.

"Well, it's certainly working in your case. You look fit as a fiddle, if you don't mind my saying so."

The waiter removed the soup bowls and replaced them with a small watercress salad.

"This salad will also help to keep you fiddling in tune."

"It's nice of you to be so concerned about my fitness."

"Well actually I was really more concerned about my own, as you had no part in choosing this luncheon menu. But now that I know you approve of my choices, I'll be free to be even more decisive next time."

Margo was pleased to know that the strong possibility existed that she could draw close to Geoffrey, as she had to Robert. She was glad to have a conservative alternative to a passionate affair with Rafael.

The waiter returned with some grilled salmon, saffron rice, and a chutney dressing.

"You see, Margo, how good I'm being? I'm consuming my quota of omega-3 oils in order to hold on to the blush of virility."

"I'll have to check with Susan to see if it's working."

"I'd feel a whole lot more secure if we did the checking together."

"Why, Geoffrey, do you think I'm some sort of expert in this field?" she said teasingly, feeling that at the very least his suggestion invited them to be on a first name basis.

"No, that's not what I meant."

"I know. Perhaps we can explore that aspect of health next time."

The waiter arrived to carry off the lunch plates and serve a cup of freshly cut fruit. The suggestive bantering changed to another subject while the server poured the coffee.

"When do think you'll be returning?" Lord Pressman wanted to know.

"I'm not sure just now, but it won't be too long. I'll let you know as soon as I find out. But right now I've got to leave in order to catch my flight."

The parting was cordial. Geoffrey took her hands in his and kissed her cheek. Margo was perky and accepted his kiss.

"You can reach me on my cell phone if you have any news or questions about my article," she said as she turned to go. "Meanwhile keep on eating salmon, if it works for you."

In the cab on the way to Heathrow, Margo thought about her lunch with Geoffrey and decided everything had gone swimmingly. He was clearly interested in her. She thought there was an excellent chance that she could return to her role as courtesan with a new leading man if she wished to return to that way of life. She promised herself that if she chose that role, it would not be as an ingénue. This time she would protect her financial future and build a career at the same time.

Lord Pressman was pleased at the tenor of the talk at the luncheon. He felt that his initial opinion of Margo had been correct. She was delightfully sexy, bright, and seemed to know the rules of the game. Having been the mistress of an important, well established man before, he wouldn't have to teach her the basics. Margo was American and therefore might be perceived by the British as brusque, crass, and over-confident, but as these were the same traits ascribed to him because of his Jewish background, he found them quite appealing. He liked her positive attitude and her aggressive, independent, single-minded pursuit of success.

And, of course, there was the way she looked.

Jim Blake reported in to the Special Agent in charge of his FBI unit, who in turn reported to the Director, who called Dr. Ivan Welland with the news that Margo had met with Geoffrey Lord Pressman for lunch and was now en route to India on British Air. Blake would attempt to find out what she had been up to in London with Pressman. Someone else would pick up the surveillance in New Delhi. The Thai police in Bangkok were checking the airlines and travel agencies to see if they could assist the FBI to discover the identity of the person who had purchased the ticket that Margo was using.

The Bureau had made sure that Margo's request for a different traveling companion was ignored. So when she had just begun to settle into her seat prior to take off, she was annoyed to find Jim Blake take his usual place at her side.

"Well, how did things go with your appointment?"

Jim continued to affect a cockiness that was supposed to make him seem like an ordinary guy struggling with an underlying inferiority complex. He wondered if he had gone overboard in making himself seem too puffed up. He decided to tone down his portrayal of the ugly American businessman. He had been instructed to try to elicit some specific piece of information that could be used to convict Margo Watson as an accomplice after she had led him to the Viper.

"Things went well with Lord Pressman. Thank you for asking. I think he's going to buy my story."

"Congratulations. Let me buy you a drink to celebrate," Jim said. He was getting into his new role as an enthusiastic supporter and confidant.

"Okay. Why not?"

Margo decided to give him another chance. Perhaps he was less of a Babbitt than she had thought.

"What's your article about?" Blake asked her, hoping he could keep the conversation centered on Margo so he could let up on the imaginary business interests.

"It's about an experience that I had a short time ago."

"Oh, what was that?"

Margo didn't see how telling this shlub anything about her story would help or hinder its sale, but she didn't want to get into the gory details of Robert's death.

"I'm not permitted to discuss the contents of the article until after it appears," she said.

"Sort of like those actresses who are not allowed to tell the story of a movie before it's released to the public."

"Yeah, just like that," Margo said.

"Here's the stewardess. What would you like to drink?"

"Scotch and soda, please. You know you shouldn't call them stewardesses. These days they're referred to as flight attendants."

"Oops, I know that, but old habits are hard to shake for an old guy."

"You don't call your employees *waitresses* any more, do you? No, you call them servers. Right?"

"Right, but let me give this server our order now."

Blake ordered two single malt scotches from the smartly uniformed first class server. Then he turned back to Margo.

"Shouldn't you be able to tell me something about your story without giving the whole thing away, sort of like the actors do to hype their films before they are released? Come on. What harm can it do? Who's ever going to know?"

"Well, it's quite a personal story. It's different when you write a true story for readers you don't know. But when someone tells an actual true story face to face to another person, it's quite another matter. Do you know what I mean? It's embarrassing. It's the difference between a witness and the court reporter in a trial."

"I see what you're saying, but can't you put in a little warning like they do on TV? Like, *the following program may contain scenes of violence, nudity,* or something like that, so that this hearer can be advised?"

"I'm afraid not."

"Well, at least tell me the genre of the story. You can do that, can't you?"

"It's a story about a murder and a hostage taking."

"Wow. That's fascinating! So, since I can see you're not murdered, are you the murderer or the hostage in the story?"

"Well, I can tell you that I'm not a murderer."

"That's something, then, isn't it?"

He made it sound as though he was relieved, but actually he would have been far more comfortable had he been sitting next to a murderer so he could simply slap the cuffs on her and be done with it. It was the subtleties that tried his patience.

"So you were a hostage?"

"Actually, yes I was."

"That must have been terrible. I can imagine that being under the complete control of some strange, violent man must have been unbearable for you."

"In my case it wasn't all that unbearable. I wasn't actually deprived of food or sanitary conditions or anything like that."

Blake had read the transcript of her police statement and knew that she had claimed to be repeatedly raped, but he had to be careful not to let her guess that he knew more than he should and betray that he was not what he pretended to be. He felt he was making some progress, however, for he had gotten her to open up at least a little bit. He hoped now that the drinks had arrived that she would loosen up even more and perhaps reveal some information that could be useful to building a case. He probed further.

"You make imprisonment against your will sound not so bad, but what about your freedom? Could you go and come as you pleased?"

Margo was conscious of the fact that he was making increasing inroads into the story that she had said she couldn't talk about with him. She attributed it to his sort of clod-like, never-take-no for an answer personality. It never dawned on her that he had any agenda other than exhibiting curiosity and hoping to pass the time hearing a spicy story told by an attractive young woman.

"No, of course not. I was a prisoner in a nice house, that's all."

"Well, what did your kidnapper want? I imagine the guy wanted a huge ransom to release you unharmed. How much did he ask for?"

Blake said this with a prurient smile on his face, hoping to anger her and thereby get her to blurt out something she didn't want to say.

"I can't tell you that," Margo said with a playful smile. Inside she knew that he had struck a nerve. She presumed he had accidentally hit on the weak spot in her story.

If the Viper had been paid off by someone to release her, it would have sounded reasonable. As it was, her statement that he had used her only for sex and then let her go free, brought into question the truth of her whole story. She had admitted being an eyewitness to the Viper's murder of Robert Thomaston. Why would he simply release her?

It was a question that Ivan Welland had already thought about when he arranged to have the surveillance put on her movements. He had to know whether Margo Watson was an accomplice who might have aided and abetted the Viper to commit a revenge murder, or if she was just an innocent bystander. Her plane trip was doing nothing to improve her credibility with the authorities.

Margo suddenly clammed up and refused to discuss the matter any further. Blake took her silence to be a sign of her involvement, but it was not evidence of it. Since he could get no more information about her past activities, he decided to work on her future plans.

"So I guess I'll just have to wait until the book comes out, won't I?"

"Yup."

"So why are you going to Thailand?" Blake asked, hoping to get some information that would help the Bureau to track down the Viper. "Are you working on another story, or is this still part of the first one?"

"You sure ask a lot of questions. You sound like an FBI agent, or someone from Interpol."

Jim Blake laughed, taken aback.

"Everyone says I ask too many questions. My dad used to say that nobody learns anything by talking. I've always proceeded with that in mind. So why are you going to Bangkok?"

Margo liked Blake better this time. At least he wasn't talking about his stupid restaurants. His perseverance was challenging her ability to lie, and that was a lot less boring than their earlier conversation.

"I'm working on an article about expatriates in Thailand, if you must know."

"What is your point of view about them?"

"I don't know that I have a point of view, at least not yet. I'll have to see what they tell me."

"Well, do you know any expatriates who live there?"

"I know one who will introduce me to others."

"Well, I hope they'll meet you at the airport. Bangkok is a rabbit warren of a city, and the taxi drivers are crooked as can be. By the time they get you to your hotel they can build up a pretty large bill if you don't know the city. What hotel are you staying at?"

"Luckily I won't have to worry about that. I have a friend who's meeting me and I'll be staying with her."

"Two women alone in sin city! I wish I could join you, but unfortunately I have work to do in India."

Blake thought that if he made it clear that he wouldn't be going on to Bangkok it might encourage Margo to be open about her plans, knowing she wouldn't be seeing him again. He had intentionally tried to annoy her all along, hoping she would say something that would trip her up and lead him to his primary quarry. She had been cagy, but he felt his approach was working to some extent. Unless she had been lying about everything, he had already found out quite a few things that could aid the Bureau in arresting the Viper.

"Are you familiar with Bangkok?" Margo said, hoping to change the subject.

"Not really. I was there once. In a decade or so Thailand may be a market for my company, but at present the standard of living and the volume of tourists are too low to be of any interest to me. It's a good place for certain types of expats, though."

"Oh? What types?" Margo asked, shifting the burden of the conversation into his court.

"Since I'm not in the policing business I'm only going on hearsay, but I've been told that criminals on the run, like pederasts, or deviates, or brothel lovers for example, favor Bangkok as a place to live. The fabulous Buddhist temples are interesting to the handful of tourists who are interested in Eastern religions and architecture and such, but there aren't too many of these. Most tourists are looking for forbidden fruit."

"Sounds like just the place to supply me with interesting material for my article, don't you think? Sex and danger are the subjects that sell stories and books these days."

"You're probably right, but in a place where corruption thrives and money can buy anything, you should be very careful. You should watch your step, know what I mean?"

"Thank you for your concern, but I think I'll be okay."

"You probably thought you'd be safe in Costa Rica too."

The words had slipped out of his mouth. He knew he had made a big mistake the instant he mentioned Costa Rica.

Margo knew immediately that she hadn't mentioned that Costa Rica was the place where she had been taken hostage. How could he have known that if she hadn't told him? From that moment on the atmosphere between them changed, and though they each continued as though nothing had happened, no further interchange of information was made. They said goodbye on the plane before exiting in Delhi, and Margo never saw Jim Blake, if that was his real name, again.

She took a seat near the gate for the flight to Bangkok. While she waited she inspected every other passenger, trying to discern if any of them were watching her. She couldn't detect anything fishy. She had no way to contact Rafael to tell him about her experience on the plane. She was certain now that Blake, in spite of his protestations, was a cop of some sort. Whether he was after Rafael, or her, or both was inconsequential. She just couldn't shake the feeling that she should disentangle herself from the Viper's coils before it was too late. She thought for a minute about canceling her trip to Bangkok, but her luggage had been checked through. If she failed to board the flight with her suitcase, it would touch off an international terrorist incident.

She pondered her options. Her self-examination revealed some things about herself that she didn't wish to face, and wouldn't have, either, under less stressful conditions. She concluded that she was some sort of adventuress. Like most thrill seekers she had an area of specialty, and hers was involvement with big-time power brokers. Her good looks were her admission card to the playgrounds inhabited by the rich and famous. Her brain was not bad, but it was her body that always opened doors for her. Margo knew, however, that her female charms would last only so long, as age eroded even the most beautiful of women. So she must use whatever advantages she had been given before they paled and faded along with her opportunities.

Forced to look at herself honestly, Margo sat by the departure gate, charting her future course.

CHAPTER FIFTEEN

Ivan Welland, now in possession of Jim Blake's report, was organizing the details of the Viper's capture. It was obvious to him now that Rafael Alvarez was holed up in Thailand. He was out there slithering around in an effort to recapture his lost prey. Margo Watson, who was once infected by his poison, had evidently decided she was immune to his lethal bite. Ivan was surprised that an intelligent girl like this could be seduced into committing a crime such as aiding a fugitive whom she knew to be guilty of murder in the first degree.

As astonished as he was by Margo's actions, he knew from his extensive reading of literature that the heart of a woman struck by Cupid's arrow can excuse almost any failing in a lover, except for infidelity. He also knew that certain men possess Svengali-like abilities to hold their women in thrall. Such men invented social customs as their tool for controlling women, while at the same time allowing male lust to thrive and be sanctioned.

No matter how much he understood and no matter how he sympathized with Margo, the fact remained that she was in the process of reuniting herself with a murderer. It was up to the law to judge his guilt or innocence – it wasn't up to Margo Watson to forgive Alvarez his crimes and grant him absolution.

Sometimes in life a pawn must be sacrificed to achieve a higher goal. The young woman knew the hiding place of a fugitive murderer, yet she was keeping it secret. Welland was determined that the murderer she was protecting should be brought to justice. If that meant that Margo Watson, naïve as she might be, had to be arrested, then so be it. It was her choice to get involved with the Viper, not Ivan's.

The question of which government agency had the authority to conduct the operation arose inevitably during the discussion of the upcoming arrest of the Viper. The Director of the FBI was adamant that his Bureau, in conjunction with the Thai Police Department, was the appropriate agency. The Director of the FBI, the Chief of the Secret Service, and Secretary of Defense Ivan Welland were all present at the meeting that took place that day.

"We've been tracking this cold-blooded killer across several state jurisdictions," said the Director of the FBI. "And we've been tracking him internationally as well, in cooperation with several foreign police agencies. It was thanks to the work of our agents conducting the surveillance of his girlfriend, and our man Blake on the plane, that led us to Bangkok. I see no reason why at the last minute the credit for the arrest should be taken away from us."

"Our Secret Service personnel have jurisdiction in this case too," the Chief chimed in. "We were the first to get involved. This man Alvarez is wanted for an attack on a member of the President's elite staff, and the protection of these people is our responsibility. We also want him for his involvement in the killing of a Saudi citizen with diplomatic immunity in New York. Clearly we shouldn't be shut out of the opportunity to capture this suspect."

"Gentlemen, gentlemen," Ivan Welland cut in. "Even though the Defense Department has military intelligence officers and my personal investigatory team working on this case, I'm perfectly willing to cede the arresting authority to your two agencies providing you cooperate in successfully bringing this fugitive to justice. Once we have him in custody the Attorney General will have to decide how to try Alvarez. It's up to them to lay charges. They'll decide what crimes he's committed, and in what order he committed them. The important thing is for us to actually arrest him, and not waste our time bickering about who gets the credit.

It's a big case, I recognize that, and I know we'd all like to get some good PR. But I'm willing to forego the Defense Department's portion of the credit if you two will put aside your long-standing rivalries. The intention of setting up the Homeland Security Department was to avoid just such jurisdictional disputes as this, and to encourage complete inter-agency cooperation. Obviously the good of the nation has to be put before the interests of our departments, so what do you say if I call my colleague, the Secretary of Homeland Security, and tell him that you two are working in concert to arrest the Viper?"

As the highest ranking man at the meeting, Welland's sensible offer was gratefully accepted. The men moved into a more cooperative mode as they planned the dénouement of the drama involving the Viper.

Rafael Alvarez was preparing to meet Margo Watson at the airport in Bangkok, but before going there he had to ponder several matters that were based on trust. It would be nice to meet her in person so he could note her reaction to seeing him again. But if she was in the hands of the police and was being forced to lead them to him, he would be vulnerable, and vulnerability was anathema to the Viper.

He finally decided to hire a local English-speaking Thai contact to meet Margo's plane. He had spoken to several tour guides and convinced one of them to hold up a sign with Margo's name on it. The guide was to drive her to a safe spot of Rafael's choosing and wait for him to come to collect the woman, for which he was to receive a cash compensation of $100 U.S. Meanwhile he'd watch her from the foreign arrivals observation deck to see if she was being followed as she picked up her luggage from the carousel. If she wasn't being watched at the terminal, he'd follow the tour guide's car to an appointed place nearby to see if Margo was under surveillance. If she was not being used as a sacrificial lamb, he'd appear and all would be well. But otherwise he'd simply disappear, never to be heard from again.

Trusting women was not in Rafael's playbook. Even though he was quite sure that Margo was under his influence, since she'd accepted his plane ticket and flown all the way to Bangkok, he nevertheless would take no chances with her loyalty. Allowing her to live after she'd witnessed him kill Thomaston could have been the biggest mistake of his life. Margo was extraordinarily attractive to him, but he could easily find adequate substitutes if she proved traitorous.

On that particular morning, Alvarez was sitting on a terrace overlooking the harbor at his hotel, drinking a frosty beer and watching the boats plying their trade below him.

"Would you like some company?" said a voice from directly behind him.

Rafael turned and saw a beautiful, elegantly-dressed Eurasian woman.

"Why not?" he replied, after looking her up and down.

People, both women and men, were always trying to pick him up. It had happened innumerable times since his arrival in Thailand. He had always refused the offers. But on this occasion, perhaps in deference to her beauty and the fact that she was operating in the most expensive hotel in Bangkok, he decided to make an exception.

"Please, have a seat," he said, indicating the chair next to his. He looked at her expectantly, curious to see if her pitch would be in keeping with the upper crust surroundings.

She slid sensuously onto the plush chair across the table from Rafael.

"I'll have a champagne cocktail," she said to a solicitous waiter who was hovering nearby. Then she turned to him and looked him directly in the eye. "Why is a handsome man like you alone in a city full of available women?"

"How do you know I'm alone? Isn't it possible that my wife has just left the table for a minute to go to the loo?"

"It's possible, but I've watched you long enough now to know that there is no wife."

"I guess I'm caught, then."

"Yes, you are certainly caught."

Rafael didn't like the sound of that, and immediately suspected that the woman was a police officer from the vice department. Thailand's reputation as a haven for deviants was currently being challenged by the local constabulary. They were putting on a big push to round up foreigners who came to Bangkok looking for Thai women and children.

"How can I be caught? I've done nothing wrong."

"The Bible tells us that if you do it in your mind then it's the same as doing it with your body. From the way you are looking at me I think you are guilty by that standard. So what would you like to do?"

"I was sitting here peacefully when *you* approached *me*, so what would *you* like to do?"

Rafael was not about to answer her question for fear of being involved in some sting that the police had dreamed up, using prostitutes as bait.

"I'm open. What is your pleasure?"

"I'm not in the market for sex."

"I didn't say anything about sex. Do you think I'm here to offer you sex?"

"It had occurred to me," Rafael said.

"I should be insulted, but somehow I'm not. You find me attractive then? Would you like to invite me up to your room?"

"You're very attractive, but I'm not going to invite you anywhere."

"Why have you come to Bangkok, then, if not for sex?"

Rafael was becoming more and more suspicious of his new companion.

"I've come for the fishing," he said. "You must find it good here since you're obviously on a fishing trip yourself."

"What do you mean?"

"You're trying to entrap me, so you must be a cop."

Suddenly his beautiful new companion's voice slipped a register lower.

"I'm taking you in for questioning. Please do not make a fuss. Leave the money for the bill on the table, and proceed directly to the exit. I'll be right behind you, and there are others here, too."

"You can't arrest me. I haven't done anything except buy you a drink."

"I can still take you in for questioning. I'm not arresting you. I find it peculiar that you are so apprehensive. It leads me to think you've been questioned before, or possibly have a record of performing illegal sex acts. We're trying to control prostitution and child abuse and we're grilling all suspicious foreign men who have no legitimate reason to be in our country. So do as I said."

Rafael was traveling with a stolen U.S. passport, yet he had no reason to believe he would be held for any length of time. He still expected to go to the airport to meet Margo that evening. He walked without protest to a waiting police van that already had several other non-Asian men in it. As he left in the paddy wagon he looked up and noticed his beautiful companion on the hotel verandah. She had taken off her wig and was chatting with some policemen. She was, in fact, a small-boned man in drag.

After a short drive the van arrived at police headquarters and discharged its passengers into a holding room containing about fifty men, mostly Caucasians. He had no doubt that he would be released, but when he saw the number of prisoners awaiting questioning he realized that he might not be let go in time to meet Margo's plane, and indeed he was right. His plans for their first night together would sadly not come up to his expectations, but he believed that Margo would simply register at one of the better hotels, and he would be able to track her down through the tour guide later.

Margo Watson had considered all her options. She had decided that she couldn't precipitously change her flight plans without arousing the suspicions of Blake's superiors, whoever they were. She had packed an emergency overnight carry-on bag with a change of underwear, her toothbrush, and some personal items in case her luggage was lost, which had happened on more than one occasion. She decided to leave her suitcase at the terminal in the hope that she could retrieve it later. If she was being followed there was nothing illegal about leaving her suitcase for later pick-up, nor was there anything illegal about the rest of her plan. She would continue on to Bangkok as planned.

She took a business card out of her wallet and dialed the 24-hour number on it. She waited for several rings for someone to answer, and while waiting she remembered the tall man she had spoken to in the Pentagon. She guessed correctly that all his incoming calls were screened to identify the callers, and that caused the delay she was experiencing in being connected to the Secretary of Defense. At last she heard his familiar deep voice.

"Welland here, how may I help you?"

"It's Margo Watson. Do you remember me?"

"Of course I do. How are you?"

Ivan knew exactly how she was, but he kept his tone light and friendly.

"Dr. Welland, I'd like to discuss something with you."

"Very well, I'll put my assistant on the line and you can make an appointment."

"No. I mean now, over the phone."

"All right. Tell me what's on your mind."

"It's about our previous discussion. I wasn't completely forthright with you. I led you to believe I'd never hear from Rafael again, when in fact he did tell me that he'd stay in contact with me. I didn't think it was too important because at the time we spoke he hadn't been in touch with me, and I had no way of knowing if he ever would contact me again."

Ivan was happy that Margo was unburdening herself to him. Any information that she could give him that would help with the Viper's capture was welcome. In addition he wanted to encourage her to cooperate with him in exposing the various malpractices of the media, but that would have to wait until the business with the Viper was concluded. If he could persuade Margo to tell him everything and help him to catch the wanted man, he could drop the charges that she abetted the Viper in his flight from prosecution. He would like to see Margo exonerated. In his opinion she had been merely a foil in the activities of some powerful men with whom fate had put her in contact. He wanted to see if she had come to some sort of self-realization that would serve to mature her judgment. This would have been easier to do in person, but he would do his best on the telephone.

"Did you encourage Rafael to get back in touch when things cooled down?"

"Yes. I guess you could say I used my feminine wiles."

"I see. You were falling for him, weren't you?"

"I suppose I was, though it's embarrassing to have to admit that."

Ivan was glad that Margo was coming around to an understanding of her motives, as it was a necessary step to making valid behavioral changes. He wanted to help her to clarify her thought processes.

"Did you know that those emotions are fairly common threads among kidnapped and sexually assaulted women?"

"No, I didn't."

"Well it's called the Stockholm syndrome. It's well enough understood to have its own name. It's not surprising that over a period of time victims with an unknown future and no intimate human contact, will fall for the keeper on whom they depend for food, news, and every good thing. After a time a certain dependency develops that in some cases results in loyalty and affection for the kidnapper. The relationship has certain comfortable aspects, and the victim clings to these. Later, if she's offered a choice of leaving or staying with her captor, she often chooses to stay, preferring to have someone to having no one. I believe you've suffered some version of this phenomenon, which accounts for your having had nothing bad to say to me about a very bad man."

"I must say it makes me feel pretty stupid to have had a dependent relationship like this. One that is so stereotypical that it has its own name. Gee, where was my head?"

"We all must live and learn, Miss Watson. You didn't call me just to make a small confession, did you? Do you have anything else you'd like to tell me?"

Ivan was giving her an opportunity to tell him what he already knew, that she was on her way to meet the Viper.

"No, I have greater sins yet to confess."

"Go on, then."

"I think I'm on my way to meet him now."

"You *think* you're on your way to meet him?"

"I got an anonymous one-way plane ticket to Bangkok in the mail with no explanation attached. It must have come from Rafael. I foolishly decided to use the ticket because I wanted to stop off in London anyway to see Lord Pressman about buying my articles or giving me a job as a writer for one of his publications. That situation is pending for the time being, so I flew on. I'm in New Delhi now, and I'm about to board the last leg of my flight to Thailand. But I'm getting cold feet and I think someone is following me. I don't want to be Rafael's accomplice, but I don't want him to know I was responsible for his capture, either. If he finds out I turned him in, he might kill me. Can you help me?"

"I can try, but you'll have to be completely honest with me. As far as I can tell, you haven't done anything illegal yet. You're the only one who has seen the Viper, so you'll have to identify him and be a witness against him. If we can apprehend him and take him into custody he won't be able to hurt you. If he's convicted, he'll get life in prison. I can tell you that this individual, besides the killing in Costa Rica, is wanted for two murders in New York, one in Chicago, and also in connection with an assassination attempt on yours truly. All this is in addition to what he did to you, and the international drug smuggling and weapon smuggling charges that he faces. If you help us catch him, your country and several other countries will be grateful, and you'll be free of him. It would make a great scoop for a journalist."

"That's reassuring. Can you guarantee that I'll have immunity from prosecution?"

"If you help us, I can."

"Very well then, what should I do?"

"You must go to Bangkok so you can identify Rafael as the Viper. How have you arranged to meet?"

"That's the strange thing about it. I don't really know anything except that the ticket *must* have come from him. I'm guessing he'll be watching for me at the airport."

"It sounds as if he doesn't trust you and wants to make sure you're alone. He's very clever and wants to be able to walk away if he suspects you've informed on him. We'll pack the terminal with undercover people. You just act surprised when we descend on you wherever he meets you."

"My plane is boarding. Is there anything else?"

"No. I wish you luck. I'll be in touch as soon as I can. In the meantime I have a lot to do to be ready for your arrival in Bangkok."

Actually Ivan Welland had nothing to do. Everything had already been done. The only change was that Margo Watson had cleared her name and was now on the side of the good guys.

Excitement was building in the board rooms of the companies involved in merging Thomaston's interests with their own. Fleets of lawyers had been working for weeks to iron out the details whereby Robert's media empire would be divided. It was all finally coming together. Lord Pressman and Baron Fritz couldn't help being puffed up about it. They were about to pull off the largest merger in media business history. The English and the German media corporations were finally going to break into the American market on a massive scale. The information age belonged to them, and they were positioning themselves to exploit the advantage.

The plans they had made on the Baron's yacht with Robert Thomaston were coming to fruition, and even better, without the missing third partner, there would be more for the two who remained. The stock markets on both sides of the ocean were burbling with rumor and expectations that had driven the stock holdings in the two European media corporations to fantastic new highs, in anticipation of the big payoff. Wall Street underwriters were licking their chops, thinking of the huge fees they were expecting to receive from organizing the details of the financial merger.

Baron von Aragon's interest in taking over Robert's company was mainly on the print media side. The German businessman had a near monopoly on the newspapers and magazines of Germany, Austria, Belgium, Switzerland, and the Netherlands. He now wanted to extend his hegemony over print journalism to the United States. Lord Pressman's interests were centered on Thomaston's broadcasting and film divisions.

Stereotypes have to have a modicum of truth about them in order to last and proliferate. So it was that the German tendency to be ponderous, analytical, and intellectual in their thinking was best suited to the written media. The British flair for theatre and film production led naturally to TV broadcast journalism. The division of the Thomaston media empire between Pressman and von Aragon was like Jack Sprat and his wife, licking the platter clean.

Ivan Welland's team, which had been investigating the media operations of the Thomaston companies, and for some time had also been analyzing the merger, were now in full court press mode. From Ivan's point of view the death of Thomaston was no great loss to American journalism, but at least he was an American. His company was headquartered in the U.S. and subject to American law. The acquisition of his companies by German and British interests meant that the giant share of the ownership of the U.S. news production would pass into foreign hands. If the proposed merger went through, Americans would be receiving their information through the filtering prism of European media moguls.

In some ways the American media had been constantly working to dumb down the average guy's view of the world in order to sell advertising space and time, which is always based on subscription statistics and viewer numbers. In their efforts to include everyone and raise readership and viewer ratings, they played to the lowest common denominator lest any customers be missed. But no matter how silly or stupid their journalistic efforts became, they were American, so certain minimum standards of loyalty and nationalism could be counted upon. The new international media organizations that were to be formed by dividing and devouring the largest American media corporation would have no such fealty.

Ivan was not so much concerned by the nationalities of the new owners or their politics, so much as he was worried about seeing to it that the truth got published. If the quality of the news presentations were to be elevated by the merger, then well enough, but if the information to be disseminated was merely preplanned falsehoods, then they had to be stopped. A free press was a high ideal among the founding fathers from the inception of the American Republic. It was a principle incorporated in the Bill of Rights. American democracy had withstood the competition of many rival political systems, and Ivan had no doubt it would hold its own in the future if the truth were told.

Welland called together his team of elite investigators, and asked each one of them to summarize his findings. The work had reached fever pitch due to recent developments concerning the proposed consolidation of the American media giant with the two European companies.

"I'm trying to decide whether to halt this merger or not," Ivan began. "Have you any information that bears on this issue?"

Damian Rutledge led off the discussion.

"I think there are plenty of legal grounds for disallowing the deconstruction of Thomaston's organization, as well as preventing its ownership from moving overseas."

"Let's hear some then," said David Feingold.

"Well to begin with," Damian said, "this merger is contrary to monopoly regulations. If it goes ahead, it would reduce the competition to an unthinkable extent. No federal court would allow it. That's my opinion, anyway."

"We've been investigating the pants off Thomaston's group for a while now," Brooklyn put in. "And now, just before we're ready to release our findings, this merger thing pops up. The timing stinks. Was this deal in the works before Thomaston died? If the deal goes through, will all our work have been useless?"

"We can't indict Thomaston," David said. "He's dead. I don't think it's a healthy environment to work in. Maybe we can get the EPA to close it down," he added, with a wink.

"My efforts in investigating the Arab TV networks lead me to believe that Ivan's fears have become a reality," Abdul said. "Others are following the path charted by Thomaston. Media producers in the Middle East, Europe, and the Far East are now busy fabricating news films to suit themselves. When I analyzed the footage of an unsuccessful bombing attack on a Pakistani political leader, I found it to be an exact copy of a previous attack that happened three years before. There's no question about it – the film was reused. I have no idea whether the last incident was a real attack or not. It could easily have been created to build public support for the leader by showing how evil the opposition is. I believe this kind of thing is happening all over the world."

David agreed.

"The enormous film library and classification system that Thomaston's organization controls in Hollywood," he said, "has film clips of nearly any movie scene ever filmed. The latest computer technology and its editing features lets you classify, manipulate, and format film any way you like. You can slip things in between scenes, too, and it's so seamless nobody can tell the difference. You can practically remake history. If a filmmaker wanted to make it appear that the Confederates won the Civil War, it could be done in a very short time and the results would seem real to everyone."

"We can expect major opposition if we try to interfere with the film business," Damian warned the others. "They have a tremendous influence on the public, and they have plenty of money and power. Any governmental interference will be seen as censorship and defended by the ACLU, using First Amendment rights to argue the case. Before we get into it we need to have the most solid case in the history of constitutional law."

The discussion continued for some time until Ivan finally brought it to a close.

"Okay," he said, "I think we all see the basic difficulties involved, and the importance of bringing the media under some sort of control. We need an insider to testify that they have been intentionally misusing the First Amendment rights for their own purposes. We need a good constitutional lawyer, too, to make our case stick. I'll be seeing POTUS tomorrow, and I'll report back as soon as I can. Meanwhile, keep up the good work, and we'll meet again soon."

CHAPTER SIXTEEN

The overcrowded holding tank in Bangkok's police headquarters was not a place where anyone would choose to spend his time. Rafael felt he was rubbing shoulders with the scum of the earth. He hated deviants, but he had to put up with them while he waited for the police to interrogate him.

He looked at the people around him. Most were scared little men who were just as much prisoners of their sexual addictions as they were inmates of the jail. He believed that his record as a rapist of women was an entirely different matter because his victims had asked for it in one way or another. He honestly believed that women needed to be raped occasionally, and they expected it. The Viper had no sympathy or patience for his victims, or for his jailhouse companions. If he were in charge he would free the rapists and execute the homosexuals, the pederasts, the child pornographers, and the rest of the sickos. The Thai Police had evidently given the local criminals the day off, as the number of prisoners in the pen overwhelmingly favored Caucasians.

In Rafael's estimation the police would interview him, realize he wasn't a pervert like the others, and release him. The problem was that the sheer volume of suspects in their net would take so much time to process that he would not be able to meet Margo's plane. He cursed inwardly as he pondered what to do about Margo. It occurred to him that he should just forget her. He hadn't even spoken to her since he had bought her the ticket. For all he knew she might not even be coming. Perhaps being picked up for being a single male foreigner was a warning to him that he was being a fool. She might be intending to turn him in, but it would be nice to know the truth.

The Viper, however, seemed unable to walk away from his prey. Margo would surely check into one of the hotels and he could find her later. He decided there were only three possibilities – she never used the ticket and she was through with him, or she flew under the protection of the many law enforcement agencies that might need her to identify him, or lastly, she was content to return to him as his love slave. He preferred the latter option, but only if it came without risk to his freedom. He had prepared more carefully for his retirement than most top executives, and he was unwilling to compromise his future for any woman.

The Viper knew he was not like the men around him. Most of them wanted to be caught, he thought. They were weaklings, risking everything to achieve a pitiful, childish moment of obsession. Rafael told himself that he wasn't a neurotic psycho with a weakness. His fantasies came from strength, not weakness. He dominated in every situation. He was *the man*. He seemed not to have considered that mastery itself could be a weakness, and that aberrations of supremacy weren't gender specific.

Margo Watson eagerly searched the crowds in the terminal. She recognized no one. She followed the baggage icon signs towards the rumbling carousels. Just beyond the customs station in the area of the exit stood a dark little man bearing a cardboard sign with her name on it. She decided to wait for her bags to appear. She surreptitiously looked for Rafael, who she thought might be spying on her from a hiding place nearby.

Finally her suitcase wobbled down the chute, fell over on the turntable and proceeded on its course towards the spot where she was waiting. She grabbed the bag and hauled it off the carousel. She stood it on end and pulled up the towing handle, placing her carry-on bag on top of the larger suitcase, and hauled them off to the customs station. A dour agent in short brown pants took her customs statement and passed her through to the mass of people waiting to greet the new arrivals. She located the man with her name on his sign.

"I'm Miss Watson," she said to him.

"Come with me, please." He spoke in an officious, curt manner. "Your man sent me to get you."

"Where is my man? I don't see him."

"You don't have to worry. I take you in the car."

The little man almost forcibly removed Margo's hand from the suitcase handle and towed the luggage off in the direction of the street. She hoped that Dr. Welland would honor his promise to have his agents keep her in sight at all times, but when she saw the hordes of people outside the airport, she wondered how the agents could possibly follow her. Times Square seemed a placid, semi-deserted place by comparison. She felt vulnerable as she trotted along behind her guide. He led her to an old Mercedes which had managed to retain a certain dignity in spite of its having been painted yellow and having suffered many non-fatal wounds.

"My name is Manolo," the little man said, as he heaved the baggage into the cavernous trunk.

"How do you do?" Margo replied. She wondered how a Thai had acquired a Spanish name.

"Are you from Thailand?" she asked him.

"No. Just live here now."

The old Mercedes lurched forward and forced its way into the stream of traffic. Margo wanted to reassure herself that everything was normal, so she kept talking.

"Where are we going?"

"We go far from city where Mister say."

"He's going to meet us, then?"

"Mister say he be there."

Since there was nothing else to do, Margo sat back in the seat and tried to enjoy the scenery while at the same time she made an effort to memorize various signs and road markers. Without being obvious, she tried to see if anyone was indeed following the Mercedes. She couldn't see any cars behind them. She supposed that in modern times surveillances were more electronic than physical, but it would have been nice to know that some support was nearby.

The surrounding landscape impressed itself upon her. She caught occasional glimpses of the Chao Phraya River, whose numerous tributaries provide an outlet into the Gulf of Thailand for the melted snows of the Himalayas. Manolo was heading north. Bangkok's central district was not unlike that of most other cities, with skyscrapers and concentrated commercial developments. But once they left the city, the contiguous villages took over. There were dense populations on the higher elevations where the residents could avoid the annual flooding caused by monsoons. Margo wondered if the people were happy with their lives. She realized that she was a poor working girl as far as Thomaston and Pressman were concerned, but compared to these villagers she was a veritable princess.

Her decision to betray Rafael was reinforced by the sight of the poverty and crowding that gripped her heart as much as the hot humid air and stench assaulted her body. She felt a strong desire to help these people, and didn't share Rafael's ambition to live off them. They certainly didn't need another form of criminal colonialist to suck them dry. She could think of no logical arguments in favor of joining her fate with his. Dr. Welland had made it clear to her that the Viper was on the run. He would be forever hunted for the crimes he had committed, and now that she knew how serious they were and how unrepentant Rafael was, she could no longer make excuses for him. Her sexual attraction for the powerful outlaw was simply insufficient to overcome the reality of a future living on the run with such a violent, untrustworthy companion.

After Manolo had been driving for about an hour, the car left the main road and followed a dusty, semi-deserted track into a patch of mixed bamboo, rattan, ferns, and shrubs. In a few minutes they came to an open rice field that had been carved out of the forest and into the alluvial soil of the basin. Manolo pulled the car over to the side of the road, turned off the engine and waited.

"Is this where we're supposed to meet him?" Margo asked.

"Yes."

"Well, where is he?"

"Not here. We wait."

Margo didn't want to get out of the car, as she had read in the tourist literature about the dangerous wildlife to be found in rural Thailand. Even though the books mentioned that many of the larger wild animals such as elephants, rhinoceros, and big cats had been hunted nearly to extinction, the survivors of man's depredations still included crocodiles, malarial mosquitoes, and many species of venomous snakes, including vipers.

She wished now that she had obeyed the admonishment to avoid the last species on the list. The absence of the human clamor of civilization had given way to the subtler susurrations of unseen creatures slithering in the grass. They loomed larger and more numerous in Margo's mind than they did in reality. The fields, having been deserted by their human cultivators, reminded her of how quickly civilization could be overpowered by the wild nature that surrounded it.

Time passed. Margo thought of the plethora of temples they had passed on their drive to nowhere. The population of Thailand, consisting primarily of peaceful Buddhists, had suffered its share of historical human strife since at least the 8th century. This pattern was characteristic of Southeast Asia, where shifting political boundaries have done little to impede the centuries-long migrations of people from one area to another.

Just the few minutes that Margo had spent in the airport revealed the diversity of the people of Thailand. She could see clearly that the principal sources of the ethnic peoples were Indian and Chinese. The speakers of the Thai language were the main linguistic group. Chinese was the second major language, with English as the runner-up. Massive birthrates had put pressure on the economy, and those who were intent on exploiting the people through corruption or criminality were rife. Rafael had chosen well when he picked Thailand to be his new land of opportunity.

Margo kept her eyes peeled, but could see no sign of human life in the surrounding countryside. Ivan Welland had promised to have his officers available to protect her, but they were nowhere to be seen. The man she had traveled halfway around the world to be with was also conspicuously absent. She felt confused and nervous. What was she supposed to do? They had been parked for over an hour, and she could see that the driver was also becoming restless. He was probably wondering if he was ever going to get his money. She was afraid to doze off, but the jet lag and the humid heat were beginning to wear her down.

Suddenly she heard a car approaching. She looked in the side mirror and saw that it was a jeep farm vehicle. Her heart started to beat faster. Would it be Welland's men, or would it be the Viper? But the jeep never even slowed down. As it passed by, she saw a Thai couple sitting inside. The driver glanced at her briefly, but he didn't smile or wave. Soon the jeep was lost in a trail of dust.

Manolo left the car to relieve himself behind the bushes, which was something Margo would also have appreciated doing had it not been for her vision of the creatures, both human and reptilian, that could be hiding in the lush green surroundings.

Evidently Rafael was not coming for her. Perhaps he had seen the ambush that had been arranged for him. Maybe she was totally wrong and he hadn't been the one who had sent her the ticket to Bangkok.

It never crossed her mind that he couldn't come because the police were holding him for suspicion of immoral sexual behavior with underage children. Rafael himself couldn't ignore the irony of his having to keep a sensual, mature woman waiting while he explained to the cops that he was not a pedophile.

Margo spoke to Manolo when he returned to the car.

"Do you know a hotel where I could stay? Evidently my friend has been held up and isn't coming."

"What about my money?"

"How much did he promise you?"

"Two hundred dollars. *American* dollars," he replied.

Since this stupid American woman had to ask him how much her friend had agreed to pay him, Manolo figured he might as well see if he could get her to double his payment.

"I'm sorry, I can only pay you a hundred baht," Margo said. "I changed my money into baht at the airport."

Manolo pretended to be hugely disappointed, and indeed he probably was. But he knew that if he made too much of a fuss he might end up with nothing at all for his trouble, so he angrily agreed to the amount she offered.

An hour or so later the old Mercedes pulled up in front of the thirty-nine story Peninsula Hotel, which was located on the Thon Buri side of the Chao Phraya River. A bellhop looked after Margo's luggage while she paid Manolo. The pint-sized driver drove off in a pretend snit, as though he had been cheated by his passenger.

Margo followed her luggage into the cavernous lobby and walked over to the reception desk. She was relieved that they assigned her to a room even though she had not made a reservation. During the registration process she was asked to surrender her passport. Evidently the police had set up a passport checking routine for all foreign guests at the hotels. The desk clerk assured her it would be returned to her later, but she still felt uncomfortable about being stripped of her personal documents.

Upstairs in her room Margo noticed that the entirely American décor left no doubt that the hotel was part of a worldwide hotel chain. She might just as well have been in any American city as far as the layout and furnishings were concerned. Her view from the sealed windows, however, was a reality check. The white buildings were architectural clones of the structures that have proliferated throughout the world. Margo wasn't surprised, as the larger new hotels were all part of international franchise schemes whereby newly-earned Chinese, Japanese, and Arab dollars were routinely invested in real properties.

It was all part of the irony of human existence, Margo mused, that tourists traveling the world to visit ancient and diverse cultures, end up in foreign accommodations that are increasingly similar to those they left behind at home.

But at that moment Margo didn't care. She appreciated her king-size American bed, as she was weary from traveling and confused by the thirteen-hour change of time zones that had turned night into day. Her feeling of disorientation was complicated by the lack of any sort of contact by either the police or Rafael.

She threw herself down on the bed and slept fitfully in anticipation of the unknown events of the days to come.

CHAPTER SEVENTEEN

The report that Ivan Welland received from the FBI was not reassuring. The Viper had evidently smelled a rat, and unlike his serpentine namesake, had decided to flee instead of taking the bait. Combined with the known facts, Welland's instincts had fairly shouted that the fugitive was in Bangkok. He blamed himself for not having gone there and supervised the arrest. He would have done that in the old days, but now his position as Secretary of Defense prohibited it.

Whenever things didn't go as planned, Ivan always took the responsibility upon his own shoulders. Something was fishy, but what? He hated having to allow others to handle the delicate business of smoking the Viper out of his lair. But he had also wanted to test Margo's self-confessed change of heart by allowing her to prove her loyalty. He was very tempted to go immediately to Bangkok to see what had gone wrong, but he had other duties besides the capture of just one man.

His team had advised him that the European acquisition of Thomaston's media empire was primed to go ahead at any time. Ivan wasn't ready for that. He hadn't yet gathered the irrefutable proof he needed to stop the deal from proceeding. A deal of this size and importance needed to be approved by federal authorities, whose job it was to ascertain that no part of it was in restraint of trade. Under the terms of the federal monopoly restrictions, no foreign company was allowed to take over a critical American industry without approval from the authorities. This particular deal would certainly place the majority control of the media in the hands of foreigners, and it would reduce the number of big players as well, so true competition was no longer possible in this case. Ivan would have to exert his influence as a Cabinet member and see if he could arrange to delay Pressman's and von Aragon's scheme to conquer the world of words and images until he could finish building his case against them.

Ivan and his group would need to have incontrovertible evidence that the big three had continually acted in concert to create news items portraying world conditions that were editorially desirable for their interests, without any regard for the truth. David Feingold had already begun to build a database of news stories that had been intentionally tampered with by the three news giants, dating back to several years before Thomaston's death.

It seemed likely, then, that at the meetings on board von Aragon's yacht a number of cooperative agreements had been made that contravened the free press conventions of their three countries. Ivan's team assumed that the strategies evolved were kept secret. But policies on common issues had to have been defined. The three men must have agreed upon some practical operational regulations as well as some rules of succession to use in the event that a member of the triumvirate died, as had now happened. Ivan felt sure that these signed agreements must exist, but where were they?

He remembered that Margo Watson had told him that she had been on board the yacht during at least one of the meetings. He made a mental note to question her closely about it as soon as possible. He had no doubt that she was not party to the agreements, nor could she know what had transpired, but she might be able to guess where the relevant documents were kept. She might be able to provide details that would be helpful if a search had to be made. If Margo demonstrated loyalty in the handling of the Viper's arrest, Ivan would feel more comfortable about involving her in building the case against the three media giants.

The fact that neither of the remaining partners was an American citizen was a complicating factor. Search warrants and subpoenas could not be issued if Pressman and von Aragon were not physically in the United States. Ivan could only hope that revelations in the United States would inspire the other countries involved to take action according to their laws. Presuming that there were some written agreements concerning the merger plans, they could be somewhere on board the *Sternlicht*. In this case, however, obtaining them would bring into play considerations of international marine law, making it even more complicated for the U.S. Attorney General to obtain the evidence.

If a signed partnership agreement were found and did become available, then the conspirators could be charged and brought to trial. The statistical data that David Feingold was collecting would then be additional circumstantial evidence. Ivan's team believed very strongly that men like Thomaston, Pressman and von Aragon would never partner up without a charter of some kind. Once the story was released, however, all the instances of fictitious news would shock the world into a new awareness that the news they believed to be true was usually fabricated to manipulate public opinion one way or the other. Ivan hoped the results of those revelations on the consumers of news would lead to the development of new U.S. and international regulations to guide the media and enforce its honesty. It was for this reason that Ivan ordered his investigative team to continue documenting all the past instances of the media's tampering with the truth.

Rafael Alvarez sat around in the crowded holding tank for over twenty-four hours. Finally he was called and taken to a dingy little room nearby that resembled a cell which was, in fact, a room that had been converted for use as a questioning chamber. He was told to take a seat on a wooden chair that stood next to an old desk covered with papers and ink stains.

Behind the desk sat a uniformed Thai police officer, tapping his fingers impatiently. The Viper was familiar with his type. He was a self-confident man, whose considerable girth had increased along with his cynicism. His suspicious nature and propensity to think the worst of people had worked in his favor in dealing with prisoners, so he had been promoted to the job of inquisitor of the perverts. The Viper knew instantly that anything he said to this man would not be believed.

During his time with the motley population being held in common containment, Alvarez had come to the conclusion that as a heterosexual rapist he was perhaps the most saintly of the lot. His relative normalcy made him stand out from the crowd, and standing out was the last thing the Viper wanted. His strategy in dealing with the police was always to be polite, to answer their questions briefly while sticking to the truth as much as possible, and to volunteer nothing.

This approach had always worked well for him, and he believed it would work this time too. It was comically ironic that he should be caught up in a generalized police effort to change the landscape of one of the most permissive sexual city environments in the world. No night had passed during his time in Thailand without his being propositioned by several ladies of the street. Other sexual offers in varying degrees of degeneracy had also been generously suggested.

Alvarez took his seat in front of his inquisitor, made eye contact, and waited for the officer to speak.

"I have your passport here in front of me. Your picture looks too much like you. Usually these photographs barely resemble the rightful owner of the passport."

Since that was a comment and not a question, Rafael remained silent.

"Have you nothing to say for yourself?" the officer said, leaning back in his chair.

"I was not the photographer. I'm glad you approve of the likeness, but I take no credit for it. Am I under arrest for having a good passport photo? If so, I'm innocent."

"You find it funny, do you? Well, my friend, it's not funny. It's not funny at all. My country is overrun with Caucasians, one more ugly than the next. My job is to clean up the mess. When I find an exception to any norm I pounce on it. Why are you in Thailand, Mr. Ricardo? Is this really your passport?"

"It is my passport, and I'm here because I like it here."

Rafael gave a confident answer, in spite of the fact that the passport was a fake. It was a good fake, though, and only a U.S. State Department expert would know that.

"What is it that you find so likeable about my country? Is it the little girls?"

"The little girls are nice as far as I know, but I'm not here because of them. I think you mistake me for something I'm not."

"I don't mistake you. I recognize you for what you are."

"May I ask why you have arrested me?"

"We haven't arrested you. We simply want to ask you a few questions in an effort to take back the moral standards of our city from the sick foreign devils that come here."

"That's an admirable objective, but it has nothing to do with me. I have a lady friend, and you're keeping me from her by asking me foolish questions."

"Where is this lady now?"

"Well, I was on my way to the airport to meet her when your officers arrested me. So right now I don't know where she is, to tell you the truth, but my guess is that she's angry that I'm not there with her."

"Yes, by all means tell me the truth, and only the truth. Your mysterious woman, what is her name? I will check to see if she exists."

"Her name is Margo Watson. She is American. She was supposed to arrive on Singapore Airlines ten hours ago."

"I'll check your story. You will remain with us until it's confirmed, this story of yours. Are you staying at the hotel where you were picked up? "

"Why can't I be released? You have my passport. I can't leave the country without it. Why must you hold me here?"

"That is my decision Mr. Ricardo, or whoever you are. I will ask the questions. You have only to answer them. What is your address in Bangkok?"

"I don't yet have an address in Bangkok. I was just deciding where to stay when your cross-dressing officer detained me in the River Café. I had narrowed my choice to either the Peninsula Hotel or the Lebua at State Tower."

"So you have no place to stay in Bangkok?"

"Not yet, but I certainly don't want to stay here."

"Are you indigent?"

"Certainly not."

"You must have a lot of money if you plan to stay in a five star hotel."

"I have enough to pay a hotel bill."

All this talk about money made him think that the cop was working his way toward a shakedown. Police payoffs were not unknown to him, as he had bought cops many times before. But it wouldn't be wise to mention a bribe at this point, for that would only convince the police officer of his guilt. Certainly he would not pay until after he was released.

"If your story checks out you can spend your money in Thailand. Otherwise you will have no need of any money at all."

The officer pushed a bell that was under the desk, and two uniformed policemen came into the room and escorted an exasperated Rafael Alvarez back to the holding cell. The interviewer, working on an intuition honed by his lengthy experience with the dregs of society, had decided that his prisoner's explanations were too perfect. His documents, his clothing, his story, and his sarcastic, superior attitude were all too pat. Besides, the man had not threatened to call the U.S. Embassy, as most American citizens in his position would have done. Having just examined a flood of pitiful perverts, the policeman found Rafael's presence among them to be anomalous, but he also knew that anything or anyone unusual was generally worth further investigation. He had more foreigners to question in order to finish his quota for the day, however, and since Mr. Ricardo wasn't going to cause any trouble while he was locked up, he could wait to check his story until after he finished questioning the others.

Margo awoke. It took her a few minutes to remember where she was. She had been too tired to undress the night before, so she had fallen asleep in her clothes. She decided to take a shower and then find something to eat. It was 2:00 AM local time when she got into the elevator and headed down to the lobby to find a restaurant. She wanted some breakfast, as it seemed to her internal clock to be the appropriate meal.

She found the lobby abuzz with people. Evidently there were other jet-lagged tourists unable to sleep, judging by the number of guests wandering around the lobby.

She found her way to the elegant River Café. It was on a terrace facing the Chao Phraya River, whose waters were shimmering from the reflection of the moon and the lights of the buildings that lined its banks. It was a romantic locale, but unfortunately she was alone.

She was seated by a delicate, slim hostess in a colorful sari. Margo felt like a truck horse in comparison to the fine-boned Thai attendant. Beautiful women who were alone seldom came into the café, and especially at that hour of the night. Fortunately for Margo she was obviously not Asian, for if she had been she might have been refused entry to the dining area. Cruising working girls were not welcome at the Peninsula Hotel. A well-dressed, sophisticated woman might make it to the bar the odd time, but never to the dining room.

Margo herself was not accustomed to being alone in a restaurant. She felt the eyes of the other guests appraising her – some with pity, others with suspicion, and many with gloating expressions that told her they took it for granted that she was unable to get a man. Her discomfort was interrupted by a waiter standing by her table, his pencil poised to take her order.

She asked for a mango juice, and then began to read the ornate dinner menu. As she sifted through the English descriptions of the Thai meals, she did not notice that an Asian woman at the bar was watching her attentively. When she had made her selections and set the menu aside, the svelte Asian woman picked up her purse and approached her table.

"Are you Miss Margo Watson?" she asked.

"Yes," Margo replied, looking puzzled.

"May I join you and explain how I know your name?"

"I guess so. Please sit down."

Just then the waiter came and Margo ordered Pad Thai. The man seemed to take no notice of Margo's companion, and didn't bother to ask her if she wanted to order anything. Before the waiter left, Margo asked the woman if she would like something to eat or drink, a question she felt the waiter should have asked himself, unless he already knew the answer. When her mysterious companion quickly declined the offer, Margo got the impression that these two had some sort of an understanding between them.

"Let me introduce myself," she said. "I'm Lieutenant Rama of the Bangkok Special Police Detachment. We work on security issues and matters of international importance."

The officer opened her purse just enough so that Margo could see an identification card with a picture of a young man on it and a shiny pistol nestled beside it.

"The American Secretary of Defense, Dr. Ivan Welland, said that you would feel more relaxed if I used his name."

"I'd feel more relaxed if the picture on your I.D. card had your photo on it."

"I will take that as a compliment."

"I didn't mean it as a compliment."

"Well then, I'll pass it along to my dressmaker and to the people who do my make-up."

"Your disguise is fabulous," Margo admitted. "You had me fooled. But I won't be going into the washroom with you present, if you don't mind."

"I don't think that will be a problem," the Lieutenant answered, with a good-natured grin. "Now, if the matter of my credentials is concluded to your satisfaction, perhaps we can pass on to more important things."

"Okay, so where were you guys when I was out in the rice paddy?"

"We were closer than you know," the Lieutenant said. "We're as good at concealment as we are at disguises."

"I've been under surveillance ever since I arrived?"

"Yes."

The waiter came with Margo's unusual breakfast order, and the two fell silent for a few moments.

"What should I do now?" Margo asked, after the waiter left. "It looks as though Rafael is better at knowing he's being followed than I am. I mean, since he didn't show up at the airport, he must have become suspicious."

"Your charms are hard to resist I'm sure, but there could be other reasons that explain why he failed to appear."

"What are we going to do now?" she asked, pretending not to notice his sarcasm.

"We're going to wait. Good police work is at least 50% waiting."

"That may be good for you, as I'm sure you get paid for waiting, but what about me?"

"You're in my beautiful country. Why not take a look around, like any other tourist? We'll come along with you wherever you go, and you'll never know we're there. Just go and see the concierge and arrange some tours. We'll prepay them and pay your hotel as well. It will be your government that pays, of course, but let's not split hairs."

"How do you know that the man you're looking for is going to turn up? And how will he know how to find me?"

"That shouldn't be hard for him. If he contacts Manolo, the driver, he'll find out you were taken to this hotel."

"So you're using me as bait. Is that all I'm good for?"

"Well, some very important people in your country think you are valuable, so you seem to be well regarded. If I were you, I would just relax and enjoy Bangkok, and have a nice dinner."

"Breakfast."

"What?"

"This is my breakfast."

"Call it whatever you like. I'll be watching you."

He made the sign the Rangers use to signal *watch out*, index finger and pinky pointing to his eyes. Then he walked away in his sling-back high heels, moving his hips just as any other woman might have done.

CHAPTER EIGHTEEN

After two days Ivan Welland had begun to question whether keeping Margo Watson in Bangkok was going to serve any purpose at all. According to his men on the scene, the Viper had made no effort to contact her. Welland sat down at his desk and leaned back to think. Brooklyn had seen her boss do this many times before, and she knew better than to disturb him.

The U.S. military was under Welland's control, and was fully absorbed with the task of implementing the President's program to eradicate explosives. The chiefs of staff of each of the services made progress reports to him every 48 hours, and he consolidated the material into a digested summary for the President. He had organized the tasks and designated the responsibilities with great skill, so the program was moving ahead as planned.

Running the huge military bureaucracy with its immense budget had been too much for many a Secretary of Defense, but Ivan had managed to cut to the chase. His handling of previous military operations in conjunction with the U.S. Navy Seals had earned him the respect of the military brass in spite of his being a civilian. He had no ties to anyone except the President, so he was able to direct the work of the military industrial complex with wisdom and fairness based on his honesty and intelligence. His efficiency in handling the basics of the program had made it possible for him to tackle other tasks as well.

Apprehending the Viper was a job that normally would not be in his jurisdiction, but the international complexities of the Viper's case were such that his Department of Defense had become politically involved. He spent a relatively small amount of time working on the case, however, as compared, for instance, with the time needed to prepare a full military budget for Congressional approval. Likewise, the question of media honesty didn't fall into his departmental oversight, but since his department was often expected to cope with the fallout caused by the lies and fabrications of the cynical, opportunistic media, Ivan felt thoroughly justified in taking action in this case as well.

As he mulled over his options, Ivan couldn't help seeing the catalytic role that Margo Watson was playing in both cases. His character didn't allow him to simply use people for his own purposes, but perhaps he could justify using Margo if she were to get an educational life experience out of the deal. He still believed that the Viper was in Bangkok, and though he was disappointed that he had failed to link up with Margo, he decided to wait a little longer.

He tried to put himself in the place of Rafael Alvarez. Why hadn't the Viper appeared on the scene? Why would he have brought Margo halfway around the world and then turned up missing, as it were? What if he had tried to meet her but something had prevented him from doing so? It was true he might have spotted the surveillance team and backed away, but Ivan was inclined to believe what his team had told him, that the Viper had simply failed to show up. One other possibility occurred to him. What if the Viper was involuntarily detained and couldn't keep his appointment with Margo? What kinds of things could have delayed or prevented this master criminal from collecting his prize?

Ivan reviewed all the possible reasons there could be for the Viper's failure to turn up. There were a number of other things that could have happened besides the ones that had been considered. There was the possibility that he was dead, or he could be injured and lying in a hospital bed, too weak to do anything. Or he could be in jail. He liked the irony of that scenario. While they went nuts trying to arrest the

Viper, he could very well be in jail already. He called out to Brooklyn.

"Contact the Bangkok Special Agent and ask him if they checked the hospitals and jails to see if anyone answering the Viper's description was there."

"Okay boss, I'm on it."

Margo Watson was back in her room. It was three-thirty in the morning and she couldn't sleep. She hooked up her laptop computer to the high-speed connection and checked her e-mail. She wanted to see if she had received any news from Rafael, and perhaps more importantly, from Geoffrey Lord Pressman.

There was no contact from Rafael, but she hadn't really expected any. He was too wily to risk exposure that way. She did, however, have a message from London.

"Margo," it read, "we will buy your story about poor Robert's last minutes. It is very well written. Thank you for submitting it to us. We'd like to discuss the terms of a purchase agreement, as well as terms of employment and other more personal matters. Please let me know when you plan to come to London. Geoffrey."

Margo noticed that he used the royal *we* as though he were some sort of a committee, but she knew his offers were not dependent on anyone else. Her time on the yacht had made it perfectly clear that though the three men ran publicly held companies, they actually operated as though they were sole proprietors. She couldn't provide any exact information about the date of her return to London, so she sent the following message:

"Dear Geoffrey, Thank you for the good news that you will publish my article. We can discuss all details, business and personal, when I return. My plans are as yet indefinite. I'll be in touch, but I don't think it will be very long before we come together. Yours, Margo. P.S. I'm on the trail of an even bigger story."

Margo was sure that her decision to participate in the identification of the Viper was the right one for her career. His arrest would be a big story, and she would scoop all the other journalists with it. She owed Ivan Welland a debt of gratitude for helping her see the huge mistake she had been about to make in joining forces with her sexy bandido.

She was obviously much better off joining forces with Lord Pressman. She counted herself lucky to have landed on her feet with Mike Slayton, Robert Thomaston, Rafael Alvarez, and now with Geoffrey Pressman, but she was well aware that her success in moving up the journalism ladder was due more to her landing on her back than on her feet. She told herself that after a year or two with Geoffrey, her byline would be known throughout the journalism world and she would never have to compromise herself again. She was primed to become one of the world's premier international investigative reporters. She knew that Geoffrey would never marry her, but if she handled things well it wouldn't matter anyway, for she would be well on her way to independence. She wished that Rafael would hurry up and contact her so he could be caught. She was eager, ready, and willing now to pursue her new plans with Geoffrey Lord Pressman.

When the sun came up Margo dressed casually and went down to have a real breakfast at the proper Thai time for it. She was glad to see Lieutenant Rama in the dining room, but they didn't speak to each other. She wondered what the Thai policeman would do if he came up against the Viper, who was twice his size and probably twice as strong and cunning.

After a breakfast of poached eggs, toast, yogurt, and black coffee, Margo approached the concierge to make a reservation to go on the temple tour. Seeing the fantastic selection of Buddhist temples in the Bangkok area would be interesting and would occupy her while she waited to hear from Rafael. Alternatively, if the Viper never showed up, Welland would eventually have to release her from her role as decoy and she could get on with things in London.

* * * *

Just as the policeman in the downtown jail finished his round of third degrees on Rafael Alvarez and had begun to check his story about the woman he was supposed to meet at the airport, he happened to read the request from Washington that the hospitals and jails in Bangkok be searched for men resembling the Viper's APB description.

From that moment on, things began to come together on several fronts simultaneously. When Lieutenant Rama heard about the American Secretary of Defense's hunch that the Viper might already be in jail, he immediately began to think about the Caucasian he had arrested forty-eight hours before. Rama called the downtown jail and was told by his colleague that he was already looking into the suspect's case.

"I'm trying to locate a woman named Margo Watson," he told Rama. "The prisoner who calls himself Mr. Ricardo claims that he was on his way to meet her at Suvarnabhumi International Airport when we picked him up. Do you know anything about this?"

"I was the arresting officer," Rama said. "What he said is true. There is an American woman by that name staying at the Peninsula Hotel. She's cooperating with us and with the Americans to identify this man. I've met with her, and we have her under surveillance. We have an APB from Interpol about this so-called Ricardo fellow. Have you seen it?"

"Not yet."

"Please find a copy and read it. Don't call any special attention to him, but don't release him for any reason. He escaped from a prison in Colombia and he's very dangerous according to the FBI. Just hold onto him until I get there with Miss Watson. She'll be able to identify him."

Rama got on the house phone and called Margo's room. He got no answer. He asked the concierge if he had seen Miss Watson and was told that she had gone on a tour of the temples on a bus that had just left. He went to the tour bus company desk and learned the schedule of the bus. Schedule in hand, he jumped into his car and followed the route the bus would have taken. Using his flashing lights and loud siren he threaded his way through heavy traffic until he caught up to the bus and pulled it over. The driver opened the door and Rama went aboard the bus and quickly found Margo Watson.

"What's this all about?" she asked, when he approached.

"I'd like you to come with me," said the Lieutenant. "We've located someone who answers the description of the man who was supposed to meet you at the airport. We want you to identify him for us."

When they arrived at the jail building they were directed immediately to the line-up room. Several men were already standing in the observation area. They introduced themselves as the FBI special agents in charge of the investigation, and the CIA Bangkok substation chief.

Margo joined them, with Rama at her side. She was asked to take a seat behind a one-way mirror that looked into an empty room. In a few minutes a group of suspects were led in and made to stand against the wall.

"Miss Watson, please look carefully at the men in front of you and tell us if you have seen any of them before."

Margo immediately spotted the Viper in the line-up of sullen, glowering prisoners.

"There he is! Number five. He's the man that kidnapped me and shot Robert Thomaston."

The two American agents simultaneously jumped up out of their chairs, like pilots ejecting from a burning plane.

"Are you positive, Miss Watson?" the FBI agent asked.

"Yes. He called himself Rafael. He needs a shave now, but he is definitely the same man."

"Thank you, Miss Watson. We'll have to ask you to sign a statement to that effect, which will be needed in order to arrange extradition so he can be tried in the United States. When he's brought to trial you'll be asked to be a witness and to give testimony against him. I'm sure you understand that, don't you?" the FBI agent asked.

"Yes. Seeing him again isn't easy for me, and being a witness will be even harder, but I realize it has to be done."

"Good, then you may go. Please leave your U.S. contact information, so we can be in touch later. Also, I advise you not to discuss this matter with anyone until the trial."

"I don't know about that," Margo said hesitantly. "I'm a journalist, you know."

"I understand, but you're a witness to a capital crime, and also a rape victim. The press will eat it up, and you with it. Once you say anything beyond the fact that an unspecified suspect has been taken into custody, your life will never be the same. Everything you say and do will become public information, and the defense lawyers will try to destroy your credibility by damaging your reputation."

Margo wasn't sure if the special agent was telling her this for her own good, or as a warning to shut her up. She knew the media would delight in cannibalistically devouring her character. They wouldn't give a second thought to the fact that she was one of them. She had seen how the media tended to portray the victim as a vengeful, spurned woman bent on getting even with the accused, or else as one who had provoked the actions that she claimed to have suffered. The FBI agent was right – if she opened the lid even a little, there would be a heavy price to pay. She had been handed the biggest story of a journalist's career, and then been told she couldn't write it. Margo decided she must consult with someone knowledgeable who could be trusted.

"I'll keep everything quiet for now," she said finally.

"It's for your own good," the agent said knowingly.

Lieutenant Rama gave the order to have the prisoners returned to the holding cell.

"Would you like to go back to your hotel, or would you rather continue your tour?" he asked Margo.

"I think I'd prefer to go to the hotel, thank you."

As soon as Rama and Margo Watson had left, the U.S. government agents began to talk excitedly with one another. Having the Viper in their custody was a feather in their caps.

"Who found out that Alvarez was in the local jail?"

"I got orders from the Secretary of Defense."

"What, the U.S. Secretary of Defense? What the hell does *he* have to do with this?"

"Damned if I know. But it was a good thing *somebody* thought to look."

Rafael Alvarez was back in the holding tank. Nobody had said anything to him about why he had been put in the line-up. Nothing seemed to have changed since he was first brought in for questioning. He wondered how long they could hold him without charge. He wasn't sure the line-up had anything to do with him specifically. Maybe they had some witness or other on the other side of the glass, but was he the suspect? If so, who was the witness against him? Could it have been Margo?

Rafael was a realist who tended to be pessimistic when it came to people, and especially women. It was highly likely that it was Margo on the other side of the glass. He knew no one else in Thailand. Had she come all the way from the States just to rat on him? Why? She could have just not accepted the free ticket and stayed home. He didn't have much experience with a woman of her type, however. She was educated, had career ambitions, and was a modern woman. Although he knew her body had been his, he wasn't sure about her mind. Had he had more time with her he could have found out, but now he might never know.

Rafael was not the type of man to live in hope, nor was he the kind to die in despair. He would assume the worst, but he would begin immediately to plan his escape.

CHAPTER NINETEEN

Margo got on her computer as soon as she returned to her hotel room. She had no reason to be in Bangkok now that Rafael had been apprehended. She got on the phone and called Singapore Air to see how fast she could get on a plane back to London. When she was told she could fly the next morning, she booked a passage immediately. Then she shot off an e-mail message to Lord Pressman.

"Geoffrey, my work here is over, sooner than expected. I'm leaving tomorrow for London. Can you pick me up? Singapore Air Flight #587 scheduled to arrive 9 pm at Heathrow. Lots to tell you. Margo."

A couple of hours later she had an e-mail from London.

"Margo, you're a fast worker. You're welcome to stay at my place. See you at Heathrow. Geoffrey."

Margo called the registration desk to ask them to prepare her bill, as she'd be checking out early in the morning. The clerk on duty asked her to hold on a minute while she consulted her computer. In a minute or so she came back on the line to say that the account had been paid, and that a limo would pick her up at 7 AM and take her to the airport. When a surprised Margo asked who had settled the account, she was told it had been charged to a Geoffrey Lord Pressman.

Bemused, Margo thought how nice it was to have the money to make such a gesture. Robert had spoiled her too, but in a different way. In Robert's case he shared his high life with her, but he didn't support her enjoyment of it unless she was with him. Geoffrey, on the other hand, seemed capable of being thoughtful without taking control of her life. She liked that, but she felt she should wait until she

knew him better before she made a saint of him. She had
found men to be disappointing in direct proportion to the
time she spent with them. After packing her suitcases, she
went down to the café to have dinner. This time Lieutenant
Rama was nowhere to be seen, either in or out of his skirt.

When she finished her stir-fried chicken with vegetables
she decided to skip the coffee so she could get a good night's
sleep. She charged the meal to her room, thinking once
again how nice it was that Geoffrey was footing the bill.

She went back up to her room, pleased with the thought
that she would soon be seeing him again. She decided to
check her e-mail once more before she went to bed. She was
astonished to find a message from the Secretary of Defense.

"Thanks for your cooperation. My spies tell me you are
en route to London. I wish you good luck. Please come to
see me as soon as you get back to Washington, as I have
something important to discuss with you. Ivan Welland."

Margo's mind began to race. What could the Secretary
of Defense want from her now that Rafael Alvarez was in
custody? She really had no idea what it could be, so she
began thinking about Geoffrey Pressman. She knew that he
wanted either an additional mistress or a new one. He had
paid her bills and invited her to stay at his place – her part of
the deal would undoubtedly be made clear to her later. The
comfort offered to a young woman by a powerful, wealthy
mentor was hard to resist. Many great artists of the past had
been obliged to have patrons, but it was hard to know how
the quality of their art was affected. If consulted, Ivan
Welland would have quoted Samuel Johnson's dictionary
definition of *patron*: "one who supports with insolence, and
is paid with flattery."

Thomaston's death made it necessary for Margo to look
for another position. The way she saw it, she could simply
enter the marketplace and find a job like the junior staff
writer her résumé said she was, or she could take advantage
of the talent she had to encourage the generosity of men in
high places. The famous courtesans of the past didn't wish

to be thrown back into the sordid lives they had led before, so they generally switched benefactors and kept on living among the rich and famous. Margo was no different from other mistresses. She convinced herself, in fact, that she was better than they were because she wanted a career, and she had to use her charm and her contacts to get to the head of the pack. An alliance with Pressman would certainly give her status, a name, and a market for everything she wrote. These benefits were difficult to resist.

Like an athlete traded from one team to another, Margo was using what she had learned from the first team to increase her value to the new team and thereby raise her own worth. Robert Thomaston had died before she could learn much about the workings of the publishing and broadcasting business. If she had been able to stay with him she might eventually have been admitted to the inner sanctum of the operation of his empire, but as things were, she still had much to learn. Getting to know the empires of two of the most important men in the industry would be valuable in ways that Margo couldn't yet comprehend. Ivan Welland, however, understood very well how valuable she could be to the United States in its role as the leader of the free world.

When her thoughts turned to Rafael she was surprised to find that she had already demoted him to a place of little or no importance. She couldn't imagine what had possessed her to risk her career to be the companion of a fugitive on the run. She understood the sexual attraction she had once felt for him, but that had burst like a bubble when she saw him in the line-up that day. A powerful social outcast independently winning an exciting game against the powers that be was one thing, but a lowly prisoner, one among many, was something altogether different. Margo easily surrendered her plans for a reunion with Rafael, and quickly moved on to her other thoughts and plans. If he had known what Margo was thinking that night, Rafael Alvarez would not have liked the way she could so cavalierly dismiss him from her life.

At 5:30 in the morning a loud, intrusive wakeup call
summoned Margo back into the tedious, confusing whirl of
long distance international travel. She got up, showered, and
selected an outfit that would still look attractive at the other
end of her long flight. She wanted to look smart and pert,
the way Susan had looked on the yacht. In the event that
Susan was still in Pressman's life, she didn't want him to
think that she was of a lower class than her rival. She chose
a bright blue silk dress with a matching jacket, one that she
had purchased to wear during her stay in Costa Rica with
Robert. It was one of a number of nice clothes that she had
in her wardrobe, thanks to Thomaston's insistence that she
dress better than she could afford to do on her own. It was
ironic that she was using some of the cosmetic items that
Susan had given her during the yachting trip. She hoped
they wouldn't remind Geoffrey of her.

She followed the luggage cart down in the elevator and
went into the café to have something to eat. She sat by
herself at the same table she had occupied the night she had
first met Lieutenant Rama. He was not in the café that
morning, and Margo missed him. She thought he was brave
to attempt to arrest men who were twice his size, and to wear
a dress in the process. She wondered how he had ever
managed to get Rafael Alvarez to surrender without a fight.
She hoped he would get the recognition he deserved for
capturing one of the world's most wanted criminals.

The stretch limo waited in front of the Peninsula Hotel.
The bellhop put Margo's luggage in the trunk, and held the
door open for her. She tipped the man and got into the car,
which then transported her to the airport.

Ivan Welland was well aware that Margo Watson was flying
to London at that very moment. Actually he knew every
move she had made in Bangkok. He had posted agents close
to her, and they had been ready to protect her at any moment.
The fact that she didn't know how much attention had been

devoted to her safety was a tribute to those who, unseen and unsung, work the security beats of the world. In fact most of the people she had met, or who had served her in Thailand, were employed by the U.S. government either directly or indirectly. Now that the Viper had been identified and was being held in custody, some of the heat was off Margo's surveillance detail. Nevertheless, Ivan had ordered that he be informed of her activities in London. If, as he hoped, she found herself a position in Pressman's media group, then he would speak to her about another project he had in mind for her. Ideally he wanted her to be embedded in Pressman's organization so she could participate in his plan to purge the media of their lies.

Geoffrey Lord Pressman's plans for Margo Watson also included embedding her in another way. The move for the big media merger had slowly progressed, and Geoffrey was tentatively putting together a team that would assimilate Thomaston's company with his. It was a big job because the American addition was considerably larger than the existing English company. One business writer had described the merger as a snake trying to swallow a grizzly bear.

The American management team and its employees had been functioning as Pressman's competitors for years, and now they were going to be subordinated to the British company. Geoffrey didn't want the American staff to quit in protest and leave him holding an empty bag. He was planning a field trip to the States to soothe the employees and assure them that their jobs wouldn't be lost. He couldn't move too quickly, though, as various U.S. federal authorities could still put the kiss of death on the deal. Until the merger received their approval, there was in fact no deal.

As a fervent devotee of Machiavelli, Geoffrey Pressman was nothing if not stealthy. He was a psychological business warrior. His M.O. was furtive, subtle, and lethal to any who opposed his wishes. Thomaston had functioned combatively in an in-your-face fashion, but Pressman was insidious, and

business associates had to watch their backs when dealing
with him.

Surviving in the media business was nothing new for
Pressman in Britain. His family had been in printing and
publishing since shortly after Gutenberg invented the press.
He was fond of saying he wasn't called Pressman without
reason. He believed that his family had been seminal in
spreading the English language to the point where it was
now the lingua franca of the world. Therefore he felt that
because of his family, and latterly his own work, he was now
entitled to the media spoils of the English-speaking world. In
a linguistic sense he was going to retrieve Britain's lost
colonies, making himself regent in the process.

Margo reclined her seat and looked out the window.
The captain had just announced that they had reached a
cruising altitude of 39,000 feet. The occasional puffy clouds
were far below now, and the earth had retreated into
shadowiness at the very edge of her sight range. In the aisle
seat next to hers sat a lady she judged to be Chinese. The
woman was about ten years older than she was. She decided
not to speak to her, assuming incorrectly that the woman
spoke no English. She preferred to use her time rehearsing
what she would say and how she would behave when she
met Geoffrey.

Margo was about to enter *his* world. From her
outsider's position she had no idea what that really meant.
Geoffrey's exterior was calm and noncommittal. His
outward demeanor was one of concern for others and
gentlemanly politeness. Taken on the surface, using what
she knew of him on board the yacht, she expected him to be
a soft, urbane, kindly man. Certainly of the three media
giants he had appeared to her to be the most sympathetic.
Perhaps it was the fact that he was the shortest of the three,
or maybe it was his upper class British accent and superior
verbal abilities that seemed so comparatively sweet to her
when he was in the company of Thomaston and Baron Fritz.
Margo had taken him at face value, which was his intention.

She was to find out that he was like an avocado – fleshy and soft on the outside, but with a large, hard stone on the inside.

Geoffrey Pressman was approaching sixty, and hating every minute of it. He defined his physical masculinity in terms of fitness and flexibility. He spent a good bit of energy under-eating and over-exercising. He had developed a fondness for foods that took a good bit of dexterity to eat. His idea was that if the food was difficult to handle he would eat less of it. As a result he loved crustaceans. His favorites included shrimp, crab, lobster in the shell, and just about anything else that needed to be wrestled into small, edible pieces before it could be eaten. He was fond of saying that there were no fat residents in the old folks' home, meaning that the obese die young, a fate that he planned to avoid by staying lithe through diet and exercise.

Geoffrey made it a point to move his body quickly and with purpose. He tolerated no slouching, no slackness, and no vague movements. He always projected a quick, deft, energetic sort of aura in his every motion. As a result he did achieve a younger appearance than his years would indicate.

Great as his will power was, his mastery over his body was nonetheless challenged by two areas of rebellion. The first was a distinct case of pate exposure that had begun at an early age. His hair had taken it into its own head to seek residence in other bodily areas, producing hirsute bumper crops on his back, ears, and brows.

The second rebellion was not migratory in nature; it was more akin to a labor slowdown. Pressman was trying his best to prevent a strike that would cause a complete work stoppage. His favorite lifelong recreation had been his dalliances with women. His current problem was causing a distinct curtailing of his ability to pursue his hobby, and yet he didn't want to become addicted to the miracles of modern medicine. The fortuitous appearance of Margo, however, had caused him to want to perform in a passionate manner again, summoning him to renew his natural lifelong interest in his favorite activity. He was, therefore, very hopeful that his meeting with her would rekindle his dwindling abilities.

In anticipation of this liaison he was formulating a dual position that she could fill. If she pleased him, he planned to train her to look after some of his business interests in the United States. He could use her writing skills, and she would be cheaper than one of the big names in journalism circles. The upcoming mergers – his and hers as well as his and Thomaston's – had opened a position in the U.S. that Margo might possibly fill. He was anxious to explore these longer-term things with her, but he wanted his pound of flesh first. He resolved not to speak of serious business matters with her until he knew her in a carnal way. He had found that no real honesty could exist between men and women until after they had sex.

During the meal service, Margo had a short conversation with the Chinese lady in the seat across the aisle from her. She was surprised to find that the woman spoke English well. Not only well, but she spoke with a better modulated voice than her own. She had an excellent vocabulary, no trace of an accent, and exemplary poise. She was somebody, in fact, whose speech was to be emulated.

The incident impressed itself upon Margo because she had made a snap judgment that had turned out to be almost completely incorrect. She examined her memory, wondering if she had a tendency in general to make such mistakes. She had certainly done it with Robert Thomaston when she first met him. She had presumed he was a hack journalist sent to cover the same convention she was attending. It had turned out that he was the owner of many publications and one of the most important men in the media business. She had also been mistaken about Rafael's true nature because she had allowed herself to be taken in by his strength and good looks. She was so seduced by his powers that she had been willing to make excuses for his crimes and to travel half way around the world to see him again. Yes, she had to admit that she was prone to making unsound decisions about people.

By the time the plane landed, Margo had allowed her self-confidence to wither away. She ended up feeling much less secure about meeting Geoffrey than she had been when she boarded the aircraft. What did she really know about him? Since all her hopes were centered on her own nebulous opinion of the man, what could she expect? She ducked into the washroom near the baggage claim area while she waited for her suitcases to be spilled onto the conveyor.

Her reflection in the mirror should have warned her that she was inwardly scared. In spite of the way she imagined it, the scenario of her arrival in London and her reunion with Geoffrey Pressman might be a disaster. Perhaps she had overrated his interest in her. He could just as easily be cold and distant. In the end she shrugged and walked off to pick up her luggage, leaving the other ladies in the public lavatory wondering what the beautiful, well-dressed young woman was shrugging about.

Margo pulled her suitcases off the conveyor belt and proceeded to the exit gate, hoping to spot Geoffrey's face somewhere along the way. She found no sign of him, but she did notice a sign with her name on it. So he hadn't even bothered to come in person to meet her. She went up to the man who was holding the sign.

"Hello, I'm Margo Watson."

"Good evening, Miss Watson. I'm Lord Pressman's chauffeur. Would you follow me, please?"

Margo was outwardly pleasant, but inwardly she felt slighted that Geoffrey had not come to meet her himself. She was trying to control her anger as she followed his driver to the exit. He had relieved her of the burden of towing her luggage and was proceeding with her suitcase in hand, not bothering with the wheels. Just outside the main entrance to the airport they approached a sleek black Jaguar limousine. The driver opened the back door to admit Margo, and waited until she got in. Then he went around to the boot and loaded her suitcase inside. Lord Pressman had been waiting in the limo, but with the smoky windows Margo hadn't been able to see him until she was about to sit on him.

"Welcome to England, Margo, my dear," he said.

Margo was startled.

"I thought you hadn't come," she stammered, as she reached out to hug him.

"Sorry about that, but you know I can't go anywhere without being harried by the press, especially these days with the merger talks in the headlines. I was afraid we'd be mobbed if I got out of the car."

He reached over to return the hug. He thought he felt a small tear on her cheek, and he kissed it lightly.

He had put his hand on her thigh as he leaned over to kiss her. It was just the smallest of improprieties, one that could have been taken as a clumsy little accident should she choose to make anything of it. But she seemed to have no objection and didn't recoil.

"If all the reporters worked for me, I wouldn't have had to stay in the car, and we wouldn't have had this awkward moment."

Margo didn't know exactly which awkward moment he was referring to – touching her leg or being unable to meet her at the gate. It didn't matter anyway, for he had come to the airport after all, and had a satisfactory explanation for not greeting her at the gate. What's more, he was being warm and affectionate toward her.

Geoffrey leaned back in his seat and put the armrest between them. The driver got behind the wheel and guided the vehicle out of the terminal area.

"Did you have a pleasant flight?" he inquired.

"Yes, the trip was fine. It was better than the outbound flight, as there was no lay-over in India. It was a direct, non-stop flight from Bangkok to London."

"That always helps. I seldom fly on commercial jets any more, now that I have my own jet. But I do remember what it was like in the old days."

"I know what you mean. I got spoiled when I traveled with Robert in his jet. Now I'm not even impressed by first class seats on commercial airliners."

"Well, in future we'll have to see if we can continue to spoil you."

Just then the long vehicle pulled up in front of an elegant townhouse in Mayfair. The driver jumped out and opened the door for his passengers.

"Put the lady's luggage in the front hall, please. That will be all for tonight. Thank you, Holmes."

Geoffrey issued orders like one to the manor born, and it was no wonder. His family had had servants for a couple of hundred years.

Lord Pressman opened the extra wide front door and let Margo pass ahead of him. The door had a brass knocker that could have been displayed in the Tower of London Museum, for the unusual quality of its workmanship. He followed Margo inside, leaving the door ajar so that Holmes could put her suitcase in the foyer.

The building was an attached five-story row house typical of London's West End, and similar to the Prime Minister's house at 10 Downing Street. The clean, simple lines of the street entrances belied the rich and sometimes exotic interiors of the houses. Everything was understated in typical English fashion, yet it was clear to a careful observer that every room in Lord Pressman's house was faithful to the period it represented. Each item in each room was an antique of perfect quality and inestimable value.

"Let me show you around," Geoffrey said. He took Margo's arm and led her from room to room. "The kitchen and servants quarters are on the floor below. This floor contains the dining room, the parlor, the solarium, and the passageway here leads to the garden at the back."

Margo couldn't help but notice the incredible quality of the antique furnishings. The wainscoting in every room was unique and irreplaceable. He squired her to the geographical center of the house where there was a small private elevator.

Geoffrey excused himself for a minute and went and got her luggage, which he placed on the floor of the lift. The entire house had been redone to accommodate the latest electronic devices, including the security system, the HVAC humidity control system, computer hook-ups, and flat-screen wall-mounted TV sets. Every modern device had been tastefully placed so as not to detract from the historicity of the house.

They stepped into the elevator together and were silently transported from the ground floor to the first floor. Geoffrey steered Margo into the drawing room.

"This is where I do my post-prandial entertaining."

There was a beautiful, cream-colored grand piano near one wall of the drawing room, set off by two large fireplaces on each end of the long room. The parquet floor was left uncovered so that guests could dance when the occasion called for this sort of diversion. The walls were covered with the portraits of the Pressman progenitors, stretching back to the 18th century. Delicate antique furniture was spread around in tasteful profusion, leaving plenty of room, nevertheless, for guests to converse and move about without encountering any obstacles.

"I'm very proud of this room," Geoffrey said, when they emerged from the lift on the second floor. "I've been told it's the finest private library in the world. Every volume you see here is a first edition, and most are personally dedicated by the authors. The majority of these books were published and printed by my family businesses."

Margo looked around the room, which had floor-to-ceiling bookshelves and a rolling ladder to provide easy access to the higher shelves. Two leather easy chairs were placed beneath custom-made Tiffany lamps tilted at just the right angle for reading. A superb example of the best in Edwardian period writing tables stood under a window that looked out onto the garden. The outside area was warmly lit by colored spotlights that simulated sunlight. The library occupied the entire second floor.

"This is my study," Geoffrey said as they stepped out of the elevator on the third floor.

Margo's eyes widened. It was the most beautiful office she could ever imagine. It was full of memorabilia from each of the Pressman generations as they interfaced with the greats of the past and present. Photos of Geoffrey, his father, and his grandfather with kings, queens, prime ministers and presidents were hung on a wall of fame.

"This is the most magnificent office in the world," Margo said, with feeling.

Geoffrey could see that she was truly impressed. He was touched that she seemed to appreciate the significance that the room had for him. She trailed her hand over the deeply polished surface of the solid mahogany desk that had been custom-built for his grandfather by the royal cabinet maker to Queen Victoria. They took the lift one more flight up to the fourth floor.

"This is the master bedroom and ensuite bath," he said, allowing her to look around.

"I see you have a balcony that looks out over the garden. It must be lovely to lounge around in this room, if you ever have time for lounging."

"Not much time for lounging, I'm afraid. Now I'll show you to your room," he said, as he led her back into the elevator. "The fifth floor contains three guest rooms with baths. You may have any one you like."

Seeking to head off the inevitable question of what had become of Susan, Geoffrey continued, "Susan preferred this room when she was in town."

"I've been wondering about Susan, as I guess you can imagine. What happened between you two?"

"I can only give you my side of the story, of course, and I'm not particularly happy to discuss it with anyone, let alone someone I care about. But I suppose we have to get it over with, so here it is. I'm married, but not to Susan, and that was the problem. Although we've been separated for many years I can't, for many reasons, divorce my wife. Susan played the role of my wife, and very well too, I must admit, but she got tired of playacting and wanted the real thing."

"Where is she now?" Margo asked.

"Lest you think me a cad, I can tell you that she is well taken care of, and lives in the country. She always preferred the country to life in the city."

Margo was conscious that she was getting the ultra-sanitized version of the break-up. There was no way on earth that he would ever come totally clean about their relationship. Even a psychiatrist would have needed years to tease out the real problem, but he was too proud to undergo analysis. Margo certainly couldn't expect to get any straight answers from Susan, either, as gender rivalry, pride, economic interests, and jealousy issues would prevent it.

"I would never have thought you a rotter, Geoffrey. Is that how the English put it?"

"Yes. I'm glad you feel that way. I may be complex, but I'm not evil, at least *I* don't think so. So which room do you choose?"

"I like this one," Margo said, pointing to the blue room on the far right.

Geoffrey set her suitcase on a stand in the large closet where she could easily unpack it. Now that the preliminaries of place had been taken care of, he was wondering how best to proceed with more intimate details. He needn't have worried, as Margo was accomplished at overcoming the awkward gaps when new relationships move from one stage to another. She was also becoming adept at encouraging men whose performance in the bedroom lacked the luster of their exploits in the boardroom.

CHAPTER TWENTY

Rafael Alvarez, because of his high-profile crimes, was hurriedly processed through the Thai justice system and extradited to the United States. Several U.S. marshals took him in handcuffs to Washington, where he was incarcerated in the federal prison until he could be tried. The Attorney General had assigned his brightest Assistant District Attorney to prosecute the Viper. They had so many charges to bring against Rafael Alvarez that they had to prioritize them in order of those most likely to bring convictions with the longest sentences. The entire judiciary of the United States was going to be brought to bear on his case. Unfortunately for the legal establishment, there were lots of issues concerning which jurisdictions had priority.

Costa Rica thought that they should have jurisdiction because the crime of murder was committed in their country. Chicago wanted him for murder and drug-dealing charges. New York wanted to prosecute him for two murders there. Colombia wanted him for escaping custody. Other serious charges were pending, but would probably never be laid if the Viper were convicted of multiple counts of first-degree murder. Legal snarls were rife.

Adding to the confusion was the Viper's choice of a defense attorney. He chose the most famous defense lawyer in the country to be his counsel. His counselor was busily playing jurisdictions against one another to delay trial, and laying grounds for future appeals should he lose. He had a client with lots of money, so his tactic was to stall, bluff, and extend the legal combat so as to wear down the government lawyers while he collected huge legal fees.

The various lawyers from the Justice Department were vacillating between trying Alvarez for the murder of Robert Thomaston, or for the murders of Prince Umar of Saudi Arabia and his American girl friend, DeeDee Dunbar. In the Thomaston case they had an eyewitness in Margo Watson, while in the death of the Prince they had DNA evidence. The U.S. State Department wanted to see Alvarez tried for the Prince's murder as a sop to the Saudis. They hoped that bringing the murdered Prince's killer to justice would improve relations between the U.S. and the royal family in the Kingdom of Saudi Arabia. Although the royal family had kept the details of the Prince's death out of the press, they nevertheless were bitter about the lack of protection that had been provided to one of their own while he was on a diplomatic mission. The King and his bevy of princes were also furious over the incident in the Holy City of Mecca in which American Navy Seals had killed three pretenders to the Caliphate of Muhammad. Aidan DeVries, a novelist of some repute, had written about the incident in his book, *Council of Caliphs*.

Ivan Welland was not surprised at the hypocrisy of the Arab position. The Meccan incident assured the family that it would continue in power, so Ivan didn't see any reason for them to complain. Prince Umar had been very unpopular. Even his fellow princes distrusted him because of his corrupt practices in managing the oil business of the kingdom, and his use of vast sums of money to support terrorist activities. To Ivan's way of thinking the U.S. should be receiving heartfelt thanks from the Saudi royals for doing a clean-up job that the Arabs had been unwilling or unable to do for themselves. Instead, all the U.S. got from them was either serious static or lukewarm cooperation.

The fact that Islamist terrorists were trying to use the Holy City as protection while they tried to acquire a nuclear bomb seemed to be of less importance to them than the fact that the U.S. had temporarily put infidel boots in the holy sanctuary of the Muslim faith, thereby salvaging the Saudi family throne at the cost of offending the clergy.

Ivan had taken the time to become familiar with recent Saudi history and he had no trouble remembering another incident that started on New Year's Day in the year 1400 of the Muslim calendar. On that last day of the Hajj in C.E. 1979, a ragtag bunch of insurgents with rifles hidden under their robes took control of the holy sanctuary, taking many pilgrims hostage, chaining the gates, and killing several policemen. The insurgents were the precursors of al-Qaeda. They were four or five hundred in number, including some African American Muslims, and they came from several different countries. They had stolen automatic weapons from the Saudi National Guard armory and smuggled them into the Grand Mosque on biers that were normally used to carry the dead into the complex to be washed as part of the funeral ritual. The arms and supplies were distributed around the Mosque through the hundreds of small underground prayer rooms used by pilgrims.

The most important Saudi princes were put in charge of recapturing the Muslim holy place. Two of the older of Osama bin Laden's brothers were called in to supply maps, technical drawings, and electrical diagrams because the enormous contract for the construction of the Grand Mosque expansion had been given to the King's favorite construction engineering company, the bin Laden Group. The insurgents took control of the loudspeaker system and continually broadcast their demands that diplomatic relations with the Western nations be broken off and oil exports cease, that all foreigners be expelled from the Arabian Peninsula, that the society reject modernity, and that the Royal family be thrown out of power in favor of a theocracy that practiced Sharia law.

It was all extremely embarrassing to the King, the army, and the royal family. It took two weeks to resolve the conflict, during which time thousands of government forces were slaughtered by well-armed insurgents using their command positions inside the compound.

During the battle for the holiest place in the Islamic world, many instances of conveniently disregarded Qur'anic prohibitions were broken or circumvented, which included bringing and using weapons inside the sanctuary, Muslims killing Muslims, corpses unburied for days, and other infractions. They even held a phony conversion ceremony that temporarily abrogated the dictum that no non-Muslim could set foot in the Holy City of Mecca. They arranged it so that a team of infidel French commandos could pump poison gas into the compound, which proved unsuccessful anyway.

Another disgraceful tactic involved drilling down from ground level into the subterranean cells below so they could drop grenades down the holes. This resulted in a lot of dead hostages, but no dead insurgents. The stench of death polluted the air. Female insurgents shot their dead comrades in their faces so the bodies couldn't be recognized and reprisals taken against their families.

Finally the horror was brought to an end when the royals made a secret deal with the Ulema (the most important Islamic clerics). To this day no one knows what the royals offered the Sunni religious leaders to bring an end to the affair. Fifteen years later Osama bin Laden demanded the same things.

A month after the insurgency mounted by the Islamist extremists, sixty-two were beheaded in a single day. The executions took place in eight different cities throughout the Kingdom in order to maximize the deterrent effect, and minimize the carnage in any one place. Ivan thought it was naïve to throw these dangerous, duplicitous charlatans the unearned sop of publicly convicting the Prince's murderer, as they were never going to like us no matter what we did for them. Even keeping them alive and in power was a totally thankless job.

The behavior of the Royal-controlled Arab press during periods of embarrassing stress was typical. They minimized, or ignored the events in order to control the management of the information, making it more palatable to the public. With consummate skill the Arab media cranked out propaganda favorable to the regime. Thomaston, Pressman, and von Aragon learned a great deal from the Arabs and could see no reason why Arab media techniques wouldn't work in the West. It was the advent of a total contempt of conscience in the new policies of the Western media that sent Ivan off in his quest for the truth in reporting the news.

As Secretary of Defense, and as a thinking man, Ivan thought the Attorney General should first prosecute Rafael Alvarez for the murder of Robert Thomaston. He couldn't discuss his reason for that choice because his investigation of the media had not yet been completed. But if it could be shown during the trial that Thomaston had acted out of spite and had used his powerful influence in the media to have Rafael Alvarez arrested in Colombia, this case might lead the public and their representatives to consider Ivan's wider point more seriously. It was not that Rafael didn't deserve to be arrested, because he certainly did, but his arrest in Colombia was an indicator of how the media can influence government policies all over the world. After the revelations in the trial, Ivan intended to launch volumes of follow-up evidence geared to prove that the media corporations were knowingly using untruths to provoke government actions. He hoped this would stop the merger of Thomaston's empire with foreign companies.

Regardless of whether Rafael Alvarez was convicted or exonerated for the murder of Thomaston, he could be tried later for the murder of Prince Umar. Underneath it all Ivan wanted to motivate Congress to emend the First Amendment in the light of modern telecommunications, the shaping of mass media opinion, and the other technological inventions that were unknown over two hundred years ago when the Constitution and the Bill of Rights were written.

Slander and libel laws don't apply in cases where the statements made are true. Lies told by an accused that do harm to an individual are subject to fines, compensations, and public apologies. To Ivan Welland's way of thinking, the same standards as those used for judging individual slanderers and libelers should be applied to corporate liars. The public needed to be able to judge if they were receiving the truth from their news sources. The difference between fiction and truth in mass media reporting was the same, whether it came from an individual or the largest news-broadcasting corporation in the world.

Giant multi-media corporations control the content of news reports. They own most of the TV news stations, as well as the largest film-producing facilities, therefore they have opportunity, means, and motivation to couch their reporting in terms that will benefit them or whomever else they wish to promote. These companies have large legal staffs to vet reports before they are released, and to see to it that the language used is abstruse enough to cover their employers against libel suits. They have tremendous power over people's minds, and the only agencies keeping them honest are the F.T.C. and the F.C.C.

Ivan knew the Federal Communications Commission was retargeted with the passage of the Telecommunications Act of 1996, after 62 years of functioning under its original charter. He hoped he would find, among its 128 pages, a proviso that the industry it governed should tell the public the truth in its reports. He did find, among the pages devoted to licensing, territorial distribution, competition, alliances, pornography restrictions, satellite and switching equipment usage, and legal boilerplate covering operations and telecom services, one statement that "TV broadcasters are obliged by law to serve the public interest." Ivan could think of no instance whereby the public was served by the distribution of lies and fictions about the nation and world they live in.

In his position as Secretary of Defense, Welland had deep reservations about a free press that could simply ignore military victories, or if mentioned, paint them in a very poor light in order to gain some political advantage for themselves or their associates. Ivan wrestled with the "what is truth" question, and like philosophers and thinkers before him, he had trouble evolving a perfect definition. He did know a few things that it was not, however. It was not a totally fabricated state existing outside of obvious facts. It was clearly not a coordinated effort to hone the opinions of the few into the policies of all. He had to ask himself if the F.C.C. was really a guardian of *the truth and nothing but the truth* in this age of real-time telecommunications, or just an electronic traffic cop. He decided to call the head of the Commission to make an appointment to discuss the matter.

When a day later he was ushered into the Chairman's office and the niceties had been dispensed with, Ivan asked the bureaucrat a simple question.

"Mr. Chairman, sir, does the Federal Communications Commission regulate the truth of the content that the media broadcasting companies present to the public?"

The Chairman chuckled at the naiveté of his question.

"Except where we are expressly legislated to control the output of broadcasters," he replied, "such as in the case of pornography and children's programming, we let the First Amendment do that job."

"In other words, no?"

"This is a free country, Mr. Secretary. It is assumed that our companies, like our people, are innocent until proven guilty. That goes for telling the truth, too. The competition between the various organizations assures that each will tell the truth in their reporting, lest their competitors expose them. It is the beauty of free speech in the free market."

"So, in the Bible quote, *You shall know the truth and the truth shall make you free,* you would substitute the thought that it is the competition that makes us free."

"We work under the aegis of Congress here and we get our mission description from legislation they have passed. They have gone to great lengths to make certain that no one person or group gets all the say. Even in the appointment of the five F.C.C. Commissioners by the President, they have insisted on mixed political party representation. It is assumed that in the blend of opinions and facts presented to honest, free men for their judgments, they will arrive at the truth in their deliberations. It has worked well for centuries. Do you not agree, Mr. Secretary?"

"I do, up to a point. But new technologies have injected some new editorial and technical elements that I believe require that the Telecommunications Act be emended before another sixty-two years pass."

"Well, that would be a job for Congress, Mr. Secretary. At the F.C.C. we administer the law, we don't make it."

"Fair enough, but if we had a case of blatant restraint of trade in the telecom industry, you could hear the case, couldn't you?"

"Yes, we could. We would try to mediate the differences as a first step. Under the rules for competition we could pull the licenses of any offender found to be guilty of restraining trade and/or being non-compliant with our regulations. Licenses are reviewed and issued for eight year terms."

"What about international organizations? Are they subject to the same treatment?" Ivan asked.

"In the U.S. they operate under our regulations, and in other countries I assume they answer to the local authorities. We have stringent U.S. citizenship requirements covering the ownership of broadcasting licenses. But, Mr. Secretary, if your question is specifically directed to the major merger of the Thomaston interests which is before the Commission now, then I can't discuss a pending case with you."

"I understand, Mr. Chairman. I thank you for your time and for seeing me on short notice."

Ivan left the office with a goodly amount of respect for the Chairman. He hadn't exceeded his authority, but he had been informative, though he was perhaps a bit too much of a by-the-book type for Ivan's taste. If the matter of the merger were left entirely in his hands, Ivan thought it had a good chance of going through. The Chairman seemed to believe that the merger should stand, unless it blatantly breached the competition rules. The regulations and the licensing reviews prior to renewal would cover this merger; at least those were the opinions Ivan attributed to the head of the F.C.C.

In London another merger had just been completed. Margo had allowed Geoffrey's little familiarities to develop. In the end she had reason to believe that he had been satisfied by her performance when he kissed her gratefully and returned to his own sleeping quarters downstairs. She had been left alone with her thoughts, most of which were interrogative in nature. He had said they would discuss matters of business in the morning over breakfast. That established a time, but it said nothing about the content to be considered.

Still troubled by the pendulum effect of jet lag on her body, her mind was too active to allow sleep to come easily. She reviewed in her mind the recently concluded sexual interlude with Geoffrey and decided that being his mistress would be light duty compared to what Robert had required of her. She thought, with some regret, that neither Robert nor Geoffrey ever had the capacity to satisfy her in the way Rafael had. On considering the choices that life had provided, however, she had no difficulty rejecting passion in favor of avoiding poverty, and no regrets about giving up a life on the run, no matter how good the sex was.

On the floor below, Geoffrey was tossing in his bed too. He thought his problem with women existed primarily in his head. He attributed his successful performance with Margo to the fact that it was their first time together, and that he had been inactive while he yearned for her from the moment she had called him about selling her story. His sixtieth birthday was approaching and his libido had naturally declined over the years. He worried that he could no longer satisfy a younger woman, and the effect that this concern had on his performance was becoming a self-fulfilling prophecy. If he had been content to scale back his expectations of himself in response to aging, he could have had perfectly normal sex, though on a somewhat decreased level of frequency. That would have been a reasonable thing to do, or alternatively, he could take a prescription to increase his arousal. But he believed that once he started taking pills he would become dependent on them, and he had a mortal fear of that.

In Geoffrey's mind Margo was to be his sexual savior. He found every aspect of her appearance to be extremely attractive, as he had from the first moment he met her. She was with Robert then so nothing could be done about it, though if he could have had her while she was with Robert, he would have liked it even better. As it was, he regarded her as a rare find and he was grateful to the dead Robert for discovering her. Geoffrey preferred his women to be shy and timid at first. As he saw it, it was his job to get them over that stage and guide them into the unknown realms of their sexual potential. A beautiful, shy young woman who was nevertheless not without experience was Geoffrey's definition of the Holy Grail of sex.

Geoffrey had found Margo to be all he had hoped she would be. Whether she was his ingénue of the bedroom, or just play-acting, he didn't yet know – but from his point of view she had been perfect in the role. He found her to have just the right degree of reticence in the beginning, but with each of his advances her reactions escalated, moving from shyly compliant, to playfully willing, and in the end she had surrendered to him completely. Afterwards she was less shy with him and seemingly appreciative of his efforts. She seemed sorry when he told her he was going to sleep in his own bed. It had all been perfect in Lord Pressman's opinion.

Even Dr. Ivan Welland, who held one of the most important responsibilities in the U.S. government, didn't understand every facet of the American bureaucracy. He thought that because the F.C.C. controlled telecommunication regulations throughout the nation, he should try to defeat the takeover by the Europeans of the Thomaston media empire by pleading his case in front of that Commission. He knew that the F.C.C. had certain jurisdictional rules such as the proviso that majority owners of U.S. broadcasting companies had to be U.S. citizens, and that anyone owning 10% or more of the shares of such companies was considered to be an affiliate of the company and subject to special rules formulated to prevent broadcasting from falling into too few hands. But what he'd learned from the Chairman of the F.C.C. was that clever corporate attorneys representing client companies with very deep pockets could legally subvert these rules. He needed to know what other agency might have authority to quash the merger. He decided to consult his assistant, Brooklyn, the redoubtable in-house expert on governmental affairs.

"Brooklyn, can you come to my office for a minute?"

"Sure, boss. What can I do for you?"

"Your boss needs a fix."

She looked at him questioningly.

"Now, now. It's not what you're thinking. What I need is a governmental navigational fix."

"That's good to hear. Now what exactly do you need to know?"

"Things are coming to a head on the media merger, and I've got to find a way to slow it down. If we're not careful they may push the deal through the approval mechanism before we finish gathering the evidence that can prevent it. I need to know what agency I can go to in order to decelerate this deal until the team finishes its investigation and can present its evidence. I already went to the F.C.C. and got stonewalled. What else can I do?"

"You should go to the F.T.C. I think you've got your alphabet confused," Brooklyn said.

"I'm glad to see that I'm such an inspiring guy to work for. First you think I'm a dope addict, and then you think I don't know the alphabet."

"Yeah, I've always been amazed at the way guys with severe learning disabilities get ahead in the bureaucracy. It seems to be a very flawed process, this business of finding leaders."

These two individuals had a serious-comic relationship that can only happen between two brilliant people intent on solving problems by focusing on the donuts, not the holes. Ivan relied on his assistant and trusted her completely, and the feeling was mutual.

"I'll call the Chairman of the F.T.C. and get you an appointment *tout de suite*."

"Excellent, ma petite tutti frutti. The sooner I can see him the better."

"Her, you mean. The Chairman is a Chairwoman."

"Oy. She'll probably turn out to be your cloned sister."

"You should be so lucky."

That afternoon, after Google had spilled the beans on the Chairwoman's background, Ivan found himself in her office. After an appropriately short wait the tall, elegantly-coifed gray-haired lady shook his hand and welcomed him into her office. The room was decorated with distinctly feminine touches here and there. Ivan thought the attempts to soften the décor were akin to an alligator floating just far enough under the water so her teeth were not visible. Her biography had also struck him as singularly formidable, kind of like an Amazon posing as Snow White.

Her specialty, in her government position and in her private legal practice, was the area of anti-trust matters. She made numerous appearances representing both sides of anti-competitive cases that were heard by the U.S. Supreme Court. After a distinguished career, the President, in recognition of her expertise, appointed her as Chairwoman of the Federal Trade Commission for the customary seven-year term.

"Have a seat, Mr. Secretary. To what do I owe this visit, if I may ask?"

"I've got a problem. Well two, really. The first, and immediate one, is my desire to stop the media merger that is pending right now. The second is to find the legal means to regulate news reporting using the logic that has been applied to truth in advertising policies. I'd like to see the media be forced to label its products as fiction, opinion, or truth. It doesn't seem right to me that a pillow manufacturer has to list the contents of his product before a customer's head touches it, while a marketer of ideas and news reports makes no such declaration about the contents of the products that enter the consumer's heads."

"Well, Dr. Welland, in regard to the media merger, that matter is, as you say, pending right now, and therefore I'm not at liberty to discuss it. You can, of course, file an affidavit as an interested party, and the Commission will be happy to take your views into consideration as we deliberate. To advise you on your second problem I will need more information. Would you mind explaining further what it is you have in mind?"

"Not at all, Madame Chairwoman. An investigative team in my department has uncovered a pervasive scheme whereby using the most modern technological developments, the media, particularly television and film producers, have conspired to present entirely fictionalized versions of many news items to the American people. This reckless disregard for the truth has in numerous instances had an effect on my department's military operations. Furthermore it deprives the citizenry of their reasonable right to decide whether they approve of the government's policies based on the facts. I need to know if the FTC is the proper place to raise this issue."

"I see where you're coming from," the Chairwoman said. "This Commission has been, since its inception in 1914, the government's trust-busting agency. It's the place to air restraint of trade allegations and make complaints about monopolistic, anti-competitive behavior. We operate under the Senate's Anti-trust Committee. In 1938, our mandate was expanded to include many areas of consumer protection. Among the items we deal with are truth in advertising, privacy issues, identity theft, and the No Fear Act. In 1975 we were given broad powers to enforce trade rules and agreements. That is what we do here. Off the top of my head I would say that we would need to have additional legislative authority in order to have jurisdiction over the media issues you are raising."

"If I'm hearing you right," Ivan replied, "you're saying you'd need to have expanded jurisdictional authority by congressional legislation before the F.T.C. could consider our evidence of media untruthfulness. In other words, we'd need to have congress pass a new law before you could deal with this kind of consumer protection. It seems strange to me that we can prosecute a person if he lies in advertising or in presenting his product or service. But since there's no direct commercial value to the news, it is permissible for the purveyors of current events information to concoct any kind of fabrication they wish."

The Chairwoman smiled at the succinct, clear-headed summary Ivan had just presented to her. Nobody had ever spoken to her about this problem before.

"Well," she began, pondering his observation, "there certainly is a First Amendment infringement issue involved in limiting or controlling what is said in the free press, but without legislation to guide us, how would we administer such restrictions?"

"I'm not a lawyer," said Ivan, "but it seems to me that the First Amendment deals with four freedoms. Freedom of religion, speech, assembly and the right to petition the government for a redress of grievances. Isn't that correct?"

"Yes."

"Well then," Ivan continued, "what happens when one part of the Constitution countermands another? For instance, freedom of speech has obviously had its wings clipped in the cases of slander, libel, national security, and matters of sedition. Since we have some limitations already, why not put limits on untruthful statements in political reporting? I think the citizens have a serious grievance with the government when it permits unmitigated lies in the press to be passed off as truth. So I'd like to petition my government in its role as a consumer champion, to keep outright lies and deception created by one segment of the economy from dishonestly influencing governmental policies that effect all its citizens. I don't mean we should control what is said in the media, only that if it is not true, that it be labeled as fiction, opinion, or truth."

"I see what you're getting at," the Chairwoman said, "but any limitations on the free expression of ideas has always been anathema in our democratic government. I don't think we can, in an effort to doctor up the plentiful sins of the fourth estate, create a bureau of truth in media. That would be overkill that could lead to a press controlled by the government."

Ivan looked at her thoughtfully.

"Yes," he agreed, "I see the legal and philosophical difficulties involved, but we already have evidence that giant scams are being perpetrated on the American people by unconscionable, self-motivated media magnates. These people can create a war, or arrange a peace whose terms they make up and pass off to the world as if they were accurately reporting real events. Using telecommunications, computer enhancement, real time photo library access, and these types of new technological methods, they can convince the world that their version of virtual reality is true life. We can't allow science fiction to replace reality, can we?"

"We hope we can depend on competition to expose any and all instances of intentional false reporting. The Federal Trade Commission can, through its merger review process, see to it that no one company gains too big a share of the market. We can help you along these lines if you'd be kind enough to submit any information that your department has gathered that supports the denial of the merger on the grounds of anti-competitiveness. Other than that, Mr.

Secretary, I'm afraid our agency is not authorized to act on your concerns. We'll just have to depend on the wisdom of the American people to see through any attempts to phony up the news."

"Thank you for your time, Madame Chairwoman. I'll submit the information you've requested as soon as I can."

Ivan left the room and headed back to his office. He was sure now that the merger was bad for competition and bad for the country, and therefore should be disapproved by the Federal Trade Commission.

CHAPTER TWENTY-ONE

Geoffrey Lord Pressman was intrigued by the process of coming to terms with the challenge of sharing his life with a woman who was considerably younger than he was. One difference in their ages was summarized in their attitude towards the office. Geoffrey couldn't imagine not going to his office when there was work to be done, and Margo couldn't imagine going to the office if it was possible to do the work at home. The dividing line between a person beginning work PM (pre Microsoft) and one who began AM (after Microsoft) created a contrast that was even greater than the generation gap.

As they sat across from each other at the breakfast table, Geoffrey was conscious of Margo's ability to look appealing even though her hair was tousled and she had not yet applied her make-up. Susan could no longer manage that feat, and she needed a good bit of time to prepare herself to be seen at breakfast. Margo was natural and without affectation, and she was unreservedly ravenous, eating twice the amount that Susan would have eaten. He liked Margo's animal energy at home, but he believed that Susan was a more appropriate companion for him when he was in public.

This factor was the tipping point in his decision to send Margo back to America. He would enjoy her sexual services and employ her journalism skills, but he would do it in the U.S., where Margo's informal, laid-back style was more acceptable. The merger approval procedures demanded that he be present for questioning by the F.T.C. and F.C.C. hearings. He would appear with his chief counsel before the Commissions for as long as it took to get their consent. He was absolutely resolved to get the approval he needed to carry out the business coup that he had his heart set on. While the process was ongoing he told himself that there was no reason why he shouldn't make a survey of the talent he would be acquiring when the merger went through. It would also give him a chance to assess Margo's business aptitude in the same way that he had sampled her other talents.

"Margo, my dear, I'm going to America soon for a considerable amount of time and I'd like you to come with me. I have to appear at several hearings to defend the merger. While I'm there I'm going to try to do some talent scouting. You can be a big help. You know something of the way Thomaston ran his operation, and between the two of us we can decide who to keep and who will be redundant. Are you agreeable to that plan?"

"I hope you don't expect too much of me, Geoffrey. After all, I was only with Robert for a short time. But if you wish, I'll do everything I can to help."

"Excellent. I really suspect that you have unexplored talents that can delight us both."

"I can say that I'm a hard worker, a fast learner, and very ambitious, but I'm not particularly experienced."

"I can supply the experience, and you can bring the beauty and enthusiasm of youth. I've written an abbreviated version of a personal contract on this paper. You can read it after I've gone to work. My driver, Holmes, will take me to work and return in an hour. He will be at your disposal for the day. If you'd like to see London by limo you will find Holmes to be an excellent guide. I will expect you back here at five o'clock, at which time we'll get ready to go out for dinner. If you agree to the terms I've written out we can celebrate tonight. Now come here and give me a kiss goodbye."

Margo obediently gave him the requested kiss. When he had gone, she opened the neatly folded note that he had given her. On his personal embossed stationery she found the note that he had hand written with an ornate penmanship more commonly used a century ago than in the present age.

Margo Watson, the note read, *I am pleased to offer you a position as my personal secretary in the United States at a salary of U.S. $10,000 per month. Included in the compensation is the Pressman Corporation's normal executive benefit package, including health insurance, performance bonus plan, paid vacation, food allowance, and the use of an apartment in Washington, D.C. Either party may sever this contract at any time after one month's notice. Severance pay of one month's salary will be paid for every year of employment when the employer is the severer. Enclosed is a cheque for the first month's salary. Employment is to begin at once. If these terms are acceptable to you I will have a formal contract prepared. Geoffrey Pressman.*

Margo put the binding informal contract in her purse. She would have a copy made at some time during the day. In the meantime she dressed and prepared herself to see London as a pampered tourist with a personal guide and chauffeur. An hour later she was off to see the sights. Holmes delivered a surprisingly erudite historical lecture, explaining the importance of each of the famous places. Time didn't allow for lengthy museum visits, but wherever possible she made an effort to absorb the ambience of the city. She was surprised that most of the buildings were sparklingly clean. They had been sandblasted, Holmes informed her, in order to remove the grime of the centuries that had accumulated due to coal-fired furnaces.

She toured the city, seeing the sights mostly from the limo. She observed the large ravens that still inhabited the Tower of London grounds, and she understood how they had achieved their reputation as the monitors of impending doom for the prisoners inside the prison. The crown jewels, still guarded by Beefeaters in their colorful ancient uniforms, were historical oddities that daily continued to impress the thousands of tourists. The old walking bridges over the Thames gave the city a romantic charm that Margo thought was typical of many great cities whose origins were owed to their proximity to water-courses. Arterial rivers that transported the commerce of the centuries like blood through the cities, all shared this ambience. Paris, New York, Cologne, Cairo, Istanbul, Baghdad, New Orleans, Bangkok – all took life from the great water systems that had given birth to them and still continued to nurture them.

Buckingham Palace, Hyde Park, Kew Gardens, the British Museum, Trafalgar Square, and the new Canary Wharf development all materialized outside the limo's windows for Margo's enjoyment. Her eyes were busily drinking it all in, but her mind was focused on her new job.

Geoffrey hadn't spelled out her duties as his personal secretary. What about her writing? What authority did she have? If he were not challenged to define these things she would merely be a lackey mistress, although a well-paid one. She granted that it was a wonderful opportunity to move among the giants of the journalistic world. Even if she didn't have much power of her own she would receive an education at the highest levels, and these lessons would prepare her for the future. She was excited, she had to admit. As a pragmatist she also had to confess that her remarkable progress in journalism had come about not from her skill in that field of endeavor, but rather because of her looks. Margo was very conscious of the fact that her youth would fade. She had only a relatively short window of opportunity to develop abilities that could take over and keep her on top as her beauty faded. She resolved to further negotiate the terms of her agreement with Geoffrey in order to optimize her future opportunities. The flight to the States would be an ideal time to have this discussion with her boss-to-be.

Rafael Alvarez, because of his "Most Wanted" status, was being held without bail. He expected that would be the case. His trial was not of deep interest to him, as he was sure he would be convicted no matter what legal defenses were brought to bear. His intention was to escape before a verdict was rendered. He did, however, have to pretend that he cared, if only so as not to arouse suspicion. He had cut all his ties to Colombia, to his drug trade contacts, and to his family. His plan to retire and disappear with Margo had proceeded too far along, so he could no longer backtrack. Rafael had no idea what had become of Margo. He didn't suspect that she was going to turn him in. He believed the Bangkok police had just lucked out when they caught him in the net they had spread to collect perverts. He supposed that Margo had returned to the U.S. when he failed to show up. It seemed to him that it was just bad luck that the police had checked the Interpol wanted list and found him there.

Rafael could have attempted to escape from the rinky-dink jail in Bangkok, but he was sure the lame rap they were holding him on would go away when they realized that he was not a sexual deviant. He wasn't worried about Margo. He could look her up again later and pick up his plan where he had left off. Thailand was not a place to escape from – it was a place to escape to. Unfortunately, because of the blend of freedom, poverty, and corruption that existed there, a number of less than desirable foreigners had discovered the country and were rapidly turning it into child-porn world headquarters. Escape in Thailand, since he was obviously not an Asian, would be more difficult than in the American melting pot. He would stand out from the smaller, darker, local men of the country. It was better for a viper on the run to be among his own kind. A rattler would stand out in the land of the cobras, so Rafael meekly allowed himself to be shipped back to the States where he would blend in, and where he knew his way around.

The federal holding cells housed people waiting for federal charges to be laid against them. Anyone arrested by federal agents ended up in the basement cells of the Federal Court House while the over-worked U.S. Attorneys decided what to do with them. The prison population of the federal pen had a totally different demographic than state and city pens. In the land of the blind a one-eyed man is king, and in the land of prisons, the federal miscreants were kingpins.

Rafael was well aware that in general the criminals that shared his accommodations were of a different kind than the ordinary street lawbreakers, with one exception – the illegal aliens. Those who were caught entering the United States illegally, or for smuggling people across the border, tended to be ethnic Latinos. This was a population within which he could very nicely get lost.

During mealtimes Rafael spent his time studying the other men. He needed to find one who resembled himself. The candidate had to be reasonably intelligent, so he could understand what Rafael expected him to do, and he also needed to be a man who was convinced that he would be shipped back to Latin America in the near future. Hordes of aliens were intercepted by the INS, detained for a short time, and then shipped home. There were too many illegal immigrants to put in the available prison space, and it was too expensive to keep them all in jail. Drug traffickers were another thing altogether. These men would be tried, and if convicted, sent to jail for long sentences. So Rafael wanted to find a man who most resembled him, one who would most likely be released before the beginning of Rafael's trial, and one whose only crime was being an illegal entrant to the U.S.

Every mealtime he would seat himself next to a different man. During the meal Rafael would casually interview the man, seeking to find just the right one for the job he had in mind. Eventually he found the best candidate, and from then on he sat next to him at mealtime. Luis Santana was his name. He was from Chiapas, the rebellious Mexican state. He was a troublemaker at home and he had had to leave his city or face possible death from his enemies. He was attracted by the opportunities to make money in the U.S. and had paid a guide to smuggle him across the border. The guide, Luis, and several men who were with them were apprehended just a few feet inside the U.S. border. Luis was being held as a witness against the guide who was known by the Immigration Agents to be a people smuggler. As a deterrent to other human traffickers, the INS wanted to make an example of him. The U.S. government attorneys had offered to drop any charges against Luis, and send him back to Mexico in exchange for his testimony against the guide. He had agreed, and was waiting for the trial to start when Rafael met him.

Rafael's childhood desire to please his father by learning the locksmith trade had provided him with a useful skill. It had become as natural as breathing for him to look at every lock he came across and recall its mechanical functioning. Picking locks became his favorite boyish prank. He would playfully trick his father by opening locks that his dad had thought locked. His hardworking father thought his talented son would use his skill in the legal pursuit of the family trade, but that was not to be. The allure of fast money and the approbation of his peers led him step by step into the criminal world. By his teenage years Rafael had become the scourge of the local police. His advancement in criminality was like most careers based on personal merit. His good looks, quick thinking, strength, fearlessness, and brainpower had enabled him to become an overlord of the underworld in record time. Although eventually he learned to rely more on other skills, he always felt challenged by any kind of security device or enclosure that made him feel hemmed in.

The locks on the cell doors in the federal detention center were noteworthy for their size and strength, but undistinguished in their sophistication. Since the federal government had the most money, their cell locks were the first to be electrified, and then computer monitored. The government never seemed to tire of installing the latest in expensive gadgets while they simultaneously bragged about how careful they were being with the public purse. After witnessing all the versions of automated locking systems, some rare intelligent being in the Justice Department pointed out that in the case of a fire or some unpredictable natural disaster, all the prisoners would die if the electronics went on the fritz. After that simple criticism, a manual override was installed so that the locks on the cell doors could be opened in an emergency by using a key. Evidently the more things changed the more they stayed the same in the federal penal system.

Rafael Alvarez became aware of this flaw. He would play around with the locks when the guards were absent or occupied, and after a while he discovered the default and was able to open his cell door manually. He kept this skill to himself, for use at an appropriate future time. At lunch one day he sat next to his friend Luis and tried to discuss his plan of escape with him.

"Luis, listen to me, and listen carefully," he said, talking quietly. "You are here for a very minor infraction."

"*Ya lo sé, coño.* I already know this."

"Just shut up and listen," Rafael growled. "I'm not like you. You're just a petty thief, but I'm being held for several felonies. If they convict me, I'll be put away for life."

"What do you mean, I'm just a petty thief? I'm twice as good as a petty thief. You have no idea."

"Do you want to know how to make a pile of money, or don't you?" said Rafael, growing exasperated.

"I'm probably even ten times better…"

"In a matter of a few days," Rafael continued, "you'll be sent back to Mexico where you'll still be penniless."

"Penniless? Who are you to tell me this?"

"If you don't shut up I'll slit your worthless throat," the Viper hissed.

"Okay, okay. Take it easy, *mano.*"

"I'm the opposite of you. I'll have lots of money, but I won't be able to use it. So what I'm saying is that we should make our different situations work out for both of us."

"What do you mean?"

"I want you to pretend you're me for a little while, and I'll pay you $10,000 U.S. dollars."

"What are you talking about? You don't have that kind of loot."

"Not here, it's true, but I can give you a check drawn on a Mexican bank, and you can cash it in Tijuana."

"Why should I trust you, *mano?* Your frickin' check will probably bounce all the way to Tijuana."

"Let me put it this way. You spent money to pay a man to smuggle you into the States, and here you are in jail. So if you testify against him and send him to jail, do you think you'll you get a refund?"

"No."

"So do you get it? You came here to make money, and now you're being sent home without any. So far you're in a net loss position. I'm offering you your first chance to make your time in the U.S. pay, and all you have to do is trim your beard so it looks like mine, and pretend to be me for a day. I promise you on my mother's grave that my check is good."

"You probably put her in that grave yourself."

"Do you want me to help you or don't you?"

"What are you going to do while I'm being you?"

"I'm going to escape."

"Just like that you're going to escape from this jail," Luis said with a sneer.

"Yes. You'll see. Tonight I'll visit you in your cell to prove I can do it."

"Okay, *mano.* I'll believe it when I see it."

The men didn't sit together any more. Back in his cell the Viper rested and watched the guard at his desk at the end of the passage between the double lines of cells, each with its single prisoner locked inside. A few minutes to midnight the guard's shift ended and another guard arrived to replace him.

From his bunk Rafael had watched the same procedure take place every night. The new guard hung up his coat. He sat down and went over some papers that were on the desk in front of him. Eventually he took a paperback out of his coat pocket and began to read. Every hour he would walk around and punch a clock at the opposite end of the corridor. After the fourth pass he would disappear to eat his mid-shift meal for a half hour.

As soon as the guard left his post, Rafael sprang to his feet. He quickly picked the lock on the cell door using a piece of stiff wire that he had removed from the toilet tank. In the aisle between the cells he walked to the cell occupied by Luis Santana and picked that lock about as rapidly as he could have opened it using a key. He poked the sleeping man.

"Luis, wake up." He poked him again. "Wake up!"

Luis opened his eyes. Rafael put his finger to his lips to silence him. He picked up the man's shoes.

"Come with me," he whispered. He swung the barred door open silently and gestured for Luis to follow him. He led him to his cell and opened the door.

"Get in my bunk," he whispered.

He put the shoes down beside the cot and slipped a check for ten grand into the left one.

"Go back to sleep."

Rafael locked his cell door and quickly walked back to Luis's cell, where he arranged the bed so it looked as though someone was in it. Then he closed the cell door quietly so as not to awaken the other prisoners. He walked quickly to the guard's desk, removed the plastic I.D. card that was pinned to his hanging coat, and cast a glance back into the cell block to make sure that everything seemed normal.

Listening intently for voices or footsteps, Rafael moved gingerly up the stairs to the exit. He swiped the guard's card through the scanner device, and the door opened to let him pass. The guards on duty were eating their meal and noisily joshing with one another. They never even noticed the Viper slide by them.

Once he was out on the street, Rafael headed for the only place in Washington where he thought he could find shelter – Margo's apartment. His Rolex watch and his wallet with his cash and credit cards had been seized when he was arrested. Without money on him he couldn't even catch a cab, so he was forced to walk.

He had no idea if Margo would be home, but that was of secondary importance. He needed a place to hole up until he could arrange to get some money and identifying documents. Then he'd leave, with or without Margo.

He arrived shortly before daybreak at the address of Margo's apartment, which he had previously memorized. The door of the building was locked, of course, but it proved no match for Rafael's skills as a lock-picker. The door to her apartment was no problem for him, either.

Once inside Margo's small apartment, he quickly found his way to her bedroom. When he peeked inside the door he felt a pang of disappointment when he saw her empty bed. He looked around the rest of the apartment and found things in messy disarray, as if Margo had left in a hurry.

He searched the clothes closet to find a shirt that wasn't prison issue. The largest one was barely large enough to fit him, but it was the best thing he could find. It was a black sweatshirt with white printing on the front. He held it out in front of him and read, *God is dead – Nietzsche*. When he turned it over to slip it on he read, *Nietzsche is dead – God*. In spite of Margo's peculiar sense of humor, the shirt was preferable to the one that read *Department of Corrections*.

While he was in his prison cell Rafael had had plenty of time to think about the details of his escape. He got to work immediately to get himself some money. Several unsavory bankers in the Caribbean Islands were holding large amounts of cash on deposit for him. They were using the money to earn interest for themselves, which was okay with him as long as they maintained silence about the source of the cash.

Using an alias by which he was known to one of the bankers, he arranged to have some funds wired to a branch of the Wachovia bank in Washington, D.C. The next day he would go there and open an account, withdrawing some cash for his immediate use. In the meantime he would go to a neighborhood office of UPS and have them call Chicago to send a package being held for forwarding instructions to the Washington branch office post haste. He would return the next day to pick up the parcel, which contained several passports and other identification documents in various names, but all with his photo on them. Planning ahead to anticipate the unexpected was one of Rafael's strong points.

As far as Rafael could tell from the scraps of paper he found in the waste basket and lying around on various surfaces, Margo had gone to Bangkok as he had hoped she would. When their rendezvous failed to take place, Rafael thought she would return home to the States, but days were passing and he still had no idea where she was.

Using her apartment as his base, Rafael shopped for clothes, a suitcase, toiletries, and the other sundries he would need to travel to his next destination. He packed everything neatly and stood his luggage in the hall near the door. He was ready to make his departure on a minute's notice. In his spare time he searched every inch of Margo's apartment. He found her set of spare keys, which were helpful, as he didn't want to have to keep picking the locks every time he came in. Her laptop was gone, so his spying was limited to whatever papers he found lying about.

One night while he was killing time, Rafael found an unmarked envelope with some papers inside. When he looked carefully he realized it was Margo's notes for a story about what it had been like to be the kidnapped victim of the man who murdered Robert Thomaston. He read it carefully, and decided it was well written. Her observations about the perpetrator were of great interest to him. It was a sanitized version of the affair, but considering what she might have written, he was pleased to see that the article gave him the benefit of every possible doubt. He felt he had been right about his hold over her. She could still be trusted, at least to some extent.

CHAPTER TWENTY-TWO

D r. Ivan Welland's life had slowed down a bit with the capture of the Viper, and the knowledge that his team still had time to finish its investigation of the media. This gave him the opportunity to go home early enough to play with his daughter Julia before she was put to bed for the night. He was enjoying the second night in a row of this pleasure when his wife, Marina, pointed out to him that his beeper was sounding in his jacket that he had hung in the hall. Ivan looked at the display. It was Brooklyn calling, and she never called him at home unless it was an urgent matter.

"Brooklyn? It's Ivan. What's up?"

"Bad news, I'm afraid. The Viper has escaped."

"What? How could that possibly happen?"

"I've only got sketchy, second-hand information. You might want to go over to the Federal Court House and talk to the warden, or whatever they call the guy in charge of the jailhouse. I wouldn't bother you with this except that I think that someone in your pay scale will get answers faster."

"Okay, Brooklyn. I'll go right over there and raise the roof. Thanks for letting me know."

He announced to Marina that he had to leave, but that he expected to return in an hour. He ordered his car to be sent around. In a few minutes he was speeding through the dark city, heading toward the Federal Courthouse with the lights flashing.

He got out of the limousine before the driver could open the door for him. He took the long stairs in the front of the building two by two. In a flash he was standing in front of the uniformed male receptionist near the entrance.

"I'm here to see the person in charge of the detention center."

The man recognized the Secretary of Defense from the many times he had been interviewed on TV.

"Good evening, sir. You'll find him down those stairs. His office is to the right when you get down to the bottom of the steps. You can't miss it. There's a ton of people down there at this moment."

"Good. Thank you," Ivan said over his shoulder, as he took off in the direction that the man had indicated.

No sooner had he reached the bottom step than he heard the excited voices of people in the hallway. He headed in the direction of the commotion. At the doorway one man in the same uniform as the guards was fending off loud questions from several reporters shouting at him simultaneously. Ivan waded in, and because of his size, was soon at the head of the pack standing next to the chief guard. He turned to face the mob, and was immediately recognized. He raised his arms to still the clamor.

"Ladies and gentlemen, I don't think any of us will find out what has happened here if we all speak at once. I'm going to question this officer and as soon as possible we'll prepare a statement that will answer all your questions."

He turned his back to the crowd and shepherded the guard into the office, closing the door behind them.

"Whew. Thank you, Mr. Secretary, for rescuing me. I thought they were going to eat me alive."

"Believe me, I know what it's like. Now, suppose you start at the beginning and tell me what happened here?"

"This morning at around breakfast time the guard on duty discovered that a prisoner was missing. His cell was empty, but his bed was made to look as though someone was sleeping in it. A Mexican by the name of Luis Santana had occupied the empty cell. He was a material witness in an illegal alien smuggling case. There was no sign of the man, no damage, and no one was injured. We questioned the other prisoners, but they all claimed they didn't see anything. It was as if the man had dematerialized in the cell, and then materialized on the other side of the bars. We do know that he walked out of the building because he stole the guard's I.D. card and used it at 3 A.M."

"That was sixteen hours ago. How is it that I've only just been told about this?"

"It didn't seem important enough at the time. Santana was not known to be dangerous. His only crime had been to enter the country illegally. We dusted the cell lock for prints in an effort to find out if he had tampered with the lock, or if he had had any assistance escaping. But we found absolutely nothing. At first we suspected that the guard must have opened the cell door for him. It was totally weird."

"What does this have to do with Rafael Alvarez?" Ivan asked.

"Everything," the chief guard said. "Later when we got the fingerprint report back we found Alvarez' prints all over the door, but none of Santana's."

"That was strange."

"Yes, indeed. Finally one of the FBI agents decided to take the fingerprints of the guy in Alvarez' cell, and bingo! They were Santana's. That's when we realized it was Alvarez who had escaped, and not Luis Santana."

"What did Santana have to say about all this?"

"He claims it was like a dream. In the middle of the night he was moved from one cell to the other. He says he doesn't remember how he got there. He claims to have only seen Alvarez at meal times, and that he doesn't know him. Anyway, that's what he claims. It took us most of the day to figure it out, what with the print checking, questioning, and so forth. Excuse me for asking, sir, but what has this got to do with you, or the Defense Department?"

"It was our departmental intelligence that led the FBI, Interpol, and the Thai police to arrest Alvarez in the first place. He's a dangerous criminal who's wanted for several murders and a number of other felony crimes."

"We've got an APB out for Alvarez, but so far we've got nothing back. The guy just disappeared into thin air. He must have picked the locks, but we have no idea how he did it. No one has ever done it before."

"How did the newspapers find out about it?"

"I really don't know. They just showed up in the middle of it all. Mostly they're a pain in the ass."

"Okay then, let's prepare a statement for them. Maybe they can help us locate the escapee by putting his picture out and soliciting information from the public about his possible whereabouts."

Margo Watson looked out the window of Lord Pressman's jet airplane and marveled at the sight of the city of London spread out beneath her, still standing proudly in spite of the many enemies that had tried to destroy her through the centuries. It seemed a genteel city to her, but her people had always managed to change into warriors when they were attacked. The Armada, the Blitz, and now the terrorists, all had tried to defeat her, but there she stood, determined and unvanquished – one of the world's beacons of democracy.

She remembered her first trip in Robert Thomaston's private jet. She thought she had grown up a lot since then. She had played at being a young trollop because that was what Robert wanted. She was only a kid, and Robert had taken advantage of her innocence. But Geoffrey was kindlier, she thought, and she would also have a contract to protect her just in case things went sour. She wouldn't come away with nothing to show for it this time around.

The business world had supposedly changed its attitude to women, but in its deepest heart it hadn't really changed at all. It would allow women to work, to use their talents, and it would even pay them for their efforts (though usually less than an equivalent male), but they were never permitted to join the old boys' club. The new strategy of exclusion was even more insidious than the old. Basically it consisted of convincing women that what they wanted was what men had, and in order to get it they had to behave like men. As a result women became more unscrupulous and more sexually available, which is what the men wanted all along. Women were convinced that the whole thing had been their idea, and that they were gaining equality with men. While they were raising their economic expectations, they were also lowering their moral worth and paying for it with loss of self-respect. In coming down off their pedestals they gave up the high ground, winning a Pyrrhic victory for their sex.

Philosophizing was not one of Margo's strong suits, but she knew she was somewhere in the middle of the continuum of the gender struggles. She still had guilt feelings about having used her body to enter the world of the mind. And although she told herself that all women did it, she still felt her heart had been unaffected by her actions. Ivan Welland had sensed this about her, and his appeal for her cooperation would be based upon it. His e-mail message requesting her to get in touch with him was on her mind now that she was returning to the U.S. She resolved to call him as soon as she could after the plane landed.

"Margo!" Geoffrey's voice called her back from her reveries.

"Yes, Geoffrey."

"As soon as we arrive in Washington you should arrange to move out of your apartment and into the flat that I keep in your nation's capital."

"Very well," she said. She had already made up her mind that she would do it, not only because it would save her the rent money, but it would also put her near the corporate action that was intensifying as the merger date drew closer. Margo had understood from the first that there was a sexual component to her duties, and being a pragmatist about it she felt that aspect of things would be easier if she was in-house.

"For a few days I'm going to be tied up with my U.S. attorneys, so you can look after the moving details. You should go shopping and buy yourself some nice things to wear. You'll need them when we start the intensive travel schedule that will begin a week from today."

"Yes, of course. I can take care of those arrangements."

"Good."

"Geoffrey, this might be a good time to discuss some of the terms of my employment contract."

"It's not."

"It's not what?"

"It's not a good time to discuss it. You have my offer. I believe it's fair. I'll have it drawn up as soon as the lawyers have time, but right now they are totally occupied with the multi-billion dollar deal. We'll get to it in due time, just trust me for now."

"All right Geoffrey, but please don't forget."

While Pressman's jet winged its way over the Atlantic towards Washington, Dr. Ivan Welland and his investigative team were meeting to put the final touches on their report on the status of the media. The Secretary of Defense had access to the files of the military and the intelligence communities. He and his staff had organized the reports made by the U.S. officers on the site of many recent incidents, so they lined up with those reported by the press. They compared the details of fact such as dates, locations, participants, story sources, outcomes, and many other salient known points, matching them with one another.

David Feingold, the resident statistical and computer genius on Ivan's team, had worked out one of his marvelous algorithms that sorted and related events, spitting out the anomalies, stating the statistical probabilities, and producing a summary of the whole business of accurate news reporting. Abdul had done a survey of the Arab media, and his report confirmed that it, too, had begun to manufacture the news to suit its owners' positions on world events. What had once been laughably primitive efforts to hide defeats and promote pan-Arab Islamic nationalism had now begun to use Western media technology to convince their audiences that Allah, in his infinite wisdom, was turning the tide in favor of the Muslims. With their pockets full of oil money, Al Jazeera and Al Arabiya had become merely propaganda machines.

The input into David's computer had been enormous. The team had decided to use only the last year's events so that they would be fresh in people's minds. The data spewing out was painting a picture that, although not unsuspected, was absolutely conclusive. In a great number of instances there was practically no relationship between the events as reported by the media and those reported by government sources – military, diplomatic, and otherwise. The dates and sites of the event were often the only matching facts, while a novelist might just as easily have imagined everything else.

Determining the truth was going to be difficult. Could the team assume that the government's reporting through its chain of command was correct and the media's incorrect? David's statistical model included an error factor, but it was a mathematical calculation and didn't take into consideration the intention of manufactured inaccuracies. It seemed to the team that whether coming from the media or the military, the way an event was presented to the public was much more important than the event itself.

McLuhan was correct when he said that it was the media and not the message that was calling the shots. The op-ed pages of the newspapers and the broadcast commentators were choosing the issues to analyze and voicing the opinions of the media bosses. That was the fruit of free speech. It was to be expected of editorial policy, but what the framers of the constitution didn't anticipate was that simulations of reality would become so graphically representational that the audience, using only its common sense, could no longer tell fact from fiction.

The impure motives of the news reporters had come to supersede the truth. Those who worked for the government were primarily inspired to make themselves look good by spinning the news in such a way that the performance of their duties seemed flawless and praiseworthy. Those in the private sector had transitioned and now had begun to trample the traditional role of presenting events in favor of the new pro-active mode of reporting, in which they constructed events to suit their motives. Film studios had become the battlefields, actors had become the warriors, and greed was the insidious motivator that shaped all aspects of news reporting, leading to the brain-washing of the general public.

Ivan decided that he now had overwhelming evidence that the media needed to be reined in. He was ready to go to the President with his results. A policy would have to be formed to restrain the media's propensity for self-promotion and self-enrichment. The President's relationship with the media was the typically parasitic one that had governed that of most presidents since the invention of television. The presidents, in other words, were the warm bodies, and the reporters and cameramen were the swarm of mosquitoes that fed off them.

Ivan knew that the journalists were the most cynical lot in the nation, and he understood that they weren't his friends. Professionally they had long since given up trying to be neutral, thoughtful, or even-handed in their reporting. Instead, they had persistently pursued the nation's highest office holder with ill-hidden malice, seeking the scandalous bit of detail with which to assassinate the character of the man. Yet he needed the incredibly pesky horde in order to communicate with his constituents.

The relatively new Secretary of Defense was not exempt from the malicious scrutiny of the muckrakers either. The maxim that bad news sells newspapers applied to Dr. Ivan Welland as well as to the President, and the theory that if you bring down the boss's henchmen you eventually can bring down the boss, had now become a journalistic cliché. Ivan tried his best to stay out of the limelight and remain good-natured in spite of the cruel comments and unfair criticisms meted out by the media. He was an easy target for some reporters, who made fun of his being an academic who had never fought for his country in the military. They pilloried him for his height, which the cartoonists worked to death by presenting him as an exposed target symbolizing the American Defense Department's vulnerability. Ivan was at his best defending himself and his department in person. On TV he came across as witty and erudite. Interviewers and commentators quickly saw that his nimble mind, verbal skills, and calm, confident manner made him a killer debater, and after a short time no journalist would take him on when the cameras were working. His value to the government and its leader was growing apace.

Yet in spite of all the opposition, Ivan's department, in its support of the President's peace initiatives, was moving the nation and the world closer to a condition of peace and prosperity. The overt enemies of the President's peace policies were being contained in some places by reason, and in others by military force. The subversive enemies, however, were still roaming about seeking whom to destroy. The media barons, being deprived of their primary weapon, the TV, and with declining readership in newspapers due to incursions in the market by web bloggers, were being hurt in their most sensitive spot – their pockets.

Advertisers, too, migrated online. Competitive factors like the advent of national newspapers culled the surviving local newspapers back to the point where many U.S. cities were now dominated by a single newspaper. All of this had the effect of centering the control of the newspapers into fewer and fewer hands, making those who remained more powerful than ever. The merger of the Thomaston interests into the European-owned media holdings of Geoffrey Lord Pressman and Baron von Aragon typified the consolidations that were closing in on monopolies. A distinct line was being drawn in the sand between those who sought control of the press and those who opposed its falling into the hands of an ever declining number of media moguls. Leaders on both sides were girding their loins for the coming battle.

CHAPTER TWENTY-THREE

When Pressman's plane landed in Washington D.C., Margo was surprised to see Baron Fritz and his companion Hilde waiting for them. It was a sort of homecoming, and they were all jolly and glad to see one another. They drove in the stretch limo to the city center and headed for Geoffrey's penthouse apartment that was to be Margo's new home. Hilde was quick to inform Margo that she expected to spend a lot of time with her while they were in Washington. The thought of wasting time with Hilde was not a pleasant one for Margo, but she instinctively knew that Geoffrey wouldn't want any sort of schism to occur that could upset the merger.

The four arrived at the hotel in which Lord Pressman maintained his residence when he was in the United States. It was just off Dupont Circle, some blocks north of the White House. They were greeted by a very effusive concierge who welcomed Geoffrey Lord Pressman home, arranged to have the luggage sent up, and led them to the elevator.

Geoffrey pressed the button for the top floor, and the lift moved silently to its destination. When the door opened on the elegant private lobby that fronted the large entrance door to the Lord's flat, they all got out of the elevator and entered the apartment. Margo looked quickly around at her new digs and could hardly believe her good fortune. What surprised her most about the décor was its stark contrast to Geoffrey's town house in London that was furnished with the finest antiques. This apartment was decorated in the very best, most modern fashion. It was all glass, black marble, white furniture, and stainless steel.

Margo couldn't help thinking that the man who owned this place was a very different man than the owner of the London townhouse. It was hard for Margo to imagine that she knew this person, so different was this environment from the other. The stark contrasts between black and white, and the cold hardness of the satin polished stainless steel were unforgiving. It was tastefully decorated, but it was as cold blooded as the perfectly meshed gears of a big machine.

The living room was spacious, with three separate areas where small groups of people could converse without creating a din that would interfere with other conversations. Each area had a different hand-woven silk oriental carpet of museum quality. A raised area, up two steps, contained a baby grand piano. In the opposite corner was a sizeable bar, suitable for a professional barkeep. When not in use the bar had mirrored panels that unfolded at the touch of a button to close in the black marble counter. Bar stools swung out from the bar's skirt, but were totally hidden when not being used. The far end of the room led out to a commodious wrap-around balcony with a view from which the lighted Washington Monument and the Capitol Building could be seen as if they were the backdrop of a theater set.

Geoffrey had chosen to live on top of a hotel in order to avail himself of the hotel's services without having to maintain his own staff. As a result he was able to use room service for his meals, or if he chose, he could have catering services always at hand. A compact, but professionally equipped pantry kitchen, which could be entered from the balcony or the living room, was closeted in a corner. The apartment could under no circumstances be considered cozy, occupying the entire top floor of a large hotel as it did, but no one could ever say that it was not elegant. There were three bedrooms. Two were of equal size, with en suite bathrooms that had direct access to the balcony through sliding doors at the ends. The third was a spare bedroom for guests. It was obvious that Geoffrey planned to have his own bedroom separate from Margo's.

When Baron Fritz and Heide left, Geoffrey asked Margo if she would be comfortable in her new living quarters.

"Absolutely, it's fantastic."

"Good, then I think I'll turn in. I have a busy day, starting at seven o'clock tomorrow morning."

Margo thought that one of the advantages of having an older man for a lover was that he wasn't always in a state of perpetual heat, like most of the younger men she'd known. Her mind was busy thinking of the things she wanted to do the next day as she undressed, put on her Johnny shirt, and slipped between the black satin sheets. She was definitely going to take Geoffrey up on his offer to provide her with a shopping trip, but first she would return to her apartment to pick up some things and take stock of what she had in her closet. Taking a little visual inventory would also help her to decide what to buy to complete her poor little rich girl's wardrobe. It also occurred to her that she should call Dr. Welland first thing in the morning to see what he wanted.

Rafael Alvarez had received a liberal dose of American cash from his shadowy bankers. He was beginning to feel like his normal cocky self, now that he had purchased some nice clothes. His false passports, lock-picking tools, passkeys, credit and I.D. cards, and various other documents had arrived. One of his earliest efforts at making his way in the world of criminality had been as a car-jacker. Eventually he took over the business in Chicago on the strength of his talent as a locksmith. He became the inventor of the idea of custom stealing. His gang would take orders for certain cars, and he first, then his men, would steal the exact model and make of car to fill the orders, which were sold at half off the sticker price to the buyers.

He had already made his plans to leave the U.S. He still had two things to do: he needed to acquire a pistol, and he wanted to find out if Margo would be going with him. Rafael still had no idea where she was. It was he who had failed to show up, of course, but in his mind being in police custody was a good reason for Margo to forgive him. For all he knew she might still be in Thailand. He was prepared to wait, for the longer he waited, the colder his trail would become. After a while the cops would assume that he had made his escape, and they would eventually lose interest.

As for the gun, that was easy for a man with his talents. One afternoon, a few minutes before the second shift of policemen relieved the day shift cops, he took a walk to the nearest police station. The street in front of the station had been reserved for police cars. The Viper simply watched while the men going off duty got in their cars and left. The men on the second shift parked in the newly emptied spaces. Rafael made a mental note of the vehicles as he watched their owners disappear into the stationhouse.

Later, under cover of darkness, he went back and opened each car, using the passkeys that had been shipped in his box of goodies from Chicago. Wearing gloves so that his fingerprints would not be found, he waited until the street was empty, then he opened the car doors on the passenger side and reached in and opened the glove compartments. In one minute he had collected three guns. One even had a very nice holster that he could use to hide the weapon under his coat. He knew that off-duty cops liked to have a gun with them, and he knew they often kept them in the glove boxes of their personal cars for use in case of emergency. He relocked the cars after he stole the revolvers, and put the booty in the bottom of a shopping bag that he had brought along for the purpose.

Back in Margo's apartment he looked over his weapons cache and decided that cops must be poor, cheap, stupid, or inexperienced with fine pistols. His experience in gun trafficking had made him a connoisseur of weapons. No wonder the criminals were winning the battles on the streets, as they certainly had better guns than these. It crossed his mind that these guns might be unlicensed throwaways that the cops were using to make the killing of criminals look as though they had been done by the bad guys, when actually they themselves had executed a victim and didn't want to be bothered to do the paper work and go through the red tape involved in police-inflicted homicides. In any case, the guns were probably good enough to get him through until he got to his next safe house.

Pistol-toting uniformed policemen were armed with big black square-looking .45s. He guessed the cops visibly wore these on their hips as a deterrent in order to frighten perpetrators. Everyone knew that a .45 slug would make a large hole in a man, so the presumption must have been that the sight of the big guns would frighten criminals into passivity, but the professional crooks knew what most people didn't know, that you couldn't dependably hit the broad side of a barn with a .45 unless the shooter was very close to his target. The dumb cops would probably not even miss the guns he'd stolen for many days, he thought. Upon giving it a little further thought, he would have bet that the handguns, if not registered, would never even be reported as missing.

He was right.

Ivan Welland's team was busy writing their report. Ivan would take it to the President and go over the details with him. He was feeling itchy about the report because he felt it might come off as being Pollyannaish. After all, coming down on the media for not telling the truth was laughable when the source of complaint was the government, the same government that was always being accused by the media of lying. They were like two kids arguing back and forth. What was bothering Ivan was the fact that there really was no law being broken by the media's permissive view that their reporting of the news could be improved by creating the news to suit themselves. His department's report would serve to give an excellent picture of what was happening in the media business, but it would have no power of law to force any changes in their philosophy or their behavior.

His conferences with the commissioners of the FTC and the FCC had been helpful in clarifying what had to be done to keep the situation from getting worse. The merger could be stopped only by making the case that it was counter to the monopoly legislation and not by proving that they were liars. In other words, the media could continue to pass lies off as truth, but they wouldn't be permitted to do it unless others were allowed to do it to at least an equal degree. Ivan ranked the situation among the least impressive examples of the workings of the American democratic system. Like so many things that seemed at first to him to be dismal, time and further thought shone the light of brighter possibilities on the subject.

The Secretary of Defense leaned back in his swivel chair, put his hands behind his head, and looked up at the ceiling. When Brooklyn saw her boss in this position she knew that he was entering one of his solo think fests. So often the results of his reveries had led to the formulation of subsequently brilliant ideas, so Brooklyn always went into her full frontal protective mode and defended him against all interruptions, foreign or domestic. Phone calls were directed into his voice mail, and appointments were postponed. Time would pass, as much time as he needed, but disturbances would cease for the duration of his contemplations.

Ivan had based his plan for the resurrection of media news reporting on his idea that virtue must eventually prevail. He believed that temptations to alter the truth for political, personal, or economic reasons must be trumped by the moral imperative to report the truth that makes people free. Welland was convinced that when all his evidence was presented, the legislators would see the light and create inspired laws that would control the mass communication of fiction being presented as fact to the public. He now realized that he had been naïve. Neither the government nor the media was the slightest bit interested in girding up the precepts of *truth triumphant* in news reporting. Dr. Welland saw the laws about truth in advertising and he wanted to do something similar for news reporting.

If the principle of *caveat emptor* was strong enough to warrant laws to protect the consumer from buying a pig in a poke, then why wasn't the assault on the public's mind and spirit by cynical, lying media barons worth similar legal protection? In Ivan's mind this was criminal activity on a very high level and should be dealt with accordingly. His opponents would immediately trot out the First Amendment to defend their positions. They would dig up the old philosophical arguments about what is truth, and fight tooth and claw to see that things remained unchanged, not because they were righteous, but because they had loopholes which they could exploit. He chuckled to himself when he recalled W.C. Fields' comment when he was asked why he was reading the Bible. The comedian had answered that he was looking for loopholes.

The Constitution, unlike the Bible, was man-made and had provisions for its amendment. The founding fathers could not have anticipated the instantaneous transmission of the news of world events. Until Orson Welles converted the fiction of H.G. Wells' *War of the Worlds* into a radio news broadcast, who would have thought that the fiction about a Martian invasion could create mass panic? Ivan knew that in today's real-time TV news environment a broadcast of, say, a fictional nuclear explosion in Pakistan would immediately have everyone in the United States cowering under his desk. A broadcaster could easily insert footage of the Hiroshima explosion into his photo-journal report, and a fictional nuclear bomb detonation suddenly becomes reality. There were enemies of democracy in the world who would dearly love to make their dreams of a world without the Western democracies in it become a reality, especially if they could do it with words and photos. How much cheaper that would be than the cost in blood, bombs, and bullets!

Perception had indeed become reality, yet Ivan had found that no way existed to make the law the guardian of the public's right to the truth. It seemed that everyone was counting on competition to be the judge, as though having a half a dozen different views of the same event would guarantee that the truth would somehow prevail. Apparently no one in government was old enough to recall the Japanese movie *Rashomon,* in which four separate witnesses describe the same murder from entirely different points of view.

Ivan could completely understand why believers wanted to have a single source of inerrant instructions for them to live by. In the end Ivan had to admit that as a pragmatist he was going to have to work with the less than perfect tools he had on hand. In the immediate future he could see only two courses of action open to him, although neither was completely satisfactory. He would oppose the merger with its tremendous capacity to reduce competition, and he would publicize the findings of his team. Lifting the stone so everyone could see what crawly things were living under the rock of free speech would help keep the media honest, but it wouldn't stop them in their tracks.

Ivan suddenly sat bolt upright in his chair.

"Brooklyn, could you come in here a minute, please?"

"Yes, boss?" she said, appearing at the door.

"Could you make an appointment for Margo Watson to see me some time this afternoon? I think she might be able to help us do something about this media merger. But I'll need to talk to her first."

"Sure, boss. You're free at one o'clock."

"Perfect. See if she can stop by at that time," he said, sinking back into his reverie once again.

CHAPTER TWENTY-FOUR

The first sentence of the Preamble to the Constitution of the United States speaks about the efforts of the American people to form a more *perfect* union. Ivan Welland held no other aim higher than that one, unless it was to form a more perfect world. Sometimes it seemed to him that the President was the only one on his wavelength. The members of his team came close, but even those stalwarts occasionally had trouble understanding his point of view.

The time for his meeting with the President was fast approaching. Ivan had gathered all the materials that his team had produced and he was on his way from his office in the Pentagon to the White House to show them to the leader of the Western world. Perhaps the President would give him some fresh insights.

"Well, hello Mr. Secretary, how are you?" the President greeted him. "How are Marina and little Julia?"

"Everyone is fine, sir, and thank you for asking,"

"And the country? Are we safer now than when we took office?"

"Yes, sir. I believe I can safely say that we are. We've shut down the largest ammo and explosives manufacturing facilities according to your orders. Many nations have voluntarily cooperated, and our forces have persuaded those that haven't to comply. In a peculiar way I think it has been a perfect use of our military strength. The new world situation has led to smaller, but more numerous operations. We've reorganized ourselves into many smaller tactical units, as opposed to a few massive armies. We've recruited and trained our men and women to fight smarter, and to take responsibility for more specific objectives. Morale is high, and working in smaller groups to perform more specific tasks has resulted in many operational efficiencies. But you already know this, I'm sure."

"I do. Please extend my thanks to the Chiefs and all who serve under them. Now, tell me why you wanted this special meeting."

"Well sir, to put it bluntly, we seem to be involved in another kind of war. In this one the weapons are words and images, and the combatants are not nations. Our enemies are cowardly by martial standards, but if anything they are more insidious, and consequently very dangerous."

"I'm not sure I understand. Who are these enemies?"

"The media, sir."

"I agree they are annoying, always looking at the dark side of things and trying to create dissension for the purpose of selling newspapers, but I never really thought they were conducting a war."

"Let me show you some research that my investigators have come up with," Ivan said, as he passed the summary of the team's findings across the President's desk. "I think the most salient point in this report is that the media have become proactive under the direction of their top executives. They no longer wait for news to happen. They're now using powerful communication technologies to manufacture the news to suit their purposes."

"Are you saying that the news reports we see and hear are fudged? In other words, they never happened? They're just made up?"

"Yes sir. In all cases the news is vetted and pre-digested to a greater degree than ever before, and in many cases it is entirely concocted. Information technology has advanced to the point that a movie can seem so real that the media moguls no longer wait for stories to break, they just write them, refer to their film clip catalogue, select the pictures they like from their library, and insert them as though they were current."

"So perception has become reality, is that what you're saying?"

"Exactly, Mr. President. You'll see from our report that the consolidations that have occurred in the media business have put control of the press in fewer and fewer hands. The same companies that own broadcasting and publishing subsidiaries now own the movie companies as well. We have begun to see fictional films that pretend to be news, but are essentially propaganda. They're so real, thanks to the new electronic technologies, that we can no longer visually separate the truth from fiction. Film libraries have been automated and information categorized to the point where we can extract scenes from previously filmed sequences and upload them into the daily news reports. Digital information technology now permits real-time audio-visual editing, and in a practical sense they can put any words they like into your mouth and broadcast them over their networks in moments."

"My Lord. Who are these guys?"

"Our original investigation started with Thomaston's enterprises. Robert Thomaston was the leader in this movement, but as you know, he recently died. Consequently his organization is up for grabs, and Lord Geoffrey Pressman and Baron Friedrich von Aragon are at this moment trying to acquire it. This would move control of our American press offshore and into the hands of foreigners. These two men were known to be associates of Thomaston and they plan to continue to operate using his corporation as a template for theirs. The FTC is reviewing this acquisition at the moment. With your permission, I'd like to oppose the take-over."

"That seems like an essential step, but are we going to run into First Amendment problems if we're seen to be interfering with the operations of the free press?"

"I'm sure they will trot that argument out, Mr. President. I'm also sure that the founding fathers never anticipated the technologies that have enabled this travesty to exist. I don't think they ever imagined that the press would, or could fabricate phony world events, and make them believable by producing such technically perfect films to simulate the truth. At the root of all this is the question of whether there is a moral imperative for the media to tell the truth, or are they really in the entertainment business?"

"You say that the FTC will hear this case?"

"Yes sir, Mr. President. It's on their docket right now. Unfortunately we have to fight this battle on grounds other than their failure to tell the truth to the public. As of the moment we have no basis in law to oppose the merger of these media giants on those grounds. Our approach has to be to fight it on the premise that this merger would upset the normal competition that exists in this segment of the economy and would create a nominal monopoly if it's allowed to proceed. If this tactic is successful perhaps we can avoid the First Amendment issues that the ACLU and others will raise. My position is that in granting the freedom of speech the government is not issuing a license to lie. There is an expectation that the speech will be truthful, or if not, the audience should be warned if it is hearing opinions or fictions."

"I see what you're saying," said the President. "But aren't there some guidelines for the news media to follow? Generally I feel these things are done best when they're self-governed rather than imposed by the government."

"I agree, sir, but in this case the industry association must be asleep, or they are loath to clamp down on the hand that feeds them. The large companies pay dues proportional to their sales, so the media giants are their bread and butter. I'm hoping that the publicity attendant on the proposed M & A will, if we win, encourage them to improve and enforce their own standards."

"Very well, Ivan. Let's keep our eyes open. I don't want my administration to be buried under the lies of the media. It's bad enough as things are."

"Right, sir. I'll lean on the FTC as hard as I can, and then if we win, I'll make a little pilgrimage to the supposed hallowed halls of broadcast virtue monitoring, and if I have your support, perhaps they can be persuaded that it is in their own best interest to have their members report the news truthfully."

"Good. Have you anything else for me, Mr. Secretary?"

"No sir, that's it. Thank you, Mr. President."

Ivan wanted his government to do something besides try to get reelected. He knew this President felt the same way. Personally taking over the control of worldwide explosives manufacturing was proof positive that the leader had a steel spine. Powerful enemies, however, were not pleased by his policies. Magnates in the defense industry, potentates in the third world, and terrorists everywhere were seeing red as their sources of money, power and weapons dried up. All the intelligence agencies had been on red alert to sniff out potential plots against the President before they came to fruition. The media barons were not happy either. Armed conflicts were decreasing in number dramatically, and with it the gory news that sells papers and captivates TV audiences. Ivan suspected that the German Baron and the British Lord were growing more and more interested in pushing their merger through in order to increase their market share of all the news that was fit to invent.

Margo Watson had confirmed her one o'clock meeting with Ivan, but first he needed to clarify in his mind what he wanted from her. He still felt that there had to be a written agreement between the three media giants that dealt with the terms of their understanding. He was sure that they would agree with the comment attributed to Sam Goldwyn, that a verbal contract wasn't worth the paper it was printed on. He wanted to see if Margo could find the document that Baron Fritz and Lord Pressman must have signed. Ivan was also worried that she was unaware that Rafael Alvarez had escaped, and might be at large in Washington. He would have to tell her. He would watch her reaction to see whether she was afraid, or happy, or if she already knew. These and other things were on his mind, but his greatest concerns were whether he could trust Margo, and whether she'd be willing to help him put a stop to the merger and help to recapture the Viper.

Baron Fritz couldn't wait to host Lord Geoffrey and Margo Watson again. It would bring back old times, when the three veterans of the publishing wars had first gathered together on the *Sternlicht*.

The Baron featured himself as some sort of naval hero. He lived aboard his little ship and loved every minute of it. His paid captain and crew had guided the vessel across the Atlantic and up the Potomac to the Capital Yacht Club. The large yacht strained the capacity of the facilities, which normally hosted yachts to a maximum of 220 feet.

The beautiful yacht was an eye popper wherever she went, and the Baron loved to see people on neighboring yachts enviously looking at his pride and joy. Although his company owned a perfectly adequate airplane that was suitable for the transatlantic flight, Fritz preferred to use the yacht. He claimed that plane flights over the ocean were too soon over *und* the jet lag too *stark*. On a yacht one had a chance to acclimatize oneself more gradually to the time and weather changes. Living aboard made packing unnecessary, and he hated packing with a passion, so there he was on his floating mansion within sight of the most famous tourist spots in the United States. He and Hilde could just walk off the yacht and into the heart of Washington, D.C.

Fritz wanted Geoffrey and Margo to live on board the yacht with him, but Lord Pressman had his penthouse and preferred to live there. He did agree to the occasional visit and meal aboard the yacht in order to placate his friend and business associate. Margo was not consulted about the social schedule. She was expected to come and go as she was told, and to look beautiful while doing it. As a result of all these arrangements she had not been given time to go to her own apartment. One of the expectations Geoffrey had of her was to entertain Hilde by taking her sight-seeing.

Hilde was not much of a tourist, however. She didn't care about buildings and architecture, and history was only vaguely interesting to her. While the men were tied up with their lawyers and advisors, the ladies were free to do as they wished. What Hilde was most interested in were physical conditioning, bodybuilding, and shopping.

Margo took her to a spa so she could see for herself the difference between the American spas and the European ones. Neither the Watson family nor the fates themselves had prepared Margo for the extravagances lavished upon ultra-rich women on both sides of the Atlantic. Margo was pleased to be able to keep Hilde occupied in a way that satisfied her, without having to exhaust herself by taking her on long a shopping spree. Her perfect, powerful body was to Hilde what his yacht was to Fritz. She was an exhibitionist, and delighted in showing herself off to one and all. She was fawned upon in every gym, spa, and health club that Margo took her to.

"Hilde, I've got an important business appointment to keep this afternoon," Margo said. "We've been so busy I haven't even had a chance to pick up my mail, and there are also a few things I'd like to get from my apartment."

"Vell, I could go dere und get your tings vile you do ze business."

"That's very kind of you," Margo said, after thinking about the disadvantages of letting her see what a poor girl she really was. "I warn you that you may be shocked by my little place. I never lived the life of a plaything of the rich and famous before Robert came along and changed things. I had a lease and he died before I could sublet my pad. I was glad to have the place then," she added, with a smile.

"Ya, vell I vasn't born with silber spoon too. It's goot to have own place to go to."

Margo gave the address of her apartment to the limo driver, whom Geoffrey had engaged to drive them around Washington. Margo got out and hailed a cab to take her to the Pentagon for her meeting with Ivan, and Hilde went on to her apartment in the limo. She felt fortunate that Hilde had not pumped her too vigorously to tell her where she was going to do business. She didn't exactly know why she felt lucky to have kept her destination a secret from Hilde, but that is how she felt.

The tall Secretary of Defense rose to greet his visitor.

"It's nice to see you again, Miss Watson," he said.

"It's a pleasure to see you, Mr. Secretary."

"Please have a seat. Would you like coffee?"

"No coffee, thanks."

"Miss Watson, I'd like to thank you for identifying Rafael Alvarez as the Viper, but unfortunately I must tell you that he managed to escape."

"I'll bet they'll never catch him in all those Thai jungles. That's too bad, and after all that trouble."

Margo's surprise at hearing the news of the Viper's escape, and her assumption that it had happened in Thailand were an indication to Ivan that she had not seen or heard from the fugitive since her visit to Bangkok. Ivan took this as a good sign, but now he wanted to see how she would react to the rest of the information regarding the Viper.

"Miss Watson, I'm sorry to inform you that Alvarez escaped here in Washington D.C. We had him extradited from Thailand to the U.S. to face charges, but before the Grand Jury could meet, he got away. We're not sure how he managed it. One morning he was just gone, and another prisoner was in his cell. We've put out an APB, of course, but so far he hasn't been spotted. You wouldn't have any idea where he might be, have you?"

"No, of course not. Do you think he knows that it was I who identified him in Bangkok?"

"I hope not, but we can't be sure, so we're going to take every precaution to protect you."

Margo was not impressed. How much protection could she expect to get from the people who had let Rafael escape after they already had him under lock and key? She was quite perturbed and did nothing to hide it. Ivan understood how she felt, but he needed her to be strong so they could work together to recapture Alvarez. Margo's justifiable anger at finding out that Rafael had escaped, and the ensuing fear it inspired, convinced Ivan that she was being honest with him. He felt inclined to pursue his plan to attempt to recruit her as an inside ally in his fight to kill the pending monopolistic media merger .

"Dr. Welland, I think I should tell you that I've just accepted a job with Lord Pressman's company. He has promised to publish all my stuff, and give me management experience with the new U.S. division which will be formed if the merger goes through."

"Miss Watson, you seem to have an enormous proclivity for getting yourself into dangerous situations. Thomaston, Alvarez, and now Pressman. Are you a self-destructive thrill-seeker?"

"I don't see myself that way. I'm just taking advantage of an opportunity to advance my career. Do you think I've made a mistake?"

"I can only quote you something that Paul Valéry once wrote at the end of the nineteenth century. *The folly of mistaking a paradox for a discovery, a metaphor for a proof, a torrent of verbiage for a spring of capital truths, and oneself for an oracle, is inborn in us.* He was right about that. We all have our faults, but premeditated lying is more than just a human failing. I believe that those who trade in lies are people to be avoided."

"Are you suggesting that I avoid my new employer, Mr. Welland?"

"No, not at all. I had something entirely different in mind. I think this is a situation that can be fixed."

"And, assuming you're right about Lord Pressman's intentions, how can the situation be changed or fixed?"

"Well you could, short of inspiring a major conversion in Pressman's morals, do what you can to prevent spreading his lies into our country," said Ivan.

"Let's just say that I sympathized with your position, what would I have to do?"

"You could try to find the agreement that Pressman, von Aragon, and Thomaston concluded. If I could get a copy of that document, I believe I could get the U.S. government authorities to reject the merger, and do it in such a way that you won't lose your job," Ivan said.

"I don't see that as a possibility. If there is no merger there is no job for me."

"That's possible, but you could still be a freelance writer, or perhaps his U.S. Bureau Chief."

"Yeah maybe, but if Geoffrey gets a whiff of my part in sinking his dream I'll be lucky if he doesn't have me killed."

"True, but do you want to work for a guy like that?"

"Maybe not, but I do have to earn a living, and I do want to remain alive. What have you got to offer me that compares to that?"

"First let me ask you a question. Why did you choose to become a journalist?"

"I decided to work on the school newspaper when I was in high school. I really liked my English classes, and writing came easily to me, and I was interested in current events, so I went to university and majored in journalism. Then I got a job as a cub reporter on one of Robert Thomaston's papers. Mike Slayton was my boss back then. I learned a lot from him, but when I met Robert I became exposed to the media business as it was conducted on the highest echelons. Each step I made propelled me further up the ladder. Now I have reached the point where some of the most important people in journalism are aware of me and my work. That's how I got into journalism. It was quite conventional, really."

"I understand. But you've been unusually successful for your age, and your route to the top has been meteoric. What do you attribute that to?"

"I don't know, some ability and some good breaks, I suppose," Margo said, trying to appear humble but knowing full well what the secret of her success had been.

Ivan also knew that her remarkable climb to success was due in large measure to her attractiveness and how she had used it. He had seen it personally a hundred times and he knew exactly how it worked. He could have written a novel about it.

"Young, intelligent, beautiful girl attracts the attention of opportunists who desire her. Seduced by the one who most cleverly handles her, she is told of her great talent and potential, with no reference to her looks. When the opportunist is through with her, or confronted with a new opportunity, she is left to consider what went wrong. She comes to the conclusion that it was really her looks that attracted him, and decides to make them work for her in the future. Her plan does work, and she has many affairs. She finally decides she is getting nowhere by focusing on her physical charms, so she changes directions and concentrates on her other talents. She learns that though she has other abilities they aren't sufficiently great by themselves to lift her to the top. To satisfy her ambition she finds she must use both her looks and her talent. She is older now, and her looks are now not as fresh as they were. What to do?"

Ivan Welland's knowledge of Margo's personality was not really born of a novelist's imagination. He had the facts. His agents had followed her and reported to him about her affairs. His staff had researched her background and her history. He didn't need to connect the dots with India ink. And he certainly was not about to accept her construct of its being luck. She had had altogether too much luck for it to be just luck.

His demeanor changed as he realized that he was going to have to be tough on this young woman if he was going to help her abandon the banal path she had chosen, and also get her to cooperate with him for the good of the nation. If he couldn't influence her or persuade her to exchange her petty ambitions for the lofty ones he espoused, then he would simply have to use the force of his position.

He had maneuvered her into identifying the Viper, now he would have to make her turn on Pressman.

CHAPTER TWENTY-FIVE

At the very same time that Margo was undergoing a psychological battering from the Secretary of Defense, Hilde was having a life and death battle of her own. The chauffeur hired by the Baron had driven her to Margo's apartment. Hilde used Margo's key to open the door, and as soon as she stepped inside she felt a strong hand cover her mouth. An arm pinned her arms to her side, while a foot pushed the door closed.

"Who are you?" said a voice behind her.

"I am friend of Margo," Hilde replied. "Who are *you*?"

"Where is Margo?" Rafael demanded.

"She stays with her other friend now," Hilde said, hoping to anger the brute with her vagary.

"Where would that be?" the Viper growled, as he spun her around to look at her.

"Why should I tell you? If you are a friend, you should know where she is."

Hilde spat her accented words into Rafael's dark and handsome face.

"You should tell me because I asked, and because if you don't tell me, I will beat it out of you," he said, staring icily at the beautiful blond woman who had dared to stand up to him.

"Maybe you are friend of Margo, maybe not. How I know? She tells me nothing about you."

Hilde half shouted her response as her perfectly coifed hair vibrated with her angry head movements.

"Believe me, I know Margo," Rafael said with a leer. "What are you doing here, anyway?"

"I come to pick up mail and get clothes for friend, is all. What *you* do here?"

"I'm waiting for Margo."

"Why she did not tell me you are here?"

"She doesn't know. It's a surprise," Rafael said, taking a good, long look at the unexpected visitor.

"I go now and pick up letters," Hilde said, trying to push past him.

"Not so fast. How do I know that you're not armed or wearing a wire? I'm going to search you," he said.

"I search you first," Hilde said in the husky voice that always worked with Fritz.

What followed was a monumental struggle, a battle of mythic proportions, encompassing levels of psychological warfare and combat by trained mixed martial arts fighters. Rafael had never encountered a woman so large, so strong and fit, and with such a will of iron. Both Rafael and Hilde had been pre-programmed genetically to dominate. Neither of them could imagine a situation in which they wouldn't be in complete control.

Halfway through the battle Rafael offered the German woman an out if she would tell him where Margo was, but she wouldn't betray her friend. The Viper put his arm across her throat and with his entire weight on top of her, he shut off her airway and watched her death throes with the deep, triumphant satisfaction of a man who was beyond psychotic.

Ivan Welland thought that Margo Watson was actually little more than a child. Her beauty had betrayed her in the beginning because men had taken advantage of her. Lately she was betraying her beauty by using it to take advantage of men. He was not her psychiatrist, however, and any help she needed from that quarter would have to come from someone else.

What he didn't know about Margo was that she had been consciously struggling with self-knowledge for a long time, and finally had come to understand her situation clearly. She had for some reason begun to use Ivan as her yardstick for measuring important men. He had always been truthful with her, treated her like an equal, never flirted with her, and his humility was noteworthy, coming from a man in his position. What he was asking of her was perfectly reasonable – he was asking her to help him catch a murderer, help him repel a media monkey who was trying to increase his power to spread lies, and help him clean up her chosen vocation of journalism, and in these ways also serve her country.

The life she had had among the rich and famous hadn't really made her happy. The private planes, yachts, houses, and the lack of money worries were impressive, but on a deeper level she had to admit these things didn't bring her happiness. She got more career satisfaction out of writing than from imagining herself in a high managerial position. She wasn't power-driven like Robert Thomaston or Geoffrey Pressman. Being a sexual plaything for older men had no long-term potential, and it kept her from finding someone she could really love. She counseled herself that when her looks waned, her career would follow suit.

Margo was at the entrance to the Pentagon waiting for a cab when her cell phone rang.

"Hello?"

"Margo, it's Fritz. I've been calling Hilde and she doesn't answer her cell phone. Is she with you?"

"No, but I know where she is."

"Where?"

"Well, I had an appointment to keep and Hilde, in order to save me some time, was doing me a favor by going to my old apartment to pick up my mail for me. Then we were going to do some more girl stuff."

"When she didn't answer her phone I called the driver. He said he was waiting outside the building for Hilde to come out. I asked him to go inside and ask Hilde to turn her cell phone on so I could talk to her. That was fifteen minutes ago and neither Hilde nor the chauffeur has called me back."

"That's peculiar, Fritz. I'll take a cab right over there and see what's going on."

"We've finished our meetings for the day. Geoffrey went home to change, and we were going to meet you girls and have a meal together."

"That sounds nice. I'll call you back as soon as I'm with Hilde and we can arrange to meet."

"No, better than that," Fritz said, "give me your address and I'll catch a cab and meet you there. Then we can all take the limo and pick up Geoffrey."

"OK, its 512 M Street Northwest, Apartment One. It's on the first floor. I'll see you there in half an hour."

Inside the wrecked apartment, Rafael Alvarez had taken a shower and changed his clothes, leaving Hilde's body on the bed. In response to the call from Baron Fritz, the driver rang the bell of Apartment One, listed in the name of Watson, and waited for a reply. The buzzer sounded to open the door, so he entered. He had expected a voice to come over the intercom, and he was prepared to ask if the lady wanted him to continue to wait for her. He walked to the apartment door, pushed the bell, and waited.

"Who is it?" said a man's voice from inside.

"It's Miss Hilde's chauffeur. Does she still want me to wait for her?" he said.

"Come in, please. You can help her with her parcels."

The apartment door opened and the chauffeur entered. The Viper stepped out from behind the door, put a pistol in the driver's back, and slammed the apartment door.

"Walk. Into the bedroom to the left."

The driver did as he was ordered. When he saw Hilde's naked dead body on the bed he recoiled in shock, but the insistent poking of the gun in his back moved him to the foot of the bed.

"Take off your jacket," said the Viper. "Now drop your pants. Drawers too."

As soon as he had complied the Viper put the gun to the back of his head and shot the man in his favorite place, at the base of the skull. The force of the shot propelled the driver forward over the foot of the bed and down on top of Hilde's body. The Viper wiped the handle of the gun on a sheet to remove his prints, and placed the pistol in the dead woman's hand.

To an inexperienced observer it would look as though the chauffeur had been attacking Hilde and she had managed to shoot him before she expired. Rafael knew that an adept crime scene investigator would eventually figure it out, but while the forensic evidence was being analyzed in the lab he would have time to find Margo. In the jumble of clothes he found Hilde's purse. He pulled her cell phone out of the bag and stuck it in his pocket. He put on the holstered gun that he had stolen from the policeman's car. Alvarez took a last look around, and left the building.

When Rafael was across the street and halfway up the block he saw a cab pull up in front of Margo's building. Margo jumped out of the cab and went inside. A minute later another cab pulled up and a rotund gentleman got out and went inside too. Rafael continued on down the street and went into a Starbucks coffee shop. He positioned himself so he could see Margo's house in the distance and slowly sipped a latte. Shortly a police patrol car showed up, then another, and afterwards an ambulance. Rafael thought for a moment his handiwork had been flawed. Why would an ambulance be sent? The victims were dead, weren't they?

Time passed and Rafael ordered a pastry and another latte. He continued his surveillance. The number of vehicles in front of the house had grown until the attraction of the flashing lights were irresistible to pedestrians who were accumulating on both sides of the street in an effort to find out what was going on. The media had evidently heard about the murders and camera trucks were now discharging reporters and cameramen. The coroner's black Ford had now arrived.

Rafael fixed his attention on the scene. Margo and the man who had pulled up in the cab were still inside. After an hour, three gurneys, with lumpy, sheet-covered cargos were rolled out of the building – three of them. Three? Were the corpses multiplying? Then a long black limousine arrived. The chauffeur opened the back door and an effete older man stepped out and walked self-consciously to the entrance of the building.

In a few minutes he came out again, with a protective arm around Margo's shoulder. They got into the limo and drove away. This was a signal to Alvarez that the focus of the investigation was moving to the police station. He left the shop, walked to the corner, and grabbed a taxi. He had the driver take him to the Marriott Hotel, but he didn't go in.

Instead, he found a nearby upscale luggage store with a haberdashery next door. He bought himself a suitcase and took it into the clothing store. He purchased a sports coat, slacks and a few shirts, and had the clerk pack them into the case. While the clothing was being packed he called the Marriott and made a reservation in the name of Señor Miranda. He liked that name because the failure of the police to properly read him his Miranda rights had provided him with several opportunities to avoid prosecutions for crimes he was guilty of committing. He strode into the hotel with his new snazzy luggage and checked himself in.

During the time he had lived in Margo's apartment, Rafael had had time to carefully snoop into every corner, and read every scrap of paper that she had left behind. From her most recent phone bill, which he retrieved from her mailbox, he saw several calls to London. By calling the numbers in London he found that they were both the office, and personal phones of a Geoffrey Lord Pressman. Using a ruse, he was able to get an employee to tell him that Lord Pressman had flown in his private jet to Washington, and was staying in his apartment in the Diplomat Hotel.

He pulled Hilde's cell phone from his pocket, fiddled with it for a moment or two, then flashed up her screen of most often called numbers. In the first position was Fritz. Other listings were displayed for Margo and Geoffrey.

He idly turned on the television in his room while he considered what his next step would be. He was only mildly surprised to see a reporter standing in front of Margo's apartment building, describing a horrible scene within. A scene which had resulted in a massive coronary to the fiancé of the dead woman, who had identified the victim as his betrothed. The audience was informed that the names of the victims were being withheld pending notification of their families.

The fiancé, however, was recognized by reporters at the crime scene as Baron Friedrich von Aragon, the German media tycoon. Rafael recognized that his little Margo had once again risen to the top of the social ladder in the media business. Her fancy associations didn't hide the fact that she had probably been the one who fingered him in Bangkok, and she must be made to pay for that.

The Viper focused on the story that the TV reporter was relating, which was composed entirely of speculations and assumptions. The media hadn't the slightest idea of what had transpired in Margo's apartment, but they had enough conjectural information to fill hours of airtime with nonsense about the killings.

Even so, Rafael did learn a few things that he hadn't known from the reporter's original story. He learned that von Aragon had a huge yacht that he was living aboard at the Capital Yacht Club's marina. He also learned that the svelte gentleman that came to pick up Margo was Geoffrey Lord Pressman, a friend and business associate of the Baron's. The two men were reported to be in Washington to defend their proposed purchase of the Robert Thomaston media interests at hearings before the FTC.

Rafael almost choked with laughter when he heard that. After all, it was he who had made the deal possible by killing

Robert Thomaston. The Viper figured he should be entitled to a finder's fee or a commission from these guys. Money, however, was not his problem. He had U.S. cash, perhaps more than these media guys had, and it was stashed out of reach of the taxmen in different locations around the world. When the huge profits from his drug empire had come pouring in from dealers around the world, he had hidden them in twenty-foot long transport containers packed floor to ceiling with used bills. Occasionally, when circumstances were right, he would ship the containers off to safe locations of his choosing, and then he'd begin to fill another. No one in the world except the Viper knew where he had hidden the accumulated treasure from his years in the illicit drug trade.

CHAPTER TWENTY-SIX

The Viper was pacing around his hotel room, thinking about Margo. He would have been satisfied to take her as a lover for some period of time, but when she had disloyally identified him to the cops in Thailand, she had voluntarily betrayed him. That was a traitorous thing to do, he thought bitterly, and now he could never trust her again. There was no question about it – she must die. Treason carries the death penalty in all societies. Margo must have known that, but she obviously thought she could get away with it. She probably thought he could never escape, and that she'd be safe for the rest of her life while he rotted in prison. How wrong he would prove her to be! He could hear her pleading that she hadn't ratted him out, but she was the only one in Bangkok who knew what he looked like, so her begging would be to no avail.

Rafael began thinking about how he would make his escape. He remembered being told that Pressman had his own jet. He would sniff around and find out at which airport he kept the plane. He was pretty sure that nobody in law enforcement knew that he could fly a jet. He had also seen the *Sternlicht* on TV, and had considered using it as a getaway yacht. But boats were too slow, and a yacht that size required a crew. Rafael needed a quick and easy method of escape, not a naval battle.

Ivan Welland always took his responsibilities seriously, and he now felt responsible for Margo Watson. He called the Chairman of the Joint Chiefs of Staff and explained that he needed guards to watch over Margo until the Viper was back in custody. The Chief arranged for a Special Forces team to take on the job. They were briefed on the situation and stationed at crucial points around the hotel. As it turned out, they were not really needed. After the incident at Margo's apartment, the Viper correctly expected that she would be assigned police protection. It would not take a genius to figure out that she was the real target. After all, it was her apartment. The German woman was just collateral damage, and any good investigator would draw that conclusion in short order. The Viper, of course, anticipated this logic and planned accordingly. He wouldn't go near the hotel. He'd wait patiently for Margo and her new man to come to him.

The unexpected death of Baron von Aragon had muddied the merger waters. Ivan hoped that the whole situation would permanently blow away. At a minimum the deal would be delayed for months while the heirs to the German's media empire worked out the details of succession. Once in place, they might not want to proceed with the deal with Pressman. This was all to the good in Ivan's mind, but there was also the possibility that Lord Pressman could proceed alone. Thomaston's heirs and assigns would have to decide what to do as well. They might have to find another buyer, or else evolve a plan for the continuance of the business.

Ivan calculated that in six or seven chances out of ten the merger would be abandoned in these circumstances. That was the immediate result he desired, but in the long term it didn't solve the moral problem of making the media responsible for the truth in their reporting of the news. The issue of the First Amendment right of freedom of the press was still in conflict with the public's right to receive *truthful* reporting, at least as far as Ivan was concerned.

Was the First Amendment just a license to lie? It was, of course, if the information in question was devoid of fact and intended to cheat, confuse, mislead, influence, or malign anyone reading or hearing it. The trying of cases based on the First Amendment were rife, yet the matter of "intent" had not been sufficiently explored and defined by the Supreme Court, at least not in Ivan's opinion.

The work of Ivan's team's presentation to the FTC was delayed, and possibly no longer relevant, in view of the halt to the proposed acquisition caused by von Aragon's demise. Ivan didn't like the fact that so much could hang on the thread of the life of one man. The testing of the principle of truth in news reporting was now not going to happen, not because of the absence of an "intent" clause in the First Amendment or in the case law, but due to a totally different issue – the restraint of trade issue. Welland viewed this unsatisfactory result as the equivalent of permitting lying to be at the core of one of the nation's vital businesses, as long as none of the liars had a monopoly on the practice.

The previous day Ivan had been at his barber getting a haircut. An older man in the chair next to him was being attended by a young barber who was telling his customer that he had seen information on the internet to the effect that the 9/11 episode was a manufactured conspiracy on the part of the U.S. government. The young man was saying that he had seen photos on the net showing that the airplanes that had crashed into the twin towers were armed with missiles, which could be seen very clearly in the pictures.

"But airliners don't carry missiles," the older man said. "So the photos must have been doctored."

The young man had fallen silent, almost as though he were disappointed by this information.

In some circumstances, Ivan thought grimly, fiction can be more far more intriguing than truth. If this was happening in Washington, D.C., close to the Capitol building and with the Secretary of Defense in the next chair, Ivan could just imagine what the viewers in the Middle East were hearing and seeing on their own computer screens.

The average citizen had obviously lost confidence in his chosen government. They believed nothing they were being told, and ascribed the sources of the misinformation to their elected government representatives. The academic in Ivan felt as if he were watching the beginning of the fall of the American Empire. He granted that it might be difficult in many cases to discern the exact truth, but that only meant that people had to work harder. He looked around the world and saw the Dark Ages that had followed the fall of the Roman Empire beginning to surround the United States.

In a flash he had a partial vision of what he must do next to try to stabilize the world situation. Up to this point in his history with the government he had spent much of his time separating the combatants, effecting settlements, suppressing the manufacture of explosives used by the warring factions, defending against acts of terror, and trying to prevent the sources of information from becoming tainted and worthless. It appeared now that he might win a temporary halt in the battle by default, but it would take a lot more work to make the line between truth and lies less blurred.

Ivan was being challenged once again to come up with solutions that could be implemented by morally functioning governments. He felt at a loss because he was one of the few who seemed capable of seeing the big picture. In order to know what to do on a small or a large scale, Ivan felt one had to know something about the humanities. Science and technology could give us weapons, but the wisdom not to use them came from the study of history and literature. A half dozen Greeks, whose names he could recite and who lived nearly 2,500 years ago, had more wisdom than all the rebels, rockers, rappers, reverends, and rascals that ever lived. If he could just get today's men of influence to study the past, the future wouldn't look so dismal.

A few days after Baron von Aragon's death, Geoffrey Lord Pressman and Margo Watson were sitting on the balcony of his luxurious apartment having breakfast. Geoffrey lay his newspaper aside and contemplated his young paramour for a moment.

"Margo, my dear, it appears there won't be any grand alliance of the media giants now that Fritz has passed away. I see little need to remain here any longer."

"Are we going back to London, then?" Margo inquired.

"Not *we*. *I'm* going to London. You are staying here."

"What would you like me to do?"

"As Clark Gable said in one of your overblown movies, *Frankly, my dear, I don't give a damn.*"

His comment felt like a slap in the face.

"What do you mean, Geoffrey? We have a contract."

"That's what you think. You never signed any contract, did you?"

"No, but I have the contract you gave me."

"That's not a contract. It's just a few notes about a possible future contract."

"So you have no intention of hiring me?"

"None whatsoever. You were given a probationary period and I decided not to pick up the option to hire you on a permanent basis. You will be paid one month's severance. You're on your own now, effective immediately."

"What? Weren't you satisfied with the work I did?"

"I have no obligation to explain anything. You didn't pass the probationary period, and that's all I have to say."

"Geoffrey, you're a monster!" Margo blurted.

"I know, my dear. I had to be to get where I am. Now go pack your things and get the hell out of here."

Pressman was a blame-shifter of the highest magnitude. He had hoped that his sexual deficiencies could be overcome by having a new, beautiful, intelligent, nubile partner. It had worked for a short while, but the novelty wore off quickly, and before his inadequacies became apparent to Margo he wanted to get rid of her to avoid embarrassing himself. He planned to go back to Susan. She was used to him, and knew how to handle him both physically and psychologically. In typical fashion his anger at himself was directed at Margo, whose only fault was that she had expected him to act like a man, and a man of honor at that.

Margo turned on her heels and retreated to the bedroom to pack her things, but first she called Ivan Welland and told him what had just happened.

"I need to find a safe place to stay right away," she said, when she had finished her story.

"I'll take care of everything," Ivan had assured her. "I take it you're at Pressman's place in the Diplomat?"

"Yes. I'm packing right now."

"Okay. Stay put until I get there. I'm on my way."

Rafael Alvarez had been on the prowl for several days. In spite of the special security arrangements taken to protect the residents of the penthouse on the top floor of the Hotel Diplomat, he decided he was going to find a way to sneak in. As usual his plan involved a good deal of personal audacity, which was also one of his strong points. He exuded relaxed confidence, since nobody but Margo could identify him. Dressed in his new sport coat, he pretended to be a guest at the hotel and scouted the place out thoroughly. He spent some time on the floor below the lobby floor and discovered the employees' entrance, their locker rooms, and washrooms. Several of the lockers were open, and in one he found a white kitchen worker's coat with a plastic I.D. tag that read *Pedro García Pérez.* He donned the coat and joined the other workers.

Many of the employees were Hispanic, and the name on his I.D. tag was like the membership card in a club. Other employees spoke to him in Spanish, and provided him with answers to all his questions. He learned that the two floors below the penthouse were the banquet floors. Catered affairs were frequently held in the rooms on these floors, and he felt he would have no trouble flitting around the top portions of the building in his white uniform coat. He encountered a maid having her bagged lunch at the table in the locker room. He chatted with her and learned her name was Maria. She was from the Dominican Republic, and was just going through a messy divorce. She had a six-year-old daughter, and her mother cared for the little girl while she worked. Her life was obviously on a crash course to nowhere.

Rafael saw several avenues of potential in the dumpy little woman. He told her that he was employed as a sort of undercover service checker. His job was to go to all the hotels owned by the hotel chain and report back to his bosses about the efficiency of the staff in performing their duties. This week it was the Diplomat's turn to be audited by him. His job, he told Maria, covered everything in the back of the house, from the most basic tasks like the cleanliness of the washrooms, the bartenders' honesty, and the efficiency of the food servers and the kitchen staff.

Part of his job, he told her, involved dining in the restaurant in order to evaluate the performance of the staff. He explained that as a spy he was asked to bring a friend to dinner so that he wouldn't attract attention to himself. He asked Maria to be his guest, and made her promise not to tell anyone about him because if he were recognized, his value as an evaluator would be over. Maria was flattered by his invitation, and took him at his word. He was so intelligent, well spoken, and well dressed that she just knew he had to be someone more important than a kitchen worker.

On her day off she met Rafael in the lobby, and they went in to dinner. He took her plump arm, pulled out her chair and seated her. She had never in her life been treated so gallantly. He conversed with her in educated Spanish. He described himself as the black sheep scion of a Venezuelan oil rich father who had disowned him. He told Maria he had gone to a hotel business school in Lausanne, Switzerland, and that was why he was hired to do the kind of scrutinizing that he was doing.

Maria described her childhood, her parents, and her school days while Rafael pretended to be interested. At the end of the meal, he apologized that he could not take her home because he had to audit the performance of the night shift staff. He suggested that they could meet the next day after she had cleaned her last room. If she would tell him the room number he'd meet her when she was finished. Her work schedule called for her to make up room 829 at the end of her shift.

After they said goodnight and went their separate ways, Rafael called the Diplomat's Reservation Desk and reserved room 829, using a phony credit card and spinning a tale about having spent his wedding night in 829, which was why he wanted to be put in that particular room again. He stated that he would be arriving late and they should hold the room for him. It worked, and if he had been a personnel auditor as Maria believed he was, he would have given the reservation clerk a very good report.

The next day at the end of her shift, Maria waited in room 829 for Rafael. He was intentionally fifteen minutes late, just enough to enhance her anticipation. The confident, forceful rap on the door made Maria gasp even though she expected him. She opened the door.

"Ah, Maria, you're still here," he said in rapturous tones. "I'm sorry I'm late. I was so afraid that you'd have already gone that my heart was beating fast. Here, feel it and you will see I'm telling the truth."

He took her hand and placed it flat over his heart.

"Rafael, didn't you know that I would wait for you?" Maria said, her hand feeling the hard muscles in his chest.

He took her in his arms and kissed her. He had known from the moment he'd met her that she was needy, and her passionate reactions weren't a surprise to him. He untied her little heart-shaped maid's apron and laid it on the bedside table, noting the pocket in which she kept the plastic pass card that she used to open all the doors to the hotel rooms she cleaned.

Maria was exactly the type he sought when he wanted an earnest partner to have sex with. She was facially pretty in a way that was not too pretty, but yet quite acceptable. Her body type was not in a class with Margo's, but it was cutely female, curvaceous, pliant, and it offered him the relief he was seeking. Maria, for her part, felt extremely lucky that this handsome, strong man found her attractive. When she looked at him with his large, hard muscles, she felt grateful that he desired her. He pulled the bedclothes down.

"Don't worry, this room is unoccupied tonight."

"How do you know?" Maria asked, appreciating the fact that he cared enough to address her obvious concern.

"I just know," he said. "I don't want you thinking of anything else except how you will please me."

Maria imagined that because of his job he knew the room was going to be vacant that night. Later when she got up to go to the bathroom, Rafael exchanged his plastic room card for her pass card. Hotel locking systems had changed since the days when he helped his father do locksmith's work, but clever criminals always found ways to get around the keyless systems. Rafael's way was the most pleasant. While she was gone he began to dress himself.

When she returned, wearing one of the hotel's guest bathrobes, he saw her disappointed expression.

"I'm sorry, but I still have a little work that I must do. I'd love it if you could stay the night with me. We can pick up where we left off when I get back in a little while. In the meantime you can order us some food from room service, and you can call your mother to tell her you'll be home in the morning so she won't worry. What do you say to that?"

"I'm so happy that you'll come back again. I've never felt the way you made me feel and I don't want it to end. I'll wait, but you should remember that you have an impatient woman waiting for you."

Once outside the room, the Viper headed down the hall to the employee's elevator. He was glad that he now had an alibi in place should he need it. He took the elevator to the floor below the penthouse. A large catered party was just breaking up and there were still many guests and hotel staff circulating around the room. Rafael headed for the back door, and took the stairs up one flight. Gun in hand and using Maria's pass card, he let himself into the servant's entrance to the penthouse.

He was immediately conscious of the silence after leaving the clatter of the party behind. When Pressman bought the place he had insisted that the ceiling below his apartment and the floor of his space contain double the usual sound-deadening insulation. Rafael had the feeling he was entering a mausoleum, so quiet were the new surroundings. He was in the semi-dark of the large kitchen that was lit only by the timing clock on the stove.

As his eyes adjusted to the light he thought how similar all the condominiums of the rich were. In their effort to remove all the unpleasantness from their lives they had set up a dependency on servants to do all the dirty work of cooking, cleaning, and removing the garbage. The wealthy want these things to be done, but they don't want to see them being done. They spend fortunes on security systems, but they are always vulnerable because they must have egress for their detritus, and ingress for their staffs. As the storeowner quickly learns that it is his employees who commit the majority of the petty thefts, likewise the rich find out that their dwellings are most vulnerable because it is fallible people who render the services they crave. They place their desire for comfort and pleasure above security, and the talented criminal can always use this knowledge of their dependency to penetrate their supposedly safe environments.

Gun in hand, Rafael moved stealthily around the huge apartment, following the walls from room to room. He noticed a light under the ensuite bathroom door of the master bedroom. He passed by, heading in the direction of some voices he heard coming from the hall that led to the front door of the penthouse. From behind a door he could see two people talking. He moved closer so he could hear what they were saying.

"Dr. Welland, thank you so much for coming. I would have died of shame if I'd had to spend the night here."

Rafael smiled. "You would have died all right, but not from shame, Margo, you little traitor," he said under his breath.

"Is that your luggage?" Ivan asked.

"Yes, I put it here so it would be near the door."

"Here, let me get it for you."

Rafael was tempted to step out and pop the Secretary of Defense, whom he now recognized from TV interviews, but he figured he probably had half the U.S. Marine Corps down below waiting for him. He was able to reconstruct what was going on from just the few words he'd overheard. Pressman had evidently kicked Margo out, and she had called the Secretary of Defense to come and pick her up. Pressman was probably the person behind the bathroom door. How she knew such an important personage as Dr. Welland he had no idea, but he assumed Margo was doing the Secretary. She was not only a traitor, but a *puta* on a historic scale. As they put the luggage out the door and waited for the elevator, Rafael heard them conversing some more.

"Where would you like me to drop you?" Ivan asked.

"That's a bit of a problem. The cops have taken over my apartment so they can gather crime scene evidence, so now I have no place to go."

"Well, if you want to, you can stay at my house until you figure out what you're going to do next."

Just then the elevator came and their voices trailed off as the doors closed and the lift descended. Neither had known how close they had come to being murdered. Rafael, frustrated, retreated back the way he had come. He would not have minded killing the lot of them – Margo, Welland and Pressman – but he was not suicidal. The trick was to murder and not be caught.

His problem with Margo was that by identifying him, she had ruined all his best-laid retirement plans. He was, however, not new to the art of killing and not unskilled in its execution, so the Viper decided to wait patiently in the tall grass until a better opportunity presented itself. Meanwhile he would entertain himself with delicious thoughts of torture and revenge as he waited for judgment day.

He inserted the plastic card into the lock on room 829 and stepped into the room. The smell of food was pervasive. Maria had made quite a nice little spread for him, and after they ate the Viper accepted her sexual attentions as a minor consolation for his otherwise unsuccessful evening.

CHAPTER TWENTY-SEVEN

Welland and Watson had had a serious talk in the car on the way to Georgetown where Ivan lived. He was interested in challenging Margo to take part in a journalistic revival that would replace lies and prevarications with honesty and truthful reporting. The First Amendment free speech rights, he told her, should not be wasted on opportunists that use it to spread intentional lies. He wanted the media to police themselves, using their own press association. He was looking for an important journalist to champion the cause, and he hoped Margo would be that person. She reminded him that she was not a journalist at that time, as she was currently unemployed.

"Why don't you approach the Thomaston heirs with a new business plan?" Ivan suggested. "Now that they're not going to sell the company to the European combine, they'll have to run the business themselves. They'll need someone who has knowledge of their operations to see to it that they stay competitive and profitable."

"You're probably right, but they'll want someone older and more experienced than I am."

"Yes, that's a strong possibility, but if you came in with a strategy that would give the company a new direction for the next decade, and if I were to sponsor your candidacy, they might consider it. After all, I'm the youngest Secretary of Defense the country has ever had. If something as stodgy and monolithic as the Defense Department can be put into the hands of someone as young as I am, with no military background, then why can't a corporation choose a similar kind of leader?"

"Well, if I really had your support, it might be worth a try. Pressman gave me a month's severance pay so I suppose I could prepare a proposal during that time. At worst they might offer me a job. I don't have anything to lose, do I?"

"No. Start working on your business plan tomorrow, and I promise to get you a meeting with the Thomaston heirs in a month's time. If you need some help with the strategy, you can count on me. My investigative team has done a lot of work on the free speech question, and I can produce tons of information about the media to support a total change in editorial direction for the Thomaston companies," said Ivan.

"Now you're getting my blood up," said Margo. "I've already got a motto picked out that will outdo the New York Times' motto."

"What is it?

"*Truth to Tell.*"

"I like it." Ivan said. "I like it very much."

Ivan Welland and his wife Marina were the ideal hosts for Margo Watson. It was obvious to Margo that the Welland family was entirely devoted to one another. The toddler, Julia, who was just learning to speak, managed to be polite and respectful to her parents and their visitor. Margo hoped to be able to visit them from time to time, whenever she needed to have a booster shot of faith in the institution of marriage. In the meantime she had a month to do the biggest writing job of her young life. It was a formidable task to map out a strategy for the next decade of business operations for the largest media company in the world.

Rafael Alvarez was also busy formulating a new plan. He was free to run around the world doing anything he liked, and except for Margo, no one knew what he looked like. They might never run into each other again, but he knew that if he were ever arrested for any crime and the police checked his prints or his DNA, the authorities would send for Margo, and she could pick him out of a line-up as she had done in

Bangkok. He recognized that the odds of this happening were not great. He had no plans to commit any major crimes, as he no longer needed the money. He felt that she deserved to be executed for betraying him, and his machismo demanded satisfaction, but his desire for revenge wasn't sufficient to make him act stupidly. He would have liked to have the affair over and done with, but the present situation was too dangerous with regard to escaping, and it also didn't satisfy the lecherous side of his plans for taking revenge on Señorita Watson. He could wait for a more propitious moment.

Washington, D.C. was the one place on earth that was precarious for Alvarez. Since he had made his escape in the capital, he was being pursued by every law enforcement agency in the district. The various police forces would be particularly interested in men traveling alone. The Viper decided that he could only improve his chances by using Maria's unsuspicious nature again.

He called Maria and told her that he had a short job to do in Montreal, and he invited her to spend the weekend with him. He was sure that she would arrange her affairs so she could go with him, and she didn't disappoint him. Using the internet and a stolen Visa card number, he purchased two one-way tickets for a private compartment on Amtrak from Washington to Montreal. Maria agreed to meet him half an hour before boarding time the next night.

Next he drove the rented car to the airport where Lord Pressman's plane was waiting to take him back to London. The crew was standing around smoking and talking while they waited for the boss to come along. The captain had filed a flight plan for departure that evening, but Pressman was late, and it appeared that the flight arrangements would have to be postponed.

That was perfect as far as the Viper was concerned, as his plan included using Pressman's flight as a cover for his escape by train. At first he had considered hijacking the plane, killing Pressman and his crew, and landing the plane by himself, but the fuel capacity of the jet was only just sufficient to make it to London. Rafael knew his chances of escaping after landing the plane there were nil, so obviously that was not a plan. He did like the idea of involving Pressman and his plane in his escape, however. He watched the captain of Pressman's crew from a discreet distance. A few minutes later the man received a call on his cell phone, and then he and the crew left the tarmac. Rafael knew the flight was off until the next day. He got into his car and drove back to his hotel in the city center.

Rafael Alvarez had followed the actions of the Islamist terrorists with great interest. He didn't share their political or religious ambitions, but he had used their bomb-making skills in his occasional one-man personal jihads. His favorite was a device invented by Ramzi Yousef, the master bomb-maker of al-Qaeda. He had perfected a small nitroglycerine bomb that was undetectable by airport security, and Rafael admired its technical details. In his lab back in Colombia he had worked out a number of variations of the Arab's original idea, and battle-tested them on several drug dealers who had failed to pay for their product deliveries.

Back in his hotel room he located the package that he had sent to himself from Chicago. The box contained all the ingredients for a nifty little bomb that he intended to place under the seat cushions in Pressman's plane. He assembled two devices, one for the captain's seat and the other for the media baron's seat. The devices used a pressure switch that was activated when a person sat down. When the victim arose from the seat again, the pressure came off and the bomb exploded.

Rafael calculated that the explosion of the first device would cause the occupant of the second rigged seat to get up to see what had caused the first explosion. Then *boom*, the second bomb would detonate. The bomb only had to damage the plane enough to admit the rarified air surrounding it, then every person, passenger and crew member would quickly die in the depressurized cabin.

While the excitement of the explosion distracted security officers, the Viper and his innocent lover would cross the border into Canada. In a day or two the security forces would no doubt be functioning at peak levels again, but Rafael believed that during the immediate aftermath of an IED or suicide bombing the confusion factor would exceed the efficiency level of the security authorities.

The Viper was optimistic that his plan would succeed, and it would have the added benefit of ridding the world of the British media panderer. Too bad his revenge on Margo wouldn't be accomplished at the same time as his escape diversion, but he could wait for that until another time.

With his collection of miniature tools, detonators, and explosive vials packed into a shaving kit in his suitcase, he drove back to the airport and used his pilot's license and I.D. to enter the gate reserved for private and corporate flights. Later that day someone else would be standing at the gate when Pressman's real crew arrived, so most likely nobody would remember him.

Once inside the deserted corporate plane area, Rafael went immediately to Pressman's sleek Lear jet. He quickly picked the lock, threw his suitcase inside, dropped the stairs so he could enter, and disappeared into the seven-seat cabin. It was easy to tell which seat Lord Pressman would occupy, so the Viper rigged his seat cushion with the device. Then he moved to the pilot's seat and planted another bomb, using the same technique as on Pressman's seat.

Just as he was finishing his task and preparing to leave the plane, Rafael had an inspiration. He reached up, slid the ceiling panel aside, and found the emergency oxygen supply. He had seen the damage that a pyromaniac had wrought on a factory in Iowa by using an oxygen cylinder as an accelerant. He took his penknife and made a slit in the main plastic tubing near the valve. One end of the tube led to the drop-down masks over each seat, and the other end led back into the tank. When the plane rose to an altitude where oxygen could be required for breathing, the system would open the supply valve and be ready in seconds to provide oxygen to the passengers if an emergency warranted it.

The result of Rafael's spontaneous improvisation was that there would be no emergency oxygen for the passengers. The tank full of the precious gas would have leaked into the cabin's pressurized air supply and dispersed. Probably it would have no effect other than to make any fire that sprang up burn faster, but it was just another guarantee that the plane would crash.

He looked over his handiwork one last time, but he failed to notice the penknife that he had left on the shelf that held the oxygen tank. Rafael replaced the cabin's ceiling panel, packed his tools in his suitcase, locked up the plane, and headed for his car. He smiled inwardly when he remembered that the plane's manufacturer was a Canadian company called BOMBardier.

He needed to sleep for a few hours, so he drove straight to his hotel and climbed wearily into bed.

In the morning Margo was awakened by a child's voice.

"Auntie Margo, Mommy says come for breakfast."

"Okay, Julia," Margo said sleepily. "Thanks for waking me up. I'm a sleepy head, aren't I? If you hadn't woken me up, I'd have missed breakfast. Then I'd be hungry, right?"

"Yes," the child said, nodding her head knowingly as Margo sat up in bed.

"I have to stop in here first," Margo said, pointing to the bathroom.

"Margo go potty?"

"That's right Julia, Margo go potty."

The little girl waited, listened, and watched Margo as she peed, threw some water on her face, dried off, and ran a comb through her hair.

"Now you can show me where your Mommy is, okay?" Margo said, taking the child by the hand.

"'Kay," she said, and toddled off to the kitchen, towing Margo along behind.

"You sleep well?" Marina asked her.

"Yes, very well, thank you," Margo said. "You have a very charming little alarm clock here," she added, pointing to Julia.

"This is good, ya? Only trouble is she can't set alarm."

Margo smiled. "I guess not."

"You can sit there," Marina said, indicating a chair at the breakfast table. "Next to naughty little girl."

"She's not naughty, is she?"

"She wakes you, ya?"

"Yeah, but didn't you tell her to do it?"

"No. It is Julia's idea. She wants to play with you."

"That would be great, but I've got a lot of work to do, thanks to your husband. So I'd better get started right after this beautiful breakfast you've prepared."

"Is because of Ivan, this work of yours?"

"Yes, it was his idea for me to develop a strategy to get the media to have a reformation, starting with the company that I hope will employ me to direct it. By the way, where is your husband?"

"He go to work 5 AM every morning. You eat now."

Margo was glad to hear that there were still people that continue to strive hard to improve the world, and among those was the relentlessly idealistic Secretary of Defense. At that moment she resolved to be Ivan's disciple and to forego her selfish career pursuits in favor of his loftier ideals.

After sleeping for a few hours, the Viper prepared himself for a big day. If all went according to plan, he would be out of Washington, out of the United States and on his way to a perfect retirement in wealthy anonymity in New Zealand. Señor Miranda, his alias, would return the car rented in his name at the Amtrak station, meet Maria under the big clock, and board the north-bound train for Montreal. His false passport and credit cards were in the inside jacket pocket of his new sport coat. Whenever he wanted more credit cards he would just go to the nearest large hospital during visiting hours. He would walk around until he found a room with a sleeping or unconscious patient, and then he would quickly rifle through the drawers of the bedside table where, more often than not, he would find the patient's wallet. As a rule people in the I.C.U. and Oncology wards couldn't report their property as missing with any degree of alacrity, so Alvarez always got away with it.

Maria came along right on time. She was dressed in her finest, and towed a small suitcase behind her. She spotted her lover and went up to him. They kissed, and everything was perfectly in order from Rafael's point of view. They walked to the track, located the car number designated on their tickets, and went aboard. They found their compartment in one of the two sleeper cars. Rafael put their bags in the luggage rack, and they sat down facing each other across a small table.

"Maria, you look beautiful," he said.

"You make me feel beautiful," she blushed.

"I can't wait to see what's underneath your dress."

"You know perfectly well what's underneath."

"Oh, then you don't think I should check?"

"I didn't say that."

The conductor's whistle sounded to summon stragglers to get on board. A minute later the train lurched forward and the first mile of their 18-hour, 700-mile overnight trip began. After a few minutes the conductor knocked on their door to check their tickets and to ask if everything was satisfactory. Rafael asked when dinner would be served in the dining car, and told the conductor they would have a nap until it was time to eat. The railroad employee pulled down the bed, and Rafael tipped him generously. The man hung the *Do not disturb* sign on the door and closed it behind him. Evidently Rafael was not the first, nor would he be the last, to enjoy making tracks out of Washington.

Three hours later the couple dressed and made their way to the dining car, which featured an electric piano bar. The noise of the train's clattering wheels drowned out the notes, but nobody seemed to care or notice. In one corner of the car the bar patrons were watching TV. Rafael and Maria were sipping some wine, waiting for the soup course to be served, when suddenly a hullabaloo broke out from the crowd in front of the TV screen. An agitated announcer was reporting that a small private jet had exploded over the Atlantic, not far from the U.S. coast. Terrorism was believed to be the cause, and no survivors were expected.

"I'm glad we decided not to take my plane tonight," said the Viper, lightly kissing the back of Maria's hand.

She smiled and went along with the joke.

"Yes, it is so difficult to get good help to maintain things properly these days."

They ate their dinner and made small talk, just like the rest of the passengers. Many of them were traveling in the coach class and would be sitting up all night. Maria would normally have been one of them. She was not used to the elegant lifestyle that her new companion showered upon her. She kept reminding him that he didn't have to spend a lot of his hard-earned money on her. It was her intention to show him that she could be a frugal wife who would manage his money carefully should he choose to make an honest woman of her. She felt that she had already proved to him that she loved him by submitting herself to him in every way he wished. Although she had only just recently met him, Maria was sure he was the one for her.

The TV announcer was delivering the breaking news that the plane had been identified as belonging to the English media mogul, Lord Geoffrey Pressman. The Coast Guard was searching for the plane, its owner, and his three crew members, but there was little hope of finding anyone alive.

Once they had passed through Canadian customs, Maria noticed a distinct change in her companion's attitude. He became grumpy, critical, bossy and disrespectful. He lost all interest in being charming and romantic. When they were out together he was a perfect gentleman, but as soon as the door closed behind them, he became abusive. She thought of running away, but she didn't have enough money for a ticket home. She knew that she had completely misjudged this man, and she decided that she would have nothing further to do with him.

After Rafael had had his way with her that night and lay snoring by her side, she quietly got out of bed and went over to the chair where his pants lay folded. Looking frequently over her shoulder at his sleeping form, she went through his wallet and took out enough cash to cover an airline ticket back to Washington and a taxi ride to the airport. Then she quickly got dressed, leaving all her personal belongings in the drawers and closet, and sneaked quietly out of the room.

As she looked back at him one final time, she almost thought she could see a red, burning eye staring at her from the head that lay on the pillow. She felt her heart beat faster, and she almost ran to the door. As she placed her hand on the doorknob, she suddenly realized that she had left her handbag on the chair by the bedside table. She looked back again and saw it sitting there, but she didn't dare approach the bed in case she awakened the stranger who lay there snoring loudly in an even rhythm, punctuated occasionally by a disgusting smacking of his wet and juicy lips.

It was hard for Maria to imagine that she had welcomed those lips with her own half open mouth that very morning. She left her handbag behind and quietly disappeared into the starry Canadian night, unable to shake the thought that the eerie red eye had witnessed her departure and would always know exactly where she was.

CHAPTER TWENTY-EIGHT

Rafael Alvarez would have liked to kill Maria for running out on him, but he didn't want to create any police problems in Canada. He was only passing through, and he didn't want to foul up his escape plan.

When Maria relived the details of her affair with the man she knew as Pedro García Pérez, she had to admit to herself that she should have known much sooner that he was no good. He had stopped being kind and gentle the minute they had crossed the border into Canada. What was it about Canada? Maybe it was something in the water. She thought it was better to laugh about it than to cry.

Maria had convinced herself that it was just the strength of Pedro's desire that made him aggressive and violent, but she understood the truth now. She had been needy. She had wanted to prove to herself, and to the husband who had left her, that she could find another man, and a better one, too. But she had quickly become afraid of this new man, and she dared not go against his will for fear that he would hurt her. Now she was free of him, and that was the one good thing about it. It was over now, or so she believed.

Ivan Welland was sitting at his desk in his thinking mode. He was considering the irony of nearly everything in life. He had tried, although it was not in his jurisdiction, to put truth back into the forefront of media reporting. He had failed miserably on the philosophical basics, which were to make the government care about keeping the press honest and truthful, and not just *free*. Then in the face of that failure along came the unknown, unseen, ironical actions of fate that changed the entire landscape of events. It was surreal that the three great practitioners of the big lie had died within months of each other, making it unnecessary for him to take any further measures to interfere with their plans. The fact that the right result had occurred for the wrong reasons, was only partially satisfactory to Ivan. He liked it best when he was in charge of writing the play and the action developed according to his script.

His drama didn't include Margo's becoming the white knight. When he first met her he wouldn't have dreamed that she could turn into a strong ally, but as he consulted with her about her plans for the Thomaston group of companies, he began to realize that she was undergoing an epiphany. Day by day she was growing stronger in her convictions that the media needed to pay for the freedom it had been given by the First Amendment to the Constitution. The payment for the freedom of speech was to come with gratitude in the form of voluntary adherence to a code of moral precepts that she would prepare and incorporate into the new mission statement for the Thomaston media interests. By voluntarily taking the moral high ground, she was hoping to make the organization stronger and provide an example to the rest of the industry.

Ivan was proud of Margo's new idealism. She convinced him that the needed changes in the modus operandi of the media throughout the world could best be accomplished from within. Little by little he backed off the idea of seeking to legislate the principles of a responsible press. The biblical imperative to seek the truth in order to be made free was frequently on his mind as he watched Margo come round to the same position as his. The tendency of people to believe what they see on TV and what they read in print can easily be taken advantage of by charlatans and liars who use the media for their own selfish or evil motives. Even newsmen who honestly try to present the facts could be guilty of being naïve, simplistic, or deluded – a case of the blind leading the blind. Ivan could hardly wait to see the draft of Margo's magnum opus on the topic of journalistic conscience.

His mind turned to another of his unresolved problems – the apprehension of the Viper, who had evidently gone to ground. Nothing had been heard from him or about him since his escape from the federal prison authorities. Ivan supposed that was not unusual for a man on the run, but the Viper was a special case. In his mind Rafael Alvarez was something like a virus. No one believes that the Ebola virus has permanently gone away just because we aren't hearing about any cases of the disease at the moment. This line of thinking led Ivan to consider just how many cases of Ebola are misdiagnosed. Maybe it was the same situation with the Viper, he thought. Suddenly the lights in his brain went on.

"Brooklyn," he shouted. "Get the team together right away."

The four appeared in Ivan's office within a matter of minutes. Ivan searched their faces and received the comfort one gets from being with trusted friends. They had been through a lot together, and each of them knew the value of the others.

"Sit down, my friends and colleagues. I'd like to talk to you about two things that have been on our minds for some time now," Ivan began. "The first is the status of the project we've recently all worked hard on, and that is the matter of the media manufacturing propaganda that is passed off to the public as news. For some time now I've been trying to decide exactly where to go with the information we've dug up. It's true that we have, in my opinion, irrefutable proof that the media are dallying with the truth in their reporting in order to benefit themselves. You four have done a great job in getting the goods on these guys.

"Unfortunately, though, I must tell you that nobody in government seems to care about truth any more. It may be that they have too much to hide themselves, or it may be that they don't have the spine to tackle the fine tuning of the First

Amendment, but the bottom line is that my pleas to do something about the situation have fallen on deaf ears. The United States government seems to be pursuing a policy of *caveat auditor*, or let the hearer beware.

"I've decided to change the direction of our program. Instead of resorting to legal means to codify behaviors and force compliance on the media, I'm recommending that we take the more circuitous route of allowing the media to self regulate."

"Isn't that a bit naïve?" said David Feingold. "Why would they want to do that?"

"There are two aspects to the answer to that question. The first is they won't want to do it, so they will have to be persuaded. The second is that they have to compete, so if others do it, they will all fall in line."

"Okay. So tell us how that unlikely scenario will play out," Abdul said.

"In my conversations with the FTC it was made clear to me that the only protection under the law that we have in the matter of spreading false news as though it were truth, comes from the regulations governing competitive practices," Ivan said.

"How does that help?" Damian asked. "I'm not sure I understand."

"Actually it doesn't help to make anybody tell the truth. What it does do is make sure no company monopolizes all the lying. We've been reading the business news relating to the proposed merger of two huge European media companies with Thomaston's American Media Corporation. If that deal had gone through you'd have seen that these outfits would have been in a position to take over the production of news reports all over the free world.

"I was planning to use the information that our team put together, and take it before the FTC hearing to try to stop the deal from being approved. I was told that our evidence would have been seen as not relevant on the grounds that the hearing didn't concern the honesty of reporting or the moral turpitude of the petitioners. It was only concerned about whether the deal, if approved by the Commissioners, would be anti-competitive or monopolistic."

"Do you mean to say that aside from the slander and libel constraints," Brooklyn said, "a media company can just manufacture the news, report it as truth, claim that it is its editorial right to slant it any way it sees fit, and quote the First Amendment free speech provisions as the source of its sufferance?"

"I do. So yes, all the work we did would have been for naught, except for one thing."

"What's that?" David asked.

"I'll get to that," Ivan said. "First I want to tell you that the merger hearing before the FTC has been cancelled. And I want you to know that I had nothing to do with it."

"How's that?" Damian said.

"Well if I'd had anything to do with it I'd be facing a whole lot of murder charges. But as you can see, I'm still running around loose."

"You are weaving a tangled web, Dr. Welland, and I'm not sure where you're going with this," Abdul said.

"The three biggest media executives had a meeting on board a yacht at sea and decided to make a pact whereby their companies would be merged in the event of the death of any of the threesome. In the U.S. this meeting and that pact would have been regarded as being collusive and in restraint of trade, and therefore illegal. When Robert Thomaston was murdered, the other two, Baron von Aragon and Geoffrey Lord Pressman, decided to go forward with the terms of the agreement and split Thomaston's companies between them. Since then, von Aragon died of a heart attack caused by the shock of discovering his girl friend's murdered body. And then just yesterday Pressman's plane exploded in mid flight, and he's presumed dead. As a result of all this carnage, the merger of all these companies has been postponed, probably permanently."

"So your voluntary protestations of innocence pertain to these convenient deaths," Brooklyn remarked wryly.

"Exactly. It's true that I wanted the merger killed, but I didn't kill its proponents."

"Okay, boss, we'll let you off the hook on the murders, but all the work we did will go for naught now, won't it?" said David.

"Not quite. I've moved from slugging it out in the middle of the ring, to close fighting in the corner, that's all."

"Would you mind decoding that for the non-pugilistic minds among us?" Damian said.

"I've got a person on the inside, or at least I hope I will have. This person will present the evidence we uncovered to the heirs, successors, and stockholders of the Thomaston empire. I'm hoping they will see the wisdom of changing their ways, and by publicizing the changes they are going to make, they will challenge all the other players in the media business to do likewise. This is my hope, that an example of virtue triumphant will inspire others. Not so much *All the News That's Fit to Print,* but *All the Truth That's News.*"

"Well, one conversion by choice is worth a hundred by compulsion," said Abdul.

"That sounds like an Arab proverb," Ivan smiled.

"It's not, but it should be," Abdul said.

"Anyway, that's my report on the current status of the media project that you all worked so hard on. Now I'd like to discuss the second item on my short agenda, the status of the missing Viper. I've been thinking."

"Oh, oh," said Brooklyn.

"I'll ignore that Miss Brocklyn. As I said, I've been thinking about the Viper lately, and I'd like you to do the same. His real name is Rafael Alvarez, of course, but he travels under the alias of Pedro Miranda, and also Pedro García Pérez. So where is this guy? What is he up to? We brought him to Washington. He didn't know beforehand that he would be extradited to the U.S. Yet he managed to escape from the federal detention center, and he hasn't been seen again or heard from since. He left us in a prisoner's jump suit with no money or weapons. Does he happen to have confederates here? How he escaped is interesting, but the real question is, what is he doing now? As I thought about it I tried to put myself in his shoes. What would I do if I were he? I'd like us to put our thinking caps on and help recapture this guy."

Ivan had spoken without realizing that he had been within a yard of the Viper, and was only alive now by virtue of some favorable circumstances.

He began doling out assignments. To Brooklyn he assigned the task of analyzing the crimes committed in Washington, D.C. in the days after the Viper's escape. She was to piece together every criminal move that he could have made from the minute he stepped outside the jail up to the present time. She could likely trace most of his movements by consulting the blotter of the Washington police. She was to get the results of the DNA samples taken after his arrest and see if they matched the semen samples obtained from the body of the woman killed in Margo Watson's apartment.

Damian was instructed to coordinate with the TSA team that was investigating the crash of Pressman's Lear jet. Ivan asked him to see if the Viper had hijacked the plane, or if he had blown it up.

"If any pieces of the plane have been recovered yet, have them examined for prints," Ivan told him. "We have to establish the Viper's connection to the plane crash, if one exists. See if by any lucky chance he was on board."

Abdul was delegated to investigate the bomb that caused the explosion that brought down the plane. He was to use his contacts to investigate any possible terrorism connections, and report back with his findings. David was to pull all the data together and plot a time-line using his computer and listing all the reported crimes that could be attributed to the Viper. Ivan told his second-in-command to study all the passenger manifests for flights out of the country to see if the names, destinations, and times of departure fit in with the other available data, and then match them against hotel reservations.

"I suspect that our fair city has undergone a mini-crime wave caused by the Viper, and I believe if we are thorough and intelligent we can track this guy down," Ivan said, in his optimistic, commanding tone. "Now let's get busy!"

CHAPTER TWENTY-NINE

Rafael Alvarez, traveling once again under the name of Pedro Miranda, was comfortably stretched out in the first class section of an Air Canada transcontinental flight bound for Vancouver, British Columbia. He was reading the *Montreal Gazette*, searching for anything that related to his situation.

He came across an article that stated that the wreckage of the plane owned by Lord Geoffrey Pressman had been found, and the Transport Safety investigators in the U.S. were examining the pieces to determine the cause of the crash. Alvarez was surprised that the reporter was calling it a crash, as though it had been an accident. He decided that it didn't really matter to him what they called it, for with every passing minute he was getting further and further away from the scene. There was no way, in his opinion, that he could be linked to Pressman's aircraft.

The Viper was enjoying his feeling of reprieve. Maria was gone and out of his life. She knew him only as Pedro García Pérez. She had no idea if he had stayed in Montreal or had gone elsewhere. He didn't believe he could be traced through her, even in the unlikely event that she had gone to the police. Only Margo could identify him as the Viper, and she had no idea where he was. He was in another country, free and clear.

He decided to order a scotch from the flight attendant to celebrate his freedom. When his drink arrived, he looked around at the other passengers for the first time. The woman seated next to him was casually looking in his direction. He raised his glass in a toast. She vaguely acknowledged his motion, but her attitude was distinctly noncommittal.

He looked at her out of the corner of his eye. She was about forty, dark haired, very well dressed, and had a sort of no-nonsense attitude about her. Rafael noticed she was not wearing a wedding ring. Normally such a woman wouldn't have attracted the Viper because she was too mature and self-confident, but as there was no one else to talk with to pass the time, he decided to accept the challenge of engaging her in conversation.

"Excuse me," he said, leaning slightly in her direction. "I feel a little awkward and ungentlemanly having a drink without offering one to a fellow passenger. May I interest you in something?"

"No thank you," she said.

"Not even to relieve this rather awkward situation?" he persisted.

She hesitated just long enough for him to decide to move forward with his ploy.

"It's a long, boring flight. Why shouldn't we just chat amicably? I promise to shut up any time you say."

"All right then," the woman said. "But I warn you that I may hold you to your promise. I'll have a vodka martini."

Rafael attracted the attention of the server.

"Please bring my neighbor a vodka martini. Have you a little caviar as well?"

The attendant nodded.

"Very good, then bring that along as well."

"Certainly, sir."

"My name is Pedro Miranda de Santiago," Alvarez said, turning back to his neighbor. "How do you do, *Señorita*? Or is it *Señora*?"

"At present it's *Señorita* again."

"Although I'm divorced, I'm still *Señor.* Does it seem right to you that a man stays the same whether married or single, while a woman's title changes?"

"No, it doesn't."

"See? We already agree on something. What shall I call you, then? *Señorita* what?"

"My name is Rachel Huntington."

"*Señorita* Huntington, then," he said, tipping his glass in her direction. "You see before you a very happy man."

"Oh? Why is that?"

"I have just seen the dream of my life for the first time, and I'm going to have her," Rafael said, in a provocative, mysterious fashion.

Rachel hoped he was not being so corny as to suggest that he was speaking of her. If so, she would ask him to honor his promise to shut up. She was a successful woman in her own right, and not subject to petty flatteries.

"Who is the lucky woman?"

"*Señorita*, she is not a woman. She is a boat."

Rachel chuckled in spite of herself.

"Perhaps you have read in the papers recently about the unfortunate demise of Baron Friedrich von Aragon, the German media mogul?"

"Yes, I think I remember reading something about that."

"Well he has no need of his yacht, the *Sternlicht,* any more. He was in Washington, D.C. living on board his boat at the time of his death. As soon as I saw the newspaper account of his demise I contacted his heirs with a proposal to purchase his yacht. It was just a wild chance on my part, as I didn't know them. I didn't know if they wanted to sell the yacht, either. So I was happily surprised to hear that they were interested. I've just come from inspecting her, and that is why I'm so deliriously happy. I'm also very happy to have someone to share my joy with," he added, popping a cracker spread with caviar into his mouth.

"I'm glad I could be here for you," Rachel said, thinking that he certainly hadn't been boring so far.

"I'm glad, too. You could have cut me off at the knees and not talked to me, but you were kind enough to listen to the ranting of a perfect stranger. I thought at first you were too formidable a woman to enter into a conversation with an unknown man, but I'm delighted that I tried to make your acquaintance anyway."

Rachel liked being thought of as a *formidable* woman. Her entire adult life had been spent developing the persona of a formidable woman. She had had entirely too many experiences with cocky males who thought they were God's gift to women. Just because she had even features and good legs wasn't reason enough for her to have to endure their incessant, importunate wooing, so she had developed a formidable exterior to keep them at bay.

This companion passenger, however, was attractive, pleasant, gentlemanly, and if anything, too perfect a stranger. It should have made her wary, but she still cherished a modicum of hope that even at forty a woman could meet a decent man.

The chain of ski equipment and clothing specialty stores that she and her husband had built together had provided her with a good living, but she'd had to work hard to keep it profitable. Her ne'er-do-well ex-husband had taken off four years before with a young ski instructor from Whistler, British Columbia. The truth was that aside from his talent for ski boarding, drinking, and some boyish charm, he had been unsatisfactory as a mate and a veritable liability when it came to business.

When they divorced, she bought out his interest, or non-interest, in the business. He became a useless playboy without her, and she became a very successful entrepreneur without him. Being a playboy was expensive, and her husband had recently run out of money at about the same time as the ski instructor had run out on him. He had been sniffing around the trough again, hoping for a second chance at the swill. So now Rachel was doing her best to remain formidable while at the same time feeling just a little bit vulnerable to the Viper's practiced advances.

"You were brave," Rachel said to Alvarez, "to approach a woman you thought was formidable. But let's get off this subject, what do you say? Tell me more about your Starlight affair."

Rafael was slightly taken aback until he realized she was using the English name for the yacht.

"Well, what would you like to know about her?"

"I don't know that much about boats. Just tell me what she's like."

What followed was a long and friendly conversation, first about the boat, then about his effusively exaggerated, and totally concocted, biographical sketch. Rafael was a viper honing in on Rachel's pheromones.

By the time the plane landed in Vancouver she thought he was a powerhouse business man from Chile who might be interested in developing franchise ski equipment stores in the Andes in partnership with her. He invited her to take a cruise in his new yacht when he returned from the trip to the Far East that he was embarking on the next day.

Although Rachel would never have invited a stranger to her home, she made an exception in the case of the suave Rafael Alvarez. She somehow believed he was legitimate, and she wanted to cultivate the friendship of the wealthy Chilean. But for every formidable female there is an equally malignant male, and Rachel had just found hers.

Rafael gallantly helped her with her luggage and loaded it into the black Audi A-8 that awaited her in the airport long-term parking lot. She explained to her new companion that she needed an all-wheel vehicle because she spent so much time doing business in snow country. He laughed and told her that now he would have to get one too, for the same reason.

They drove north from Vancouver to the Whistler area where Rachel lived in the ski chalet that she and her husband had purchased when they got married. She opened the door, turned on the lights, and directed him to the bedroom where he was to put her suitcase.

"I'll make us a drink. What would you like?" Rachel asked him.

"I'll have a bloody Mary, please," he answered from the bedroom.

Rafael had found her underwear drawer and was tying twisted panty hose to each of the four posts of the queen-sized bed in readiness for the fun that was about to take place. He moved swiftly around the house and pulled down the blinds on every window, without regard to the beautiful views to be seen from them.

"How are the drinks coming along?" he said, entering the kitchen and coming up behind her.

She turned around to face him, holding the drinks between them. He focused his eyes on hers, took the drinks from her hands, and set them on the counter. He moved closer and gathered her into his arms. Before she could say or do anything, he kissed her.

She was taken completely aback, because she had never been kissed that passionately in her life. She would have enjoyed it more had she known the man better, but she had no choice in the matter. Her arms were locked at her side by his one arm. His mouth covered hers and she could make no sound. Rachel started to squirm to get away from him, but he was too strong. She struggled harder.

Suddenly he let her go, and when she separated from him she saw that he had taken her carving knife from its wooden block, and was pointing it at her.

"There's no use struggling," he warned her. "It'll do you no good. So take off your clothes."

She hesitated, but he took a threatening step closer, wielding the knife an inch away from her throat. She began unbuttoning her blouse as rapidly as her frightened, nervous fingers could manage. As she tried to slip her blouse over her shoulders, he spun her around and held her arms behind her with her wrists still in the sleeves.

"Let me help you," he said, as she felt the cold steel of the blunt edge of the knife against her back. He severed first the vertical, then the horizontal bra straps. The exceedingly sharp knife continued down her back, slicing its way through her belt and skirt.

"This is a really sharp knife, Rachel. And a sharp knife is a joy to me," he said, as he brandished the long, shiny stainless steel blade in front of her face.

He spun her around, using the blouse that still trapped her arms behind her, and pushed her into the bedroom. At the foot of the bed he shoved her hard and simultaneously let go of the blouse that bound her hands. She fell down on the bed, and while she struggled to free her arms he tied first one leg, then the other one to the bedposts, using the panty hose he had prepared in advance. Next he tied her wrists to the headboard posts.

"Now that's better, isn't it?"

Rafael went into the kitchen and brought the drinks that Rachel had mixed into the bedroom.

"Let's have that drink now, shall we?"

Rachel's house was far enough away from any others that no one would have heard her scream. He was so strong that she thought it best to save her energy. She was trying to think her way out of her situation. She could see that she wouldn't be able to avoid being raped, but she wanted to stay alive at all costs.

Like most women, she had read the accounts of rapes in the papers and had heard the advice from victims, police, and TV psychologists about what a woman should do in rape situations. Surprised by her attacker, she had no chance of using any of the avoidance tactics. It was too late for those. She had heard about a confident woman who had challenged her rapist to show her what he had and how he could use it. She claimed that her overt sexuality had cowed the man, and he had lost his confidence and let her go.

Somehow she didn't believe that strategy would work on this guy. He was obviously very experienced as a rapist. He knew exactly what he was doing. He hadn't hurt her yet, so maybe he would just use her and not harm her, but of course she couldn't depend on that.

He was sipping his drink slowly, and then held her head up so she could take a sip of hers.

"How nice this is," he said. "We don't have to go through all the *ifs*, *ands*, or *buts* of courting. We'll just get right to the point. Isn't that right?"

Rachel's silence was a little disconcerting to him. He didn't know whether she was going to accommodate his desires, hoping that he would spare her life, or whether she was hatching some plan of escape to spring on him. He walked around the bed, having a long look at her. For her age he found her conditioning to be very good. She was not perfect like Margo, but she would do. There was no need to rush. He could take her anytime he wished.

Rachel wanted to order her mind to ignore him totally, but she found it impossible. Why was this man doing this to her? If he had played his cards right she would have willingly given him what he was about to take. Why was the rape necessary?

From the Viper's point of view, the rape was absolutely necessary. It was not really about sex. He could sense that she would have engaged in consensual sex with him if he had approached her in the right way. But the purpose of the game that he played with women was not about seduction. It was about exerting absolute control, and it was a power trip from beginning to end. It was a throwback to the primeval days, perhaps as far back as the days before the sex act was associated with reproduction.

Rafael's particular fantasy called for the rape to be followed by gratitude and respect on the part of the woman, and her continued, absolute subjection to him. He didn't expect Rachel, at her age and state of maturity, to satisfy his fantasy of total submission, but he still wanted to exert complete power over this so-called formidable woman. As the battle of the wills continued, neither of the combatants heard the small sound at the front door.

Rachel's ex-husband had seen the lights on in the chalet, and thought he would pop in and see if Rachel had softened to the idea of a marital reconciliation. He had tiptoed up the front steps and had his hand on the knob of the front door. He listened for any sounds from inside, and heard only some stirrings coming from the bedroom.

As he thought idly about whether to ring the bell or not, his hand twisted the doorknob. It was unlocked. He opened the door and went in, thinking he would surprise Rachel and berate her for leaving her door open so any stranger could just walk in.

Once inside, he definitely located the noises as coming from the bedroom. They sounded like grunts emanating from some kind of a struggle. Suspecting that Rachel might be in some kind of trouble, he went over to the desk and opened the drawer in which they kept a loaded pistol to frighten off bears or other wild animals that inhabited the woods nearby. He was glad it was still there.

He quickly moved to the bedroom door, which was ajar. He looked inside and saw his ex-wife being mauled by a half naked man. Something snapped inside him, and he saw red. He entered the room and walked over to the bed, unnoticed by the couple. He put the gun to Rafael's head and fired, instantly killing him and spilling much Viper blood over his ex-wife. For an instant the jealous man considered shooting the woman, too. Rachel could see the anguish in his eyes.

"Don't shoot me, Richard. Look at me. I'm tied up. I was being raped and you saved me! Call 911 and I'll explain everything to you, and to the police."

The thought crossed her mind that even in a situation like this, she had to do all the thinking for Richard.

Months later, however, when the Mounties completed their thorough investigation and cleared her ex-husband of any crime, Rachel gave considerable thought to the fact that Richard's one decisive act had saved her life. It seemed ironic to her that a man could be a wastrel and a ne'er-do-well all his life, and then redeem himself in a random act of blind rage that had resulted in the unexpected death of a rapist and murderer, while at the same time granting her a new lease on life. She had spent the best and most productive years of that life developing her career and catering, she knew not why, to her spoiled husband's every need. Yet without him she might have died a premature death at the hands of a dangerous psychopath.

CHAPTER THIRTY

D r. Ivan Welland, Secretary of Defense for the United States of America, was sitting at his desk in his spacious, impressive office in the Pentagon. He could have felt proud of the power of his position and the reputation he'd earned for solving difficult security problems in the hot spots of the world, but this day his thoughts were centered on humility. Being humble was not high on the list of traits valued by those who govern the American people.

Ivan was that rare individual who was not afraid to face the fact that in spite of his great power, he was not in charge of everything. He was still striving to live up to the Christian and Judaic principles stated in the Old Testament Book of Micah, where he was instructed to do justly, love mercy, and walk humbly with his God. The recent developments in his professional life had brought him back to earth with a thump.

The case of the Viper, for instance, had been settled, but in a way that only an omniscient God could have envisioned. Who could have foreseen that the Viper, with his vast talent for evil and his incredible genius for escaping the penalties for his transgressions, would fall victim to a jealous ex-husband with a track record of success that was not much better than Elmer Fudd's?

Richard Huntington, not even a husband, but only an ex-husband, had dispatched one of the world's most wanted men. His reputation was buoyed up tremendously when he was perceived as the righteous mate that saved his wife's virtue, and probably her life. An instant of blinding, jealous rage had turned him into the heroic, decisive, thoughtful man he had never been in real life.

Rachel, the formidable, successful businesswoman, was in turn seen as an equivocating, pusillanimous female victim, who had only herself to blame for inviting this unsavory man into her home. Life is not fair.

When the RCMP had responded to the 911 call that night, they quickly got to the bottom of things. The issue of the rape became moot, since the dead man could not be prosecuted. Rachel was relieved not to have to go to court and discuss in public every detail of the one night in her life that she would most dearly love to forget. She would have liked to let some of the hero's wind out of Richard's sails, but not at the price of having to admit to the embarrassment of having been raped.

The Mounties knew the truth because they had taken semen samples from the sheets on the crime scene bed that matched the DNA of the Viper's body – this in spite of the victim's unwillingness to submit to the added indignity of a rape kit analysis. Canada's policemen, like the citizens they served, were circumspect and didn't feel the need to release this information to the panting, prurient press that hounded them for the gory details as soon as the news of the Viper's death was released.

Had the reporters been patient, however, they eventually would have found out that Rachel was pregnant. Her first reaction was to terminate the pregnancy, as she was not at all happy with the idea of living with a constant reminder of the ugliest, most repulsive experience she had ever endured. But she was unable to motivate herself to go to an abortion clinic and do the deed. She struggled for weeks to try to figure out what to do, but Rachel, the formidable decision-maker par excellence, was paralyzed by indecision for the first time in her life.

Then one day she felt the life of her baby quicken within her, and the matter was settled once and for all. Her baby may not have been conceived in love, but Rachel discovered, to her utter amazement, that she felt almost overwhelmed with a feeling of hopeless, bottomless love for the child she was carrying. She realized, suddenly, that she was entirely prepared to lay down her life for this child, no matter who the father was or how the baby had come into the world. All she knew was that her child was a human being in her own right, and that she, Rachel, had taken a giant step toward becoming more of a human being herself. She decided to take everything one step at a time, starting with the creation of a new life in some distant community where she could reinvent herself and raise her child with the love that had been so decidedly lacking at the moment of her conception.

When the news of the shooting and the accompanying photos appeared in the newspapers and on TV, Maria saw them and realized that the father of the child that she, too, was carrying was the very same man who had raped her in Montreal. She called the FBI and obtained their promise to keep her statement a secret. She then provided them with an account of most of the Viper's last movements, which helped to verify the details of his travels across Canada.

The Royal Canadian Mounted Police are roughly the equivalent of the Federal Bureau of Investigation in the United States, and the two cooperate closely with each other, as well as with Interpol. It was quite a coup when the Canadian law enforcement officers finally determined from fingerprints and DNA samples that the dead rapist was in fact Rafael Alvarez, aka the Viper. There were a truckload of coordinating details to be handled with law enforcement authorities in all the places in the world where the Viper was being sought. Many cold cases were closed out as the result of just one bullet fired in Canada. That one bullet had legal repercussions stretching from British Columbia to Bangkok, from Costa Rica to Colombia, and from Chicago to Washington, D.C.

As soon as Ivan heard the news of the Viper's death, he called Margo Watson and informed her of the situation. She was able to visually identify the body from photos that were sent from the RCMP to FBI Headquarters. The murders that had occurred in her apartment were now solved and verified by DNA matches.

Eventually the Transportation Safety Board recovered the remains of Pressman's Lear jet from shallow waters off the coast of Maine. In the retrieved jumble of human detritus and airplane rubble, the investigators found the pilot's seat with the tell-tale evidence of rigged booby-trap explosives that provided the TSB with proof that the plane crash wasn't accidental.

A particularly conscientious investigator discovered a penknife in the ceiling of the plane. On the chance that it might have been left there by the person who planted the bomb, the knife was sent to the FBI to be checked for prints. The report also verified that the fingerprints were identical to those of the Viper.

Margo Watson was able to convince one of the heirs to von Aragon's estate to allow her to search his yacht for certain business documents that she believed might be useful in detailing the history of the great failed media merger. During her search of the *Sternlicht* she found the contract that had been signed by Robert Thomaston, Geoffrey Lord Pressman, and Baron von Aragon, which proved that the three media giants had indeed conspired to rewrite the future history of the world – a conspiracy that Ivan Welland had suspected from the beginning. When Margo presented Ivan with the one-page document, he told her he would frame it and hang it on his office wall.

"This little piece of paper," he explained, "is for me a historical document of inestimable value because it presents the opposite spirit to the one that produced the Declaration of Independence and the Bill of Rights. We hardly ever see such a glaring example of why we should value and defend our democracy. There will always be those, like these three men, who would strip us of our most precious treasures, so we must be prepared to fight them with words that are just as effective as our weapons."

Ivan was still marveling at the fact that the Viper could travel first class around the world doing unspeakable crimes, and yet the greatest military and the most technologically-equipped country in the world had been unable to put a glove on him, in spite of making his capture a very high priority.

But the one-man crime wave that the Viper produced was nothing compared to the one represented by the leaders of al-Qaeda, who also remained at large. When dealing with Islamist extremists, Ivan sympathized with the admonition from the Apostle Paul to the Ephesians that he was not wrestling against flesh and blood, but against principalities, powers, the rulers of darkness in this world, and the spiritually wicked ones in high places. His lack of success in tracking the Viper wasn't reassuring to Ivan when he thought about how many young dissolute Muslim men were out there just waiting for a chance to kill Americans. He had gotten lucky in the Viper's case, but he couldn't expect to have only good luck. There was also bad luck, but he was determined to do everything in his power to serve his country well in spite of the many obstacles that existed, and would always exist, to prevent him from achieving his goals.

Margo Watson did manage to impress Thomaston's heirs with her plan. They felt, however, that she was too young and inexperienced to be in the upper echelons of corporate management. On the other hand, she was too good to just let her get away, so they gave her the responsibility of overseeing the editorial staff. In that position she would have the final say about all matters of truth and accuracy of reporting for the Thomaston group of media companies.

Ivan counted that as a victory, and he would take all the victories he could get. The Thomaston Corporation changed its motto to *Truth to Tell,* and that was a big win for America and for all those who held her values in high esteem.

AIDAN DE VRIES

Council of Caliphs

If you enjoyed reading *Contempt of Conscience,* you will also like *Council of Caliphs,* the first book in the Ivan Welland series by Aidan de Vries. First editions are available at www.erserandpond.com, or you may send a check or money order for $24.95 (please add $1.50 sales tax plus $4.00 for postage and handling) to Erser and Pond Ltd, 1096 Queen Street, Suite 225, Halifax, Nova Scotia B3H 2R9, Canada. Checks and money orders should be made out to Erser and Pond Ltd.

If you enjoyed reading *Council of Caliphs,* you will also like the second book in the series, *Cruise Control,* about an attempt by Islamist terrorists to sink the world's largest cruise ship on her maiden voyage. First editions are available at <u>www.erserandpond.com</u>, or you may send a check or money order for $22.95 (please add $1.38 sales tax plus $4.00 for postage and handling) to Erser and Pond Ltd, 1096 Queen Street, Suite 225, Halifax, Nova Scotia B3H 2R9, Canada. Checks and money orders should be made out to Erser and Pond Ltd.

If you enjoyed reading *Council of Caliphs* and *Cruise Control,* you will also like the third book in the series, *The Peacemaker,* about a U.S. President's unusual approach to ushering in world peace and security. First editions are available at **www.erserandpond.com**, or you may send a check or money order for $22.95 (please add $1.38 sales tax plus $4.00 for postage and handling) to Erser and Pond Ltd, 1096 Queen Street, Suite 225, Halifax, Nova Scotia B3H 2R9, Canada. Checks and money orders should be made out to Erser and Pond Ltd.

www.ingramcontent.com/pod-product-compliance
Lightning Source LLC
Chambersburg PA
CBHW070540260626
47161CB00002B/458